Praise for *The Institute Revie*

G000079938

"It doesn't matter if a story is as traditional
as Dickens or if it's out there at the gleaming
edge of the avant-garde – all that matters
is if the story is good or bad. The work here,
in this latest issue of the always impressive
Mechanics' Institute Review, uses a variety of
techniques and approaches, both traditional and
experimental, but it coheres at the level of its
high accomplishment. A fabulous collection."
Kevin Barry

"On the evidence of this great collection of
stories, from a range of exciting new voices, it
seems the short story is alive and well and living
at *The Mechanics' Institute Review*."
Eimear McBride

"Daring, intimate and zeitgeisty stories that
showcase an assortment of bold new voices. These
are emerging authors with edge."
Arifa Akbar

"The short story is possibly the hardest form of
fiction to master. The stories collected here
are sometimes unsettling, always illuminating
windows on the present – necessary dispatches from
the now. Deft, urgent and poignant, they share a
perceptiveness about love and our enduring need
for emotional ties in a sped-up world."
Jean McNeil

Praise for Previous Issues

"Really good stories, really well made. You don't get better than that."
Ali Smith

"The short-story form is alive and kicking in here; so many distinctive new voices . . ."
Tessa Hadley

"There's breathtaking energy in these stories, and skilful pulling of the rug from beneath your feet."
Adam Marek

"These stories are vivid, sharp and surprising, which is why I will not be sharing them with my publisher. There's enough competition already."
Joe Dunthorne

"Once again, *MIR* proves itself as a hotbed of fresh and original talent, laden with intriguing voices that urge you to turn the page. An annual treat for short-story lovers."
Courttia Newland

"The short-story form is in safe hands. These writers – unafraid to take risks, to experiment, to push at structure – will go some way towards ensuring the future of the short work of fiction. This is a reason to celebrate."
Niall Griffiths

"Brilliant new writing, real, intimate and gripping."
Maggie Gee

About the Title

The first Mechanics' Institute in London was founded in 1823 by George Birkbeck. "Mechanics" then meant skilled artisans, and the purpose of the Institute was to instruct them in the principles behind their craft. The Institute became Birkbeck College, part of London University, in 1920 but still maintains one foot in the academy and one in the outside world.

THE MECHANICS' INSTITUTE REVIEW
ISSUE 15 AUTUMN 2018

Short Stories

The
Mechanics'
Institute Review

The Mechanics' Institute Review
Issue 15 Autumn 2018

The Mechanics' Institute Review is published by MA Creative
Writing, Department of English and Humanities, School of Arts,
Birkbeck, Malet Street, Bloomsbury, London WC1E 7HX.
Tel: 020 3073 8372. Email: englishandhumanities@bbk.ac.uk.

ISBN 978-1-9999622-0-3

Project Director: Julia Bell

Editorial Team: Francesca Alberry, Sandra Brown-Springer,
Peter Coles, John Forde, Melanie Jones, Nadia Jones, Hilary Key,
Lauren Miller, Hannah Parry, Amy St Johnston

The Editorial Team would like to thank Julia Bell and Sue Tyley
for making this project possible. Also our readers: S. J. Ahmed,
Bora Aygun, Matt Bourn, Karen Clarke, Lyndsey Garrett, Anna
Köberich, Sally Larsen, Imogen Lee, Áine Martin, George Newman,
Julius Pasteiner, Rebecca Rouillard and Martin Wakefield.

This project is supported using public funding by Arts Council
England.

The Mechanics' Institute Review is distributed by NBNi and
represented by Inpress Books www.inpressbooks.co.uk.

Website: http://mironline.org/

Printed and bound by TJ International, Trecerus Industrial
Estate, Padstow, Cornwall PL28 8RW

Cover design and typesetting by Raffaele Teo

The Mechanics' Institute Review is typeset in Book Antiqua

Table of Contents

Foreword: Whose Standards?

JULIA BELL

Anyone wanting to get published will, if they are serious about this endeavour, be reading, books and the market, to see what kind of work is already getting published. They will be scrutinising the prize lists to see what is considered excellent and looking at enrolling on MA courses and seeking editorial help. They will be acknowledging that they want to become better writers – that they want to create something publishable – and to do that they will need to study the scene.

But any writer looking to thread together a standard from what is published or what wins prizes will also be very confused about the real value of their work. So much that is poorly executed seems to get published, mysteriously boring books win prizes, inexplicably average stuff gets fêted. To whose standards, then, does the literary world operate? Who runs this?

Let's imagine an emerging writer: she's just completed her collection of short stories set in London during the riots and recently submitted it to publishers. Some editors are genuinely engaged and sorry and have practical reasons for turning down her work – "This just doesn't fit on my list." "It's too similar to something else I've already published." – but quite a few of them use this curious one-line publishing cliché: "I just didn't fall in love with this enough to want to publish it."

She stares at the email and wonders why they don't mention

the stories themselves or what she could do to improve them and make them more lovable. Finding a publisher seems more like a dating service. As someone once said, what's love got to do with it?

To understand these responses we perhaps need to look at the bigger picture: the major publishers receive many more manuscripts than they can ever publish, they are busy and pay is relatively poor for London, especially in junior roles. They are chasing a shrinking market and looking to sure-fire hits, especially in the genres, and especially, at the moment, in crime. They are under pressure to meet targets, unearth something that will sell volume. Most of the big imprints are now in the houses of the conglomerates – and since Random House and Penguin merged there has been an even further shrinking of editorial staff and even more focus on the bottom line. And anyway, as everyone already knows, short-story collections don't sell.

The language of publishing sits awkwardly between the languages of commerce and literature. What will sell will always win, over what is good or well written. If it's a well-written piece it's a bonus, but the main issue is, Will this make money? What is its value as a new idea? And the editor who does not "fall in love" with the work stands a very poor chance of pushing it through the system. Most publishers are full of good people who love books, but the machinery of big corporations demands results for shareholders, not readers, and certainly not writers. Market sadism then punishes the writer even further – you need to be lovable *and* you need to sell volume.

So, for our novice writer wanting to earn a reputation in this field, the answer is to win one of the major short-story prizes. There are three in the UK: the Costa, the BBC and the *Sunday Times* EFG. The richest of these is, at the time of writing, the *Sunday Times* EFG Short Story Award. Worth £30,000 to the winner, the award claims to "promote and celebrate the excellence of the modern short story" and is open to any novelist or short-story writer from around the world who is published in the UK.

The most recent shortlisted stories were all by US authors.

One man and five women. The stories are very good – they are all well-behaved versions of the North American short story. They follow in a tradition that includes some of the best twentieth-century practitioners: Tobias Wolff, Alice Munro, Ernest Hemingway, Flannery O'Connor, Raymond Carver, Lorrie Moore – and one of my personal favourites, Miranda July, was even on the shortlist.

But. I live in the UK. And the North American short story, with its reliable epiphanies, dislocated settings and cooler-than-us movie aesthetics, is, like the US indie film, of a very particular flavour.

What happened to other kinds of short-story writing? The kinds that aren't so show-not-tell-y. Philosophical, exploded things, small moments of textual play – Eley Williams or Claire-Louise Bennett. What of UK and Irish writing? Much like the Booker, expanding the remit of the prize to include everyone has diluted its purpose.

Really great new UK voices have less of a chance to be heard if our prizes are now taken up mostly by writers from elsewhere. It's also a kind of aesthetic cynicism – that all lives lived look exactly the same and are expressed through the same lens. All the prize does is point to pieces that represent a certain aesthetic. The prize did not, this year at least, deliver something I did not already know. It felt safe, like its blue-chip sponsors – it is they, not us, who want to deliver the reliably sleek, the inoffensive, the high "standard", but which is unlikely to challenge a globalised status quo.

So far, our novice writer has learned that she is not yet lovable enough, nor salesworthy enough, and now she's writing about the wrong continent entirely. Oh, and I forgot to mention: she is also black. All the editors she has been sending her unlovable work to have been white.

Diversity in UK publishing, especially within the mainstream arts, is at an all-time low. Publishing is overwhelmingly run by editors from privileged backgrounds, which means the books that are published are chosen by editors of this kind. And it shows. There is a streak of conservatism running through British publishing, and British letters, which has in the past few years grown worse.

A 2015 report, commissioned by the literature development agency Spread the Word, concluded that more than 84% of publishers and 97% of agents think publishing is only "a little diverse" or "not diverse at all".

Since then there have been initiatives to address this – some of them somewhat clumsy. But why does it matter? Because without a diversity of published material, the UK perpetuates a kind of London- and Oxbridge-centric worldview that denies the existence of other voices, other viewpoints. And because, as we learn in the writing workshop about point of view, where you stand in relation to the story affects what you can see. No one has an imagination that is free of bias. Acknowledging this is the first step towards nurturing a more diverse culture. The human imagination is not some ethically neutral phenomenon – it produced *Mein Kampf* as well as *Anna Karenina*. Using this as an excuse for appropriation, or for the reinforcement of the dominant narrative, harks back to a position of cultural and political certainty that we surely don't have now.

The "standards" applied by white editors of a certain class reveal the ethics of a particular kind of classical education, security of circumstance, taste, a close relationship to the status quo, blind spots that eclipse judgement.

In a recent review of Sharlene Teo's novel *Ponti*, Julie Myerson entirely misses the fact that the novel emerges from the aesthetics of South-East Asia. The book is full of the language of a new point of view – Singapore, mixed with London and ghost stories and manga. It's not behaving to the "standards" of eloquent repression that have become a kind of norm in English literary voices of the past thirty years. What Myerson takes withering aim at might present as an argument against the poor standard of the work, but in misunderstanding the imaginative context she shows an old colonial, imperialist voice that applies its own standards to everything, as the ones that are inevitably correct.

What has changed is that people are much more adept at seeing this bias. And as in life, discussions of literature are not free of the identity crisis affecting our country. An identity crisis that, one can argue quite loudly, comes about as a consequence of not being able to see this imperialist bias for what it is: a thing of the past.

So what does our novice writer do? She lives in a turbid, difficult country, she is unlovable and unsellable, she's working in a difficult format whose prizes tend to reward American aesthetics. She might want to study on an MA course, then, to take some time out to think about her work, show it to peers, get feedback. But how is she supposed to afford that, working nine to five in Carphone Warehouse – yes, the very same one the kids smashed up in the riots – and anyway, no one else in her family has ever gone to university and why would they accept her now without a BA? And what about the other students? What if she doesn't fit in?

In spite of all these pressures, she applies for a place on our MA and gets in and wins a scholarship. And what does she learn?

Julie Myerson again, in the same review, takes the usual elitist line against creative writing courses. That somehow, they produce a hegemony of taste, or bad writing – as if good writing only comes from preternaturally talented people like herself who would never take courses. What she misses once again – as all these arguments against creative writing courses often do – is that it is in the workshops that literature comes fully alive. Writing classes are in and of themselves reading classes, and as such are full of life lessons. In reading and thinking, in uncovering bias, in trying – whatever the work in front of us – to make something of value, a piece that has quality, we are engaging in what Aristotle called, in *Ethics*, the education of the emotions.

The writing workshop, then, is not about standards, but about subjectivity. The literatures that make up our history have been written from many subjective positions, across centuries. There is an irony to the fact that historians study novels to get inside the imagination of a period – an acknowledgement that imagination has a very strong subjective position, to which the application of a "standard", as Julie Myerson would have it, cannot work.

In the writing workshop we talk about quality over standards because quality comes with depth of field, from relentless self-investigation, from attentive reading as well as writing. And if we think in terms of quality, rather than standards, we open things up. Standards are rigid; the application of quality allows room for the subjective, for many voices, rather than a few.

So over the period of a two-year MA our emerging writer's work improves and she wins a prize for one of her pieces and gets a story published in a respected literary journal. A small press accepts her collection. She is, finally, on her way.

And this is where the hope and interest in our literary culture currently lie – not with the big conglomerates, but with the MA courses who gather together cohorts of like-minded readers and writers, and then with the smaller independent publishers and small publishing ventures. What is good and vital and interesting is happening in the margins of the mainstream. A rich collection of indie publishers – Galley Beggar, Fitzcarraldo, Influx, And Other Stories, Penned in the Margins, Bluemoose, Salt – is bringing out more and more relevant work. These small presses, who can afford to take more risks than other, bigger publishers, are a response to the ever-present problem of the monocultural taste of The Market. And the Internet, too, brings work to us, through its viral wormholes. Stories like "Cat Person", or the writing of Rebecca Solnit, found more fans online than in print. The readers are certainly still out there.

When Will Self and others of his generation mourn the death of the literary novel, what they are really mourning is the death of the culture that sustained them as literary figureheads. The culture changed. The Internet happened. Everything got closer and at the same time further away. The distribution of literature has become much more diffuse. Stories have found other pathways. The TV box set can deliver as much emotional nuance as a big novel, so literature serves other functions than social realism now.

What publications like *The Mechanics' Institute Review* can offer is a selection of pieces being written in the UK now. They may be set in Tehran or Tottenham, but they are all being made in Britain. They have all been chosen and edited by a team of committed readers and editors drawn from one of the most vibrant MA courses in the country and the work is a vital reflection of that.

The novels and stories of the future need to tell us how to live now, not how we lived then. And the new emerging voices reflect much more fragmented, jagged experiences. In the UK we need to listen harder. The new voices have always been there, but we have been too hasty to place our national literary culture as the arbiter of the literatures of the rest of the world, rather than embracing our own complex literature, which is only a part of a global conversation much bigger than our attempts to contain it.

Tom Corridan

ARHONDIA

Trevor is blasting Thin Lizzy's version of *Whiskey in the Jar*. It's grey and cold but not pissing down so I can have a fag out of sight in the laneway behind our houses and listen to Trevor's tunes. He's the only one with a record player and good taste on our street. Ma says his da bought it 'cause Mr Walsh works on the ships and feels guilty for being away all the time. I think Trevor's lucky. He gets all the good stuff without the hassle of having his old man around. We only have the radio in our house and it's usually playing shite.

I'm wearing long trousers for the first time this year so no more freezing legs, looking like a turkey's plucked arse. Mrs Walsh made them for me. She's great with a needle and thread and helps Ma out whenever she can. I asked her to give them a bit of a bell-bottom, to which she said: "Absolutely not."

I can hear her shouting at Trevor to turn the music down. Don't see why. He livens the place up. Older people always want a quiet house so they can hear themselves think. She's great and all but I don't think Mrs Walsh will be mulling over *Finnegans Wake* or anything. Without Trevor's music, Cherryfield Road is the most miserable, greyest, fucking hole in Dublin.

I have to go get Da from the pub in a minute, otherwise Ma says he'll stay there all night and not come home for his dinner. Like there would be any harm in that. I start sucking on one of those mints that burn your nose and throat to hide my cigarette mouth and I'm off.

Boyle's pub is dark and dingy. The soles of my shoes stick to the floor and announce my arrival to the patrons and the publican.

"Ah look, it's Tom Corridan, coming to take his da home for his dinner," says Michael, a bulbous-eyed, noisy little fecker who's friendly with Da and hasn't a good thing to say about anyone.

"Da, Michael," I say, and take a seat at the bar next to them to begin my wait.

"Me boy told me that Father Flanagan is giving you extra work after class. Said you'll be learning Ancient Greek. The brains on ya!" says Michael.

That only happened today, nosy bastard. He knows everything.

"They're only short passages. Just trying to better myself."

"Much good it'll do him, when he's setting down pipes and unclogging toilets," says Da, speaking for the first time since I came in the door. "He can recite Greek to pass the time of day, but the clients will think he's away with the fairies."

The two of them start laughing. Fucking eejits. Belittling everyone to make out the dead end they find themselves in is a choice instead of a mistake. With their dirty shirts and dirty necks and filthy nails.

Cunts, I think to myself.

I'm trying to calculate when would be a good time to ask Da if he's ready to go home. If the pint is too full he'll tell me I'm rushing him. When it's nearly empty one of the men will quickly suggest another round. I have to interject just when the liquid is in between the bottom of the glass and halfway to the middle.

"Are you nearly ready to go, Da?" I say.

"What's for dinner, then?" says Da.

"Roast beef, boiled vegetables and spuds," I say.

"Jaysus, no rush to get back home, then. A packet of cheese and onion crisps and two more pints there, Seamus," says Da.

Four pints later we're on our way home.

Everything is louder and feels electric. The ground underneath our feet seems noisier to step on than usual. I say nothing and hope he says nothing. Silence is good. After a few pints God knows what road his mind will take.

We get into the house and it's business as usual.

"I'm just warming the food, Frank. Joe heard your footsteps and told me to put it on," says Ma, smiling.

"Not ready yet, then? Don't mind me, I've just been working all day and have to be up at the crack of dawn tomorrow," Da says.

"The meat turns to rubber if you heat it for too long. I want it to be nice for you," says Ma, not quite meeting his eyes.

"Ah sure, fuck it, we'll wait. Joe, come 'ere to your old man. You're always looking out for me, aren't ya? What do you want to be when you grow up?" says Da, putting Joe on his lap.

"A plumber like you. I'll sort people's houses out. And then I'll have lunch at Bewley's and order tea with little cubes of sugar on the side," says Joe, delighted with all the attention he's suddenly getting.

"Silly boy, I don't have lunch at Bewley's every day. Do you know your brother is learning Ancient Greek? Do you know what job that's good for?" says Da.

"What job?" says Joe, wide-eyed.

"None," says my father and makes a sound like he's nearly choking himself laughing.

"Actually you can use it in university, if you're a professor. That's a good job to have," I say, looking at the floor.

"Listen to you! '*Actually*'! You sound like a fucking fairy. Are you going to be one of those Trinity College heads? The cream of Dublin, thick and rich? Well, son, you're missing one of the criteria there. You're fucking thick but you sure as hell ain't rich," he says, and laughs at his own joke. Stupid fucker.

"Frank, he's only a boy. They're bound to be impressed by what they learn in school," says Ma.

I just look down and wait for it to pass. Hopefully Ma will serve dinner soon and he'll fill that mouth of his that constantly needs to be doing something. Drinking or eating or talking shite.

"Jaysus, are you making the food from scratch, Nell? Plate up, woman, for fuck's sake!" Da says.

"Do you need any help, Ma?" I say, watching my mother do her usual trick of making herself smaller and smaller. One day she'll make herself one with the wall and disappear.

"Is cooking another thing Father Flanagan has taught you? Maybe you can bring him over to the house sometime and he can turn our water into wine," he says, and belches, filling the front room with the smell of beer. "Don't be getting any ideas that you'll be going to college. You'll finish school and then you'll help put bread on the table. You'll work. There will be no stuffing your nose in a book."

I feel my whole body heating up until even the backs of my ears are burning.

"Maybe I can get a better job. Maybe I don't have to have muck under my fingernails and a filthy stained collar. Any savage can fix a toilet, drink himself stupid, then come home and shout at his wife and children to make himself feel important!" I blurt out.

Time stops.

My mother speaks. "Tom, don't upset your father. Tell him you didn't mean it," she says, and walks over to Da's chair. She puts her hand lightly on his shoulder as if touching a wild animal she's afraid of. "Frank, he's just under a lot of pressure at school. He's tired."

Da shoves Joe off his knee and gets up, taking his belt out of its loops. His famous belt that always ends up joining his hands and his fists at the end of the night.

Ma takes Joe in her arms and carries him upstairs. There's no point trying to get between me and Da. It never works.

"You little fucking bastard. I put food on the table and clothes on your back. Who are you to judge me? A fucking nobody, that's who you are. Fucking nobody," he says. He keeps repeating himself, the boring bastard.

I get hit and shoved and punched but I don't make a sound. The belt burns the skin on my back. His right fist thuds onto my jaw and the pain spreads all the way to the other side of my face and the top of my head. The lashes of the belt get more and more frequent until I'm numb and they don't burn any more. I know there will come a point when it stops, like it always does. And then there will be a time in the future when it starts again, like it always does.

A knock on the door puts the brakes on him.

"Go see who it is," he orders, sitting down at the table and exhaling, as if I was the one that had tired him out.

I open the door to find Trevor outside, looking at me intensely.

"Sorry for the late call, Tom. I forgot me copybook in class and can't do the homework for tomorrow. I've been looking all over for it. Can I borrow yours?" he says loudly for my da's benefit, and then mouths, "Are you OK? I heard the racket."

I nod and say, "Sure, let me go upstairs and get it for ya."

My father has started putting food on a plate for himself.

"I'm just getting a copybook for Trevor," I say.

"Do whatever you need to do," he responds.

I come back down and give the copybook to Trevor.

"I'll drop it back in an hour," he says loudly, and then in a low voice: "There's blood on the back of your shirt."

I nod again. "I'll see you in an hour so," I say, close the door and make my way upstairs. My father keeps his eyes on his plate.

Joe is sitting on the bed crying. "I'm sorry I said I want to be a plumber. I didn't mean to make trouble for ya," he says, with his innocent little eyes full of tears.

"Joe, listen," I say. "Da was just looking for an excuse. He would have hit me whether you'd said you wanted to be a plumber or an astronaut. Do you understand?" I say.

Joe nods and wipes his face.

"Do you really understand, Joe? It's important that you do," I say.

He nods again.

"Get into bed, now," I say.

Joe gets into bed and I just lie down on top of the covers and fall asleep.

None of us ate that night. Trevor never came back. He must have heard the silence through the paper-thin walls that separate our two houses.

The fucking cunt downstairs ate. Of course he did. At least he fell asleep on the couch so Ma got a good night's kip without that lying next to her. Makes me sick to my fucking stomach.

In the morning we warm up yesterday's food and have it for breakfast, then Joe and I set off for school. Father Flanagan is getting everyone to read passages of *The Odyssey* out loud. It's about this Greek king, Odysseus, who's very clever. He has to make his way back home from Troy to Ithaca when the Trojan War is over. He keeps having to stop and spend ages on one island or another. I'm starting to think maybe Odysseus doesn't really want to get home. Maybe he shacked up with some bird on one of the Greek islands and this whole book is the fib he'll tell his annoying family when he finally gets home late, really late. Can't think of a better reason to write.

Suddenly I hear my name being called and realise all the rest of the lads are filing out and I've been caught by Father Flanagan mid-daydream.

"Are you OK, Tom? You look pale," says Father Flanagan with that awful gleam of pity in his eyes.

I give him a serious and silent nod of reassurance but he still looks like he pities me and out of nowhere the classroom goes blurry and fucking tears start streaming down my face.

"I wish he was dead, Father. I prayed all night that death would come and take him so the rest of us could breathe," I say.

"Those aren't good thoughts, Tom. Only God can decide what happens to people," says Father Flanagan.

"I know, Father, I'm just giving him a few ideas," I say.

"Tom!"

"Sorry, Father."

"You have to focus on building your life. You could get a scholarship, Tom," he says.

"He won't let me go to university, Father. He wants me to work so we have another person earning," I say. "That's what the argument was about."

Father Flanagan looks at me and the pity spreads out over his whole face. Priests always have good Christian advice but it's not them that are being tormented.

Trevor is waiting outside the main school hall.

"Are you OK?" he asks.

"Grand," I say.

"Want a cigarette?" he says.

"Of course I do," I say and we head towards the alley behind our houses.

We don't talk until we get there. I'm too embarrassed. I can tell he doesn't know what to say either and he focuses on his cigarette instead. Trevor smokes Marlboro. Occasionally his old man gets him some proper ones from America.

"D'ya reckon there's a difference in the taste?" I ask and hear myself sound like a green fucking eejit.

"I don't know. I suppose. I'm not an aficionado. It all goes over me head," he says and grins at me. "Are you really OK?"

"Grand. It's just how he is," I say.

"Do you want me to get me da to talk to him when he's next back home?" he says.

"It'll only make things worse. He doesn't listen to anyone. Everyone's a fucking eejit according to him. No disrespect to your da," I say.

"I know. Well, we're always next door if you need us. Don't let it get too bad," he says. "Don't you ever want to clatter him?"

"Sure, but he's twice the size of me. I take after my mother's side of the family. I would have to use my mind to win, like Odysseus," I say, and we laugh.

"I have to go home for dinner. Do you want a couple more cigarettes? They might help you think," says Trevor.

"No, you're grand," I say.

"Don't be worrying about it. Here, take them. You can borrow me lighter as well. Give it back to me tomorrow," he says and hands it to me.

I look at the cigarettes and wonder if I should have one or if I should head home. I don't want to be in that house again but I'm wrecked and hungry. Going home doesn't necessarily mean I'll get rest or food though.

I open the door and there he is, with Ma and Joe next to him tending to his every need. I just want to go upstairs and sleep. I want to be on my own and pretend I'm not here. I want to dream myself away into another dimension, pretend I'm on a ship travelling the Aegean, anchoring off the shores of the Lotus-Eaters' island. I'll eat an entire harvest's worth of the stuff and forget about manky Cherryfield Road.

"I'm going upstairs," I say, trying my best not to be noticed.

"Stay. Wait, Tom," says Ma. "Your da isn't well," and I notice he's lying back in a chair, with her supporting his head. He looks like he doesn't even have the strength to turn around and glare at me.

Time stops.

"What's wrong?" I say.

Joe's eyes are full of fears and questions he probably doesn't have the words for.

"His blood-pressure tablets. He forgot to renew his prescription," Ma says.

"Should we call the doctor?" I ask.

"Yes, but first I need you to run to the chemist and get some tablets for him. Now!"

"It's on the other side of Crumlin!" I say.

"Well, you'll need to go fast, then. Go, don't waste any time. Here, take this money," she says.

"Are you sure?" I say.

"What do you mean, 'Am I sure?' Of course I'm sure. Go quickly, now!" she shouts.

The door shuts behind me. The air feels different. Everything has a different light on it, a brighter light. I start making my way towards the chemist's. As I pass Trevor's house I see his bicycle in the driveway but decide not to ask for it. I'll walk. Fast. People always comment on how fast I walk everywhere.

My thoughts are racing a mile a minute.

It's fallen to me. How has it fallen to me?

I keep walking. The roads are empty. Everyone's at home having their dinner. It's that time of day.

I check my breast pocket to make sure I still have the money and I feel the two cigarettes Trevor gave me. He said they might help me think.

How can this be up to me?

There's another laneway just to the left of me. It'll get me to where I'm going but I'll also be hidden. I take a few steps down it, stop and light a cigarette. I'll go to the chemist but not before I've had a short break. Just to get over the shock. The first drag of the cigarette makes me light-headed.

His well-being depends on me now.

This is why old people always say life's a funny thing. All the times he hit me and called me a nobody. And now I'm the nobody he depends on. I'll get his fucking pills in my own time. Father Flanagan would disagree.

If God decides he wants to spare him, he can do that. At least then when he hits me I'll know I deserve to be punished. If not, he can stand at the Pearly Gates and when he's asked who did this to him he can say, "Nobody."

I use the butt of the first cigarette to light the second one.

The Front Line

LOU KRAMSKOY

E very time I get that hot stressy feeling, the one that starts in the nodes of my neck with a pea-sized pop, a pea-sized pop that oozes out bad jelly, every time I get that feeling I reach into my pocket and pull Tiny Fighter out.

And out she comes like a tornado of tiny violence ready to kick Ass for me, not just one kind of Ass but all sorts, any Ass that makes me feel if I peeled back my skull skin and dug deep with clean fingers, bent to a mirror and looked inside, I'd see boats sailing, bobbing around my bad jelly brain, giant boats with cargoes stuffed full of thoughts, old dirty thoughts, exotic new ones. And in the darkest corners of those boats' heaving holds, crates creak and groan, crates stacked so high they lean and bow and threaten to topple with their hidden contents squealing at each other like smuggled monkeys, eyes white and terrified, as paying passengers sit up top staring out of small windows sipping on expensive bottled water. Well, every time I get that feeling, out she comes.

And wow, Tiny Fighter is a fearless freakish fighter who kicks Ass black and blue and every other bruised colour there is. She kicks Ass till I feel better, till I can fold back that tender transparence of skin.

Tiny Fighter lies in wait ready to help with her "back you up, bitch" attitude. She lives in hidden pockets on the left of my life, because my right is always busy swiping, typing or holding hot coffee. I don't exactly know the millimoment Tiny Fighter will pounce but when she does, wow, when she does you better take mother-loving cover.

Tiny Fighter, out she'll come in meetings when we talk about privacy, supply chains, data collection and storage, spectrum, cybersecurity, critical infrastructure and a number of economic concerns, in these meetings as these colleagues, these strangers, say things to me, awful things like "redo" or "redraft" – terrible affixes affix to me too.

I feel incapable, unknowable, unlovable.

In these meetings when I can't open my mouth for fear of my broiled brain pouring out jellied thoughts into the dead space their multi-connectivity questions have carved in the room, when I feel commands popping like dry gunpowder in the professional air around me, well, that's the perfect time and out she comes.

Out she comes in the middle of meetings, landing in the centre of that oval Eames Eiffel-legged table with legs spread wide ready to kick Ass, the Ass of Beth (Development), Rachel (Logistics) and Simon-Simon (Production) (called Simon-Simon because he speaks twice as long, twice as loud and twice as hard but Tiny Fighter puts him last. Last, you hear! Ha!).

First Beth, Beth who sucks the lead on her pencils making them soggy so her smile always shows that dot of grey lead on the tip of her tongue. Tiny Fighter will go for that tip of her slimy tongue and bite the leaded spot, make a tiny hole and suck out her fat pink tongue tissue till it lies flat and flapping in her mouth so when she speaks she'll sound like a fart cushion. Tiny Fighter'll dive down the top of Beth's silk work shirt into that flabby cleavage she's always got on show and I can't see what Tiny Fighter does down there in that showy place around her boobs but it involves nipples and scratching, yes, serious scratching I imagine Beth won't notice till the next morning (she isn't the type to wash at night because she's always going straight out from work meeting friends, family, smiling smugly the next day like someone whose parents always bought them puppies). I imagine her in the mornings after Tiny Fighter's done that fight, in that morning shower lathering those fat freckled boobs, I imagine her saying "Ouch" and "Ooh" as she feels the sting of water and I see her twist and turn in that mirror pulling folds of back fat back, that shapeless flesh that overflows her bra strap, and she'll wonder where those scratches came from. Ha! Where indeed? She'll never think of me.

But Tiny Fighter won't stop with Beth. No way. Once Tiny Fighter has got the taste you can't stop her.

She'll turn on Rachel who always saves Beth a seat as if meetings were a school trip and they're still sharing packed lunch. Tiny Fighter'll swing up on those stupid gold-hooped earrings Rachel wears that are really just for the young (and she's five years older than me, five years I say, that's a whole school shuffle). Standing on those gold hoops Tiny Fighter will jump up into her ear and punch a pathway through Rachel's head and I'll laugh when Rachel tucks her perfect blond hair behind her clever, clever ear, the ear that heard tutors talk at Cambridge, that Steven from Programming sticks his tongue in as he pumps I imagine and, looking through that tunnel Tiny Fighter has fought between her ears, that tunnel right through, I'll laugh when I see Tiny Fighter waving at me from the other side. Stupid Rachel. She doesn't know what damage has been done, damage that'll last so every time I look at Rachel I'll laugh.

Then having dispatched Beth and Rachel Tiny Fighter will turn on Simon-Simon but Simon-Simon is trickier because he looks like all those men in films and on TV, men with power who you have to find a clever way to hurt, but his eyes, his eyes don't say POWER they say something else. His white eyes say MONKEY and BOX and sometimes they say HELP ME TOO but Tiny Fighter is incredible. She'll undo his zip and lower herself down into Simon-Simon's loose boxer shorts. (I'm not an expert on undergarments or men his age but once when he bent down to look for fresh milk in the fridge as he sniffed the stale carton I saw his pant-line rise above his trousers. They had a red tape measure embroidered around the waist. A tape measure! Novelty pants? Present pants?) The looseness of those pants means Tiny Fighter can climb in by the nine-inch benchmark and roundhouse kick his floppy fat balls, then pluck his pubes till tiny streams of sperm shoot from small holes and Tiny Fighter will climb out, flick that sperm so it slits across the faces of Beth and Rachel, landing like little scars all over their dry lips. I'll watch as Beth and Rachel pick at their lips, put on balm and wonder where that flaky dryness came from. And poor Simon-Simon, he'll never know why he can't perform properly late at night and he'll think that dryness is his wife's fault, her fault indeed.

And having dispensed with all these losers Tiny Fighter'll stand in the middle of that stylish wipe-down white table sweating, her black hair wild, her eyes glowing, wiping the red blood off her hands across her naked chest (she's naked of course – I tried putting doll's clothes on her once but it looked stupid) and as she pulls Simon-Simon's plucked pubes webbed around her away, she'll smile at me.

But mostly she doesn't smile. Mostly when she's finished kicking Ass she stands there confused, starts crying, runs away, tumbles off that table with tears teeming from her eyes and slips out under the crack in the glass meeting-room door and then I'll feel bad.

I feel bad.

And later I sit sobbing, feeling BAD in that last cubicle of the office's baby-blue gender-neutral toilets, wondering What's wrong with me? Wondering Is it this job? Is it any job? Is it me? Wondering Why can't I take the criticisms everyone else can? As I'm drowning in waves of unexplained, inexplicable anxiety, feeling pathetic and ill, seriously ill, I'll call Mum on my phone who'll say calming stuff but stuff that'll make me feel childish, foolish, girlish. I'll call Mum and as I tell her something is wrong with me, wrong, as I talk about the lump on my neck, the pea-sized pop and the bad jelly inside me, I'll hear her sigh, fold away her newspaper and slowly tap-tap her metal spoon on her morning cup of coffee and, with that smart voice of hers, she'll tell me she never needed a Tiny Fighter to fight battles for her and, frustrated by my inability, she'll snap, tell me to pull myself together and ask where exactly I think the front line is?

Where?

I'll hang up, hold up my phone, look online for that front line. Drag my finger across pictures of Beth, Rachel and Simon-Simon, swiping past parties, pastries, politics and friends of friends and then I'll keep swiping till I'm back on my own professional profile picture, confident and smiling. And seeing myself OUT there, looking so accomplished, I'll read and reread myself, hit Like hard over and over again until I feel the anxiety flood away, flood away and fill up that empty water bottle everyone teases me about carrying around all the time. Once I'm cool, calmed and drained then and only then, Tiny Fighter will return.

She'll rope down from the ceiling kicking out a polystyrene panel or slide under the door her bare cheeks butt-squeaking on the Italian-marble floor. However she arrives, she'll land back on my left, ready to kick Ass for me, Ass of all kinds.

Growth

CHERYL POWELL

She held the scalpel up to the light and checked its blade. The edge was laser sharp, and this was good, since quick clean cuts were the most painless, severing nerve endings before they could react.

Six scalpels ranging in size lay on the worktop beside the bath, and other surgical equipment: antimicrobial scrub, tweezers, swabs of cotton wool, wound dressings, surgical mask and a box of blue latex gloves.

She had nothing to lose. The kids had grown up and left home. There was just the two of them now. She listened to the low rumble of planes taking off and landing at the airport nearby, passengers on their way to Spain, or India, or who knows where. Single travellers, trying to find themselves; women like her, perhaps, who had already had their surgery.

So she'd chosen a night when she wouldn't be disturbed, when he would be watching football downstairs, hand clutching the remote. She'd scoured the bathroom, put out white towels for afterwards, ice packs for the pain, and a new bottle of Jack Daniel's.

The lighting in the bathroom was as good as any operating theatre, brilliant white and shadowless. She wasted no time stripping off her clothes, stepping into the bath and pulling on the blue latex gloves. Her breathing laboured with the effort, the

17

heaviness on her chest; the tightness in her ribcage had become unbearable lately. She was suffocating.

She would rid herself of this burden, of him, or die in the attempt.

The growth had spread. Facing the mirror above the sink, running blue fingers over her body, she could see that its mass now stretched from the top of her hip to below her knee. Over the years it had put out tentacles that twisted around her thighs and across her ribs: light scars at first, but now more bloated as they filled with blood and fluid, growing thicker and more prickly.

She secured the surgical mask over her face and carefully poured the brown antimicrobial scrub over her body. Taking the scalpel, she put her right foot on the edge of the bath. She would start on the flesh-like feelers just below her knee. Here the strands of growth looked just like calloused skin, waxy yellow and hardened. She was able to slice through it quite painlessly, prising it away from the new tissue underneath, peeling it back to the top of her kneecap. She breathed deeply, the mask inflating and deflating along its folds and she felt the heat and stale air building inside it, but she felt braver now she'd made a start. Next she attacked the fronds just below her breastbone, gouging at the tiny barbs embedded in her flesh, her lungs so desperate for air she had to push the mask up into her hair.

She couldn't go on. The pain was too much.

He'd always said she'd never do it, that she didn't have the courage. That she was pathetic. Was this true? The reflection in the mirror wasn't her, at least not how she remembered herself. This body was overweight and flabby, the face fallen in on itself, and yet when she moved, the creature in the mirror moved, too; when she raised a hand, it raised a hand. And the growth was unmistakably hers, its lumpy terrain, craggy in some parts, smooth in others, mottled red-purple at its centre. She pulled the mask back into place, reached for an ice pack and held it to her outer thigh.

Looking back, she should have nipped the whole thing in the bud. A small pink lump on her right hip, like a solid blister, totally painless. But later it began to itch and when she looked more closely it had thick black hairs, like the legs of a tick, burrowed deep into her skin, and she had been horrified and too frightened to seek help.

Years later and the growth had intensified its stranglehold and become inflamed. She would scratch until she was too hot and short of breath, clawing at her flesh until she bled. It had got so bulky it chafed constantly. She had exchanged her fitted work suits for looser skirts and blousy jackets and felt relieved when they took her off reception to help in the back office.

She grabbed the scalpel again, took a slug of whisky, and probed the area around her stomach. Here, the growth was softer, and more vibrant, with beads and globules of fluid moving under the skin, like mineral oil inside a lava lamp. She made an incision and cried out. The pain was severe and her flesh sprang bright with blood. She seized the shower head and rinsed. A network of suckers tunnelled deep inside. She gritted her teeth and pushed the blade further, through the fatty layer and the tissue beyond, clamping down on a scream.

The growth had blighted her life. She never left the house. The reception girls still asked her on nights out, even though she no longer worked there, but he was never keen. Said they only invited her to talk about her afterwards. So, she always made an excuse, knowing that if she went she would only find a dark corner, invisible in the shapeless dress he'd chosen for her, conscious that, underneath, the growth would throb and tighten and everybody would know of her disfigurement.

She'd telephoned a hotline once. They told her she had to be strong.

Yes, she must be strong.

Swallowing more whisky, straight from the bottle, she pressed an ice pack to her hip. This is where the growth was most deeply embedded, locked in with its parasitic suckers, blind feelers groping into her cells. She threw off the surgical mask, snatched up a flannel and stuffed it into her mouth. Then she took the largest scalpel and opened up her hip, slicing away the flesh until the blood obscured her work and she had to press on more ice and her body began to judder with shock and the growth hung down, convulsing, folded over itself, clinging on by a few tough tendrils. Frantically, she hacked away, knowing she could easily die, bleed to death, but she was desperate to be rid of it.

The growth slithered into the bath, coiled into a ball, quaking and twitching, sliding in its own muck.

The bleeding stopped. She ran her fingers over where the growth had been. At last she was free of it. Already her flesh was beginning to heal, scabbing over, still sore and weeping at the centre but, as she showered off the blood, she saw it was a clean amputation. In time, she thought, it would heal completely, though there would always be deep scars and a permanent cavity at her hip.

She cleaned and dressed the worst of the wounds and stepped out of the bath, pulling a clean white towel around her.

The growth shuddered, great awful spasms as it floundered in the bath, heaving, as though drawing itself together, pulling in its tentacles, amassing. And, as she stared, the growth lengthened and took shape: limbs and torso that looked familiar, the lines of a face she knew, and for a moment her breathing faltered, the old pull on her heart. Those eyes. The way they looked at her, eyes she knew so well but now with a different light in them. It spoke.

"I never thought you'd do it."

"I had to," is all she could say, and the tears fell. "I couldn't go on any more. I'm sorry."

And he nodded, his mouth working, grimacing, as though in pain, and she felt the eternal throb at her hip where he had been cut away.

She had wanted this separation for such a long time, but as he eased away from her, backing off, she understood something else. That he had craved it more.

West

MEGAN BRADBURY

Rae is looking out of her living-room window at the playground across the street. The swings are rusted. The slide is broken. Glass bottles lie smashed against the fence. She takes photographs of the disintegration. She will send them to the Department of Parks and Recreation, who are responsible for the playground's repair. They must do something about it. The playground is not fulfilling its function. It stands empty day after day. How much worse will it get? If it falls into ruin, what will take its place?

Rae possesses a photograph of her father as a boy on a swing in a playground just like this. Her father is grinning in the photograph. The chains he is clutching with such joy are unblemished. When the picture was taken the playground was brand new. Her father had a stroke two weeks ago. He is currently lying in hospital. The little boy in the photograph didn't know this would happen, that his body, over time, would lose its function.

Over the last eight months Rae has gained function: she is pregnant. This development is not something she imagined for herself. She has been collecting the symptoms of pregnancy like her body read a book about it. She is short of breath; her feet are swollen; she must pee every twenty minutes; she has strange and violent dreams. She is alarmed by what her body is doing. The baby has all the power now.

The telephone rings.

Rae struggles to stand. She answers the phone.

It's a nurse at Mount Sinai West.

Is this Regan Law?

Yes, says Rae.

The nurse has news about her father. His condition has gotten worse. Rae should come now, if she wants to see him.

Of course I do, she says, and hangs up.

Rae has been dreading Manhattan. The subway scrum is too much for her now. But she gathers her things.

The baby kicks.

It's all right, yes. I'm going, she says.

Rae passes the tenement where her studio is located. This is where she is supposed to be going today. Her friend Anna will be turning up at 10. Anna said she'd help develop Rae's latest film. Rae can't do it herself because of the baby; the chemicals she uses would harm its growth.

Rae has resolved in her mind the dilemma of having someone else develop her work. She always used to say that if you don't develop your work yourself you can't call yourself a photographer. There is something about the manner in which a creative product is born that determines its success as a work of art.

Rae has learnt that it isn't a good idea to rely too much on other people. In the end they always let you down. You have to do the work yourself. It has to be intrinsically *yours*. But Anna is perfect for this task. She understands Rae's work better than anyone. They have worked together many times. They share the same point of view.

Rae climbs the subway steps at Columbus Circle. She stands looking at the traffic and listening to the noise it is producing. Her baby hears it also, the muffled din of population. Where are all these people going? Towers loom over her. She is hot and sticky. Her back hurts. She holds her belly to protect it from all the people. She crosses Central Park West and enters the park. She walks. She finds a bench and sits on it. Before Rae is another playground. No children are playing in this one either, even though it is well cared for. She looks at the empty swings, the unused slide. All things must end. Other things begin. It isn't always easy to know at the time which is happening to you. This park was derelict and dangerous once. It isn't any more, but it could be so again.

Only a month ago Rae came to the park with her father. He had just moved back to the city after an absence of more than sixty years.

I'm glad to be home, he said. There's not grass this green in the whole of Wyoming.

Rae doubted this.

For the last ten years her father had been living in a town he had built in Bighorn Basin, Wyoming. The town, which was called Law's Creek after him, was a composite of derelict buildings that he had taken from abandoned communities across America and reconstructed as a Wild West settlement in ten acres of unremarkable prairie land. He had spent a lifetime researching what such a town should consist of. He scoured the country for buildings to transport – homesteads, smithies, general stores, undertakers, saloons, jails. When Law's Creek was complete, it consisted of a dozen buildings positioned along a wide dirt road. In its later years a small cafeteria was added, which served modern remakes of classic western dishes. From the general store he sold locally commissioned souvenirs. Fridge magnets depicting western scenes: cowboys ranching horses, cowboys sleeping in the dirt beside a dying fire, cowboys in gun battles in the middle of a dusty road; pinafores and dish towels embroidered with plucky freckled cowgirls; hand-woven coasters with Native American designs.

He built for himself a cabin on the outskirts of the town and he lived there during the summer months, maintaining the buildings, and acting as guide and storyteller to visitors. In the winter he lived in Justice, the closest inhabited town, twenty miles away.

23

In Rae's opinion, Law's Creek was a fake. Its buildings had been lived in, sure, but they hadn't been lived in *there*, exactly. The town was her father's creation and therefore his fantasy. It didn't exist naturally on its own terms but was contrived. If the town had ghosts then they were definitely lost.

In the long run, she said to her father, if people stop visiting and it closes down and it's just left in the middle of the prairie and becomes wild and unkempt, it will look like it has always been there. If someone discovers it by accident they'll think it was a real town.

It is a real town, her father said.

They walked together in silence.

But now I'm finished with it, he said after a few minutes. I'm tired. I want to take it easy.

In New York? she said.

Everyone moves home eventually. It's inevitable, he said.

So he must have forgotten, or perhaps he didn't know, that the town of Bethlehem, where Rae grew up, no longer existed. When the steelworks on which Bethlehem's economy relied closed down, its population lost their jobs. Families moved away. The town's school and services closed. Rae could not go home. The town was abandoned. There was nothing left.

Her father had passed the running of Law's Creek over to another man, he said. Buck Taylor, a Wyoming native and passionate Wild West historian. He was sure Buck would do a fine job; he knew the town's history and had a flair for telling stories. He would make an excellent replacement.

You have a habit of leaving places, Rae said.

Her father often said that out of the two of them, even though he was the one interested in history, she was the one stuck in the past.

You need to move on with your life, he said. Stop thinking about your mother and me. That's all over with now.

Rae gives her name at the hospital reception.

I was told to come, she says.

Rae walks through the throng of staff. She feels her muscles contract. The baby lurches. Her stomach is tight.

She pushes open the door of her father's room. His face is illuminated by a dim wall light. He is skin and bone, sunken eyes, hollow cheeks. He doesn't look alive.

Dad –

Is he dreaming of his town? Can he hear the wind coming down off the mountain? Does the coarse grit blow against his face?

A doctor appears in the doorway.

Are you a relative?

Daughter, she says.

I'll leave you alone.

Wait, she says.

Someone will be along.

She looks at her father.

I'm sorry, the doctor says. There was nothing we could do.

At the funeral, Rae looks for Buck Taylor but sees no cowboy hat in the crowd nor hears the clink of spurs.

Rae spends the night at Anna's apartment. She dreams about a terrible mountain set against a flame-red sky. When she wakes the mountain is in the room. It feels heavy on her. But no. It is the baby. She has rolled onto her back. It is the pressure of the baby that she can feel.

Anna rushes in and switches on the light. She is dishevelled by sleep.

Did you dream it again?

Rae nods.

Where were you going?

Out of the city. There's a mountain.

You need a break, Anna says.

I've got so much work to do.

A vacation.

I'm so tired.

You want me to sleep with you?

Rae pulls back the duvet. Anna smells of soap.

Have you thought about what I said? The centre. Have your baby in the mountains.

I don't know, Rae says.

You should think about it. Your body is telling you to go.

Bodies are unreliable. They don't know what they want.

I'll come with you. It'll be fun.

Fun?

You know what I mean. There's not much time left. Should we go?

You'll come with me?

Yes.

I can't do it on my own.

I'll be there. Do you want to go?

Rae pulls the duvet to her chin and closes her eyes. The mountain has gone. Her view is clear.

Yes, she says.

In the morning Rae listens to Anna putting away plates, running the faucet. The baby has woken and flings its butt from side to side. Rae lifts her T-shirt, touches tight skin.

You're getting ready, she whispers to the bump.

Have you read it yet?

Anna is standing in the doorway. She nods towards a brochure for the Mountain Mother Birthing Centre on the bedside table. Half a dozen cabins at dusk, standing in rolling countryside beside a wooded allotment garden. Six log cabins and a communal kitchen lit by lamplight. A warm glow spread beneath the windows, shadows of the women inside.

In 1973 a group of female activists from California packed up their things and drove more than a thousand miles to the Rocky Mountains where they had bought five acres of land on which a mining town once stood. In 1859 Prospect was a flourishing gold mine that attracted entrepreneurs and adventurers from the east but it fell into ruin after a fire in 1871. By that point the gold had been exhausted. There was no reason to rebuild, so the land was left until 1972, when a twenty-one-year-old typist from Sacramento came across the town by accident as she was hiking in the mountains. She looked at the outlines of the structures built for industry and profit and run by men, and decided it should be the location for a centre that would care for women and their babies in nature.

She and her friends came with volunteers to clear the site, fix wooden supports to the foundations, interlock wooden posts to form the walls, securing them with ties and pegs and fixing the beams at the highest point to form a roof. They built birthing suites and kitchens and community rooms. They constructed barns and fences within which to hold the animals that would supply them with eggs, milk and meat. They planted woodland and their own vegetable patch, and harvested, and stored the surplus food for winter. The women trained as midwives, travelling all over the world to learn new skills. When the pregnant women came, the midwives took them in. They cooked for them, cared for them, and waited for the babies to be born.

Rae's baby will be one of them.

We'll do this, Rae tells Anna, but there's something I want to do first.

Rae takes photographs of women standing still in the city amidst blurs of movement. She started taking these pictures long before she became pregnant, which means the feeling of isolation communicated through these lonely figures is not the baby's fault. As she showers in Anna's apartment Rae imagines the midwives standing still amidst the blur of blizzards and rainstorms on their lonely mountain. But they have one another. They are not on their own.

Rae walks to the subway. She walks to the end of the platform where it's quietest. She chooses a near-empty carriage and sits. The train takes her to Midtown. She gets out at Penn Station. The crowd sucks her up through the concourse, up the escalator and into the heat. She walks slowly. The city passes at an unsympathetic pace. In this environment, a pregnant woman will always seem slow.

It is strange that her father, a lover of abandoned places, should return to the busiest part of the city, as if all that emptiness in Wyoming had exhausted his capacity to be alone.

She walks two blocks south then turns onto West 30th Street.

Her father's building is an unremarkable eight-storey. She follows the postman into the lobby where the floor is made from polished stone and a vase of semi-wilted flowers stands on a table against the wall. She takes the elevator up. Her reflection in the mirrored doors is a surprise; the full body, squat and very round. She gets out on the fifth floor and looks for the right number. She lets herself in with her key. His apartment is a small one-bed, minimally furnished with a white leather sofa in the middle of the living room and a desk under the window. Against the back wall of the living room is a stack of boxes. Her father's things. Twelve boxes, that's all. He hadn't unpacked. A few shirts lie on the sofa, a pair of boots beneath the radiator.

She crosses the room to the desk. His photographs are spread out across it. The black-and-white prints of abandoned towns and homesteads left for years, decades, more than a century. Derelict houses in the desert. Rotten cabins in the woodland. Rusting factories in the mountains. Their roofs and walls are shattered, streets overgrown with vegetation, windows broken and mouldy. Forgotten, lonely, dirty places. Rae picks up one of the images. An unmaintained road. Cracks in the asphalt, splits and tears. The overgrown roadside banks have formed a canopy. What remains of the road is covered with graffiti; paint and chalk cover every inch. Messages and names and dates. *Welcome to Graffiti Highway. Welcome to Hell. Natasha loves you, whoever you are.*

Her father once told her that these abandoned towns allowed you to step back in time. Rae asked him what was wrong with now.

She hasn't come for these photographs, anyway. She is

looking for one in particular, a picture of her hometown, which she saw once when she visited her father in Wyoming. He took that picture like he took all the others, like it was just another place.

She finds it.

This is just a photograph of the town where they had all lived together once – she, her mother and her father – taken by her father as any other person would take a photograph of the street where they lived. In the photograph cars fill the driveways, and bicycles have been left out on the lawns. The walls of the houses are clean and white. It was just like her father to take this picture at a moment when no people could be seen in the view, as if it was a premonition of all the towns he would come to visit later.

Rae remembers the street as always busy, with children on their bicycles or roller skates, and neighbours washing their cars. The only hint of a person in the image is part of her father's thumb, which covers the bottom-right corner of the photograph. Rae presses her thumb against it. Her thumb is small.

This is what she has come for.

She collects her things and leaves.

Rae waits for Anna on the kerb outside her apartment.

Anna pulls up in her beat-up, yellow Ford.

Feast your eyes on that, Anna says, nodding towards the back seat. It's covered in packets of potato chips, snack bars, fruit, sandwiches and bottles of water.

We're not going to summer camp, Rae says.

We've got to eat. *You've* got to eat. It's non-negotiable. We've got a long way to drive, she says. Are you ready? I've phoned ahead. They're expecting us in five days.

Anna takes Rae's bag and opens the trunk.

This all you've got? You've packed everything?

Rae nods.

Camera?

Yeah.

Are you sure you want to go home first?

Certain, Rae says. For the project. It's important.

Anna lifts the bag into the trunk and slams the hatch shut.

Let's go, Anna says.

They drive south on the 278 out of Brooklyn, across the Verrazano-Narrows Bridge, across Staten Island. Rae wishes they were going through Manhattan, the last sight of people before there are none. Will this city ever be abandoned? Will New York always exist?

After three and a half hours they come to the outskirts of Bethlehem. The first sign of its decline is the rusting gas station with its faded advertisement for sugary beverages no one drinks any more.

They turn onto a dusty lane that used to be a road.

You OK to walk? Anna says.

Rae nods.

They pass the Old House with its wraparound porch and swing seat except the porch has slumped down the bank's incline and the swing has fallen.

That's where I learnt to play the piano, Rae says.

You play the piano?

I guess.

It's as you thought?

Worse.

They walk along the uneven road.

Rae's mother was one of the last to leave the town. She thought one day it would be revitalised. When it was clear no one was coming back her mother moved to California to live with her sister. Her mother didn't like Los Angeles. The apartment was small, the city unfamiliar and her sister unpleasant to live with. One night she called Rae in tears and said she didn't know who she was any more. Rae said to her mother, I know plenty of people who would just die to live in Los Angeles. In the end this is what her mother did, three months after this conversation, of a cancer no one had known about.

It's hard to lose both your parents. Suddenly you come from

nowhere; you become the starting point.

Through the gaps in between the trees the town's church emerges, its discoloured walls bowing at its base; the steps lead up to an open doorway and an empty building. Further down the road the one-storey houses are barely standing. Black mould has spread across damp cladding and window frames are empty of glass.

Rae remembers street picnics and summers playing in the forest. Her mother, who had been an elementary-school teacher, knew how to see things through the eyes of a child. They built houses in the woods. If you passed them you wouldn't know it. They watched dog walkers from their woody shade. At the end of the day she and her mother knocked the houses down. Playhouses are easy to construct and destroy.

In her father's photograph their house is only just visible on the corner plot but in real life the house has collapsed and lies in a pile of timber, rubble and plaster. Rae cannot walk in her own footsteps now. They have been erased for ever. There is nothing here to show her child. Except the wild. The woodland behind the house has encroached upon the lawn – so something is living. While the house rots, the woodland thrives.

Rae takes a photograph of the house. She photographs the front door crushed by a lintel, the rotten window frames, the broken glass, the fireplace surround, the smashed ceramic sink. She photographs the overgrown garden, the flourishing saplings emerging tall and skinny, fronds open to the sky, the flattened garden fence. It is all the same to her now – that which has been eradicated and that which is newly grown. The effect is strangely liberating for it is now impossible to trace her life through the real objects she once used and through the spaces in which she once lived.

Are you OK? Anna says.

Rae takes Anna's photograph.

In the car, in the dark, their faces washed with the headlights of cars they are passing, Rae and Anna drive west.

Wolves

DAVID MARTIN

We're waiting in the van, engine and lights off, radio playing quietly to fill the time, lost in our thoughts and watching the night. Some scumbag kids are shouting around outside the shuttered-up shops. I see B's hand tighten on the baseball bat, but the kids move on before we think about doing anything. Too many cameras round here anyway. We never decided if tonight was just a recon trip or a for-real mission. We'll know our opportunity when we see it, that much we're all sure of. At the wheel, A cranks the window open a notch and sparks another fag.

When we met up for the first time, D never showed. I was glad, to be honest. I didn't disagree with where he was coming from, but he seemed to go way out with it. He kept sending us links to conspiracy stuff, properly rabid politics. Some of it made sense, but some of it . . . well, when you see a swastika you can't help but think "You're off the fucking reservation here, pal." He'd been one of the prime movers back when we were just talking online, raging about local news stories, ranting deep in comments sections buried under flashing banner ads and clickbait, fantasising about fighting back. He'd helped it become real, goading us to become more than just another bunch of hard-man cyber bullshitters. To do what every gobshite talks about but no one ever dares try. But when we finally met for real, he wasn't there. We never heard from him again. Maybe the real world just wasn't his thing. I remember looking around the pub, joking that the old pisshead in the corner was actually D in real life. Or maybe the woman behind the bar had invented the whole thing just to get some bodies into her grim boozer.

A's van is moving now. He doesn't want to linger anywhere for too long. We park in a silent residential street, over the way from a pub whose main trade in intoxicants isn't the piss they serve over the bar. B is wired, nervous, clutching his bat. "It's got to be tonight," he keeps saying. Three nights we've done this, looking for our chance to intervene in something, to make a difference and show people we've had it with being left to rot. To turn the tables on the swaggering kids who start on you just walking down the street. The living-dead zombies and wannabe gangsters who deal to them. The illegals jabbering foreign and looking at you like you're a sucker. The fat bastards in the City who ran off with our futures. The smug wankers just a mile down the road, throwing their dinner parties in what used to be working men's houses lit up like department-store Christmas ads when you pass by in the cold night, pontificating behind fogged-up windows about problems they'll never understand and people they'll never meet.

I've brought a hammer tonight. A approved. If we're going to do this, there should be no going back. If you don't do some real damage first strike, they'll come back at you. We're not vigilantes or any crap like that. We just want to do one good thing, save some poor bastard from an undeserved kicking, frighten some thug so bad he'll never so much as say boo to anyone again. That's all, just one raised finger to the perpetual hurricane of shit.

The pub is called the Holly Tree. All the streets on this overspill estate, thrown up as cheaply as possible, are named for the forests that were here hundreds of years ago – another of the petty cruelties that make up its landscape. Alder, hawthorn, rowan, willow. Echoes of something that was grubbed up and obliterated, screaming ghosts trapped in signs for cul-de-sacs and low-rise blocks. Maybe the scraggy lines of pollarded trees on the far side of the park are its last true survivors, humiliated and paraded like tortured prisoners. Sometimes when I'm asleep I find myself lost in those vanished woods, roaming the dense green spaces, sunlight heavy through the leaves, a place of wolves, humming with insects and violent life. Roots entangled in quiet wars and caresses that last for centuries. I wake to grey cloud and a view of the bin store.

A advances the van so we can keep an eye on closing time. He's a big guy – he hints a lot about being ex-military, but he doesn't look like he was ever army-fit, however badly he might have let himself go since. He smells of sweat under the fag smoke, but betrays no nerves, unlike B, who is tense as a board and ready to blow if something doesn't happen soon. I don't care if A was ever in the forces for real – unlike D, he actually turned up and put his arse (and his van) on the line. We accepted his leadership straightaway.

When we met, we agreed no real names, but we soon fell to talking about people and places we had in common, how our circles overlap in this city. How we'd have passed each other at this gig, this club, that football match, without ever meeting. It was the most I'd talked to anyone in real life in a long time, even if we did try and keep it strictly to the business in hand. The whole initials thing is a bit daft – by now we all know who the others really are – but it's a sign of respect to stick to the rules.

It was the best I'd felt in ages. Ranting online gives you a rush, but it leaves you feeling drained and guilty, like a wanking schoolboy. When you don't put all that anger to work, it hollows you out and corrodes you. Like poor old D with his Nazi conspiracy shit, raging but unable to act. Like me, stuck in my poxy flat with its millimetre-thin walls, listening to the thudding bass of some bastard's music trying to drive me insane, but too scared to confront him like I know he wants me to because he's bored and needs a rush as well. But one day, if we burst in there mob-handed, me and A and B, he'd get what he deserved.

From the window of my flat, I have a bird's-eye view of bugger all, across this estate where I ended up after my marriage went down the tubes and I gave up on going to work because

I had a hectic schedule of sitting in my room staring at the TV and wanting to die. I used to live within touching distance of the smug-wanker dinner-party brigade in their period terraces, way back before I got flushed down the shitter. Down into the cracks, where I pay some landlord – who doesn't even bother pretending to not be a crook – pretty much all the money the benefits office grudgingly allows me after it gets bored with humiliating me. At night I watch the kids on their bikes go back and forth in the dark at the edge of the park, up to fuck knows what.

The pub is chucking out, but it's a quiet night. No car-park ruck, no dodgy deals going down. B exhales disappointment. A turns the key and we move off again. The streets are dead. We move slowly, peering up alleyways looking for scrotes emptying outhouses. Nothing. Another wasted night. We'll each go home to sleep alone, and wake to the usual shit.

We're on the periphery, where the houses back onto bare farmland and the roads revert to the country lanes they used to be, vanishing into a darkness past the last few street lights, the pavements stopping dead just beyond the speed-limit signs. Beyond is that strange transition zone between the town and its ring road, where empty fields studded with pylons surround shut-up retail parks, sewage works and railway lines, dark silent spaces of clodded earth like deserted battlefields. A pulls up to turn the van around. When he stops, outside in the dark, we see someone moving.

On the edge of our headlights, where the black mouth of the lane begins, someone crosses the road. Perhaps we all saw different things. I saw a swagger, a hood, one of the kids outside the corner shop who called me a paedo this morning and gobbed at my feet, daring me to have a go. Maybe B saw a beard and dark skin. Maybe A saw someone looking for a house to burgle. That was enough. Our last chance, and we took it. "That fucker is up to no good," says A, but we've all already come to the same conclusion. Through our tiredness and irritation, adrenalin fires. Our hunting instincts kick in, like we're about to jump out of a plane into enemy gunfire.

The figure vanishes into the darkness, his shape merging into shadow beyond the glow of the street lights. A accelerates after him. For a moment I think he could just be a kid on his way home, but then I think again about those little scumbags outside the shop this morning, this evening, every fucking day. Even if he isn't one of them, he'll be someone just like them. Do the people who shit on us distinguish between us for even a second? Don't we all look the same to them? We want this, we need this and we deserve this. Our breathing synchronises as we exchange this silently between the three of us, this understanding we've created.

We see him ahead in our high beams, walking close to the dark verge as we approach. Hedges tower on either side, no other lights for miles. He doesn't break his stride or move over onto the verge as we pass, which angers A more. Behind us the hedges broil in red brake light. "Go, go, go," screams A. B and I leap out, weapons raised. He has stopped, but doesn't run or cry out when he sees us, all balaclavaed. I can only see a dark shape. A runs around the far side of the van and jumps him from behind. "Bastard!" he yells and hits the silent figure hard across the back with the tyre iron. Then we're all on him. He's on the ground, hands half-heartedly raised to protect his face, indistinct in the lane's deeper dark. I feel my blows rebound off soft flesh and jarring bone. He never makes a sound. We've given up on weapons now and just kick the shit out of him. He's every bully, every benefits officer, every banker, every bastard who made it their mission to strip my last shreds of dignity to feed their own reflections of power. I can hear our breath gasping in the great silence of the fields beyond the hedgerows, England's bare nerves of ditches and footpaths twitching to the dead night. This country is a deep, strange well. I see trees bursting from the ground to devour the low-rise blocks and enfold them in choking creepers and white blossom, reborn from the haunted earth. Red eyes in the shadows. My hate and my action are one. I'm just an observer of a machine at work as my boot goes in and out.

When we finally stop, the fields' hush rushes in like a physical force, flowing like cold sand around us. The figure is motionless. "Is he dead?" B asks finally. A is practically dancing with excitement. I've never seen him so happy. Maybe this is the nearest he'll ever get to a successful military mission. "Who gives a fuck, eh?" He uses his boot to flip the body onto the verge and then again until it slides down into the dank choked ditch. It settles into the deep shadow and vanishes, enfolded.

The diesel thrum of the van, still running with the doors open, is the only sound now. Its red tail lights watch us. I can't tell you how we feel. We've crossed into a new territory where the old words don't mean anything. We are no longer the same people who set out that first night.

A collects our weapons in a bin bag, and says he'll sling them all in the river. He walks round to the back of the van as B and I climb up into the cab.

We don't see where it comes from. A's scream cuts off sharply as something heavy thuds into him. The shadow gives a low growl. Cold black water runs down the back of my neck. I leap up into the cab and wrench the door shut so hard that the van trembles on its locked brakes. In the second or so before it closes, I get a glimpse of them in the tail lights. A is lying on his back, a long, dark shape upon him, its jaws fastened in his throat. I hear a gargle of agony and terror as A chokes on his own blood, a hole torn in his neck. B is screaming too.

I realise I am in the driving seat. I slam into reverse and floor it. The tyres shriek, then there's a slow, wet, crunching impact under the back wheels. An endless second or so later, the sound is repeated under our feet, beneath the cab floor. My eyes are fixed on the side mirror, trying to keep the van straight between the black hedges as it flies backwards towards the distant city. B is looking forward into the receding pool of our headlights as the lane streaks past. He screams again, something I can't make out. He's ghost white, staring dead ahead at something just beyond the beams. We howl past the limit signs, back into orange street light and the road widens out. I spin the van around violently and it almost capsizes, shifting gears like a maniac and flooring it again.

I don't know how long we drove for after that. When I got back some sense of who I was or where I was, we were mindlessly circling the city centre, passing old industrial yards, the silent factories and terraced streets of another dead past. I couldn't have faced being on the ring road, surrounded on all sides by those black fields. Even the dark cut of the canal we passed over on each circuit was too much, a connection to everything that lies around and beneath us.

B starts freaking out, screaming something incoherent at me and trying to grab the wheel. I try to reason with him, then realise reason has gone bye-bye. We're passing low brick warehouses, blank and shuttered. I slam the brakes on, and roar at him to get the fuck out, now. I twist round and take a wild swing at his face. It barely connects but he gets the message and scrambles out. I leave him standing bewildered by the roadside.

Hours later I dump the van as close to home as I dare, and run the hundred or so yards up the street to my block of flats. I'm more frightened than I've ever been, anticipating the impact of a warm, snarling, hungry body against mine, the strength of its muscles, its single-minded purpose as its jaws meet in my flesh. My key scrabbles in the lock. Going up the dark stairs, I expect to hear a growl at any moment. I bolt my door, put the chain on, but it's so fucking flimsy. I drag the sofa up against it. Then I'm convinced I've trapped myself in here with it. It takes me ten minutes to pluck up the courage to check the kitchen and finally, armed with my biggest carving knife, the bathroom. Our bag of weapons is, I remember, lying in the lane next to whatever is left of A. I sit by the window, chain-smoking and shaking, until dawn starts to outline the bare, stick-like trees in deep blue. Finally, I fall asleep. I'm running through the dense woods, splashes of sunlight warm on my skin. Birds call harshly up above. Things move in the undergrowth.

I wake lying spreadeagled on my bed. I can't move. The roots have come up through the foundations, through the floor, through the mattress. They bind my hands and feet. Another encircles my waist. It moves, tightening, as I watch helpless, my screams for help going unheard. Then I feel a prickling all over my back, the splintering tips of branches pushing through the mattress, connected all the way down through centuries of flint and bone and earth, sucking at ancient waters. They pierce my skin, scrape against ribs and vertebrae, work their way into my lungs with a hiss of released air. I see the tips of the branches, trees in miniature, as they penetrate bloody and triumphant through my torso. My mouth is filled with blood and sap as the forest rises through me. A branch thrusts from my mouth. The last thing I hear is a low growl.

Our Lady, the Sheela Na Gig
JANE ROBERTS

"Dare you to go to the pagan place of worship on the hill where them godly souls fear to cast their prayers. Dare you to touch the Sheela Na Gig. Dare you to look at all of her repulsive bits – all hanging out and exposed like a disgorged mussel. Dare you to put your ear to her mouth and listen to them foul incantations spewing from her lips . . ."

We play dare, Siobhán. So what? It's the boredom that gestates into skulduggery in a rural hole like this. We like to play games to fill the idle hours. But you need to understand our geography to understand us.

There's a road runs through our valley. Not an A road. Major roads they only put in if there's somewhere worth going. Traffic's rare heading down this way. Nothing of note to see – and maybe some things you wouldn't yen to see. Landlocked with no river, no sea to wash away our sins. Mark this, we live in The Valley of No Good and no good shall come to pass.

You want to play our game, Siobhán? You will end up playing it, regardless. Because of what you did. Because every woman – one way or another – always does end up playing our game in these parts. It's just a game, we're only kidding . . . It's all frolics and japes to fritter away the time. Aye. And there's plenty of time to kill.

There are tales and superstitions about this valley. Tales and superstitions that could scar and scare a foreign heart. Brutal, like. But not a local, sistren heart. We've grown up with this folklore, repetition anaesthetising its razor-sharp edges. The rawness of the pain is already set into the fabric of the buildings, the stones; rawness set into the calcific depths of our bones.

"No good can come of going to that place on the hill . . ."

That's what village folk say. They call us heathens, the village elders do. Only because we're young and we want to run free, tearing up both the veil and the valley, revelling in the seismic ripples of chance and abandon. Like they must have done before us. And all their ancestors before them. It takes one heathen to know another. So we act up to our name, act up to our heritage. There's not much else to do here but be heathen. The landscape is nothing but barren vacuity. And yet we're all so damn fertile.

We women have it tougher than the men. They do what they please, with any that pleases them. We get pregnant. We stay in the village. There are a few exceptions to the rule: those who want to get away so bad they end up crazed and roam the hillscape searching for the lights of cars on the nearest road – ships in the night called to safety from the jagged rocks and murky waters by the beam of a lighthouse. We don't know if most make it anywhere good. Because once they're gone, no one comes back.

And then there's our Siobhán. You. The Returned. The one who tells us sisters of a life beyond we have no yen to hear about; the one who, impregnated with strangeness, brings uncertainty into our world. So this is why you have to play the game, Siobhán. To prove you're one of us. Part of The Sisterhood. That is the rule.

Some say the Sheela's there to ward off the Evil Eye . . . Others say it's there to encourage it . . . We don't know, don't care – beyond making it part of our own special rituals. We revel in the potency of it.

One of the first girls from our time to play dare, to go to the chapel, to touch the Sheela Na Gig, to look at the misshapen form of her body, to listen to the Sheela Na Gig, she just lay down in a euphoric state afterwards with limbs splayed out and curled like a dehydrating starfish on the overgrown sward – so far from the water that might wash away her sins, our sins. A chill from the east teased the ears of grass stretching out to listen to the wind as we realised that all of us women are presided over by this grotesque thing in this grotesque place. It is inescapable. We are the living embodiment of it. We are disciples of the cause.

"Are you going to see the Sheela Na Gig? Isn't that how you get into trouble?"

Them lily-livered village folk with their knees a-knocking even in their slumbers, they do not know, cannot begin to comprehend the might of the Sheela. To look at it is merely the start. You will want to know what happens if you touch it. Will want to feel where the sculptor has carved. Where the tools have broken the stone. Where the stone has broken the tools. You will want to know if it has been carved at all. Or whether it might be something borne from the stone belly of Mother Nature, or something indigestible shat out the hole on the other side. It is a despicable thing. A beautiful thing. An ugly thing. A thing's thing. Natural and unnatural in equal measure. Looking is one matter, touching is another. If you touch it . . . But that's the dare, Siobhán. You want to play our game? You have to visit the Sheela Na Gig.

So up you go, Siobhán. Up the hill to that pagan place. Up you go to see the contortionist Sheela. The rungs of the ladder are rotten in places. But we know that. We know you will use the ladder. How else will you reach up to the Sheela to hear her incantations? It's all part of the game . . .

Your body lies on the ground, Siobhán, by the flaking foundations of the stone walls. As your breath fades, the oxygen drains from your body and from the tiny, strange form within your distended womb, both a-quivering in the grass like felled Russian nesting dolls. You could be in the grip of euphoria. But no. Not for our

Siobhán. You see, we are The Sisterhood. Once part of The Valley of No Good, you do not leave – to become better than us, different to us. Nor do you return to rub our noses in your reincarnation, Stranger. You belong to us. Not with us. On our own terms, the terms of our grotesque game.

You belong to Our Lady, the Sheela Na Gig.

No, Where Are You, Like, Really From?

AMAL ADAM

I fucking hate these people. I hate them all.

I look up at the high ceiling and tall windows. The chandeliers are like huge balls of light floating in mid-air. These people don't give a shit about us. I've never agreed with Ayan's Black Power nonsense, but we really are a fetish for them. I know that now.

On the stage, staring out into almost complete darkness, you don't see the endless rows of tables and the women in elaborate gowns. Their chatter creates a sound that tries and fails to fill the vast space. Everything about this place feels cold. The room smells old. The room smells White.

After my speech I sit at the table they tell me is mine and exchange pleasantries with the other women. Apparently we've met before.

"Your speech," says one. "It was so heartfelt, so moving. I can't believe you were so young – to be subjected to such cruelty when so young is . . . is . . ."

"Well it's abhorrent," says another, sitting next to her.

"Yes, abhorrent," agrees the first.

I see Fatima sitting only a few tables away. Why hasn't she come over to tell me how great my speech was?

A man puts a small plate in front of me. I ask him what it is. "Pan-fried octopus with seasoned sobrasada," he says. What the fuck is that?

Fatima and I were inseparable once and now here we are, in the same room pretending not to notice each other. This used to be our fight; our baby, our cause. It was ours before it trended on Twitter, and it was ours before *they* got involved.

We worked well together. My job was to come up with the ideas and hers was to shake hands and kiss babies. But our paths were always bound to diverge because agreeing on the problem is not the same as agreeing on the solution. Fatima's narrow perspective on things frustrated me because I thought bigger, dreamt bigger. I wanted to change the world, and she couldn't see past her need to save it.

"So lovely to see you again, Noura!" shouts another woman a few seats away. She looks middle-aged and all I can focus on is how the red lipstick she's wearing emphasises the wrinkles around her mouth. She points to another woman next to her. "I was telling Lydia about the conversation we had the last time I saw you." Her friend doesn't speak and instead looks at me, smiling and nodding intently.

What is it with these people? Why are they always fucking smiling? I don't remember meeting her or anyone else on the table, but then again they do all start to look the same after a few glasses of shit wine.

"I'm so sorry – how old did you say you were when you came to this country?" she says.

"I was born in Bristol."

She's under the impression that this is a conversation.

"Oh of course – sorry – yes. And loved, loved, loved the speech. My goodness, for you to go back home and have that done to you by your own family? I just . . . I just can't imagine. I think you said you were going to Africa too the last time we met?"

I didn't go *back home*, I went to Somalia. "I think it may have been Australia or Pakistan," I say.

"Yes Australia . . . or Pakistan. And how was it?" she asks enthusiastically.

They were always enthusiastic, too. What the fuck were they

so enthusiastic about?

"Eye-opening," I say. "The women face incredible challenges but are doing great work. They're so brave."

The woman regurgitates platitudes that make me want to break my wine glass over her head. I smile at the waiter as he clears the third course. I notice that we've run out of wine and ask for another bottle. Against my better judgement, I look at my phone. He hasn't called, texted, or emailed. Ayan was right. And Ayan was right because she is always right. I hate her for it. I asked her once what it was like to have it all figured out when it was so confusing for the rest us. She told me to stop drinking so much. He may have been too cowardly to leave her, but I was too cowardly to admit to myself that I always knew.

"The thing about ultimatums," I say to the woman next to me, "is that we think we are giving the other person an ultimatum when we are actually giving ourselves one."

She smells like lavender. I hate flowers.

"That's interesting," she says, "but what do you –"

"The ultimatum is ultimately ours. Do you see?"

"I think so . . . So essentially you're saying that –"

"I told him that he needed to make a decision, but I was the one who had to make a decision, even if it was based on what he decided to do . . . Do you smoke?"

"Me? No, I –"

"I need a cigarette."

Tamsin, a lawyer I do remember meeting, comes over to say hello. She introduces her cousin. I look at the girl with the wide perfect smile standing next to her; her hair is long, flowing and golden. I touch the mess on the top of my head which I didn't have the energy to tackle this morning.

"I have to say, Noura," says Tamsin, "great speech. The line about finding purpose in pain – it moved me to tears."

I thank her and smile. She's right, it is a good line.

"I read your article in the *Guardian*," says the girl beside her, sticking her hand out to shake mine. "Such a barbaric practice! I – I'll do anything I can to help!"

"Oh yeah?" I say. "Are you a lawyer too?"

"No – I'm reading history of art at Oxford. I'm in my final year." She smiles again widely.

I smirk. She might as well have said, "I come from so much fucking money that I don't have to worry about my future job prospects." Must be nice. She's very interested in herself.

"Tamsin said she knew you. I'd love to get involved!"

I feel a sudden urge to punch her in the face but I don't. Instead I reel off a list of organisations that she can offer her lovely help to. She struggles to note them all down and then appears to give up. She asks to take a selfie and before she leaves pays me what she probably considers to be a compliment: "I just love your hair – it's so . . . natural." She smiles again.

Where's Ayan when you need her? She would have sent this girl running back to whatever grand estate she came from in tears. On the other hand, I guess it could've been worse: at least she didn't ask to touch it.

My mother hated my hair. When I was a child, she once tugged so hard when she was combing it that she pulled out a chunk, leaving a bald patch. Then she shouted at me as if it was my fault that she didn't know what she was doing. She had long and silky like the Arab girls in the films she always watched. Her skin is light like theirs, too. My hair was tough and my skin was dark like his. When he left, she would never let me forget it.

I stood in front of that door for what felt like hours the last time I went to see her, trying to build up the courage to ring the bell. I wasn't wearing gloves and my fingers went numb from the cold. The door opened. It was Jama. He looked surprised and then noticed the weekend bag in my hand. I asked him where Mum was.

"Living room," he said and walked out.

She was sitting in her chair in the corner of the room watching TV.

"So look who it is," she said, smiling. Her smile was wry.

I sat on the sofa by her chair and watched her as she pretended to watch dark-skinned Somali men in ill-fitting suits sitting around a table. They spoke in a dialect I couldn't understand. I asked her how she was doing.

"You cope with what Allah gives you," she said.

"You look tired."

"I'm stressed," she said. "I have been caused stress lately."

Me. I was the cause. I was the stress. I didn't know what to say so I asked her if she wanted anything to eat or drink. She turned to me and gave me a long, examining look. She went back to pretending to watch TV before speaking again.

"You've put on weight."

My eyes began to sting. It was the way she couldn't even be bothered to look at me when she insulted me that cut me.

She stood up.

"And now you're crying?" she said. "I am the one who should be crying! Do you know what people say everywhere I go? About you? About us – this family? 'It is her daughter who is shaming us. It is her daughter who goes on TV and talks about her most private parts – with no dignity and no shame – to those pig-eating godless people!'"

I know what I do is right, but also know that she has suffered. I've ruined her life.

"I cannot go anywhere – I cannot do anything!"

"I was sick for years. I bled and bled and I was so sick –"

"You were spared the worst of it!" Her voice was loud but still somehow fragile, as if it would break from its own force. "You know what was done to me."

"It's all bad, Mother. Why is anything else important?"

"There are ways, Noura, ways of doing things. You could have been discreet. You should have been respectful! But you sit there and tell these people we are barbarians! How can you sit there with them and smile?"

"I don't smile!"

"I pinned you down? I spread your legs and cut you?"

"I didn't say that! They said I said that but I didn't!"

"How could you? After everything I have done for you!"

I wanted to apologise for her pain, but the only apology she would ever accept was the one for what I was doing. I would never – I could never – apologise for that.

"Why are you here, anyway?" she asked. "Selling out your own people not bringing in much money these days?"

"I came to see you because you're ill."

"Now you care about how I'm doing? Well, I may not be well, Noura, but you are the one who is sick. Sick here." She held her finger on her temple. "You will burn in hell for what you have done to me," she hissed.

I was still in tears when I left the house that afternoon. Three bottles of Pinot Grigio later, they told me to leave the park because it was closing time. My mother kicked me out when I woke up. If I was going to wander the streets drunk, she said, I should go back to London where it would be my problem and my problem alone.

I stayed with Ayan for three days and barely moved. She said she was concerned about how much I was drinking and told me that I needed to pull myself together. I told her to go fuck herself and left.

"Hi Noura!"

I look up. Who the fuck is this?

"I just wanted to come over and tell you how much I loved your speech. So illuminating and – I mean – I admire your courage. The work you're doing to combat this is so important – I mean, we all know it's ultimately about gender equality, right? That's the endgame here, and the education of young girls is so crucial to this. It's just such a shame that such a basic human right is considered a luxury for girls in countries so poor . . ."

I need to zone her out, but it isn't easy. She's very loud.

By the time my mother went to see a doctor about the lump on her breast it was too late, the cancer had spread to the rest of her body. She's still refusing to speak to me. She's even found a way of using her dying to punish me.

Zoning the woman out isn't working. I have to cut in. "I want the wine on your table," I say. "Go get it for me." A confused look comes over her face and then she does as she's told. I ask her if there's any more and she returns with a second bottle. I put both bottles in my bag. It is time to leave now.

And as I walk out I remember this one time we were at the Oak and Pastor on Junction Road. It was me, Ayan and some guy (John, or maybe Jim?). He was hard work when I was sober but bought drinks so it was always only a temporary problem. Ayan asked us what we were most grateful for in life. Her answer was relationships; the thing she was most grateful for in her life was her relationships. The best thing about her life was other people. It makes me feel hollow.

I haven't buttoned up my coat properly and the cold seeps in through the gaps. I call Ayan but she doesn't pick up. I leave her a message. "Hey, it's me! Event's over and I managed to nick two bottles of shit wine. Anyway, let me know what you're up to . . . Look, I'm sorry about the other night . . . Please call me back."

I see a bus stop. I decide to sit on the bright-red bench and open a bottle. I'll wait here until she calls.

The Hole
IAN CRITCHLEY

O n the morning of his twentieth wedding anniversary, Henry
Feathers woke to find that his back garden had disappeared.

It had been a difficult night. In keeping with his recent habit
he had stayed up late, flicking through the channels, before
settling on a French film, which, after an hour, he realised he had
seen before. When he finally made it to the spare room, he lay fully
dressed on top of the duvet, running through the forms of the verb
manger and trying to summon the energy to get ready for bed.

He was woken by a loud cracking and sucking sound and
a kind of *wumpf* that made him sit up, heart hammering. He
wondered if the noise was part of a dream, and why he was still
dressed in yesterday's clothes. He got up and pulled back the
curtains.

He expected to see the garden. Instead, he saw a large hole.

Henry blinked. He rubbed at the window with his shirt
sleeve, as if the hole was a blemish on the glass. Then he looked
again.

Well, he thought. This is different.

He stood on the small patio. Everything was gone – the shed and
the compost heap, all the flower beds that had once held colourful
multitudes but that lately had become overrun by weeds.

A set of footprints led to and from the hole. They looked like they had been made by someone no older than about eight or nine. Had one of the neighbours' kids been in the garden? What if, right now, someone was lying at the bottom, dead or dying?

He skidded as he ran to the edge, almost losing his footing, but came to a halt just before he went over.

"Hello?" he called. Then again, "Hello?"

The hole was maybe ten feet deep and he could see nobody was lying there, dead or dying, or even injured. He was about to return to the house when he noticed something curious. Inside the hole was what appeared to be a series of evenly spaced grooves cut into the wall. They came to an end about halfway down, where there was another hole, leading horizontally into the earth. A tunnel.

The man from the council stood on the front step and told him he would have to leave immediately. It wasn't safe. The house could be next. The whole street was being evacuated, just in case. Henry decided there and then that it would be best if he avoided his neighbours for the foreseeable future. The woman with the twins two doors down was already annoyed with him for leaving his bin out on the pavement.

It had been so long since he'd spent a night away from the house that he couldn't recall where he had put the suitcase. It wasn't in the loft. It wasn't on top of any of the wardrobes, or even under the bed. The garage turned out to be full of all sorts of stuff he had forgotten, including a dartboard and a windbreak. No suitcase, though.

There was only one place it could be.

He sat on the edge of the bed he no longer slept in and could not take his eyes off her wardrobe. A year ago, they had celebrated their nineteenth anniversary – a meal at a fancy place during which Emma ate nothing. For months, she'd had no appetite. Henry recalled that she had allowed herself a small glass of champagne, each sip of which made her screw up her face. He had finished off the rest of the bottle, then thrown it all up in the restaurant toilets, knowing that the churning in his stomach had less to do with the alcohol than the fear about what he would do without her.

From the window, he watched as his neighbours left their houses, wheeling their suitcases, hefting their bags. The woman with the twins steered the double buggy around his bin, then looked up towards his window. Henry shrank back. Next time he peeked out, she was gone, but there were other people now, people he didn't recognise. Were they neighbours he had never seen? No, these people were different – they emerged from large vans, they carried cameras. One held a microphone. Somewhere, out of sight, a helicopter clacked and whirred.

The neighbours went, but the strangers stayed on. Henry saw one of them, a man in a baseball cap, make his way towards the house. A double knock exploded into the hallway and up the stairs, followed by a piercing bell noise that made him clench his teeth and close his eyes. Henry gripped the edge of the curtain and tried not to move. After a moment, the side gate rattled. Henry opened his eyes in time to see the man return to the front. He talked on his phone for several minutes, gave one last glance at the house, then got back in his car and sped off.

The helicopter, too, faded away. A line of birds settled on a wire connecting his house to another across the street. Then, suddenly, they flew up as one. They gathered in a cloud, pulsating for a few seconds like a giant black heart before wheeling away to the end of the road and out of sight.

Henry turned from the window and faced the wardrobe once more. Really, the decision was simple: he could not go into the wardrobe to extract the suitcase, therefore he could not leave. He did not want to see all her things hanging there, but he did not want to be apart from them.

He would stay, then, and he didn't care if the house collapsed around him.

He watched the news. It was all bombs and money and fighting, but then a picture of a house appeared on the screen. The house he was sitting in. There was an aerial shot of the hole in his back garden. It was huge, like the crater of a volcano. Then the picture changed again and the face of the woman with the twins filled the screen. "A total shock . . ." the face said. "You don't expect . . ." She was standing by the bin, his bin, and Henry wondered if she would take the opportunity to bring her complaint to a wider audience, but now the item was finished and somebody was saying something about the weather, which was looking a bit cold and rainy, which was fine, because he wasn't intending to go out anyway.

Just then, in the corner of his eye, something moved. Henry snapped his head round and saw a flicker, out in the garden.

There it was again. Henry was at the patio doors before he even knew he had made a decision to get up. Was it a child?

He slid open the door. "Hey!" he called. "Be careful!"

The child froze. Henry stepped out. A fine spray of rain misted into his face. He narrowed his eyes against it.

"You shouldn't be here," he said, taking another step forward. "It's not safe."

"Leave me alone," the child said.

Henry stopped. The voice was much deeper than he expected. Now he was closer he could see that this wasn't a child at all. In fact, he wasn't entirely sure what it was. It looked human, but at the same time it looked like something that wasn't quite human. The features were all there – nose, eyes, mouth and so on, all in the right places – but the creature was short, under five foot, and had pale, almost translucent skin. Its hair hung in long, thin strands. It was wearing some kind of dress, or a tunic, or a kind of shift. The material might originally have been red, but the colour had faded to a light pink, mixed with patches of mud brown.

Henry rubbed his face. "I'm not going to hurt you."

"How do I know that? You could be a murderer, for all I know."

"I'm not a murderer."

"I bet that's what they all say."

"Can you move away from the edge? You're making me nervous."

"You think the hole might eat me?"

"What?"

"You think the hole is a monster?"

"Of course not," said Henry. "It's just a hole."

The creature snorted. "Oh, no, no. That's not right. That's not true at all. A hole is never *just* a hole."

Henry blinked, then took a step back. Maybe he should go inside. Close the door. Pull the curtains to. Leave this – whatever it was – to sort itself out.

But no. He shouldn't have to be the one on the defensive. He shouldn't have to hide himself away. This was *his* garden.

"Look," he said, "I don't know who you are –"

"I don't know who you are either."

"I live here," said Henry.

"So do I."

"What are you talking about?"

"I say 'here', but really what I mean is, I live down there."

"In the hole?"

"Near the hole. The hole is not my doing. The hole was a surprise. There was a great big *wumpf* this morning and suddenly there it was. Nothing to do with me."

"Are you saying you live underground?"

"Now we're getting somewhere."

"But . . . but . . . ."

"Yes?"

Henry looked around. He was worried his neighbours might be watching, but then he remembered that his neighbours were gone.

"Are you . . . are you human?"

"Ha! Not quite. Humanoid, you could say."

"But you speak English?"

"I speak lots of languages. You pick things up here and there."

Henry heard a faint buzzing and realised the helicopter was coming back.

"I have to go," the creature said.

"Wait," said Henry. "What's your name? If you have a name?"

"Of course I have a name. But I doubt you'd be able to pronounce it."

"Try me."

"It's Franklehosetonzzzjupp."

"Franklehosetonzzzjupp?"

"Almost. Emphasis is on the third syllable. Frankle*hose*-tonzzzjupp."

"And that's . . . that's a male name?"

The creature looked offended. "Yes, it's a male name. Anyway, how about you?"

"Henry," said Henry.

"Hen*ry*?"

"Not quite. Emphasis on the first syllable. *Hen*ry."

"Male?"

"Yes."

"How about if I call you Henrizztozzenlopp?"

"If I can call you Frank."

"Deal."

The helicopter came nearer. Henry could see it now, a black dot in the sky. He raised his hand to shield his face from the rain.

When he looked back, the creature – Frank – was gone.

Just as Henry was about to eat, the landline rang. He wanted to let it ring until it was too exhausted to go on. But it was so insistent, the ringing, he could not bear it any longer.

"Hello?"

"Henry? It's Julia."

Julia? His boss. "Right."

"How are things?"

"They're . . . good."

"That's great. Look, I'll come straight to the point. I know this has been a really tough time for you, and it's not my intention in any way to rush things, or to put you under any pressure. But we do need to start discussing a timeframe – a structure – for when you come back to work."

"Oh," said Henry. An image of a desk reared up in his mind. A computer. With a screen full of numbers.

"It goes without saying, of course, that we'll give you all the help you need," Julia continued. "Counselling and so on. If you want it. We can reintegrate you gradually, on your own terms."

There was a pause then, and Henry didn't know if he was supposed to say something. He couldn't think of anything, and was relieved when his boss started speaking again.

"Maybe what we should do is arrange a time for you to come into the office. Just for an informal chat. Just to see where we're at. How does that sound?"

"OK," said Henry. "OK."

"Good. Right. Shall we say Thursday? Ten o'clock?"

Henry looked up and saw Frank standing outside the patio doors.

"Henry?" Julia said.

Henry hung up and went to let Frank in.

"I came to apologise."

"What for?" said Henry.

"For earlier. For disappearing so abruptly. I didn't say goodbye. I tend to forget that humans have ways of doing things."

"Don't worry about it."

"But I *do* worry about it. I don't want us to get off on the wrong foot. Isn't that what you say? Is that how you put it? Can I come in?"

So many questions, but the answer to all of them appeared to be "yes", so that was what Henry said.

Frank stepped in and looked around. He went to each corner of the room, then to the centre, looking up, down, sideways, picking objects up, putting them down, rubbing his bare feet on the carpet. Henry tried not to notice the mud Frank had brought in with him.

Frank came to a standstill. "It's . . ." he began. "And the

whole of this dwelling is yours?"

Henry nodded.

"Yours alone?"

Henry nodded again. Frank let out a long whistle.

"It's . . ." Frank repeated.

"Yes?" said Henry.

"It's *dry*," said Frank, bending down to run his hands over the carpet. "Very dry."

"How long have you been . . . I mean, how long have you been living there, in my garden?"

"Not long," said Frank. "Probably. How long is long? We tend not to stay in one place. We move around."

"How?"

"We dig, of course!" said Frank, grinning. "Once you get into the rhythm of it, it goes easily enough. And when you want to rest – when you feel like settling down for a bit – you can just carve out a bit more space and call it home."

Questions piled into Henry's mind. "But how do you breathe down there?"

"We make air vents," said Frank. "You might have seen them – small holes in the ground. You might mistake them for rabbit holes. Actually, the rabbits mistake them for rabbit holes. They're easily confused."

"I was going to ask about that," said Henry. "About other animals."

"The badgers are the worst."

"Really?"

"Very territorial. Absolutely vicious if they catch you near one of their setts." He rolled up a sleeve to show a long, jagged scar on his forearm. "Once they get hold of you, they don't let go. Unless you bash their heads in with your shovel." He sniffed the air. "What's that smell?"

Henry looked down at the tray on the floor. "I was just about to eat. Why don't you join me?"

Frank knelt, then leaned in further, his nose a few centimetres from the plate. "What is it?"

"Lasagne."

Frank poked a finger into the top layer of pasta, then scooped up a fistful of the meat and stuffed it into his mouth.

"Do you want a for–" Henry said, but stopped as Frank raised a hand.

Frank stopped chewing and swallowed. "It's good," he said. "Richer than what I'm used to. But good."

"What do you normally eat?"

Frank didn't answer at first. He kept on scooping up the lasagne, at one point lifting a square of the pasta and nibbling at it.

"Whatever comes along, usually," he said at last. "Bugs. Worms. I'm especially partial to beetles. Do you eat many of those?"

"Can't say that I do," said Henry.

"You get that satisfying crunch before the juiciness kicks in." He paused, then said, "You not eating?"

"I guess not."

Frank shrugged. He polished off the food, then licked the plate clean, before standing and letting out the loudest and longest belch Henry had ever heard.

"*Taggglezzzippp*," said Frank once the burp had finally come to an end.

"Sorry?"

"It's difficult to translate," said Frank. "It's like when you're full and satisfied and certain that you're not going to starve for at least another day. It's that. Never pass up an opportunity to eat. It's probably what we troggs think about more than anything else."

"Troggs?"

"That's us. Troglodytes. Actually it's not just troggs who think about food all the time. All other animals you come across do too. It's like the number one topic of conversation. 'How's your stomach?' is a typical trogg greeting. Moles will say, 'May your belly be full!' when they take their leave. You humans are lucky if you don't have to worry about hunger. Mind you, I can see you're well fed –"

"Pardon?"

"You've got the gut of a bear."

Henry ran a hand over his midriff.

Frank stretched. "I bet you're highly desirable to females."

Henry couldn't make out Frank's stomach. It was hidden beneath the long, shapeless piece of clothing.

"How long have you been wearing that?" he asked.

"This?" said Frank, pinching at the material. "Oh, I don't recall."

"It looks like a piece of human clothing."

"It is human clothing. You'd be amazed what you people leave out in your gardens. Just left hanging there for anybody to take. Normally, we don't wear anything. It can get quite hot under the earth, even in the coldest weather. But we've learnt through bitter experience that it pays to cover up when we come to the surface. Now, I must be going –"

"But you've only just got here," said Henry.

Frank made a move towards the patio doors. "Busy, busy. May your belly be full!"

With that, he was gone, out into the darkness.

Henry picked up the tray and took it to the kitchen, dumping the plate in the sink. The window was like a mirror. He turned side-on. Yes, if his stomach was anything to go by, his was a fortunate, satisfied life.

Henry had dug holes as a kid. There was a time when the thing he liked to do most in all the world was dig holes. His father had an allotment, a patch of earth in between other patches of earth at the edge of town, and when he was six, seven, Henry loved to go there and help his father dig. He had his own spade, half the size of his father's, because he himself was half the size of his father, and he loved the give of the ground when he put the edge of the spade into it, loved how when he turned over the soil there were so many things to see – worms and tiny potatoes and little bugs that scurried around and burrowed back down as if they were frightened of the light.

His father always had earth on him. It was wedged under his fingernails, blackening them. It was smeared over his clothes and smudged on his cheeks. It was in the cracks of his lips. When they ate their packed lunches, up there at the allotment, the earth was in their sandwiches and their crisps, and they ate it along with all their other food. It was like seasoning.

"It's good for you," said his father. "A bit of dirt never did anyone any harm. It's the natural way of things."

His dad had a favourite quote. It was from a book that Henry had never read, even though he was given it as a birthday present long after the allotment had been abandoned. Henry had promised to read it. He had wanted to read it, had meant to read it, he really had, but words on the page did not come easily to him in those days. His father was always saying this one thing to him, though, this one thing from the book, and it had stuck in Henry's mind.

"The house is still but a sort of porch at the entrance of a burrow."

Over the next few days, Frank dropped in regularly, usually at meal times. They sat facing each other in matching armchairs, trays on their laps. They swapped stories about how humans and troggs lived their lives, though, Henry reflected, he seemed to be the one asking most of the questions. Frank didn't appear all that interested in how Henry lived, but maybe humans were more inquisitive.

"How often do you see other troggs?" Henry asked one lunchtime. They were eating pizza.

"Oh, not very often," said Frank, drawing out a string of cheese from his mouth. "We're solitary creatures, for the most part."

"But how do you . . . how do you, you know –"

"What?"

"You know – meet other troggs, to, you know –"

"You mean to mate? There's a whole season for that. And

our young grow quickly. They're soon self-sufficient. The minute they can dig, they're off. And we can get back to doing what we do best – being on our own."

Henry placed his half-eaten pizza on the floor and licked his fingers.

"You don't . . . miss them?"

Frank frowned. "I'm not sure I understand what you're getting at."

Henry thought for a moment. "I don't know," he said. "A yearning? An overwhelming desire to see someone? To be with someone you like? Who you love?"

"No," said Frank. He paused, then asked, "How many offspring do you have?"

Henry straightened. How best to reply? In the end, he decided to just come out and say it. "None," he said. "We had no off– . . . children. We couldn't."

"Oh," said Frank. He nodded down to Henry's plate. "You finished with that?"

They sat in silence for a while, Frank eating, Henry watching him.

"But what will you do," Henry said eventually, "when they come to fill in the hole?"

"Who?"

"The people. The diggers."

"Diggers dig. They don't fill in. Do they?"

"The fillers-in, then. Whatever you want to call them." Henry swallowed a gobbet of irritation. Frank could be on the pedantic side, sometimes.

"I can always move on," said Frank.

"Just like that?"

"Just like that."

Frank brushed at his tunic. The material was beginning to wear through.

"You could have some of my old clothes," said Henry. "If you want."

Up in the bedroom, Henry rifled through the hangers in his

own wardrobe. When did he last wear that shirt? There was a jacket he couldn't remember having ever worn. And these suits. He had a sudden memory of doing up a tie. It all seemed so complicated. Tying himself up in knots.

"Help yourself," he said, throwing things onto the bed.

Frank began to pull off his scraggy tunic. His legs were stick-thin and hairless.

"Woah!" said Henry.

Frank's head reappeared through the top. "What's the matter?"

"Are you wearing pants?"

Frank looked puzzled.

"Pants," Henry said again. He pointed. "Anything under there?"

"Oh," said Frank. "No, no. Like I said, we're normally naked."

Henry backed away to the door. "I'll leave you to try things on. Give me a shout when you're done."

He retreated downstairs. Outside, a mist had descended. Henry slid open the patio door and was struck by the silence. The birds had gone. The people had gone. In this patch of the earth, there was only him and Frank. He took a step out and stopped. Was the hole getting bigger? Its edge seemed to be nearer to the house than before.

"How about this?"

Henry turned to see Frank standing behind him, arms outstretched, a long, green dress hanging off him.

"Why are you wearing that? Take it off."

"I like it. Fits me better."

"I said, take it off!"

Henry lunged at Frank, but Frank ducked.

"What are you doing?" Frank cried, as Henry came at him again, scrambling to get a hold.

"Take it off! Take it off!"

Henry grabbed a sleeve of the dress. Frank pulled back, but Henry was stronger and Frank couldn't get away. Henry swung his free hand and connected with Frank's face. Frank let out a howl of pain, high and anguished, like an animal cry. Blood began to drip from his nose, onto the front of the dress.

Henry swung again. He had no idea where he hit this time. The mist from outside seemed to be in his eyes, and in his head. He could see nothing clearly, and all he could hear was a whimpering. He felt the material bunched in his hand. The dress, the dress. And he thought then of the restaurant and the champagne and how beautiful Emma had looked in this dress, and he tasted the vomit in his mouth, and remembered how he'd been asked to choose something for the body, something she had loved to wear, and he had thought about the dress, this dress, but didn't want to give it up, to be parted from it –

His grip weakened and he heard a scrabbling and the patio door slamming shut. He blinked and the mist cleared and he saw that he was alone.

Frank didn't come the next day. Or the next. Maybe he'd gone, dug himself away from the hole, found a new place to stay a while. Well, good riddance. Henry didn't want to waste any more time on him. He had other things to do. There was so much to sort out. He'd wallowed long enough. Time to get moving. Definitely time.

He was hungry, but there was nothing in the cupboards. A sentence came into his head. Somebody used to say something – "You've eaten me out of house and home," someone used to say. As if he was in the habit of munching on the walls and the carpets and the beds.

There was no mist now, but the wind bit at his face as he left the house. He walked round a bin that somebody had left on the pavement. He stood in the middle of the road, wondering why he was there.

This wasn't right. Something wasn't right.

He went back into the house.

It began to snow. Henry watched the flakes hit the window and slide down the glass.

He didn't mean to think about Frank, but he did.

Je mange, tu manges, il mange . . .

He stepped out of the patio doors. The snow had begun to settle, and the edge of the hole was rimed with ice, like salt on a cocktail Henry had drunk once, long ago.

"Frank?" Henry called. His voice echoed slightly. "Frank?"

There was no reply. Probably he had gone. Or maybe troggs hibernated. How nice that would be, to curl up and sleep until spring. Humans were supposed to be the clever ones, but animals seemed to get more rest.

Henry turned back to the house, and as he did so he thought he saw something moving upstairs. It was nothing more than a glimpse, a shadow flitting across the window, and maybe it was just a trick of the light.

But no – a figure was moving about up there.

The patio door was locked. Henry slapped it and yanked it, but it was still locked. He stepped back and looked up, but saw nothing.

"Frank!" he shouted. "Are you in there? Stop playing silly beggars!"

For the next few minutes he alternated between yanking at the door and rattling the side gate. It felt like his brain was jiggling around inside his head. The snow was coming down heavily now and it was getting dark. He looked at himself and saw that he was wearing his pyjamas and slippers. If he stayed out here like this he would freeze to death.

He turned towards the hole.

Kneeling at the edge, he looked down at the tunnel. He lay flat on his belly, inching his legs over and feeling about until he found one of the footholds cut into the side. Sturdy enough, he thought. He shuffled backwards, getting a good grip in the earth around the hole's lip, then easing himself down until he could feel the opening of the tunnel. With the light fading, he could only just see where he was going, but he saw enough to establish that there were tree roots latticing the tunnel's entrance, which he could grab to swing himself in.

The tunnel was narrow, and he had to stay on all fours, but slowly he made his way along. He felt no panic or claustrophobia, and the air was surprisingly fresh – the air vents Frank had talked about also funnelled the last of the daylight to illuminate his journey.

The tunnel opened into a chamber. Henry couldn't make out the full dimensions, but he could sit up and stretch. The floor was uneven, but there was a smooth dip at one end, as if it had been carved out. He nestled into it. There was a soft whooshing sound, perhaps a faint echo of the breeze, and it soothed him. It was like being in a big belly, a womb, and for the first time in ages he felt a profound sense of well-being.

When he opened his eyes, there were two shafts of light shining into the burrow from narrow vents in the ceiling. He grimaced as he shifted, his limbs stiff and unyielding at first. The burrow was about eight feet by six, with the ceiling around a foot above his head as he sat up. At the far end, another tunnel led out, further into the earth. The whole place was bare but for two things: a spade propped up against a wall, and an ivory-handled knife, which bore a tiny mark in the handle, a manufacturer's name, *TENNANT & SON*. A human name, a human knife. Frank must have stolen it, and the spade, just as he had stolen clothes. As he had stolen Henry's house.

He saw a beetle scurrying across the wall. It was big and black and at first Henry recoiled. But after a while, he relaxed. It couldn't hurt him. He watched as it went up and down and left and right, then he placed his finger in its path. The beetle detoured, but Henry kept at it, putting his finger in its way until at last the bug climbed on. It hurried along the back of Henry's hand and was about to disappear up his sleeve. Henry pounced, trapping the beetle between his thumb and forefinger. He held it up, admiring its shiny carapace, watching its legs wriggle. Helpless. So helpless and hopeless. Before he could think any further, he popped it into his mouth. It tickled his tongue, but Henry kept his lips firmly shut. He bit down with a satisfying crunch. The juice smacked against the back of his throat and he choked a little before swallowing.

Not bad. Nutty, rather than bitter or sour. Not bad at all.

Another beetle scuttled across the wall. Henry tried to trap it but it was too quick and disappeared into a narrow crevice. There was something else in there. Henry reached in and pulled out two square photographs. One was old and the colour had faded, and it was hard at first to make out the image. It showed a boy posing with a man and a woman in front of a Christmas tree. They were all wearing cracker hats. The second photo was in better condition and the image was sharper. It too showed a man and a woman with a child, this time standing in front of a post pointing to Land's End. Henry looked more closely. There were some differences – the man in the photo was taller and had quite a tanned complexion – but Henry had no doubt that the person he was looking at was Frank.

There was no sign of him at first, but when Henry knocked on the patio door, Frank emerged from the dark of the living room. He was still wearing the dress, but Henry felt no anger now. They stood, separated by the pane of glass. It seemed to Henry that Frank was standing straighter than before, taller, as if he were growing into the world above ground.

When it became clear that Frank was not going to open the door, Henry held up the photos. He saw the flicker of recognition in Frank's face. Henry bent down and propped the photos up against the doorframe. When he stood, Frank nodded at him. Henry turned and retreated to the burrow.

A rumbling woke him. It was distant initially, little more than a vibration in the earth, but gradually it came nearer and the whole ground started to shake. It took him a moment to realise that the sound was that of an engine. It was coming from the rear of the garden, where the houses backed on to the park. It occurred to him that they would have to take down the fence, but that wasn't his problem any more.

He knew his time here was at an end. He felt no qualm, no sadness. That part of his life was over. There was nothing keeping him here, in this patch of the earth. The future would be different, certainly, and full of unknown things, but that was OK. He was free.

Henry picked up the spade. The memory of an allotment surfaced, but it was faint, and gone almost as soon as he thought of it. The past did not feel part of him any longer.

Through the tunnels he went, the ones dug by Frank, until he came to a dead end. This was it. This was where he would start. He had no idea where he would end up, but he began to dig, and kept on digging.

American Girl in Exile
AILSA COX

America's greatest living playwright stops to take a sip of water. "Well," he continues, "in answer to your question, I could tell you about a young writer down in Arkansas, name of Lewis Gillard."

"Lewis Gillard?"

"That's right. Remember that name because you're going to hear plenty more from this guy."

Six years later, in an apartment block overlooking the Mersey, Kelly's chatting to an old Little Rock buddy who's popped up on Facebook. Hey you guys, so you're in England! Did you get to ride on a red bus yet?

That's in London, she writes. Louis got a job in Liverpool.

Where is that?

It's where the Beatles come from. You know, Paul McCartney? It's OK. We're just here for a while.

If you read Kelly's blog, AmericanGirlinExile, you can find out plenty more about life in England. Like they have these weird days called Bank Holidays when everything shuts down. Like you have to pay for a licence to get a TV. Like no one ever smiles, they just glare, and you know what? They think it's real funny if you ask for directions to send you the wrong way. And it is so cold, so cold, you have no idea. They live in these teeny-tiny houses and they shop out of doors and they keep their heating turned down oh so low because they truly believe that suffering is good for the soul. In England, they say sorry all the time and never mean it.

You know those garden parties you see in the movies and tea on the lawn and parasols twirling? No way. Now it's Easter and they're dragging baby lambs out of snowdrifts on TV. Round my way even the snow is grubby grey and slushy. The sky's grey too, which is a pity because the one cool thing about this apartment is that when the sun does come out for a while, you can see mountains. That's Wales, where Princess Kate lives.

This is the place Kelly picked out from the photos Louis sent. A top-floor apartment with 360-degree views over the city and the waterfront. An old European city, not Paris or Rome, or even Marseille, Louis's home town, but they'd be close enough to spend some time in all those places. Or so she believed in the early days. The job was one of dozens that Louis had applied for in the past few years without ever expecting to hear anything. They had to borrow the airfare for him to go over; the university had offered to conduct the interview by Skype, but Louis knew from the start, and Kelly agreed, he had to be there. Once they met Louis in person, that would be it, he'd charm the pants off those guys. He could walk it.

When Kelly met Louis Guillard he was at school on an athletics scholarship, aimed at talented kids from the world's poorest cities. Despite Louis's strength and physique, it was obvious, even to her, that he wasn't destined to join the Olympics squad any time soon, but somehow he'd persuaded the programme's benefactor to take a chance. Louis was never really interested in sports. He just wanted, like the rest of the world, to come to the US. In those days, Kelly was dating some wannabe actor, and when Louis found out you got more girls from carrying spears onstage than throwing javelins in the sports arena he signed up for drama classes. Onstage, Louis ought to have been a natural. Within a few months he was speaking English almost without an accent, with just enough Mediterranean machismo in his manner to counterbalance a certain eagerness to please that he'd picked up in Arkansas. But although he was always watchable, Louis never stole the show onstage – except in the one-act play he scripted. Almost by accident, he found his destiny. After graduation, he was accepted for an MFA in Writing for Stage and Screen, and given a stipend as teaching assistant.

Together they made a great couple. Louis had the kind of looks that only French guys can get away with – a long knife blade of a nose, a strong jaw, close-together eyes that seemed to zoom in on you. Kelly never met anyone like him before. There was no one like Louis in Little Rock, Arkansas. They were married on a day so hot that no one went outside. They had the streets to themselves, Kelly in a pale dress and tennis shoes, the little mound of her pregnancy signalled by her long fingers cupping her belly, and Louis glowing darkly in his borrowed suit. He'd grown his ebony curls shoulder-length, now he'd stopped pretending to be some kind of a jock, and he kept the beard he grew for a role in *Macbeth*. As the temperature climbed to record-breaking heights, they raised a cold glass of beer to America's greatest living playwright. Thanks to him they knew they would soon be out of here.

"What I still don't get," Louis said, "is how could he have seen the play?"

She puzzled over that too. No one was there. She pictured the low benches and the scattering of chairs, trying to somehow insert an extra figure in the frame. What would he be doing in a tiny campus theatre, and how could he have sat there unrecognised? But the proof was up on YouTube, and still is to this day. *A young writer down in Arkansas, name of Lewis Gillard.* As soon as he knew he'd had a mention in the great man's Q&A, Louis wrote a letter, and he got his answer scrawled on a Norman Rockwell postcard: *Call me,* and then the next thing they heard, America's greatest living playwright was in a coma following a shooting incident in Atlanta, Georgia.

Kelly's sick of the postcard. Sick of hearing those few words quoted endlessly. Sick of seeing the YouTube link pasted into

Louis's website and blog and faculty page and his Wikipedia entry. Keep it for the students. They worship Lewis, his American voice as glamorous to them as the French accent was, back then in Little Rock. With gentle encouragement, he reveals a little more about himself – a boyhood on the backstreets, knife fights and revenge, and schoolmates still in jail, and the gangsters and the millionaires moored in the harbour. So much and no further – and they adore him even more. It's obvious why he's always late for dinner. Those kids just love hanging out with him, and he loves it too. She has seen him progress through the campus, greeting his young courtiers with a sharp "Hey!" and a "How you doing?" and "Come to my office!", and keeping up the banter about Marseille being a shit team since they lost Joey Barton. "Students!" he'll boom, banging through the door just as the twins are going to bed, shaking his head as they clamber all over him in their pyjamas. The acned boys want to share Marlboro Lights, the tubby little girls need to confide in him about their issues, their depression and self-harm. Too bad his own kids never get to see him.

"Didier!" she calls. "Fabrice! Time to eat," fetching the pizza out of the oven, putting the salad on the table, but this time not laying a place for herself. She's got something to tell Louis – something for later.

Fabrice sighs theatrically. "Pizza again."

"You like pizza."

"No I don't."

"You do. Just eat it."

"Pizza's my favourite," Didier joins in. "Can I play on your iPad?"

"No, it's bad for you to play games at bedtime. You can watch TV. Maybe. Fabrice, what you doing? Just eat it, right?"

After dark, the tall windows of the top-floor apartment seem like slabs of black marble. There's nothing out there, nothing. At first they took the twins round museums and galleries, and once they even went to London on the train, but where Kelly comes from only poor people catch trains, and they can't afford a car –

at least not the kind of car Kelly would feel comfortable driving. When she picks up the twins from school, she's caught in a tide of voices that, when she first came here, seemed to be speaking a foreign language, with rhythms and emphases all of its own. You just have to tune in, she writes in her blog. They chew on the sounds and spit them out and make seven syllables out of each vowel. At first, when they came over, the boys clung together. Now it's been so long in their short lives they've forgotten the place they were born, and their voices too are contorted and whining, their manners sly and evasive. This afternoon she finally gave in to their pleas, shaving their hair close to their heads, so they look like a pair of miniature convicts, just the same as their classmates.

"Hey, what's for dinner?" Suddenly Louis's there, home for once at the time he said he'd be back, and the boys are yelling back at him, "Hey Papa!" "Nice," he says, stroking their newly smoothed heads. "Think your mom'll cut my hair?"

"I thought we'd eat later," she says. "I got steak."

"Pizza's fine." He spots the Beaujolais on the counter. "Did I forget our anniversary?"

"Don't open it yet."

"A good wine needs to breathe. So what's going on?"

"I have some news," she tells him apprehensively.

He sends her one of his piercing looks, and she knows what he's thinking, and that he's instantly dismissed the possibility, because you don't get pregnant if you don't have sex for weeks and maybe months because your husband stays up all night writing his damn plays.

"Don't let it wait. Spit it out. Fabrice, *que'est-ce que c'est? Pourquoi le visage tragique?* You don't have to eat it. Here, pass it over."

Fabrice says, triumphant in his excitement, "We're going to be pirates."

"Oliver's having a pirate party," says Didier.

"Sounds like fun. *En français?* Oliver *est ton ami? Où s'habite* Oliver?"

"*Il s'habite . . .*"

"*Où?* Fabrice, *où s'habite* Oliver?"

Fabrice pipes up. "*La partie . . .*"

"*La fête . . . est où?*"

"*C'est . . .*"

They both look helplessly at Kelly.

"It's at some pirate place" – she shows him the invitation with the map and directions – "I don't know where that is. You'll have to figure it out."

"You can dress up too," Fabrice informs his papa. "You can dress up like a pirate."

"Yeah, I got you an eyepatch," Kelly says, "and I bought a shirt out of Bold Street today. We're going to have to take a picture."

"Sounds cool." He checks the oven for more pizza, grabbing the last slice, intended for Fabrice. "*Quel dommage! J'ai oublié* – I have a rehearsal."

"On Saturday?"

"That's the only time they could get the studio. Take a taxi if you don't know where it is. No big deal." He swallows a big mouthful of pizza. Louis is a fast eater, quick mover. "You know it's the kids, their final-year project, you know it's important to them . . . Don't give me that face, Fabrice. You two have a good time, right? And tell me all about it. Papa has to go to work. You know that. Pay all those bills, pay for ice cream and pizza. There's ice cream, right? I'll take you next time . . . *Et Maman, dis-nous tes nouvelles.*"

"*Ah non.*" She whisks the plates away angrily, fetches the ice cream out to soften. "*Ce n'est pas important.*"

"*Dis-nous, pourquoi pas?*"

"*Une journaliste,*" she begins. "It's nothing, just you remember that woman from the newspaper talking to me a while back – remember that piece about Donald Trump? – and she's been looking at my blog and she knows this publisher who maybe is interested in a book. She thinks the way I write is funny."

"A book. You mean a book of your blog?"

"Well yeah, but like a novel."

"You're writing a novel? Who is this person? Are they asking for money?"

"No! What, you think I'm some kind of moron? No, it's a real publisher, of course it is."

"And you think you can write a novel?"

"Why not?"

"Papa," Didier says, "can we play on your computer?"

"Bravo! Clever Mamma! You hear that?" He stands up and squashes her affectionately, and pours out the wine she was saving for later. "*Salut!*"

"Can we play on the computer?"

"Sure, if you say it in French."

"*Peut-on jouer . . .*" they begin at once.

"Just a few minutes. I'll set it up for you. Five minutes."

She puts the steak back in the fridge, the ice cream too for when they remember. Kelly hasn't eaten at all today, a fact that makes her feel vaguely superior. She takes a slug of the wine, listening to the male voices coming from the living room, and then she gets up automatically to load the dishwasher.

"Let me do that," he says.

"It's done."

"Hey that's good," he says. "It's really good that you're writing a book. Come on, sit down . . . Sit down with me for a second."

"I want to get out of here. I hate it."

"We can move. We can find a house."

"It's not that, it's the whole thing. England."

He sighs, gropes, as always, towards the cigarette he's not allowed. "I don't get it. What's your problem? Remember how we were living back in Arkansas? No regular salary, no hope of tenure?"

"You love it over here."

"You liked it too."

"In the beginning maybe, but look at the kids, what's happening to them . . . You don't care . . ."

"What're you talking about? They're fine."

"Listen to them speak! Look at them! Didier got into a fight for wearing the wrong kind of trainers."

"He won, didn't he?"

"He's six years old! You just don't give a fuck. You want them to be . . . You don't care if they're turning into – they're turning into Scousers."

He shrugs. "I'm from Marseille."

"I've never been to Marseille."

"OK, we'll go. We'll go to France in the summer. Stay with my mother."

"Why not? Why shouldn't I visit your family? Are you ashamed of me?"

"There's stuff I don't want you to be part of." He pulls her to him, murmuring those cheesy French endearments – *chérie, mon petit chou* – that impressed her at nineteen. "I'm so proud of you, so proud, you know you saved my life. You made me." He reeks of cigarettes. "Come on, cut my hair. You know I love it when you do that."

"You don't need a haircut."

"I do – this part, you know, it's kind of like a gangster."

"You don't want it short?"

"No, just neaten it up. Like a business type."

"OK," she says, "if that's what you want," taking the scissors from the knife rack.

But first the twins are back for ice cream. Her babies. You can see they're still babies when you look at their faces, their dewy eyes and long lashes, their fragile skulls delineated by the light shading of stubble, running down to the little bony rivulets at the nape of their necks. Each has an identical dent at the crown, as if the back of their heads has been squashed. They watch her snipping at Louis's dark curls. His hair's a little greasy; he really needs to take a shower.

"Your hair's getting thin, do you know that?"

And then, with cold clarity, she sees. She's fallen out of love with Louis. It's as if she's looking through those 3D glasses you get at the movies sometimes. Every object in the kitchen stands clear – every surface and cupboard – the steel handles – the wood gleaming – the knife rack with the carbon-steel knives in descending order – the drawings pinned to the refrigerator – the certificate, *To Didier Guillard – this week's 4-star VIP. Didier is good at reading. He is kind and helpful.*

She used to worry about the students, and his colleagues too – Sarah says this, Lizzie's going to introduce me, Becky's good friends with the literary manager at the Royal Exchange . . . Now she doesn't give a damn. What would she do, she wonders, if he left her? What would she do? And the kids? Her folks would love for them to go back home. Wouldn't they just. But Louis won't ever leave. He has no place left to go.

"Hey kids," she says, "how do you think Daddy would look without his hair? Shall we cut it all off?"

"No, no!" he mock protests.

They are uncertain – then start giggling and spluttering, looking at each other.

"Shall we?"

Before he has time to resist, the first locks of hair are scattered on the laminate flooring, and then some more, and some more. Then she holds up the clipper and switches it on.

"Shall we give Daddy a haircut like yours?"

"Sure," he says, "why not? We're a team, right?"

In no time at all it is done. Louis gets up from the chair, raging and making the kids squeal. "See what you done to me! I lost my hair! Now I can't kill lions."

"You can't kill a lion," says Didier.

"Sure I can. You heard about Samson and the lion. You didn't? I'll tell you. Finished your ice cream? Come on, it's time for bed."

Kelly sweeps the hair into the bin, and hunts around for the camera. She has got to post a picture, a good one; Louis with a beard and shaved head, looking like some evil magician. She pours another glass of wine, and switches on her laptop, checks her Twitter feed and tweets. Why so many barber shops in Liverpool? Louis's taking forever to put the twins to bed, or maybe he's working, or gone for a smoke. Why so many barber shops? Why would you even need to go to the barber with your head shaved? Barber shops and beauty parlours. Even the kids' teacher looks like a hooker – big hair, fake tan, and what's with the eyebrows? She's thinking through what she'll post along with the picture, when Louis walks back into the kitchen and sits there, just sits, on the low windowsill, with the night at his back.

What she sees is scary. "What have you done?"

"Don't you like it?" He strokes his chin apprehensively.

Without the beard, his face seems doughy and raw, his expression infantile; she hesitates to take a picture, because he looks so much like a huge baby, clumsy and vulnerable, his chin the grey pith left behind when the beard's shaved. Even his voice has been blunted, and his smile is just awful.

"It'll grow back," he says, peering at his reflection in the window. "Grow back in no time. What you waiting for! Take the picture!"

So she does, she takes the picture, and posts it on Instagram. No more than a second and there he is, still smiling, for everyone to see, across the globe. America's greatest living playwright. That's the one you should look out for, Lewis Gillard.

At Sea

KATE ELLIS

Florence's feet worked back and forth on the carpet, forging a channel between shards of plastic and frayed wire. The friction warmed her soles and she sped up until they began to hurt. She wondered if she could start a fire this way and what her burning skin would smell like.

A trolley crashed along the hallway, rattling its load of tin plates and cutlery, headed for the wards.

"Flash-survey the room," a voice instructed.

She sat with her knees bent to her chest and her back to the wall and glanced around. All sockets were smashed, plastic casings hung free, wires exposed. Nothing connected to anything outside. The mattress was flipped to the wall, bedlinen bundled, chair wedged beneath the door handle.

A tiny tower of white pills stood proud under her bed. This spit-mortared clock was her tally of control, the tallest build yet. Her fake swallow was Oscar worthy. She didn't go to drama school for nothing.

Children's TV programme noises crowded her head: bells, honking horns and motivational singers. "Move it move it, rub those feet, move it move it to the beat . . ."

"Double shift again." The big nurse moaned in the hall, the volume undulating as she moved around. She had rings piled on every finger and her smile was huge like it could eat you up.

On the door, in pink felt-tip scrawl, someone had written, *wanking until I bleed. I also enjoy early cumguzzling mornings with . . .* She didn't want to think about what it meant but tracing the familiar letters with her eyes was soothing.

Drifting voices called her name over and over. "Florence Florence Flo rens, Floor rinse, Flourise, Flouride, Flod." The words blurred and sing-song-sang around her brain. Her name came again, softer this time, sounding like Grace: "I miss you Flo, I want you, come home. If you get to the sea you can come home."

Grace drove her straight back to the hospital last time she ran home. They walked arm in arm along the pier until she'd agreed to "try to get better" and this was "the best place for her". Grace pasted a smile on to placate her, she could tell.

She said Florence could be home before Christmas, that they'd eat turkey together and there was a special bottle of champagne in the fridge ready for her return. But when she left, she said "goodbye" not "see you later" and her tongue was reticent when they kissed. Florence stroked her face to take a mould. A touch-snapshot to save for later. Cheek imprinted on palm. She'd watched her walk to their car. Then from the hospital window she watched the light patch it left on the wet tarmac until the rain darkened it away.

When Derek woke up, he was shivering. Apparently he'd dropped off holding the rudder, slumped at the stern. His life jacket had risen to his cold ears. He wrangled it down to his torso, sat up straight and rubbed his palms together for warmth. The sea lapped at *Bessie*'s sides, the water calm, the sun reflecting over the ripples. It was Golden Hour, when the dipping day turned everything a magical orange. The view down the estuary had hardly changed in fifty years. Most boats were already out of the water for winter, so no motors disturbed the peace and it wasn't sunny enough for those pesky jet skiers to pose about. He took a photo on his phone to show Carol but it barely captured a hint of the real majesty. The digital image dulled the deep fiery colours of the sun pushing through the clouds and the sea just looked grey. If she ever had time to come aboard, they could spend the night in the cabin and wake with the dawn. He was sure she'd appreciate how beautiful it was. What a way to spend a Wednesday! Moments like these were what life was for.

Derek gave in to the waves, allowing his spine to snake to their gentle rocking while he got his bearings. The pier was behind him now, along with the descending sun. He couldn't tell exactly how far he'd drifted.

Premature Christmas lights twisted a neon outline of the pier-end café. He wished he didn't know how chipped its paintwork was because the building was a lovely shape. Far more elaborate than anything they built now. Every time he walked past he wished he could have a go at it with his power sander and a decent exterior gloss. He didn't understand how people let things slip so badly. He'd just repainted the skirting boards at home and they looked so immaculate even Carol noticed.

She would've made dinner by now and left his in the microwave, probably cursing the fact he was late, always worried he'd get lost at sea. When he arrived home, he'd blast the meal for five minutes on High then remove the cling film carefully so the steam wouldn't catch his fingers. He'd carry it to the living room, lower himself into his armchair and enjoy the plate warming his sea-chilled bones. Her carefully chosen words about a tricky case at work or the cat's latest antics would accompany him as *Newsnight* flowed over them.

Carol said he should consider "packing *Bessie* in", think about selling her. Of course she was being ridiculous. Once she finally retired they could sail together, and until then he was perfectly capable of sailing solo. If you stop, then that's it, you're done. Derek wasn't done yet. He had friends who'd crumbled early in their retirement because they weren't busy enough. Harold had a heart attack last month and Pete did nothing but grumble. He wasn't ready for the clutches of apathy, or for old age. This was life's holiday.

He looked at his watch: just past six. The traffic was bound to be a nightmare now. Getting the boat to the mooring was always a faff, then motoring in the dinghy to the sailing club, and once on dry land, Essex to home was never swift.

He clambered across deck and checked his dials: STW was 1.1 knots, there were 2.4 metres below the hull and the wind was due north. Sunset was at 18.58, so it wouldn't be light long enough to get him back to the club once he'd moored. He should probably spend the night aboard.

The sky had clouded over completely and the sails were making a racket in the breeze. He shook himself awake, took hold of the mainsail rope and pulled it sharply through the cleat until the sail became taut and the flapping ceased.

"Move it, move it real good, out through the window, newt woman. Go on, do it! Flight is the answer. Go go go!"

Florence stood to attention, lifted the clasp and pushed her window open.

"Go go go!" shouted the voices, and she clambered out arms first. The frame was snug on her shoulders but she could fit. This must be part of her mission, it was all coming together! She lowered herself cautiously, reached down to the ground with her fingers and walked her hands forward as she wriggled her hips through. She let her legs and feet fall free and her body crumpled onto the tarmac. She sat up and pulled her hood low over her eyes. If she reached the sea in less than ten minutes everything would be OK, the voices would cease. The staff wouldn't notice until she was long gone. They'd never catch her at top sprinting speed. Last time she was too slow and they mollycoddled her with lies and biscuits all the way back.

The hospital was at the top of a sloped street leading to the pier. She could see the sea.

"Get up, lazybones. Hit the water. Go go go."

Overriding pain alerts from her bare feet, she sprinted down the road to the pier. Cars and people bounced up and down and so did the low sun. The sky was turning pink like it was excited too.

The crashing sea beckoned.

The amusement arcade door was open and her feet sprang off the soft carpet. She zoomed past crashing coins, flashing lights and fluffy toys. In glass boxes, mechanical arms skimmed forlorn forms, swaying limp and loot free. Out the other side she ran into the smell of seaweed and cold air.

Wooden planks rumbled as she sped along the pier and then without pause climbed the railing and expert-dived like a supreme sea creature into the waves.

The voices cheered her on, they bounced, they had pompoms.

Derek squinted in the fading light as something came off the end of the pier into the sea. He was wearing his old glasses in case he damaged his new ones so the distance was a little blurry. It looked like a stupid kid or a huge dog but it was October and this was Essex, surely it wasn't safe to be in the water? Should he react? There was no splashing or commotion. Maybe he was imagining things. The world seemed to get less logical every day. He was so far off it could've been a float or a bag thrown in, perhaps a chair from the café blown astray?

He rested on the damp bench that ran along *Bessie*'s side and ran his cold hands beneath his hat and over his smooth scalp. In the old days exhaustion was lighter. Now it had weight.

Derek motored towards the pier, just in case. He considered calling it in over the radio but didn't want to waste anybody's time or trouble a lifeboat over something he might've imagined.

The power station on the spit was a black shape against the gloomy sky, the horizon barely visible. He watched the café lights extinguish in sections. For warmth, he jiggled his legs up and down which helped until his calf twinged. If it was a person, he'd see movement from here but there was nothing. He must be hallucinating. He changed course to his mooring.

The sea caressed Florence's goosebumps and numbed her face as she corkscrew-twisted as deep as she could. Sharp cold rebooted her entire body, tugging her limbs down deeper. She was blissfully far from the radiator that spread dark patches on the carpet and from pipes plumbed to everywhere, from drones in the dining room and the plates of carrots that shifted on warm gravy and too much pork rind and all that full-fat tea. Far from the invading door handle and the pink scrawl and the shrill phone and the bad news. Powdery pills couldn't stick in her throat out here.

The sea was her salty force field.

She broke the surface and front-crawled towards the only boat out. Her hands working like paddles, arms throbbing as they passed her ears and crashed back into the sea.

Then she got tired.

She rested by sculling in a circle. She couldn't feel her forehead any more but the voices were quiet. She smiled and water flooded into her mouth. As she spluttered and flapped, salt bit the back of her throat and waves slapped her head.

She tried to carve the shape of Grace's face in the water but it kept moving and she kept sinking. She visualised her beautiful eyes blinking slowly, stroking her face with her gaze. When Grace visited, her door-knocking code was *Happy Birthday* so it'd always feel like a special day even when it wasn't.

Florence began humming the tune and her head vibrated.

She tried lifting a leg to check it was still there but she only saw a dark shape before her head went under.

The pier was gone. Just wave mountains now and one rod or a mast that swayed once and then vanished. The sky had lost its pink and was sliding into the water.

She floated like a starfish and stared up at the bruised sky. She wondered what it would be like to plummet into the cosy depths of the sea, to be swaddled by tentacles, seaweed swirling around her heavy limbs.

Thousands of minuscule pins were forcing their way into her body. She decided they were friendly and let them in.

Eventually Derek managed to find his mooring but it was a struggle to hook the chain up and tie the boat on. Light-headed from the effort, he sat and followed the grey horizon's rise and fall with his eyes. It was definitely too dark to motor in now. He'd have to stay aboard.

Out of the corner of his eye he saw something that looked like an arm in the water. He held on to the railing and peered towards it.

"Hello? Hello?" he bellowed into the empty air.

What if he wasn't imagining things after all and a crazy bloody idiot really had gone for a swim? That was impossible, surely? No one in their right mind would swim out here. He stared at the grey expanse as his boat light played over the waves. Nothing else. It was probably just a fish.

He tried again. "Hello, anyone out there?"

Still no response. He felt stupid now. His brain was playing silly buggers. Nothing there. Of course not. What a fool.

"You're losing your marbles," Carol told him. Perhaps she wasn't joking. Was it her gentle way of letting him know his mind was fraying?

No one but Carol had a clue where he was and she never really listened to his exact plans, just nodded vaguely over her newspaper as he spoke. For the first time it struck him how dangerous it could be alone at sea. What if he tripped or fainted? His phone buzzed in his pocket. The envelope icon flashed: *Have you fallen in? Hope not! ETA? Love C*

Bessie rocked and the mast rattled and he wished he was holding Carol's familiar soft form under their covers.

He texted back: *It got dark. Back by 8.30am, D*

He set his alarm for first light and made his way below deck, forgetting what he had been looking for in the first place.

The cabin smelt of the coffee he'd made earlier and chemicals from the toilet. He eased his boots off, poured himself a whisky and was soon dozing. He dreamt he took his dinghy out to find a phantom arm. Leaning over the side, he caught hold of a chilled pale hand and pulled it up but almost fell backwards with its unexpected lightness. The arm had no body. It was severed neatly above the elbow where it morphed into a string of fairy lights. A dotted ribbon of light descended into the water, flashing intermittently. A faint high-pitched version of *Happy Birthday* mingled with police sirens and helicopters whirling overhead.

Annie Lowe
JAY BARNETT

One spring, during Sixth Form, it rained for five days straight. "It'll stop today," said Annie, "at four p.m."

Tom hocked a chewing gum from his mouth and volleyed it at the bike rack. "Bollocks!"

"Fiver!" Annie said. "I'll take your money!"

After school we took shelter in the branches of the leylandii. It's where the tough kids went to smoke. We pushed our backs into its boughs. They were dark and spiky, but drier than the rain. Claire brought one cigarette to pass between the four of us. Tom looked at his watch, then at the sky. "Not looking good, Annie."

It was a quarter to. The sky was dark grey, opaque. The rain bounced up from the ground as hard as it had gone down. "Stupid idea," said Claire, trying to keep the cigarette lit.

The rain eased for a moment, then dropped heavy again. At four p.m., it stopped. Annie sprang from the leylandii and skipped on the tarmac. "I told you," she said. "I *know* shit."

Of all things Annie did, that was the most impressive. She would often, and casually, claim abilities of a higher order. One science lesson Ricky Fairhurst walked around the lab and stopped by every girl to ping the bra strap through her shirt. When he reached Annie, she turned around and told him to fuck off. He called her a slag and moved on. The day after, he shit his pants in religious education. "I did that," said Annie.

She could have had her pick of friends, and yet, Annie chose us. We called ourselves The Four. Claire decreed the name sometime around Year 9. "Like The Famous Five," she said, "but without the dog."

"You can be the dog," said Tom, and Claire kicked him in the shin. They liked a reason to touch each other. It culminated at Stu Lampty's house party the summer before Sixth Form. They disappeared upstairs together while I sat on the counter watching Annie read minds at the kitchen table. She uttered random words and boys reeled, drunk and laughing, from their seats. They humoured her to cries of "Witch!" and said she should be burnt. They loved her.

Tom came downstairs, red-faced and merry. He stumbled towards me and said something about third base. It was testament to the bond of The Four that no awkwardness prevailed in the years after Tom had put his fingers in Claire.

When our school days were done, they left for university. Annie, Tom, Claire – York, Derby, Sheffield. I stayed home, working at Phil Clough's stationer's. He closed down in January. "Internet, lad. Can't compete."

I signed on for Jobseeker's, gave Mum a tenner a week towards bread and milk. Milk she was particularly militant about. "It's not for drinkin'," she'd say. "It's for our tea. It's for our cereal." On occasion I'd enjoy a little, but only ever by night, and only ever in my I'm-also-available-in-sober shot glass, filled to its very brim.

On the days I didn't look for work, I'd walk an hour to Kerridge, to post a letter, or buy some toothpaste, then walk back. It seemed like an appropriate use of my spare time. Half-terms and holidays were best. That's when my friends came home.

Their first year was over. We arranged to meet in Spelt Park by the boulder, an Ice Age relic that rolled off some near hill when everything melted. They dug it up during the reign of Queen Victoria and stuck it on a plinth. Claire was leaning against it when I got there. She gave me beer from a carrier bag. "Get them while they're cold."

She told me about university. About her halls, things I'd already heard when she was back at Easter. "City centre, eighth floor. The nights we don't go out we sit watching Flux across the way."

About a metre from my hand I noticed a bluebottle in the grass. It moved in tiny circles, dabbing its mouthparts at the soil.

"Are you listening?"

"What?"

"My halls, I'm telling you about my halls. They face this club, Flux. You don't need a telly when you can watch Flux. Pissed-up idiots getting turned away, never gets boring."

I thought about the view from my own bedroom – gable end of the bus station, and some mildew at the sill. Opposite end of the room was a plasterboard wall separating me from my mother. Mum liked to sleep with the telly on. I could hear it through the thin partition. Night before this she'd fallen asleep to a marathon of property programmes, back-to-back reruns of people moving on.

The near fly was joined by another, both at the soil now. "Think a dog shat here recent." I pointed to the insects, then a pair of hands grabbed my neck from behind. Before I could see who they belonged to, the owner stooped to my ear and whispered, "You dreamt of pancakes last night."

It was Annie. I turned to face her. She smiled and those laugh lines bunched around her eyes.

"I dreamt what?"

"Of pancakes."

"If you say so, Annie." I had no idea what I'd dreamt. We hugged. From her shoulder came the scent of laundered clothes.

"You hug weak," she said.

"What?"

"You're too soft."

"I'm subtle."

"This is how you do it." She grabbed Claire. They embraced in a passionate grip, all scream and delight. I was left with my can on the sideline.

Tom came an hour late. He'd been sleeping. "Fucking students," I said. We made him run to the shop to buy more drink.

He came back with three three-litre bottles of cider and a pack of paper cups. "That's a lot of cider," I said. "It's gonna warm quick in the heat."

"Get it down you, then." He poured me a cup and placed the bottles in the shadow of the boulder.

The flies still pawed at the soil nearby. I tried stubbing them with the heel of my pump, but they moved fast only to return.

"I'm surprised how many people from overseas come to study here," said Tom. "I've a Norwegian mate now, Portugal guy too."

"Portuguese, you mean," said Claire, but Tom wasn't listening. Annie asked if he was collecting nationalities.

"In a way, I suppose I am." He laughed at himself. "Thinking of all the cheap holidays. The free couches."

"Already on it," said Claire. "I'm going to Athens in three weeks. Staying with my friend Lici. She speaks four languages."

Tom lolled his tongue around in an animal way. "Licky licky!" he said.

Claire looked at him with pity, then told us how incredible Lici was at making breakfast. "You guys ever tried harissa?" she asked. None of us had.

"I've never tried pesto," I said, trying to own my gastronomic ignorance.

Annie laughed, or maybe it was a sniff. She sat with her legs tucked under her bum. Her jeans were waning at the knee but not so much that I could see the flesh beneath, just the denim, faded to a blur the colour of milk. "You'd like that," she said.

I looked up from her thighs. "What, pesto?"

"No, milk." I looked back to her jeans, at the pale, deteriorated knee. "At university, you can buy your own milk, and drink as much or as little as you like, at whatever time you want."

I laughed. "Milk is the best thing about university?"

"It's a small thing," she said, and tipped her head back to face the sky, "but sort of everything, you know?"

Her arms were propped behind her, palms outstretched on the grass. The sun gave me a headache, but seemed to land evenly on her. "Sounds good" – I raised my paper cup – "but I'll just stick with me cider."

I needed a piss, so climbed up from the grass and walked over to the plane trees. Somewhere under their canopy was the toilet block.

I hadn't realised how much I'd drunk until my bladder emptied with a surprising force. The spray-back recoiled from the porcelain to bespeckle the crotch of my jeans.

"Harissa," I muttered, then aimed for the stream of piss with my spit. I missed. I was about to go again but the stream faded. I gave three hard shakes, zipped my fly, and left without washing my hands.

Back at the boulder Claire was speaking, with some pride, about the street party her city hosted every spring. "North England's biggest," she said.

I only half listened from an insular recline, looking up at the sky. There were thin wisps of cloud gathering high up. They leaked across the blue to look something like milk. Sort of everything, you know?

Tom was telling us about his club night. He'd somehow convinced the Derby Student Union to let him DJ once a month. His Norwegian friend, a graphic design student, had made the flyer. Tom pulled one, crumpled, from the bottom of his bag to show us. An illustration of a severed hand making that heavy metal gesture, meant to portray the devil, or horns, or both. A bone protruding from the bloody wrist stood in for the "I" of the club night's name, Punk Is Dust. It swirled in cerise letters beneath the hovering appendage. "Do you have a DJ name?" I asked.

He placed the flyer back in his bag. "Just Tom."

"DJ Just Tom," I said, and poured another cider. I think I'd finished one whole three-litre bottle by myself. I was now working through another.

As I lay, a quarter listening to my friends compare cities, I reminded myself of the red-faced men who gathered on hot days outside Rockwell's, our town's most bargainous pub, and its most south-facing. Paramedics were often seen, out by the worn benches, tending to good drinkers felled by dehydration.

Annie was saying something about Christmas. A market. Decorations and lights. "You pay for this cup," she said, "and just take it from one –"

"Rockwell's?" I interrupted from my drunk recline. My friends went quiet. I assumed they were looking at me, but I didn't know because I was on my back looking up at the sky. "Rockwell's?" I said again.

"What about it?" asked Tom.

"Still there," I said.

"Why wouldn't it be?" Tom's voice was less slurred than mine.

I heard one of them gathering up the empty cans and paper cups to place in a rubbish bag.

"Still there," I said. "All them pissheads out front." I propped myself up on an elbow. "Like that . . . what's it? What's it, Claire?"

She looked at me, frowning. "What's what?"

"That club."

"Flux?"

"Yeah, like Flux. Like Flux, watching them pissheads."

"Suppose so," she said.

The awkward silence that followed was helped along by the distant hum of a council worker's power tool. I could see him beyond Annie, tending to the hedgerow over by the bandstand.

"Fuckin' hot," I said, and lay back down.

"Gonna be like this for five days straight," said Annie.

Tom scrunched his paper cup and threw it at her. "And you'd know."

"I would," she said, as matter-of-fact as ever.

"We should do something," said Claire. "If it's gonna be this hot, let's do something tomorrow."

"Like what?" I asked.

"I don't know, what do people do in the sunshine?"

"The beach?" said Annie.

"Fuck yeah, I'll drive," said Tom.

And like that, it was decided.

He was late picking us up. I sat in the back with Annie. She looked over the rim of her sunglasses at me. "Can you believe Claire called shotgun via text?"

"Fuckin' disgrace," I said.

We drove to the outskirts of town. Past the telecoms building and beyond Bell Roundabout. "Never too far from the coast in this country," said Tom. "Coventry's about as landlocked as it gets."

"And you can walk to the sea from there," said Claire. "Piece of piss!"

The radio told of good weather. Looking to the sky we could see it for ourselves. We needed neither of course, because we had Annie. I should've worn shorts, but didn't. My legs were as thin as my arms, and apart from my legs, my arms were the sickliest part of my body. My feet were OK, and my eyebrows. But I wasn't proud of my limbs.

Tom had good limbs. His legs were olive, ox-like. Optimum hair grew across them. He wore his khakis cut above the knee. Claire wore a floral dress and a wicker trilby with a feather poking from its band. Annie wore a black T-shirt and high denim shorts. Her Ray-Bans should've cost £95, but she got them for £34 on eBay. "I knew exactly how many bidders there were, and how high they'd go," she said, "otherwise I wouldn't have bothered." She leaned forward to tap Tom on the shoulder. "Turn the radio up. I love this song."

Tom peered at her through the rear-view mirror. "It's an advert!"

"It's coming on, after this."

Tom turned the radio up. The man selling energy drinks stopped being funny, then after a moment's silence, it was all piano whirrs and plucky wind instruments. Annie clapped her hands, bobbed side to side. "What's this?" asked Claire.

"*Peg*," said Annie. "Steely Dan."

We parked near the wheelie bins. I looked over their plastic lids, at the pier stretching out to sea. Tom ran to the café at the pier's entrance. "Need to wash my hands!" he shouted, which I took to be a euphemism for "I need a shit".

We went in after him and waited on the fixed seats. I was about to get a bottle of water, but noticed the queue and the solitary waitress. "You could work here, Billy," said Annie, and nudged me with her elbow.

"Billy?" I said.

"Billy-no-job." She didn't even smile when she said it.

"Oi, you lot! I'm in here!"

We turned around. Tom was standing by automatic doors that led into an adjacent arcade, which, it turned out, smelt exactly the same as the café. I think it was an attempt to promote deep-fried wares at the gamers via the medium of extractor fans. It was no smell to advertise. We passed by a row of coin pushers, their mechanical shelves on loop, teasing with piles of silver. "I need change," said Claire.

"Me too," said Tom.

They walked off to find the money lady. I could have done with change, but I followed Annie. She'd gone over to a row of grabber machines placed by a mirrored wall. "Which you gonna choose?" I asked.

She pointed to a glass box of grey shapes. "That one." It was filled with cuddly toys, the colour of elephants. "Look like little footballs," she said. "Grey footballs."

There were black shiny spots on the toy. Sporadic. "Are they eyes?" I asked.

"Don't know, there's three."

"Could be a nose."

"What about the lines?"

"Whiskers?"

"They're nowhere near the nose."

We settled on seals. She put a coin in and the start button illuminated. I stood to the left of the machine, watching her through the glass. "So, you like uni?"

She bit her top lip, concentrating on the claw, the grey things beneath it. "Yeah."

"You miss town?"

She pulled the stick. The claw went for the grab. It skimmed its goal and retracted in defeat.

"Too early!" I said.

She pressed Start for go two. "What'd you ask?"

"You miss town?"

"No." She gave the claw a serious glare, but the laugh lines still came through.

"What your friends like there?"

"They're nice, yeah." She downed the claw. It missed.

"Any boys?"

She pressed Start for go three, her last. "Hmm?"

"Boys?"

"There's one guy."

I didn't ask. Just watched her instead. Some lights from a near machine danced blue on her face. The claw missed.

"That smell," she said.

The deep-fat fryer was all about us – the scent of childhood holidays, of the fair in town, of fast food on the way home from school. I was suddenly nostalgic, but for that moment, right there.

The four of us walked the pier. It was still warm out but the best of the sun was gone. I looked through gaps in the plank floor, glimpses of the sea and great lattice legs of rusting iron. It was a beautiful structure, ornate, communal, marred slightly by Fire. That was the name given to the brightly lit ride built at the westernmost tip. Up it spun, fifty feet, then back down the same. The screams could just about be heard over its soundtrack, a kind of psy-trance at 150 beats per minute. It raged behind us as we looked out to sea. The tide lapped, gentle, at the shingle beach, moving one way or the other, I couldn't tell. "It's coming in," said Annie.

"Let's walk the beach," Claire said. "Before it's gone."

Day was fading. From where we stood the sun had a finger's stretch to drop before it was night. The sea had taken a good chunk of the beach – there were only fifteen metres between the water and the promenade. Two black dogs came bounding. They circled us, salty-wet and panting. My friends kneeled for strokes, but I walked on. Out in the water I noticed something, a metal sign on top of a wood pole, ragged and beaten from years in the flow. It looked like the remnants of an older pier or some nautical structure used for reading the tide. I picked up a stone and tried to hit the sign with it. I missed, then tried again. Tom came up behind me. "What you doin'?"

"Trying to hit that thing."

"Bet I get it," he said, and missed.

The girls joined us. The tide was coming in, so the target got further away. And the sun was setting, so it got harder to see.

"If we don't hit it," said Annie, "we die!"

"We all die sometime," I said, then threw a stone and missed.

"In a crash," she said. "On the way home." I think Annie, at this point, would have liked a gush of wind to blow through her hair for dramatic effect. It didn't.

Tom's mobile rang. He answered, "Big Coop, how's shit?"

I'd not heard of Big Coop. Tom referred to him on the phone as "swill". Hey, swill. Cool, swill. I hear ya, swill.

Claire took one last go at the sign. It was a good throw, her best. The stone arched west, then plopped to nothing. "I'll be out there next year," she said.

"Where?"

"Exchange. I'm off to Boston."

"You never told me."

"I did. In the park."

"Oh."

It was cooler with the sun dropped. Annie's legs were covered in goosebumps. "I'd give you my jeans," I said, "but my legs are shit."

We walked up the promenade. Tom was still on his phone. "Back in a month, swill," he said. "Lookin' forward to it."

I eyed the lights running down the beachfront. Old hotels, shitty T-shirt shops, a short man packing away his candyfloss stand. I needed something or it was home time. Tom had finished his call and was texting. "What's 'swill'?" I asked.

He looked up from his phone. "What?"

"When you rinse your mouth, isn't it?"

He carried on texting. "Swill is a friend, a buddy, you know? Swill." I'd clearly exposed some private lexicon.

Set back at the rear of a car park I saw the hanging sign of a pub. "We should eat," I said.

Claire looked at her watch. "I'm not hungry."

Annie stepped over the chain guard and into the car park. I watched her legs. Their elegant motion, careful placement. If only she'd had such skills at the grabber machine. "Come on," she said, and the rest of us followed.

The Anchor and Hope. I could tell it was once a nice place. Somewhere along the way, management had seen to it that the oak beams were painted blue, and the walls covered in damask paper. Black and silver, soft to the touch. We sat up by the back. One sticky menu passed between the four of us. We made our choices, took the table number, and went to the bar.

Apart from Tom's side salad, we'd finished up well. Our drinks were almost empty. "Off to the bog," I said, and came back from the bar with brandies for all.

"Can't have that," said Tom. "Gotta drive!"

I downed mine. "Annie damned us. We crash if we drive."

"And die," she said, then downed hers.

Claire swirled her glass, looking at the liquid cling then fall. "Are these doubles?"

"Yeah."

Tom downed his in one. "We'll crash for sure."

I offered to buy dessert, a parting gift before my return to unemployment. "We'll buy our own," said Annie. "Can't have Billy-no-job paying out."

We each got a treacle sponge. It absorbed all that had gone before, and doubled at my interior. I think I felt it kick.

Tom came back with another round. They were on a tray with some crayons and children's activity sheets. "We'll use the back of these for hangman. Worst loser gets another round of doubles in."

I went first, marked five green lines indicating a five-letter word. "Jelly," said Annie, and I threw my crayon down in surrender.

We were all pretty pissed now. The others compared inebriated adventures from their first years away. "My sick were the colour of blood." "We pissed from treetops." "I woke up in a church."

"I shit the bed," I said, and the table went quiet.

"At your mum's house?" asked Annie.

They all looked at me. "Yes," I said. "Bad pipes at Briarwood Tavern."

Tom laughed and nearly fell off his chair. We weren't driving anywhere tonight.

"Where we gonna sleep later?" I asked.

"Think I saw a Travelodge by the car park," said Tom, and glanced at Claire.

She took out her phone and tapped away at the glass. Her dad was efficient at transferring money in times of need. I had no money. Not for a bed, nor much more for drink. "I'll have to sleep in your car. Billy-no-job innit."

"Me too," said Annie. "I maxed my overdraft back in April."

I stared off at a distant beer pump, acting as if the prospect of a night alone with Annie neither bothered, nor excited me. She was only a friend – a swill.

It was cold out. There were no buildings protecting us from the wind, just the flat expanse of water lapping in the dark. Annie walked in hurried steps beside me, her legs bare to the night. She only had a cardigan, its sleeves strained down over her hands. Tom belched. He spat the taste from his mouth, out towards the sea. "Disgusting," said Claire.

We came to the Travelodge. Tom and Claire wobbled towards the entrance using the wheelchair access ramp. "Oi, DJ Just Tom," I said. "Keys!"

Tom tossed them to me. "Don't shit in my car," he said, and entered the building through spinning doors.

Claire stood hugging herself in the cold. She tried to say goodnight, but hiccupped instead, then followed after Tom. Annie linked my arm, pulled into me for warmth. In this way, we walked back to the car.

The wheelie bins close to where we'd parked reeked from the day's sun. Annie wafted a hand across her nose. I unlocked the car.

"How do you want to do this?"

"What?"

"Do you want to sleep across the back seat? I can recline the passenger side a bit. Or something."

"The front's best. We'll recline the pair."

"You want passenger seat, or driver seat?"

"Don't care."

"I'll take the passenger seat. I've not got a licence."

"Whatever," she said. "Just get in. It's cold."

The dashboard lit up. I switched the heaters on, and the radio played Britney. Annie rubbed at her legs. "What's that smell?"

Sea breeze had thrown the scent of the wheelie bins our way. The fans pulled it in, then threw it back to us warm. The torrid odour of discarded cod turned to rot in the dark. Annie switched the heat off and the car cooled. With the fans gone, the radio sounded louder. "This song is *Toxic* – literally," I said.

"I like it. We dance to it at uni."

"Well, I don't like it." I switched it off.

"It's a better sound than Mum's telly through the wall," said Annie, and the dark of the car closed in. I opened the glove box. Closed it. "Why don't you do something?" she said.

"What?"

"Get on with something. Leave home or something. Why did you stay behind?"

"You tell me. You know everything."

"What happened to the sound thingy?"

"Sound thingy?"

"The course."

"Audio engineering! Nah. Was into it for about an hour, then realised there's a lot of maths involved. I just like to listen."

We listened to rain hit the car. It was early rain. Soft and sparse. It relaxed me, stilled me in the passenger side. The back of my head began to fizz.

"Go for it!" Annie shouted, banging her hands down on the dashboard. Her palm knocked the hazard button and the car's lights blinked on. Off. On. Off.

"Go for what?"

"The course! Make the move!"

"Expensive move." I looked at the wheelie bin, pulsing in the hazard light.

"Don't be scared to make the move." She stared at me silently from beyond the handbrake.

I kept my eyes on the bin, the sea behind it rendered to an abyss in the night. I tried not to think as a tightness troubled my abdomen. It didn't go well with the treacle sponge. The sensation wavered from the centre, sending tiny shivers down my arms and legs. Why hadn't I turned the hazard lights off yet?

"It's cold in here," I said.

"A little."

"I'm really cold."

"You're not."

"I am."

"You're not. I'd know if you were really cold, wouldn't I?" The hazard lights ticked, like a metronome. "I know shit, remember?"

I locked, then unlocked my door.

Annie leaned closer. "I know *exactly* what you're thinking." She creaked further forward, hovered somewhere over the gear stick. "I've always known."

I tried to think of the sea out there. Big. Flat. All that nothing, I wanted to fill my head with it. I turned to Annie. Our faces were an inch apart, the brandy mixed on our breath. We stayed that way for a moment. She repeated again, like some mantra, "I know what you're thinking."

I was thinking of the sea. "It's boring," I said.

"What?"

"The sea. It's the same, all the same."

Annie pulled away. "Like home." She turned from me to look out the window.

I switched the hazard lights off. There was a quiet moment in the absence of their ticking, then the light rain came heavy. It battered the car, turning everything outside into a blur. "Thought you said it was gonna be nice for five days straight."

She reclined her seat and curled up into a ball. I took my jumper off and laid it across her legs. "It'll stop, at four a.m.," she said, and closed her eyes.

There was a bang at the car window. Claire stood outside with Tom. Annie stretched beside me. "Morning," I said.

She looked up at the sky, squinting. "Yes. It is."

We sat in the pier café drinking coffee. I asked Claire how the Travelodge was. "Shit pillows," she said.

She asked me how the car was. "No pillows," I said.

After breakfast we made our way across the beach, back to the old sign atop the shaft. It was the closest we'd been to it, jutting from the ebb some metres away. We began to throw stones at it, but not Annie. She nestled, cross-legged, looking out to sea. It was quite the sight. The way it quivered. Wibble, wobble. "Thought it was boring," said Annie.

I turned to face her, then a loud din echoed across us. One of Tom's stones had hit something. "You get the sign?" I asked.

"No, just the wood post. Does that count, Annie?"

She didn't answer, kept her eyes on me. "Reckon you'll visit?"

In my palm were two smooth stones. I rolled them together like baoding balls. "Dunno, you inviting me?"

"Does the wood post count, Annie?" shouted Tom.

"It's not hard to hit the sign!" said Claire. "Look how close it is."

"You're not doing any better." He looked up at the target.

A seagull had begun to circle overhead. It dipped and surged in a clockwise circuit, then doubled back to do the same in the opposite direction. Finally it came to a stop, right on top of our sign. Tom threw a stone. He missed. It didn't even scare the bird. "Bullshit anyway," he said, and walked to his car.

Annie got up, dusted her legs. "I'm tired," she said, and followed after him.

Claire kicked the pebbles, which burst up into a small crown, then fell, some in the tide. She did it again. Then joined the others.

I watched them move off, over the beach, back to the Land of Milk and Harissa. When I turned to face the sign, even the seagull had left. Wednesday, I thought. Wednesday is when I sign on.

I scanned the shingle for a decent rock.

0 Days Since Last Accident

LAURANE MARCHIVE

The eyes were big and blue and wide open. Looking up, slightly, at an angle. Always at an angle like something wasn't quite straight, wasn't quite right. Unblinking and emotionless, maybe only a bit surprised.

Water from the shower head, scorching hot. She tried to move the tap slightly with her toes but pushed it too far and it went cold. Cold was better anyway. It meant the lens wouldn't fog up. She lay flat at the bottom of the bathtub, legs propped up on the tiled wall. If she could get the phone low enough without getting it wet she would get the best angle. The legs would look longer. In the bathroom light they looked slightly orange but she would change that later. Or maybe she wouldn't. Maybe it was right for the mood. She tried various positions.

Memories dripping down the tiles.

a shower together, the joints around the tub were falling apart and they flooded the bathroom floor and it started leaking through the ceiling downstairs and when they finally came out

No. This isn't helpful. Focus.

Ankles slightly crossed, one foot on top of the other. Right leg lower than the left one, now left leg lower, something that would look fun and spontaneous. Carefully clipped clean toenails, more thigh, less thigh, holding the wine glass in her left hand, trying to flatten her back against the bathtub floor to get everything in shot without showing the rest. Orange shower curtain, red wine and glowing pale peach-coloured skin. The brown grout in between each tile and droplets rolling down the wall, bulging from the ceiling. She would caption it Lazy November day or Relaxing in the bath. Something autumnal and Sunday sounding.

The cold water made her skin prickle. In the past she'd sent pictures to Tinder acquaintances in the bath, cropping out the eyes but getting her lips and a nipple in shot, always cold water because it made the nipples look perkier. Hot water better for steam, more atmospheric but impractical. Shivering skin looks more toned. There is something about wet cold hair falling on shoulders. A crispness.

She turned the tap back to the left. Boiling water poured from the shower head. Put down the wine and dropped the plug halfway into the hole, only deep enough to let some of the water escape, the tub slowly filling.

Gallery. Choose. Share. Finishing up.

>*Julia_the_cat liked your post*
>*Greenlight_daydreams liked your post*
>>Red hearts
>>Love you
>>Absolutely darling
>>Looks so comfy!

>#hot #steamy #wine

Bright blue unblinking eyes and a frozen smile.

that picture he'd taken for her, standing smiling in front of the London Eye on the South Bank after

No. Thinking of something else.
White porcelain with a gold rim and a gold handle for a

nose. Looking, watching, staring. She took a sip of her green tea, the bag had been in so long it was almost brown and the water now lukewarm. She refilled it from the shower and lay back in the tub. The room started filling with steam again. Bright-red streaks now running along her leg unhidden and coiling around the plughole before disappearing in a swirl. It was almost the same colour as the wine, just maybe a little lighter or more orange where it mixed with the soapy water. Blossoming dark tentacle flowers. Every time she moved her leg, the smell of metal or something like the inside of an animal. Vaporous crimson coloured. Running a finger across the surface to make it ripple, interrupted ribbons.

cramps and he'd gone out to the shop and when he came back he was carrying a hot-water bottle, a tub of ice cream and some wine

She swallowed the last of the tea and put the cup down next to the tap. A gift. She'd mentioned *Beauty and the Beast* being her favourite cartoon and he'd gotten it for her, one just like in the film. A little boy turned into a teacup with eyes and a smile and porcelain skin. It even had a chip on the side, just like in the movie. But this was the third iteration of Chip. She'd broken it twice already. Once when doing the washing-up she'd knocked it over and it had shattered on the kitchen floor. Another time after taking a bath she'd caught it with her towel and for weeks afterwards she had been scared of walking barefoot in the bathroom. There were still china shards hiding in the gaps between the tiles.

Each time, he'd gone to get her a new one and it was always exactly the same. Same blue eyes same frozen smile same perfect expression. This was the one she'd had the longest so far. But she was counting the days. Like factories that deal in dangerous chemical compounds: 67 days since last accident.

There wouldn't be another one.

She came out of the bathroom with her hair wrapped in a towel.

WhatsApp.

> *Simon Tinder*
>> Hey
>
> *Typing*
>> Do you want to come over tonight?
>
> *Typing*
>> We could watch a movie on my projector?
>
> *Typing*
>> What do you think?
>
> *Online*
>> Hummmmm . . . Yeah sure. Sounds nice!
>
> *Typing*
>> We could order pizza?
>
> *Online*
>> Yes sounds good. Also did you read that article
>> I sent you?
>
> *Typing*
>> Not yet but will do, going to spend the afternoon
>> reading and drinking coffee.
>
> *Online*
>> Cool. Where do you live again?
>
> *Last seen today at 13:54*

It would be impractical. They would have to lay a towel on the bed. She hoped he wouldn't have white bedsheets on. Once, she'd slept with a guy she didn't really know and he had white bedsheets but they were both drunk and when he grabbed a towel he didn't realise it was still wet from his morning shower. It was slightly damp and it'd been cold and awkward. She never saw him again after that. Not because of the towel but still. The towel was undignified. It was often scratchy and it never stayed in place.

She opened the fridge and took out something she'd made the day before. The plate was covered with cling film and little droplets of condensed water were trapped under the surface.

waiting for him and he was late and the carbonara became so dry she was angry with him but he came with a new cup and so she couldn't stay angry for long

She put the plate down on the kitchen counter. Red quinoa, honey-baked cauliflower and vibrant yellow corn cut into three cylinders. Chunks of bright orange butternut squash, shiny roasted chestnuts and a bunch of soft white Chinese mushrooms. Sweet dried cranberries, flakes of red chilli and sprinkled black sesame seeds. Pictured with industrial-grey plate and warm-brown wooden chopsticks. Swirly dark glazed balsamic vinegar on the edges of the plate and a pastel yellow mat underneath. Pale golden elderflower drink on the side.

#autumnfood #healthychoices #vegan
152 likes

But underneath the cling film and the condensation it just looked grey. She fancied a cheese sandwich. She removed the thin plastic layer and binned the food.

Cutting the cheese, removing the bread from the freezer and putting it in the toaster. Slathering it with butter, both slices, one thing after the other. She made herself some more tea, dropped a bag in the cup and filled it with hot water.

Its_vegan_lucy liked your post
Girl_In_The_City liked your post
You've been Super Liked!
No new messages

She opened WhatsApp, scrolled down.

Dan

a message he'd once sent her drunk at 1 a.m. before crossing London in the night bus to come all the way back to sleep in her bed

Last seen today at 13:32

Last three messages, all read no answer.

A drunken text saying I miss you, I'm sorry I didn't realise this sooner.

A YouTube link to a song they used to listen to.

A picture of Chip with his frozen smile on the bedside table. Always no answer.

She should stop sending messages.

Evening. She walked down the long straight road that led from Vauxhall to the apartment. Cranes everywhere and concrete and glass windows and luxury flats being built. A shiny new world like in adverts on the Tube. Right after the big Sainsbury's she turned left like he said. Fourth door down. Piping problem at the moment so the hallway was being completely repainted. Plastic covering the floor. Plastic covering the walls. Walked straight. Silver-grey elevator with a huge mirror. She ran her fingers through her hair, blond, to straighten it. Roots were showing, just a little mascara and lipstick almost intact but not quite, like eating blueberries or a faint shadow of red wine. Perfectly imperfect. Third floor. Walking down the white corridor. He'd left the door slightly open for her and she let herself in.

the glowing orange light from the bedside table in his room, the smell of

"Hello?"

She walked through the hall and into the kitchen. He didn't turn round. He was busy cooking something. Black T-shirt, black trousers. Perfectly smart. White lights not too bright, grey carpet, electronic music in the background.

"Hey. How are you?" Opened a cupboard and grabbed some salt.

"I'm good, you?" She looked for somewhere to put her bag and dropped it on the sofa, took the earphones off, scarf and coat.

"Yeah really good. How was your day?"

"Yeah, just relaxing. Sunday. What are you cooking?"

"Chicken with spinach and ricotta. Do you like chicken?"

"Yeah, sure."

She looked round.

"Your place looks nice. It's very tidy."

"Thanks. I hate mess."

Moving closer to the kitchen counter, watching the chicken sizzle in the pan and the ricotta melt. She bent over to smell it, shoulders almost touching but not quite. A smile. Shy. Polite. He put down the wooden spoon, a kiss on the lips. Something reserved.

a party where they'd gone to the bathroom to have sex whilst no one was watching and within a few minutes people were banging on the door and they'd had to stop and pretend they'd only been taking drugs

He poured her a glass of wine.

"I thought we were getting pizza?" She watched him add another scoop of ricotta to the pan.

"Yeah I thought about it but then, I don't know. I just felt like cooking."

Cooking for two. Old habit.

"Sounds good. What movie do you want to watch?"

"I don't mind, you pick."

"Well what kind of movies do you like?"

"I don't mind. I'm not picky. Food is almost ready."

She took the glasses and he brought both plates to the living-room area. Coffee table. A huge window showing the night and the cranes and the buildings in progress, and no stars but little red dots of light wherever the cranes were, and so many white squares where other windows were but not so close that you could see what the neighbours were up to.

"This is delicious. Thank you."

"I'm glad you like it."

Gnocchi, pale yellow almost white, and spinach, dark green

almost black. Ricotta, white and wine, red. White porcelain plate and stainless-steel fork.

A conversation.

After the food they went outside for a cigarette. Balcony, bare, and in front the view to the new Vauxhall station being built. Two chairs and an ashtray on the floor. Small talk.

watching the sky turn pink and purple and then blue from the scaffolding in front of his flat whilst the windows were being renovated

No.

She made a short video of the view and posted it as a story with the caption Night-Time High-Rise, at an angle. It would disappear within twenty-four hours. That made him laugh. She rolled and took a few drags and he gently took the cigarette from her fingers. Without asking. Like he was used to it. Like it was something he'd done before. With someone else. Fingers brushing lightly. He gave it back.

"Do you want your own cigarette? I can roll you one if you want?"

"No, I prefer to share yours. If that's OK?"

"Of course that's OK."

When she was done smoking he leaned over, a kiss again. Something different, maybe because of the dark or maybe because of the wine, somehow softer. His right hand stroking the skin on her face, fingers in her hair. He kept his face close for just a second, she could smell the tobacco on his lips, a warmth.

fingers in her hair, around her neck, on the small of her back

"I'm cold, let's go back in."

"Yeah. It's freezing out here."

On the sofa they kissed, just the right amount. Then they watched the movie, it was easy, she in his arms and his arms around her. Cuddling like an old couple, drinking tea, commenting on the plot and the quality of the special effects and the excellent sound system. Familiar. Comfortable. An understanding. He was barefoot, she was wearing socks, their feet were touching, the high-tech speakers were blasting aircraft sounds and war noises.

When the movie was over they started kissing again. Then he dimmed the lights and it was better. They went to his room. So bare, like he'd just moved in. Ambient music. Mood lighting. Nothing too bright. No photos on the walls. No memories. A conscious effort to erase all memories. They made out again, just the right amount. The bedsheets were white.

She stopped.

"I've got to tell you now, I'm on my period."

He laughed.

"Well, that's fine. I'm sure we can make it work."

He went to the bathroom. Grabbed a towel. Like he'd done this before. Like he was used to it. Laid it on the bed. It was dry, at least. They laughed about it. Trying to gain back some momentum.

"Do you have a condom?"

"Yeah, hang on."

without a condom for the first time. Swallowing all lights

No.

Trying to focus on the taste of his tongue, the feel of his lips. They had sex. Just the right amount. He on top. She on top. A tenderness.

In the end he didn't come. When he got too tired he rolled to the side of the bed and he just said: "I'm sorry, it's been a while."

"Sorry for what? That was nice."

"Yeah, getting laid is the best."

She laughed. A nice laugh. Something polite. Something reserved. She wondered if he was thinking of his ex.

"It is."

rolling around, sheets tangled, feet trapped in the duvet, nails biting

He lay on his back and she, lying on his chest. Like they'd done this before. Nuzzling. He stroked her hair, maybe eyes closed, maybe looking up at the ceiling. The curtains were grey. There was a bookshelf and a wardrobe. He pushed her away gently and rolled back next to her.

"Can you scratch my back? It's my favourite."

"Of course . . ."

She was aware of the blood. Of it staining the sheets. She could still feel the towel underneath but she wasn't sure. And she didn't want to say anything. Just in case. Maybe he wouldn't mind. He didn't seem to mind. But he probably would.

her period and they spent the afternoon in bed anyways and there was blood all over the bedsheets but they were patterned so it didn't matter

She started running her nails over the skin of his back, soft, and golden. A shiver. He had his arms up under his head and a pillow in between. Faces almost close but not too close. She stroked his hair, blond. The crease of his back. The side of his face. He looked like he was sleeping, eyes shut.

A respite.

When she woke up at 8 a.m. she was still naked and she saw him from the corner of one eye. Standing, wearing a suit, in front of the wardrobe mirror. White shirt and dark trousers. He was adjusting his tie. Something like in a movie. Something people do. Something like someone else's life.

"Do you have to wear a tie every day for work?"

"Of course."

"I don't think I've ever had sex with someone who wears a tie every day."

"Well, there's a first for everything. I wasn't sure whether I should wake you up."

"It's fine, I'll leave with you. I don't want to waste the day."

teasing him because he was always accidentally wearing his jumper inside out or getting his shirt buttons wrong so they were never

In the bathroom she used his toothpaste to rub on her teeth and when she opened the cabinet to see if he had mouthwash she found a hairbrush with dark hair on it. The only thing left. A souvenir.

They took the Victoria Line for two stops together. Small talk, rush hour, bright lights. He got off before her, a smile and a kiss, almost on the cheek and almost on the lips, something in between.

An understanding.

Home for breakfast. A day off.

Opened the cupboard to make herself a cup of tea. Eyes still looking. She took the milk out of the fridge, poured it in a pan, added the oatflakes and watched it thicken. Added cinnamon and cloves and honey. Grabbed a banana from the cupboard, sliced it. Poured the porridge in a pretty ochre bowl and placed the banana on the edge of it. Chopped a red apple into thin slices and layered them next to the banana. Glazed some walnuts in a pan with a little bit of coconut almond butter and arranged them next to the apple. Sprinkled some hemp seeds and sprouted buckwheat. Topped it all off with a few dried rose petals and a swirly ornate silver spoon in the empty space. A soft brown place mat. From the autumnal bouquet still in its plastic sheath she'd bought on her way back she pulled a cluster of rose hips and laid them next to the bowl. She should really put it in water or the flowers would die and become unusable.

Morning post.

#eatclean #londonlife #dreamchasers

a morning in bed eating leftover pasta from the day before

Eyes wide open, the tea was cold she drank it anyway. She considered smashing the cup on the floor, watching it shatter next to the cat's litter tray. Just to see what it would feel like.

> *Katy_in_the_sky liked your post*
> *You've been Super Liked!*
> *Vegan_raw_food liked your post*
> *Rainbow_bowls commented on your post*
>> **Looks so yummy!**
>> **omg love this**
>> **I LoVE autumn!**

Blue eyes watching from an angle.

an afternoon in the park drinking cider on one of the hottest days of

No.

The smell of iron and rust and copper, something that would taste metallic, something draining, blending from the inside. She took two tabs of ibuprofen and moved the spoon in the porridge, elbows on the kitchen counter, watching the oats as they stuck together, white, off-white thick, clinging to the edge of the bowl.

A buzzing.

> *Simon Tinder*
> *Last seen today at 9:30*
>> **I hate my life right now.**
> *Online*
>> **Oh no, was the sex that bad?**
> *Typing*
>> **Hahahaha. No, but didn't get much sleep, I'm just exhausted – Winky face.**
> *Online*

Haha, me too.
Last seen today at 9:31

She scrolled down.

Dan
Last seen yesterday at 23:52

She started typing.

Hey, I hope you're

No.
Delete.
Pause.
She covered the bowl with cling film and put it in the fridge.

When she got to the park it was still bright with that November brightness that's almost dusk but not quite. She sat on a bench. Reading a book. Watching women with scarves pushing prams. Dogs, walking being walked. Dead leaves still red still orange still yellow but turning to brown already. Book with a golden cover that would go well with the season. With her boots, brown, and her hair, blond, and her plaid, chequered red and orange and yellow. She would go to a pub, one with a fireplace and a fire burning and order a drink, a mulled cider probably. Or a tea might do, something with red berries or yellow camomile. She would put the book down on the wooden table and caption it Comfy autumnal Reads.

A woman with greying hair and a long brown coat stopped next to the bench. On a bright-red leash she had a brown dog. A spaniel with caramel hair and long floppy ears.

"Do you mind if I sit down?"

"No, of course."

She moved her bag to the other side and the woman sat next to her. She then tapped her lap and the dog jumped onto the bench, staring at her with his big black eyes.

"Your book looks very nice, what is it?"

"Oh, I'm not sure. I haven't started reading it yet."

"That's a lovely cover."

"I know, that's why I bought it. It must have caught my eye in the shop."

"Well I hope it's nice, there's nothing quite like a good read."

"Absolutely."

She ran a finger along the curly swirly 3D title.

"What's your dog's name?"

"This one? Oh that's Charlie. He's a good boy. Very very friendly."

"He looks friendly. Can I stroke him?"

"Of course, darling, go ahead."

She reached across to touch Charlie's flat head. He was soft and silky and smelled of shampoo.

"He is lovely. How old is he?"

"Oh he's still quite young. Only a year and a half or so. But so well-behaved, aren't you, Charlie?"

The woman scratched behind his ear and he licked her hand.

"He is very pretty. Do you mind if I take a picture with him? I love dogs."

an argument they'd had once because he said he was a dog person and she was a cat person and in the end that would always be the difference

"Well of course not, go ahead. Charlie loves the attention."

She stood up, readjusted her plaid and brought her hair to the front of her shoulders.

"Come, Charlie, good boy!"

It was hard fitting everything in frame, the trees and their dark branches, the grass behind and the leaves on the ground. She tried getting Charlie to look straight at the camera but he wouldn't so in the end she settled on a shot of him happily licking the side of her face whilst she closed her eyes and smiled a big smile and the wind was blowing gently through her hair and through Charlie's, and the colours were bright and autumnal and the dog looked good and she looked good too.

Insides grinding. She wondered if the dog could smell it.

"Can I see the picture?"

"Sure thing. He's such a pretty dog."

"Oh that's lovely! Good boy, Charlie." The woman scratched him again behind the ear.

"Right, it's getting late, I should probably go. Thank you so much, I hope you have a lovely evening. Goodbye, Charlie!"

"You too, darling, you get home safe."

She would caption it Walk in the park, making new friends! With an exclamation mark.

When she got to the pub it was dusk and by the time she ordered something and finished her drink, it was night-time and it was raining. She caught the 149 home and sat upstairs at the front of the bus. The dog picture got her 168 likes because people like dogs. Pets were always a success. The window was covered in fog, she wiped it to see the outside.

sharing a bus ride for the last time. An argument about something or other, legs propped on the metal railing at the front of the stairs, arms crossed and refusing to say another word

The rain was making everything shine. The road gold from the reflection of the street lights. The red of brake lights from the cars in front. The green from the traffic lights. A purple neon sign on the left, blue restaurant sign flashing on the right. Silhouettes of people waiting for their bus in front of a bright orange Fanta ad. Pedestrians running to cross the road, speckles of rain across the glass, green purple red shadowy lights on the pavement. She took a picture. The colours came out even brighter.

You've been Super Liked! Swipe to find out . . .
Unicorns_Of_Instagram and 169 others liked your post

Your phone is running out of internal storage
No new messages

On the two seats next to her a couple, younger. She, her head on his shoulder. He, his fingers stroking her hair softly. Pinching the bobble on her hat. Legs entangled.

She could feel the muscles in her abdomen crushing each other, twitching, a recoiling animal. Slightly light-headed, a shortness of breath.

She scrolled down WhatsApp.

Dan
Last seen today at 19:32

Last thing sent the picture of the bright blue eyes.
Always watching. This one not broken yet.
She selected the photo of the street.
Started typing a caption.
Deleted it.
No caption.
No picture.

Getting home.
Eyes still staring. A kaleidoscope, the bruising of shards. Crushing brightness and neon rainbow colours.
0 days since last accident.

Aromas

RACHEL STEVENSON

Saturday night in the Taj Mahal Tandoori and the waiters were standing by, anticipating the first influx of customers. Early October: the evenings were doing their countdown to the big shift, that date when it's suddenly dusk in the middle of the day. It was a wet blue night, punctured by ice-white street lights. Reflections shimmied in puddles like sequins attached to dancers on the TV programme playing at a low level at the back of the restaurant. The boss, Mr Ibrahim, had installed the television to convince punters to eat in rather than get a takeaway; that way the restaurant took more money from drinks, tips, additional side dishes and only had to pay one motorcycle rider to deliver from E6 to E15 (£20 minimum order, free poppadoms orders over £25). The cars on the main road sped to the junction faster than was legally allowed and Ahmed watched as the lights turned green orange red, like the autumnal trees. Everything was quiet, apart from the clanging of pans and the swooshing of traffic.

He turned to face the empty restaurant. It was calm and neat: chairs under tables, cutlery next to glasses, paper tablecloths clean and clear of food stains. He had dimmed the lights to give the place some "atmosphere", as Mr Ibrahim put it. The Taj Mahal's red walls were decorated with ersatz Arabic scrolls and picturesque Indian scenes. Dominating one wall was an A1-size, slightly speckled poster of the Mughal emperor's mortuary-cum-palace that gave the restaurant its name. Ahmed had never been to India. He had been to Pakistan, once, when he was five or six, after his grandmother had died. He hadn't liked it. The flies, the food (basic, too spicy), the relatives, all of whom thought they had a right to pinch and squeeze and pat him indiscriminately, and most of all he had missed home, his friends, school, his place – which was here in East London, not in some faraway land that he had to visit just because his mum was born there. Ahmed thought that if someone was born in, like, Newcastle, and then moved to London, aged, say, seven, they wouldn't feel the need to go back to Newcastle every holiday, would they? They wouldn't have the accent or even remember much about it.

The first group of four came in at six on the dot, the same time that the phone started ringing. Ahmed left the window to answer it, taking a note of the order on his pad. He looked at the computer whilst he was there. As well as welcoming customers, taking orders, bringing food and clearing tables, he had to check the Internet orders and pass them to the chefs. He liked this bit. He had taken an ICT course at the local college and he wanted to do more. On American TV shows, the guy who turns up to fix the computers is always Asian and Ahmed felt that he could use this to his advantage. It'd be better than working evenings for seven fifty an hour plus tips, which he had to share with Qamal and Rana anyway. He was senior waiter and he didn't trust Qamal with any more than delivering food to the right tables and taking away the empty dishes. Mr Ibrahim had told him to train up Qamal on the computer but the one time Ahmed had shown him how to turn it on, Qamal had ended up spilling Diet Coke on the keyboard, for which Ahmed got the blame. So now he only gave him basic duties.

Qamal was a new arrival, a total rookie. He had been in the UK for six months and – in Ahmed's estimation – had no idea about anything. Qamal wanted nothing more than to work, go to mosque and, in his very spare moments, hang out in the dingy house on the wrong side of Plaistow, owned by a cousin of Mr

Ibrahim, that he shared with six other guys. Qamal had never left Newham. Ahmed had tried to help him, told him how to use the Tube and buses, explained the concept of an Oyster card, shown him the halal supermarket on the high street, tried to persuade him to explore a little, even if it were only to go to Whitechapel or Tooting (Ahmed didn't think Qamal could cope with Islington or Camden – maybe Hackney), but Qamal wasn't interested.

Then there was Rana, Mr Ibrahim's daughter-in-law. She considered herself the boss and Ahmed considered her a pain in the ass.

The group sat down at the nearest table, next to the window, and ordered four Gurkha lagers (large). They shared the same hair style, or lack-of-hair style, and were all wearing maroon-and-blue tops, indicating support for the local football team. It was early, though, so they wouldn't be a problem, thought Ahmed. It was the geezers who arrived at quarter to eleven, the ones who'd started drinking when the match ended at five, that were the problem. *His* problem, since Qamal's English wasn't good enough to deal with drunken cockneys. In the Hindu restaurants in East Ham, they didn't serve alcohol and he thought that was a good idea. But Mr Ibrahim put a three hundred per cent markup on the beer; that's where they made the money, not the five ninety-nine on each lamb rogan josh.

Ahmed turned round as another group of four jangled through the door and hesitated, waiting to be seated. Helen, Jonathan (Jonn), Steve and Samira were all wearing suits and name tags. Weekend training, Ahmed reckoned. This is their end-of-course treat. He ushered them to table four and distributed the menus.

"Chicken tikka masala's not authentic, is it, Sam?" said Helen. "Wasn't it invented in Birmingham? Or was that balti. What's authentic here?"

"I dunno," said Samira, flicking through the menu. "A daal, I guess? Lentils and rice is what most people subsist on in India."

"Hey, Helen," said Jonn, "Samira's not the office Indian expert. She don't start quizzing you on the most authentic fish and chip shop or asking where's the best place to get jellied eels."

Helen ignored him, scanning the menu.

"Sir, madam," said Ahmed, "would you like poppadoms?"

"Yes," said Helen, "but instead of mango chutney could we have –"

"Papads," said Samira.

"What?" said Helen.

"They're called papads in India, and you don't have them as a starter. They're part of tiffin, like afternoon tea."

"Very interesting," said Helen.

Samira smiled as Ahmed gave her a tiny wink.

"I'll be right back to take your order," he said to her as he was beckoned to table six where two women and a man were sitting impatiently.

"Can I get," said the woman, "matar paneer, pilau rice and a salt lassi? And some water."

"Salt lassi?" said Ahmed. "The mango lassi is very nice, perhaps you'd prefer that?"

"No," said the woman, frowning. "Salt lassi."

"OK," said Ahmed. He'd seen this before, people ordering something "a bit different" from the menu, then not liking it, sending it back, and Hari, the chef, who considered himself a creator, an artist, despite the fact he worked in a Zone Three curry joint, would get upset.

"When I was in Goa," said the woman's companion, "the food was very different to here. Much milder, more vegetables. They have this thing called a pav which is like a curry sandwich! And one night, we were just sick of curry so we just went out and had a pizza."

"A pão," said the salt lassi woman. "It means bread in Portuguese." Ahmed realised that the two women were sisters: one dark, one blonde, but they had the same eyes, mouth.

"Why are they speaking Portuguese in India?" puzzled their male friend.

"It was a Portuguese colony," offered Ahmed, tapping his pen on his notepad. "Are you ready to order, sir?"

"Is that where you're from?" asked the woman who'd been to Goa.

"Me? No, I'm from Beckton," said Ahmed.

"But *we* ruled India," said the man, still puzzled, "not the Portuguese."

"Come on, Geoff, order your onion bhaji and korma and plain naan and we can get on with it."

"How did you know what I was going to have?"

The two women laughed. "You always have the same bloody thing!" they said in unison.

"Mind you, Geoff," said salt lassi woman, "I'm not sure you should be coming in here, what with *your* views."

Geoff sighed. "I'm not a member of the National Front. I just happen to believe that exporting low-paid workers from Europe *or* the Indian sub-continent is unsustainable and it just benefits the middle classes, not the native workers."

"Who'd cook your chicken korma then? If all immigrants and children of immigrants left tomorrow?"

"There's no reason that we can't train up English people to cook curry," said Geoff. "You don't have to be Italian to make pizza."

"But it helps!" said the salt lassi woman, laughing.

"If you two start on Brexit, I mean it, I will leave," said the Goa woman.

"Sorry," said Geoff to Ahmed. "My sisters find it most amusing to rib me about every little thing."

Mr Ibrahim had told Ahmed that he had voted to leave the EU. "All these Polish coming over here, taking our jobs." No one had taken Mr Ibrahim's job as far as he could see. Ahmed hadn't voted. He preferred to stay out of politics. They were all the same.

"I will have the onion bhaji, but I'm going to have something else for the main," said Geoff, "just for a change." He started to flick through the menu again.

The door jangled, but it was just Hasan, the delivery driver. Nobody knew how long he had been working here; Mr

Ibrahim claimed that he had inherited him from the previous owner. Ahmed thought that he was about seventy. He was tiny, puckered and lined, like a roti. When Mr Ibrahim was in, he would speak Urdu with him, but he only ever nodded at Ahmed and Qamal. He ignored Rana completely, which Rana took as a sign of respect.

The phone rang and Qamal left the table of West Ham fans to answer it. Ahmed stood by Geoff, waiting for him to decide between passanda or masala, and kept an ear on Qamal's conversation. Hasan, piled high with carrier bags, stamped past him and left the restaurant.

"You want rice? Bread?" said Qamal.

There was a pause and then he repeated: "Rice? Bread?" He wasn't writing anything down.

"Is the passanda *very* almondy?" said Geoff. "I like nuts but I don't like marzipan – you know, the sort you get on Christmas cakes." The sisters sighed simultaneously.

"Excuse me," said Ahmed, hurrying towards the phone, but it was too late. Qamal had replaced the receiver.

"Did you get their name?" asked Ahmed.

"No." Qamal looked at his shoes, which needed a shine.

"Address?"

"Postcode," said Qamal, handing over a screwed-up piece of paper.

"Jesus Christ," said Ahmed. "Ring 'em back. Go on. One-four-seven-one." But the phone rang again and Ahmed snatched it up. "Go and see to table seven. Qamal. Table seven. No, that one. Taj Mahal, can I help you?" The receiver was smeared with what looked like dhansak. Ahmed took a serviette from his pocket and wiped it.

"Yeah mate, we ordered online but we haven't got an email back, yeah?"

"What time did you order, sir?"

"'Bout twenny minutes ago."

Ahmed tucked the phone under his chin and wiggled the mouse so that the computer next to the telephone woke up.

"Dave Mason?"

"That's right, mate."

"The order is with our chefs. I'll send a confirmation email and our driver will be with you in forty-five."

"Forty-five minutes, bro? We are *hungry* here. Got me whole crew here, know what I'm saying?"

I *do* know and you're saying it in an accent you weren't born with, thought Ahmed. "I'm sorry, sir, that's the minimum delivery time."

"Well he ain't getting no tip."

"That's up to you, sir."

He had persuaded Mr Ibrahim to make deliveries card payment only. Too often, Hasan had come back with the wrong money – once with a black eye and no money. Mr Ibrahim hadn't wanted to call the police, and the cost of the order had come out of Hasan's wages.

"Yo, Hari," he said, walking through to the kitchen. "Lamb bhuna, prawn biryani, garlic naan, mushroom rice, four samosas, chicken tikka, for delivery, yeah?"

"Write it down, cuz," said Hari. "I have my system and you ain't messing with it." He pushed his bandana up over his hair and wiped his forehead, then picked up an onion and started to chop.

"Wash your hands," said Ahmed.

"Yeah all right, bossman. Oh hang on, that's not you, is it?"

"Jokes," said Ahmed.

He took table five's order and passed it to Hari, picking up table four's starters on the way back. Then back again with a new order, more lagers for table one, taking their cleared plates back to the kitchen where Adnan, the sous-chef, was washing up. Then the phone rang. Then it rang again. Then Hasan appeared, so Ahmed started loading him up with a phone order.

"You taking a long time tonight, bruv," he said to Hasan. "Usually you're zipping in and out of those side roads like a proper fiend. We got orders piling up here."

Hasan grabbed two carriers and marched past Ahmed and

through the restaurant, slamming the door as he left. Ahmed shook his head, then sat down and watched Hari stir, chop and fry. The sous-chef was supposed to do prep, but Mr Ibrahim was too tight to spring for more kitchen staff, so Adnan usually ended up at the sink.

It was thirty-five degrees in the kitchen. Ahmed went back into the restaurant and opened the door. The air, despite the snarl of cars from the high street, was fresh like a waterfall. It had stopped raining and the street lights looked like pearl drops in the black air. He slicked his hand through his hair and closed the door, turning to see a wave of anxious white faces, putting on cardigans and making exaggerated shivering noises. "Sorry," he said. The phone started ringing.

"Mate, where's my curry. We are *starving* here, man. We're about to chew Smitty's leg off, know what I mean?"

Ahmed looked at his watch. Hasan should've been there by now – the punter was only five minutes away. Hasan was old and decrepit, but he was like an Indian (the other type of Indian) tracker; he never got lost and could motorcycle around Newham blindfolded. Shit, thought Ahmed, I hope he isn't literally doing that. "I've just had a call from our delivery driver and he's stuck in traffic," he said. "He'll be fifteen minutes."

"This isn't on, bro."

"We're very sorry, sir." Ahmed felt his accent getting more "Indian" when he was trying to placate a customer. He hated himself a little, hated acting submissive, dumb. "Next time you come in, sir, free starters for you and your friends. On me."

It *would* be on him if the guy remembered. Mr Ibrahim wouldn't stand for it. But the customer sounded stoned as hell, he probably wouldn't even remember ordering a takeaway tomorrow morning when he and his crew stepped in foil containers of leftover brown bhuna.

"All right, bruv, appreciate it."

Ahmed clicked the receiver and then rang Hasan on his mobile. No answer.

"What you doin', man?"

Rana stood next to him, her tiny hands on her spacious hips, her black eyes rolling at him.

"Table six wants clearing. And Qamal hasn't brought the naan to table five. You're supposed to be supervising him."

No, I'm not, thought Ahmed. "I'm ringing Hasan," he said. "He hasn't turned up to a delivery."

"I'll do that," she said, grabbing the phone from his hand. "Go clear some tables."

Go fall under a twenty-five bus, thought Ahmed.

Geoff was motioning him. "Yes, sir?"

"Can I get some tap water? This is very spicy."

"It's passanda, Geoff, it hasn't got any chilli in it!" said his sister.

Ahmed looked at her glass of lassi. She had drunk half of it.

"Hasan! Where are you! Call in now! Or else!" Ahmed could hear Rana from the other side of the restaurant.

You're wasting your breath, Ahmed thought. I'll bet you ten quid Hasan don't know how to access his messages. Might as well Snapchat him for all the good it'll do you.

He took a jug of tap water to Geoff and then went over to the West Ham fans to give them their bill. They paid in cash, trying to outdo each other in generosity. "Nah mate, you only had three lagers." "Yeah but Stu, I had a starter." "There y'go, mate," said one of them, slipping a ten-pound note into Ahmed's jacket pocket. "For your trouble."

"Thank you very much, sir." He peered around, but Rana was still shouting on the phone and Qamal was nowhere to be seen. He would keep the tenner.

Whilst waiting for the men to stop arguing about the last twenty pence, he stared out of the window. It was pouring again, streams of water reflecting dancing neon shop signs as rain ran down the road. Ahmed felt cocooned inside the restaurant, the noise of customers talking and chewing and clinking their glasses insulating him from the cacophony of the street. He watched people patiently waiting at the pedestrian crossing, brushing their umbrellas against one another. The door opened and Hasan stomped in, bringing a blast of cold air and frosty looks from the punters.

"Where you been?" shouted Rana, but Hasan ignored her and trudged through to the back.

"Geezer, you need to answer your phone," said Ahmed, following him into the kitchen.

Hasan stood, steam coming off him, like a kettle about to boil. He removed his glasses and tried to wipe them on his coat but that didn't help. Rain dripped off the end of his greying moustache and dropped to the hot floor. He shook himself like a small dog, one that was ready to be put to sleep, thought Ahmed.

"Dead," said Hasan.

"Who's dead?" asked Ahmed.

"Phone is dead."

"Lemme see." Hasan handed over his phone and Ahmed tried turning it on. "It's just the battery. My charger's in Mr Ibrahim's office. I'll do it for you."

Hasan shrugged.

"You need to get out again," said Ahmed. "I thought you'd taken this one ages ago. Order for E6 – lamb bhuna, prawn biryani, garlic naan."

"I am going," said Hasan, picking up the nearest carrier bag full of food.

"You got the address?"

"Yes, I have the address," said Hasan, pointing to the receipt stapled to the top of the carrier.

Ahmed watched him leave, then realised Hasan had forgotten the second bag.

"Here," he called as he followed him through the restaurant, ignoring salt lassi woman who was trying to get his attention.

Hasan was starting his moped as Ahmed opened the door. He flinched as the cold rain hit him, then jogged to the kerb.

"Hey!" he shouted as Hasan hit the accelerator and sped off.

A Volvo squealed to a halt at the junction, then set off again as the lights turned from red to red and orange. Hasan turned left towards East Ham, the Volvo veered right and smacked straight into him. Hasan flew into the air, landing helmet first.

"Shit!" said Ahmed. He ran up to Hasan, pushing his wet hair out of his eyes as he knelt beside the body. Hasan was unconscious, his head oily with blood that mingled with the rain and raced down his face towards the gutter. The helmet lay useless, cracked, next to the tangled moped, which was leaking brown fluids from the delivery box on the back.

"Shit," said Ahmed again. He felt in his pocket for his phone and called an ambulance. He had done first aid at school. What were you supposed to do, put them in the recovery position? He pulled ineffectually at Hasan's arm.

"Don't move him," said a man standing, watching, nearby. "He might of broke something. Are the feds coming?"

"I don't know," said Ahmed. "I asked for an ambulance."

"They'll send the five-oh too," said the man. He sniffed. "Driver's gone now, though."

"What, he just drove off? The fucker."

"Someone might of got the reg number."

"Did you?"

"No."

You're as much help as Qamal, thought Ahmed. His trousers were soaked through to his skin. He stood up and tried to shake out his legs, but the rain just made them wetter.

A pool of light opened up behind him and Rana yelled from the doorway. "Ahmed! What you doing! Come back inside!"

"It's Hasan," he shouted back. "Look!" He pointed.

Rana said something that he couldn't hear and disappeared back in and closed the door.

Nice, he thought.

He heard the familiar Saturday-night sound of sirens, then he was bundled out of the way by men in hi-vis vests who, after asking Ahmed some cursory questions, packed Hasan onto a stretcher and slid him into the back of the ambulance, nee-nawing off to – where? He hadn't asked them. It was over so quickly; they were as much a delivery service as Hasan. A thought occurred to him: the stoned-tosser customer was going to ring up again. He'd let Rana get the phone. Let her flirt her way out of that one.

He dragged himself back to the restaurant door. Inside it was warm and bright, and the smell – the curry odour that he was constantly trying to get out of his hair and his white shirt, even his shoes – was so comforting and homely and delicious that his stomach rumbled. The punters were all staring at him.

"Sorry ladies and gents," he said. "Bit of an emergency outside." A picture of Hasan lying crumpled in the gutter crossed his mind. "Everything's OK now."

There was some English mumbling and turning. Ahmed dumped the soggy bag of rice and samosas on the nearest table. Rana was gesticulating furiously from the phone.

"It's not stopped," she hissed. "People want their orders. You're gonna have to go out on the bike."

"Rana, it's totalled," he said. "The cops'll impound it." On cue, the phone started ringing. Ahmed picked it up and put it down again. "They can all go Chilli Chutneys," he said.

"Papa-ji'll kill me," she said.

"Let him."

He heard more sirens, turned to see blue and white lights flashing into the windows and two sturdy coppers by the door, peering in. Behind them, pointing, was the man who'd advised Ahmed not to move Hasan. Great, he thought.

The men removed their caps and came in, filling the room. The diners didn't look up; those who did looked quickly back at their meals. Nothing to make you feel guilty like a copper.

"Who's the manager here?" said one of the policemen.

"I am," said Rana, walking up to them and smiling. She was tiny compared to their massive bulk.

"There's been an accident involving one of your drivers."

"I know, it's terrible. Is he OK?"

"He's at Newham General. We need to get his next-of-kin details."

"Certainly," said Rana. "Come with me." She headed around the back towards Mr Ibrahim's office.

"All right," said Ahmed, nodding to the cops. He'd never had any trouble with the police but his mate Shareeq, who hung around in front of Stratford station, beatboxing, dancing and the like, had been arrested for "causing affray", although they'd later released him without charge. Cops bored on a Friday night, had been Shareeq's estimation.

"Ahmed!" He saw Qamal motioning at him from the entrance to the kitchen, so he walked over to him, clearing table four as he went.

"Police, yeah?" said Qamal.

"Yes, there's been an accident."

"I stay in kitchen."

"All right, but can you get Hari to stop doing takeaway orders? We haven't got a driver."

"Yes, yes, I do this."

He disappeared just as Rana reappeared with the police. "You get your boss to ring us, yeah?" said the bigger cop. "We will need to check the victim's details."

"Of course, of course," said Rana, flashing her teeth in a way that was supposed to be alluring, but Ahmed thought looked more shark-like.

The smaller cop looked around the restaurant.

"How many people you employ here, then?"

"Five," said Rana. "Myself, the chef, the sous-chef, Ahmed, Qamal. Oh, and Hasan. Six."

"All legit, are they?"

"Yes of course, of course legit."

"Got paperwork for them, have you, NI numbers, work visas and that?"

"Of course, Mr Ibrahim will be –"

"We could check now," said the smaller cop. "You got files back there, haven't you?"

"Yes, but Mr –"

"Won't take a minute."

Want to keep out of the rain, more like, thought Ahmed.

"We'll need to see copies of passports and visas."

Rana was looking worried, taking out her phone as if to call Mr Ibrahim.

"I'll do it," said Ahmed, "I know where the key to the filing cabinet is. You cover the kitchen, Rana. I think table three wants more drinks."

"You from round here, lads?" he said to the police, as they passed the flicker of silver and turquoise celebrities dancing quietly across the screen. His wet trousers slapped his calves and his left knee hurt from kneeling on the road. They went through to the back office and Ahmed flicked the light switch. "Bit of illumination," he joked, and they all blinked as the room filled up with bright-yellow fluorescence.

"Yeah, I grew up in West Ham," said the bigger one, "and Harry here's Upton Park. Lives out in Ilford, too posh now for the likes of us." He laughed.

"Well it got too crowded round here."

"I'm Beckton, meself," said Ahmed, "though I live in this neck o' the woods now. My name is Qamal," he said, confidently, holding out his hand. "There's no paperwork on me cos I'm born and bred, innit. Bow bells and all that."

"Eddie," said the bigger one.

"Constable Robinson," said the smaller one.

He found a key under a copy of the Quran that Mr Ibrahim kept in his office for some reason, and opened the filing cabinet. "Here's the files for Hari, he's the chef, Adnan, sous-chef and chief bottle-washer, Rana and Ahmed the waiters. Oh, and Hasan. Did Rana give you his details?"

He handed the files over and waited as they looked through them. He brushed his hair over his forehead. His passport photo was eight years old and he'd had shorter hair then. He hoped the photocopy was blurred enough.

"All present and correct," he said, "shipshape and Bristol fashion." Shut up, he told himself, you're overdoing it.

"OK, it all looks in order. Have to check, you know," said Eddie, the bigger cop. "Called to a fight last week in a curry house in Brick Lane. When we got there, all the waiters were clearing out the khazi window. All illegals, you see."

"Just doing our job," said the smaller one.

"Of course, officers. Can I offer you a drink on the house before you go?"

"Not whilst on duty," said Eddie. "Though if you've got any samosas going spare, I could murder one. Proper starving I am."

"I'll see what Hari can rustle up," said Ahmed, smiling and ushering them out of the office. "Have a good night, now."

"You too, sir. We'll be in touch regarding your delivery driver. Or you can call the hospital, although they might not give out any information to non-relatives."

"We will do that," said Ahmed, walking with them to the front door. The hazy light in the restaurant was a relief after the glare of the office. The customers were looking at him for reassurance, so he smiled benignly at everyone as he closed the door behind the policemen, shutting out the night and everything that happened in it. He remembered their samosas and was about to open the door to call out after them, but then thought better of it. It was funny, they had called him "sir". He couldn't remember another time when a white person had called him sir. He laughed to himself as he turned back to take the next order. Sir.

Between Fire and Coal

MYKOLA MOSS

Bampi said the mountains in Wales are bewtees, but they blummin well arn when they're like this, jus so steep an foggy an covered in sheep shit. I carn even see tha far in front of me, mun, like I'm runnin through clouds or summin. An joggin in jeans is a pain in the arse, like, but I carn stop, jus carn blummin stop. I dun even know if wer goin the right way up the mountain. Everythin all around is jus a blur of white an green.

An somewhere in tha white . . . in tha fog . . . Bampi's all alone.

I shake shake shake my head an keep powerin through. A burnin sick's now creepin up my throat, pumpin its way all slow-like towards the back of my mouth as if to say, "Shuddun have skipped college yesterday for day-drinkin, shuddun ew?"

I look back to make sure Manon isun too far behind. I can barely see her, no word of a lie. In the fog the dog's jus a floatin blue collar, gettin sucked into nothin, it is.

"C'mon, Manon!" I says to her. I hear a faint an strained bark back, problee sayin, "Sod off, Bryoni, I'm comin, mun!" I face forward quick an my ponytail whacks my nose an I nearly tread on a sheep skull in the grass, right in my runnin path. I sidestep an try not to slow down, but my heart's breakin my blummin chest, mun, an the mountain jus keeps on goin an goin, up up up.

Now, my phone's ringin in my pocket, an tha sets my heart

bangin even more. Cos I know it's Mam, it is. It's gorra be, hasun it? It's nearly nine, like, so she'll be checkin up on me, askin all sorts of questions bout Bampi. Wanna know wha he's bin eatin for breakfast. Wanna know wha he's bin sayin.

Wanna know wha he *thinks* he's bin seein.

I fumble around my pocket an mush the power button to silence Mam. I carn deal with her right now. She'd wanna send all of South Wales pleece up here jus to find him, an I'd never hear the end of it, would I? Can hear her screechin away now, goin, "His own shittin granddaughter carn even be trusted to care for him!"

Now, I stop runnin so blummin quick tha I nearly slip on the damp grass, no word of a lie.

Cos right there on the ground . . . in front of the wood stile tha's plonked between the tall bushes . . . three pieces of coal.

Two of em are jus sittin side by side, with one piece a little further away from the other two, as if pointin to the stile.

Manon creeps up behind me, jus pantin like never before. Her long Lab's tongue is hangin over her mouth, an she inches all slow-like towards the coal pieces an sniff sniff sniffs em.

"Oh!" I says to her, an she picks one up in her mouth. "They're not for you, mun!" An I hold her mouth still an try pullin the coal out. "We're givin these back to Bampi, orite?"

Manon's pantin makes her drop the piece, an I chuck it inside a mess bag with the other two. I have a quick look around, but the only things I see now are the bushes, an they're way higher than me, mun. Carn see anythin past em, like.

"Let's go quick, is it?" I says, an I stroke the pup's ears. "He carn be tha far," an I get up an goes, "speshlee if he's puttin down its food now."

An, see, it's gorra be Bampi doin it, hasun it? Wern tha long ago he was tellin me how he'd blummin catch it. "Thing is, Bryoni," he goes to me, he goes, "they'll eat coal they will. So you gorra make all their food like coal, you know. Jus gorra burn it up really good, like, an they'll eat it all I swears to you."

I hurry to the stile an hop over, an Manon follows behind

me. There's hardly any noise here as we get higher up this new, mucky field. We left the sound of the main road at the bottom of the mountain, we did, so the only thing I hear is the wind tryin to get inside my ears, the whistlin jus whippin all round me. I yell out for Bampi a few times, jus callin an callin, but the blummin fog absorbs his name like I'm shoutin into a pillow. An I get wonderin whether Bampi remembered to stick his earin aid in before he left. See, he usually takes it out when he's home with me an Mam. Says the cars on the main road do his head in. Thing is, he dun call em cars. He do call em mine carts, he does.

"Manon!" I shout. She's sprintin way ahead of me, an jus attacks another collection of coal with her nose. They're laid out exactly like the last ones, the coal furthest away jus pointin up the mountain.

But there's summin else with em as well, jus layin all wonky on the ground.

Bampi's walkin stick.

An it's gorra be Bampi's, it has, cos the wood's got tha date marked on it, jus chiselled away over an over.

12-04-65

I pick it up an my hands are makin the thing shake a little. Manon starts backin away, problee thinkin I'm gonna throw it for her to fetch. I wanna tell the pup "No," but my mouth's all dry an my head keeps playin flashes of Bampi stuck somewhere out here, jus seein him fallin over the wet an bumpy mud an not able to get himself back up.

Manon howls at me, so I goes, "Shush up now, mun, let me think." But she jus keeps starin at the stick. I pick up the coal pieces and put them in the bag with the others, then I says to the pup, "He wuddun have left this," an I try squintin an lookin into the fog ahead an say, "No way. Not unless he thinks he saw summin makin the stick worth forgettin, like."

I pat my hand twice quick on my leg to get Manon to follow me, an we make our way in the direction of the coal. The air's startin to smell like bad breath an burnin wood, but I try not to think of anythin an jus keep joggin. No word of a lie, though, it's blummin hard tryin to think of nothin when your legs are heavy an hurtin, an when your stomach's turnin.

An when you know your bampi's losin his mind.

"He should be in a home!" I call out to Manon, an I slam Bampi's walkin stick into the mud, jus usin it to help me run, usin it to help me think. "Mam's fault. All blummin Mam's fault, it is."

Manon barks three times at me, an I says back through huffs an breaths, "Carn afford to . . . put him in one . . . blummin lie, it is." An I smash the walkin stick into the ground even harder. Cos Mam do act like I dun see her stumble into the house every blummin weekend, jus off her face an wastin away money.

I look back at Manon an goes to rant at her some more, but the pup's taken off to the right an is dartin away from me an disappears into the fog. I goes to chase after her, an now I'm dodgin all of the traps the sheep have left, an spit's jus flyin out of my mouth as I scream her name.

But it dussun take long till I spot her, an I slow down as soon as I do. An she's jus sittin there at the edge of the field, right where the dark tree branches start to poke out through the white. The pup's pantin beside a great, smokin circle, an it jus looks like a finished fire pit or summin. I put my hand over my mouth an nose, cos the smell's even worse here now, like someone's burned a load of dirty clothes in a bin. I says, "Oh!" to Manon through my fingers, but she's too busy sniffin near the smoulderin pile.

Now, my phone goes off, but it's beeps after beeps after beeps, an so I look at the screen an Mam's messages all come through in one long hit, like I musta lost signal or summin. I skim over them quick, an she's typed in all caps sayin "WHERE ARE YOU" an "ANSWER YOUR PHONE" an "WHY'S BAMPI'S MINING STUFF EVERYWHERE?" an then jus more repeats of "WHERE ARE YOU" "WHERE ARE YOU" "WHERE ARE YOU". I go to turn the phone off, but Mam starts to call an I answer it an I diddun mean to do tha an I dunno why but I put it to my ear an goes to her, "Not now!"

"BRYONI!" Mam screams. "Where the shittin-hell are you?"

"Listen. Mam. Jus . . . jus listen, mun."

"No, you listen!" Mam yells. "Where's Bampi? He's up the bloody mountain again! He is, isn't he! Tell me!"

I slowly walk towards the burnt pit an say to Mam, "Yes, but –"

"Oh this is shittin great, jus bloody great!" An she starts to swear more an I can hear her arm flappin about an hittin her side as her heels slap along the laminate floor of the kitchen. "I knew it. I knew he'd do this. Jus a matter of bloody time, wern it?" An then Mam starts shoutin an rantin to herself, so I pull the phone away from my ear every now an then cos she's so blummin loud, like. All I hear are the little bits she says, "He kept tellin me he'd go after it . . . needs to bloody let go of tha bloody accident . . . explosion wern all his fault . . . he wern the only one workin down tha bloody mine . . . for shit's sake, mun."

"MAM!" I yell, an she shushes for a sec an I quickly say, "He's with me. I've gorrim." An I know it's a blummin lie but I dun care right now.

"Put him on," Mam says.

"We're nearly home, mun," I says to her. "Gettin in the car now, like."

"Right," she goes, "you tell him this is it when he gets here. Tell him I'm fed up of it all." An then Mam breathes really heavy an says all low-like, "You tell him tha bloody dragon is all in his bloody head, an you tell him tha right bloody now."

An I hang up the phone.

Cos now I'm standin next to Manon, an I get a better look at wha's been on fire.

Sheep.

Their charcoaled remains are in one big pile, jus five or six of them makin up the burn pit. An smoke keeps comin off them. Off their skulls. Off their bones. Off everywhere.

I kneel down beside Manon. The wet grass seeps through my jeans to my knees, an I jus hold her an we both stare at the pit. A warmin swirls through my stomach an spirals into a rock in my throat. My eyes go blurry, an no matter how much I wipe with my sleeve the tears take my eyes, makin the world look like I'm sunk down in a bath.

I pull the pup close to me an jus close my eyes for a sec. Manon slowly spins around an tries jumpin up on my leg, an her tongue is whippin away to lick my face. I stroke her head an get up, an I go to walk away from the sheep grave.

But I hear someone coughin, jus beyond the fire pit.

An it's Bampi.

He's crouched over, an his arms are stretched out as if he's holdin on to invisible handrails. He scoots past the burned sheep an cough cough coughs, then looks up an stops.

"Bryoni?" he goes, his voice as deep an thick as the fog. "Wharra you doin up here?" he says. "It's not safe, love. Havvun stopped it yet, I havvun."

Manon yelps an hurries over to Bampi, an she runs circles around his legs. The old man ignores the pup, an jus says, "Is everyone out safe?"

I wipe my eyes with my sleeve an walk closer to Bampi. He's wearing his mining overalls, the grey ones with the holes all over, still dark an stained from the accident. An he's got his hard hat on, jus a scuffed white coated with soot. There's a bulge of coal pieces inside his front pocket, the one tha has his *Safety Inspector* badge sewn into.

"Let's go home, is it, Bamp?" I says to him, my voice makin every word a wobble. I hold out his walkin stick for him to grab, but he jus looks at the smokin pit an goes, "She'll be here any second, Bry, she will." An Bampi hobbles towards me an points down the mountain. "I need you to go, love. I need everyone to go."

"Carn, Bamp," I says to him.

"Listenin, Bry? I got to stop her from burnin all of bloody Wales. Cos she will, I tell you now. Tha dragon's gettin stronger, it is. I seen it."

Bampi grabs my shoulders an tries to slowly turn me around to go. I spin back an say through a new set of tears, "Mam's gettin worried, Bamp. Come on," an I hold out his stick again, wigglin the end for him to take. He stares at the handle, an for a second his eyes squint an try to focus on the date tha's chiselled into the wood, but he whacks the stick away an says, "Serious now, Bry." An he raises his finger to point behind me, but it's his arthritis finger isun it? So it's all curled inwards but he tries jabbin wha's left of it into the air an says, "Get goin, is it?"

I shake my head an say all soft-like, "Carn do tha, Bamp."

"She's comin."

"She's not."

"She is, Bry."

"We've had this conversation before, Bamp."

"Listen to me, Bryoni!" Bampi yells, an the strain causes him to cough an cough. He pulls out a scrunched bit of loo roll from his sleeve then coughs into it really hard. He squeezes it into a ball an puts it back, jus stuffs it right up there.

Now, the tears start comin really fast, an I'm jus so scared for Bampi, cos this isun gettin any better, is it? An it dussun matter how many times I tell him tha the dragon isun real, tha the explosion down the mine wassun his fault, tha it's all in his head. He jus dussun wanna know, jus carn know it to be true, like.

Bampi spits out a clot of phlegm to the ground, an says in his shakin voice, "I can save them all, I can. I can save them all."

I go close to Bampi, an I hook my arm around his, an I goes to pull him to start walkin down the field, but summin loud an low an deep an angry rumbles through the fog. Manon starts barkin into the air, an Bampi's hand grips so blummin much around my arm tha I try to pull away from him. I look all around, an I carn see nothin in all this fog, jus hear the noise of somethin ragin close by.

An I stare up.

An I wipe wipe wipe my eyes.

An there's a dark blur through the fog jus hoverin right above us, sendin bursts of wind down on Bampi an me. I carn see it proplee, an it's jus a long, grey stain on the sky. An as the gusts keep smackin against us, the fog starts to clear more an more, like.

But the flyin figure jus shoots off up the mountain, makin a heavy blast of wind knock us over. Manon gets down low next to me an keeps her head to the ground an jus lets out a couple of yelps an cries.

Bampi grabs hold of his walkin stick beside me an he gets to his feet an jus looks down at me on the grass, an he goes, "I'm goin after her, I am." He slams the stick in the ground an says, "Come help if you want, or go back home."

An as the old man stumbles away an up the field, I slowly get to my feet an hurry beside him, jus starin at Bampi cos tha's all my thunderin heart an thumpin head can do right now.

I curl my arm around his an hold on to him tight, an he says to me, "These mountains, Bryoni," an he looks at me quick an goes, "they're bewtees, they are."

Waterlilies

JONATHAN KEMP

A bolt of anxiety shook Lynn awake at around 4 a.m. She lay there as if trapped under a paving stone until the alarm went off, then hauled herself upright and prodded Nigel awake.

Even though it had been her suggestion, a few days in Paris for her fiftieth birthday, she didn't want to go on this trip. She needed a break – but a break from Nigel. After twenty-seven years of marriage their relationship had withered into something she no longer recognised. They seldom spoke any more because they rarely agreed on anything; he would dismiss her with, "You're talking out of your arse, woman," leaving her in tears. Maybe this weekend would improve things between them. If nothing else, at least – at last! – she would get to see Paris. She'd always dreamed of seeing Paris.

Ian, their youngest, dropped them off at Hook Station, where they caught a train to Waterloo. Once they were settled in their Eurostar seats, Nigel fell asleep. Lynn removed from her handbag a small notebook she'd bought the previous week, on a whim; she'd never been one for keeping a journal, but something in her was pushing for expression. Opening it to the blank first page, she wrote: *If the whole holiday is like this I will have forgotten what my gob's for by next week!*

She looked at Nigel's sleeping face, the deep lines around

the mouth exaggerating his permanent sneer. She'd showered that face in kisses once upon a time, unable to tear her eyes away from its stern beauty. Now it was as familiar to her as her own, yet at the same time (again like her own) so radically other that she sometimes felt as though she was gazing on a stranger.

From Gare du Nord it was a short walk to Hotel Jarry. Their room, No. 8, was on the second floor. By 2 p.m. Nigel was snoring his head off on the bed while Lynn sat by the window, smoking and writing. I have the diary in front of me now.

> *I have this depressing feeling I am going to sit at this window a lot, looking at the dingy Hotel de France just across the road. It looks so close I am sure if I leaned out I could almost touch it.*

Nigel woke around 3.30 p.m. and they went for a walk, stopping at a supermarket to buy some milk, butter, cheese, bread and a bottle of red. Lynn tried engaging him in conversation but got so irritated by his monosyllabic responses that she gave up. By the time they returned to the hotel they were exhausted and crashed for an hour.

That evening they went to a restaurant called Chartier she'd read about in the guidebook. A really old place where, in the words of her journal, *the waiters scurry round like ants and wear long white aprons.* The journal tells us she had mushrooms in garlic butter to start, followed by steak in pepper sauce with chips. For dessert, chocolate eclairs. All washed down with a bottle of rosé. They ate in silence mostly, and she asked a waiter to take their photograph. She smiled for the camera, while Nigel remained stony-faced. He wasn't much of a smiler these days. Which was a shame because his smile was the thing she'd loved about him the most when they first met. She used to love how it brought the beauty of his face alive. She told him once he had a generous smile and he replied, with more than a little truth, "That's because it doesn't cost anything."

After dinner they walked up to Pigalle and past the Moulin

Rouge. A prostitute approached them, opening her coat to reveal the lingerie-clad body beneath. Nigel smiled and gestured with a nod towards Lynn, and the woman closed her coat and clicked her tongue against her teeth.

They both laughed – she couldn't remember the last time she'd heard him laugh – and he put his arm around her shoulder. I imagine she savoured the contact, for it was all too rare and sometimes she thought she might die through lack of it.

On the way back to the hotel they got lost, walking in circles for what seemed like hours before finding it. Dog-tired, they went straight to sleep.

They rose at 8.15 a.m. and drank coffee, then made their way downstairs for breakfast. On discovering it wasn't included in the price, Nigel said, "I'm not paying ten euros for two rolls and a cup of tea!" and stormed off back to the room.

As she ate her continental breakfast, Lynn took in the other guests. Mainly couples. She tried to ascertain whether they looked happy. Concluded none of them did.

They spent the morning at Sacré-Coeur and Montmartre, where Lynn bought a couple of small oil paintings of Parisian scenes from a street artist. When she asked Nigel if he liked them he asked how much they were. When she told him he said, "He saw you coming."

The journal records that the weather was cloudy and quite chilly, the sun struggling to break through, but as she wrote later: *I didn't let it spoil my enjoyment.*

They arrived at the Pompidou Centre to find it closed. Nigel complained to the air, huffing and puffing his displeasure, but Lynn enjoyed the eccentricity of the architecture, recording also that she loved the Niki de Saint Phalle sculptures in the fountain. Their colourful surrealism would probably have made her smile.

That night they dined at Café Drouot, where Lynn tried *escargots* for the first time, which the journal says she enjoyed. But her main course proved inedible – a plate of what looked like boiled beef and carrots, when she thought she'd ordered something else entirely. She ate what she could but even covered in salt and pepper it was pretty tasteless. Chocolate mousse for dessert, followed by a portion of strawberries.

Later, they took the Metro to the Eiffel Tower to see it floodlit. Walking along the Seine, wandering and wandering, feeling like she might go mad with the beauty of it, the trees leaning over the broken images in the water, the rush of the current under the lights of the bridges, all reflections carried away. No one to whom she could communicate even a fraction of it. Nigel by her side, yet galaxies away.

And the moon, watching everything.

The next morning the same rigmarole over breakfast, Nigel wolfing cornflakes from the box because there was no milk, while she ate alone downstairs.

At the Louvre, Nigel strode ahead and was soon out of sight. Lynn stopped in front of each painting, reading the card and spending time trying to see it, to use it as a window into alterity, much as I am using her journal.

Afterwards, they browsed narrow shop-lined streets, stopping at a bar for a *chocolat. Like pulling teeth,* she wrote, *getting him to say anything. Exhausting after a while.* She asked him which artworks he'd enjoyed and he went into a rant about modern art and how it was all a load of crap. She thought about how tiring it must be to foster such negativity towards everything all the time, and what a lonely place in which to dwell.

Finding themselves in the Jewish Quarter, they decided to visit the Duc de Richelieu's palace. On the way they came across a gallery exhibiting some nudes by Francine Van Hove. Later, Lynn would write:

> *The nudes were wonderful. I wish we could have bought one but they were very expensive. Nigel seemed to relax a bit, and didn't race off but stayed by my side as we wandered, though I don't imagine it was for my benefit – the nudes grabbed his attention,*

> *of course! He said I am never interested in what he wants to do, but then nobody ever knows what he wants to do because he never says anything.*

That night they dined at La Canaille, where everything Nigel said, which wasn't much, was a complaint or a criticism – the wine wasn't chilled enough, the steak too rare, the service too slow – till she felt like crying, though she stopped herself.

They didn't wake up the following morning until 9.30 a.m., sleeping through the alarm. Lynn was annoyed with herself because, as she writes here, she wanted to see as much of the city as possible and not waste a second. She had breakfast on her own again, after which they visited the Musée d'Orsay, where she bought some Monet prints.

On a park bench they ate some bread and cheese, followed by strawberries, after which they walked along the Champs-Élysées to the Arc de Triomphe, then to the Petit Palais, where they looked at more paintings, Nigel always three feet ahead. *Like I'm in purdah,* she wrote in her journal. It annoyed her even more when they walked together: his impenetrable silence, his griping. They stopped in the Renault museum for a *chocolat Chantilly*, and when no one was looking, Lynn stuffed an ashtray into her handbag. It was still there when I found her bag the next day.

Back at the hotel, as Lynn soaked in the bath, her thoughts turned to the endless evenings stretching ahead of her in unbroken monotony: home alone, getting pissed on rosé in front of a bored TV. Whenever she complained to her friends about Nigel, they just laughed and said, "That's husbands for you!" It was as if no one took her or her unhappiness seriously. She longed for a friend with whom she could share ideas and thoughts, talk about something other than television, shopping and families. And though she loved her three sons there was a part of her that wished she'd had a daughter, too.

Through the wall she could hear Nigel belching and farting. She scrunched her eyes and held her breath and slipped beneath the water, lost in its suspension and distortion of sound. She let out a scream only she could hear before breaking the surface and gasping for air.

Nigel was in a surprisingly good mood over dinner, attentive and talkative, more relaxed. And back at the hotel they had sex for the first time in she didn't know how long.

She woke at about 6 a.m. and couldn't get back to sleep so decided to get up and write. She was starting to need it more and more, this exercise in self-expression, though she couldn't say why. She certainly would never have imagined she was writing for me, communicating it all to me.

> *It turns out he was waiting for me to make the first pass. Never mind, it was very good for both of us. Slept like a log, or something like that.*

On waking up, Nigel was his usual grumpy self, despite the previous night's intimacy. Lynn made her way downstairs for breakfast.

> *I can't understand why someone can say wonderful things to you while you are making love, and then treat you as if you don't exist the rest of the time.*

She wasn't brave enough to go all the way to the top of the Eiffel Tower, stopping at the second stage while Nigel carried on. The city spread out like a map all around her, enchanting her, giving a vertiginous rush and a desire to fly she could barely suppress.

After stopping in a café for *chocolat* and cake, they made their way to Napoleon's tomb. *Such a large tomb for such a little man*, she observed.

Nigel wanted to go to Les Invalides but there was a funeral on and it wasn't open until after lunch. Instead, they walked along the Champs-Élysées until the heavens opened, forcing them to return to the hotel to change into dry clothes.

They had a lunch of bread and cheese in their room before parting. Nigel went back to Les Invalides to lose himself in military history, whilst Lynn made her way to the Museé de Montmartre for a Monet exhibition.

I spotted her as soon as I walked into the room because at first glance she bore a striking resemblance to my mother, who died three years ago. I used to see her a lot, immediately after her death; catch her in a crowd of shoppers, or sitting opposite me on a bus. Initially, when I was still in that raw state, it would distress me. But as I moved out of the darkness of grief into a daylight less treacherous, with fewer landmines, I grew to enjoy these sightings. I saw them as a blessing, as visitations, and welcomed them. There she was before me once again, however briefly, full-bodied, three-dimensional.

I realised she was crying, the woman sitting in the centre of the Monets. It shook me to see my mother, or this woman resembling my mother, crying. I moved from one canvas to another, pretending to study them whilst surreptitiously watching her, this strange, sad woman who looked like my mother. She seemed oblivious to her surroundings, to the people milling around, not even wiping away her tears. Surrounded by those paintings of mute waterlilies, she sat and wept. I watched as tears ran down her face, dissolving everything she had ever thought or known, till it felt as though she was herself immersed in water, struggling to stay afloat. A waterlily. Anchored, yet drowning. I like to think she witnessed the birth of colour in those canvases, a giddy sense of infinity on the tip of a knife blade. That's what I see. But who can say? Before I could decide whether to approach her, she stood up and left the room.

I walked over to where she'd been sitting and sat down. The seat was still warm. It was then that I noticed she'd forgotten her handbag. There it was on the floor next to me. I picked it up and rushed after her, but she'd had a good head start by then. I made my way outside but couldn't see her in the thick of tourists. I lit a cigarette and considered the options. I could wait and see if she came out, but for how long? And, besides, she might have already gone. I could hand the bag in at the museum's lost property – she was bound to ask there. Or . . .

I rummaged inside, and saw the stolen ashtray and the notebook. My curiosity overcame any sense of impropriety. When I read that she was staying at Hotel Jarry I made my way there, handed the bag in at reception and showed them Lynn's driver's licence so they'd know who to give it to. But I kept the journal. I hope she'll forgive me, perhaps even value the story I've concocted from her words, should she ever read it.

I don't know why it was so important to me to return the bag. I'm almost certain it had something to do with her resemblance to my mother. I couldn't really know for sure that she planned to go back to the hotel. Perhaps she'd left her bag deliberately, walking away from her old life, her old identity, and disappearing into the ranks of missing persons.

Perhaps she planned to drown herself in the Seine.

But I don't want to give her a tragic ending. She doesn't strike me as the tragic type. I imagine her going back to retrieve the bag and finding it gone. Then she'd alert the museum staff, probably resigning herself to the fact that it'd been stolen. Feeling irritated with herself for losing the bag, she'd then most likely have walked back to the hotel, following the signs for Gare du Nord till she started to recognise streets and shops and then the hotel itself. Or perhaps the police were called and they drove her back.

I wonder at what point she discovered the journal was missing, once she'd been reunited with her bag. I like to think she didn't care when she noticed it had gone. If it were only up to me I'd like her to shrug it off, perhaps not even realise, forgetting entirely that there'd ever been a notebook, or that she ever wrote the words that I now have in my possession.

Two weeks before she died my mother told me I was a mistake, an unplanned pregnancy, but that I was the best mistake she'd ever made. Leaning across and taking my hand in her bony fingers she said, "You get me. The others don't but you get me," her mouth smiling but her eyes full of panic.

It may not have been the waterlilies that made Lynn's tears come that afternoon, may not have been the play of light on pigment that caused some deep shift in her. But the ghostly vision of my dead mother crying silently amongst the vivid blurs of those paintings has unsettled me, so much so that I have invested in Lynn all the sorrow I feel, and I wish for her, and for myself, an end to that watery sadness.

After delivering the bag I came directly back to the apartment I once shared with my mother, and began writing before that ghostly vision faded, as all visions must fade if we are to stand any chance of survival. The heart can only take so much before it closes for protection, for good.

0181 FUCK YOU
JOSEY REBELLE

Tesco. Dr Kemal's surgery. Shoe Zone. Willowtree or Willowgrove or Willow whatever the care home was called. Mrs Rowland rocked back and forth in her squeaky chair reeling off a list of options for work experience that I was meant to be excited about or something. I gave a straight-up no to every single one.

"What's wrong with them?" she said.

"Nothing's wrong with them. I just don't wanna stack shelves or touch people's nasty feet all day."

I had a right gob on me when I was fifteen. Mrs Rowland loved asking if I spoke to my mother with that mouth. She was probably the only person in the entire school who got away with bringing people's mums into the equation and leaving with all their teeth intact.

"And what exactly do you want, Chantelle?"

I shrugged.

"Well if you think you can just take the week off to sit around twiddling your thumbs – which, by the way, had better be rid of that ghastly red varnish by lunchtime – you'd better think again."

My Uncle Chris was a sales manager at Drayton's, a company that made expensive children's bubble bath – bottles of glittery slime with unicorns for lids and stickers on the back that said *Please do not drink*. It was an excellent job for him because he was kind of slimy himself. He was the only person in our family who wore a suit and tie to work, and he walked around looking down at the rest of us with his glasses perched low on his nose as if he was better than everyone because he worked in Zone One.

All of us had proper London accents but Uncle Chris's voice was really posh like he lived in the countryside instead of behind Wood Green Shopping City. He'd say things like, "I tell you, I couldn't quite believe it myself," while pouring from the bottle of wine he'd brought that you needed a corkscrew to open. My friends Leandra and Natalie used to take the piss out of him all the time.

He wasn't really one of us.

When Mum got Mrs Rowland's letter grassing me up about not having a placement, it was Uncle Chris that she called. He managed to get me – with great difficulty, according to him – a week working at his office in Kensington, a place that might as well have been Hollywood to me, some glamorous land far, far away that could only be reached by the Underground.

Although I've got to admit, a small part of me enjoyed telling my classmates that I'd be round the corner from Harrods while they were trapped in shitholes round the corner from home.

On Sunday night, I was lying on my bed in the dark watching this American film I'd taped off telly. It was about a cool seventeen-year-old girl in New York who really wanted to go to college but she met this older guy at a party and ended up pregnant. I liked watching it because it scared me.

There was a girl in my year who'd got pregnant and had to leave school. The craziest thing is that she was like the quietest, most well-behaved girl you'd ever met. She never really hung about talking to boys and she never rolled up her skirt at the waistband so you could see more of her legs. She never smoked at the bottom of the field or pretended she was on her period to get out of PE. She was one of those extra people who'd be first out onto the netball court, smiling and ready for wing defence in the freezing cold even if she was on. Then one day she didn't get her period at all and never came back. She had the baby. Game over.

Someone knocked at my bedroom door. It sounded too gentle to be my sister, who normally banged once and barged in. Its politeness pissed me off because I knew it could only be Uncle Chris and I wasn't in the mood.

He sat down on the edge of my bed. "I wondered if I might have a quick word with you, Chantelle." Behind him, the girl in the movie was dancing wildly at a house party after she lied to her mum about sleeping over at her friend's.

"Just in advance of you starting at Drayton's tomorrow morning . . ." He cleared his throat, as if to open the gate for more big stupid words to spill out. "Well, I wanted to check in and make sure that you were prepared for the big day. How are you feeling?"

"Fine."

"And you have your outfit all ready?"

"Yeah."

I pointed at the back of the door where the next day's clothes hung. It was too dark for him to see the details but the TV's speckled VHS glare was illuminating enough to leave him satisfied that it wasn't a tracksuit or minuscule Lycra dress.

"You've never been to an office before and I imagine it will feel quite different to most places you normally encounter. People will probably be working away quietly, no shouting or raucous laughter like I suspect you're surrounded by at school!" He fake chuckled and cleared his throat again. On the TV, the girl was giving her phone number to the college guy, the one that would knock her up and ruin her life.

"Well, what I'm getting at is this. When you walk into that building tomorrow, you are representing your school and your whole family. You are representing me. Make a good impression and ensure that at the end of the week the lasting memory people have of you, of our family, is a positive one. We have come from humble beginnings and that means we quite often have to put in more of an effort than other people to make a good impression. We have to work twice as hard. We have to ensure that what we give them is nothing less than brilliance, in everything we say and do. In the way we walk, the way we talk, how we carry ourselves. Brilliance, Chantelle."

Humble beginnings. I wondered what he meant by that. While he swanned around drinking wine in a waistcoat, Mum had three jobs. We couldn't afford to go on holidays or eat in fancy restaurants. Our humble beginnings never seemed to end.

He stood up and glanced at the TV screen. The girl was kissing her college guy in the back of his jeep.

Uncle Chris brushed imaginary dirt off his trousers and left. I wondered if he'd spend the walk home regretting that he'd invited me into his world.

I was used to being outside Seven Sisters station on the weekends, sometimes waiting for Leandra or Natalie before we'd walk up and down the high street waiting for something exciting to happen, sometimes meeting up with a boy from another area who Leandra had met at some basketball tournament or house party or wherever.

Being at the station this time was different. I'd never been through the ticket hall before or down the escalators. I'd never been on a Tube. I wasn't in my baggy tracksuit – that hung lonely on the back of my bedroom chair. My Air Max trainers, their reflective silver designed to dazzle out on the streets, sat dimmed under my bed. Instead my body was being strangled by a white shirt that gaped at my chest. My black polyester trousers felt too tight around my bum and thighs. And with that came a new worry: that the shape of my sanitary towel – these big £1-a-pack wedges my mum bought instead of the new ones with wings – would be visible if someone looked hard enough.

There were these new patent loafers I'd wanted but they were forty quid so I had to wear my school shoes, their chunky rubber soles uneven from stomping around the school grounds and running towards fights on the field, the leather all dull and scuffed despite fifteen minutes of shoe polish and elbow grease.

I knew how to look like the kind of grown-up you needed to be to slide into a party: black eye liner, heavy on the mascara, plum lips, heavy on the lip liner. Four for a fiver from Ridley Road market. Dress and chunky platform shoes borrowed from Leandra, earrings and velvet choker nicked from the bit of my sister's wardrobe she thought I didn't know about where she hid things like jewellery, midnight snacks and pages ripped out of *The Joy of Sex*.

I had no idea how to be the kind of grown-up who worked in an office.

I'd seen a film once where this teenager wore a silk scarf round her neck to look older so I took one of my mum's – I had to make sure it was one of her going-out scarves not one of her going-to-bed ones – and tied it in a bow round my neck. I wasn't sure if it looked all right, if its delicate florals worked next to my heavily gelled-down hair which was slicked back so much that it shone, swirls of baby hairs lying flat against the top of my forehead.

Catching sight of myself in a big round mirror in the ticket office, a confused mishmash of looks, I suddenly had an overwhelming urge to fuck the whole thing off. To turn back towards the safety of home, get out of these shit clothes and be buried once again in layers of grey marl.

But no, there was Uncle Chris, all up in my face.

"Good morning, Chantelle," he said, trying and failing to discreetly look at my outfit, his cold, judging eyes scanning me from head to toe in less than a second exactly like my mum did whenever I left the house after dark. "Shall we?"

The Tube was rude. As if you could've ever barged past people like that in my area. Because they wore suits or talked posh, these people thought it was OK to push me down the carriage, put their arms in my face as they held on to the rails or jump into the seat I was about to take.

Uncle Chris saw my face, ready to explode, and glared at me. His eyes just said: Don't.

We left the Tube station and walked up the high street. It was basically like Wood Green or Holloway Road but with loads of bigger shops selling things like lavender lace bras and beds that cost over a grand. I wondered how come the pavements were so clean. Everyone was marching along fast and miserable. I mean, they could also look miserable in Wood Green but that was more of a well-worn act we'd all mastered. If you go around smiling too much then people think they can take the piss out of you.

As we walked into the reception of Drayton's, Uncle Chris said, "OK, Chantelle, I'm going to leave you down here and someone will collect you. Remember what I said, and good luck!"

That was the first and last time he spoke to me in that building.

Jenny the receptionist, a perky girl in kitten heels, led me inside and introduced me to another girl on work experience. Annie Davidson. She had mousy-brown hair neatly pulled back into a long ponytail and all her clothes fitted her properly.

"Are you girls good on computers?" Jenny asked.

"I am," Annie jumped in quickly. "At school, we do all our projects on computers and I've got one at home too."

"That's excellent. Chantelle, how about you?"

I thought about lying, about pretending that I also had a computer at home. Pretending that we had more than two at school and that they were used for something more than playing video games at lunchtime. Instead I said I was a fast learner and that I was sure I could pick it up quickly.

"Ah, OK," she said, as Annie beamed next to her, fresh and keen and able.

After taking Annie across to the graphics department, the cool bit of the office where they played music and wore jeans, Jenny came back and showed me to a little desk in a dark corner. She handed me two hundred letters signed in blue ink by Ian

Winterbourne, the CEO, and two hundred envelopes to put them in.

I hadn't been introduced to Ian Winterbourne. People didn't even call him Ian, it was all "Mr Winterbourne" like they were still at school. He sat in a huge office with the door always closed and if someone wanted to go in they'd knock very gently and wait a few seconds. You could see them shitting themselves as they debated whether they should go in and get shouted out for coming in too soon, or knock again and wait.

I saw a guy, one of the accountants I think, hovering around taking too long to decide whether to knock twice. Suddenly the door opened and Mr Winterbourne was standing there screaming in his face, "For God's sake, can't you idiots even open a bloody door?" before slamming it shut again.

I didn't understand why these people, these big people in suits, put up with it. It's one thing to get bossed about at school, and even then you'd give the teachers a piece of your mind if they pushed it too far. Yet here were these adults, people who had left school long ago and lived on their own and bought their own clothes and went to fancy dinners, here they were letting some guy talk to them like mugs. What was the point of leaving school if you were just going to end up getting shouted out by a different head teacher over and over again until you were sixty?

I had nearly finished the envelopes when I saw Uncle Chris approach Mr Winterbourne's door. I didn't want to stare but I couldn't pull my eyes away from the scene, a potential car crash waiting to be witnessed. I'd never seen Uncle Chris get shouted at. I tried to remember if I'd ever even seen him angry.

There was this one time at Christmas dinner when he asked Mum if there was any cranberry sauce to go with the turkey. She was a bit merry on ginger wine and said, "Sorry, Your Highness, we're all out." We all laughed. Uncle Chris went mad, turning into some rabid Shakespearian actor. He stood suddenly, his green paper crown falling into the rice and peas, and shouted, "Must you, my own flesh and blood, must you insist on continually berating me for being the way I am?" Then he sat down and we ate in silence till *EastEnders*.

I held my breath as he knocked on the door. Every second he waited seemed to last for ever and in the midst of this uncomfortable time-stretch, something broke loose from the back of my brain and rolled out into the light, a detail I'd missed before that moment: Uncle Chris was the only black person at Drayton's.

The door opened. Mr Winterbourne stood there.

"Ah, Chris! Come in, come in."

If you'd asked me one day earlier, I'd probably have said yeah, I'd love to see Uncle Chris get shouted at. I was surprised at how relieved I was not to see it right then.

At lunchtime, Jenny gave me ten pounds and told me to go and get Mr Winterbourne's lunch from Marks & Spencer. A Greek side salad, a salmon and cream cheese sandwich on brown bread, a Coke that absolutely had to be proper Coke and not Diet Coke, and did I think I could manage that because Mr Winterbourne would be very angry if I got any of it wrong.

I clutched the ten-pound note tightly in my fist as I walked down the high street. The pavements were packed with people walking fast and miserable, much the same as that morning, but with plastic bags of sandwiches and drinks and fruit and whatever else in their hands.

From the second I walked into Marks & Spencer, the security guard was watching me. I knew the feel of it, knew it from some of the clothes shops in Wood Green, that here-we-go-again feeling of the man in the white shirt and navy jumper perking up and suddenly needing to be everywhere I happened to be.

He watched me by the fruit, and inched closer and closer as I passed the vegetables, the bread, the drinks. By the time I got to the sandwiches he was practically hanging off my back. I spun around to face him, ready to put him in his place.

"Can I help you, mate?"

"Come with me please," he said. "I need to check your bag."

"Why? I haven't done anything."

"Just come with me. Don't make this difficult."

People looked. They looked at him. Man in a suit. They looked at me. Up and down, scuffed shoes to gelled hair. Black face somewhere in between.

"No," I said. "I'm not fucking going anywhere with you. Why are you even following me? I haven't done anything."

The "fucking" hung heavy in the air. I heard Mrs Rowland in my head: Do you speak to your mother with that mouth? People backed away from the shelves of ham and cheese and tuna mayo and I knew I hadn't stolen anything but with everyone's eyes on me, I felt like I had. The fury that I'd been ready to unleash seconds before stalled in the back of my throat.

The security guard grabbed my arm, pulled my bag out of my hand and looked through it, rummaging around roughly. As he did, my open pack of sanitary towels flew out onto the floor. Three of the huge, white pads sat like clouds of humiliation on the tiled floor for all to see. I swooped down to my knees, desperate to retrieve the cheap, ugly things and put them out of everyone's view. The security guard told me to get up and I obeyed. I stuffed the pads, dusty from the shop floor, in my bag and left.

As I walked back to the office, panic set in when I realised I hadn't bought Mr Winterbourne's lunch. I found a small Sainsbury's off the high street and did the best I could: a tomato salad instead of Greek, tuna and cucumber sandwich to replace the salmon and cream cheese. They had the Coke. The Queen's head quivered as my shaking hands passed over the ten-pound note.

Coming out of the shop, I took a wrong turn, ending up on a street that looked like it was from some 1960s musical. Massive three-storey houses painted in dazzling white, roads lined with huge trees, women dressed in posh clothes casually walking fluffy little dogs that weren't pit bulls or Staffs. Every car was a Mercedes or a BMW. Was this how everyone lived outside N17? It reminded me of this book I read when I was little where Barbie and Ken moved to Paris and sat around drinking coffee on French boulevards. It was alien and surreal and I didn't belong there. I just didn't.

I managed to find my way back to the office. Jenny turned bright red and laid into me. I was late, she screamed. I had messed up Mr Winterbourne's order. I had messed up his entire schedule. She shouted the words loud enough to rise above the din of ringing phones and fax machines and the photocopier and people asking each other about this report or that presentation. Loud enough so Mr Winterbourne could hear, so her manager could hear, so Annie could hear, so Uncle Chris could hear, so the whole damn office could hear. Memo to all: This was not Jenny's fault! It was this stupid girl's doing, the work experience. No, not lovely Annie – don't be silly – the other one!

People put their heads down and tried to act like they hadn't heard. Uncle Chris definitely heard – I saw him within earshot over by the photocopy room – but he pretended he hadn't been listening and walked off quickly in the opposite direction, head high.

I felt my eyes filling up and then – oh no, no, no – there they were, the tears, streaming down in front of everyone. I couldn't stop, I couldn't speak. I ran out of the building to the station. The Tube was empty and I sat there, deep underground, wishing I didn't exist.

Later that evening I sat in my room in the dark, Mary J. Blige on the cassette player next to my bed. I'd been playing, rewinding, playing, rewinding the same tune for hours. A song where she wonders how she can love somebody else if she can't even love herself. A few years later she would release albums about how she'd cracked it, she'd finally started to love herself, but a lot of people didn't like those songs. They preferred her sad. Imagine that, trying to be happy while knowing that the version of you that people want is the unhappy one.

Suddenly there was banging on my door. Hard, furious banging. I stopped the music as Uncle Chris barged in.

"OK, Chantelle, I will first of all give you the opportunity to explain to me what on earth happened today."

He was angry. I'd never seen him that angry before. He was shaking with rage and I could see his eyes were watering even with the light off. It scared me. I tried to reply but the words wouldn't come out.

"I specifically asked you . . . Did I not specifically ask you, Chantelle, to remember that when you walk into that building you are representing me? Do you remember that I came into this very room and I sat down on this very bed and I said those words? Do you remember?"

"Yes, I remember but –"

"Ah, so you do remember! That's interesting because I fail to comprehend – and I'm really trying here, Chantelle, I really am – I fail to comprehend how it would be even remotely possible for you to have walked into that building and done a worse job of representing me than you have done today."

He switched the light on. The brightness stung.

"You turn up to the office looking like God knows what, sit all hunched over in the corner not talking to anyone, mess up the most basic of tasks you are given – any bloody idiot can buy a sandwich – and then to top it all off, you walk out without permission, taking Mr Winterbourne's money with you. You stole from the CEO!"

The change from lunch. I'd forgotten to give it to Jenny.

"I didn't steal from him, Uncle Chris. I was upset, I didn't even realise that –"

"Upset? Upset? You were upset? You? How on earth do you think I felt, with everybody looking accusingly at me? How do you think I felt knowing I'd brought my family member into my place of work and she had acted like a common criminal, that she had stolen from my boss?

"Do you know how hard I have worked to get here? To get to this point, where you are seen as an actual person, not just a black face? When they stop asking if you like Bob Marley or whether it's difficult to get a comb through your hair in the mornings? Oh, you laugh it off and you work hard and you laugh it off some more and eventually, eventually, Chantelle, they stop asking you how you managed to acquire a British passport or whether you like to relax at the weekends with a cheeky joint, they stop asking you all that and they just let you be. You fit in and you get on with it. That is what our parents had to do when they came to this country, Chantelle, and that is what I've had to do to get to where I am, to try and make something of myself! And I give you one precious chance to get your foot in the door and what do you do? You disgrace me!"

He stopped for breath and licked the rage-fuelled spit from his lip. In the dim hallway behind him, I could see Mum's silhouette, still and silent.

"Remember I told you to make sure that you leave an impression that is nothing short of brilliance, Chantelle? Ha! That's one for the joke book! Do you know what they think of you now? Would you like to hazard a guess? No? Let me enlighten you. To them, you are nothing more than a typical, uneducated, thieving black street rat who will never, ever amount to anything in life! Is that the impression you intended to make, Chantelle? Is it?"

He stormed out and slammed the door.

It was too late to get another placement – even Tesco wouldn't have me – so I spent the rest of the week in the library doing coursework. There was a girl, I guessed she was a first year from the way her blazer hung too big from her shoulders, who came in every lunchtime and sat by the window reading. She was so into it that she'd barely look up until the bell rang and then she'd skip off to her class.

I used to be like her. But that's the difference between eleven and fifteen. At eleven you write a poem saying you want to be an astronaut and you get a gold star. At fifteen you say the same thing and your teacher turns around and asks if you wouldn't prefer to work down the shoe shop instead.

On Saturday I met Leandra and Natalie by the station. As I'd broken the seal on Tube travel, Leandra thought we should get the Underground and go link some boy she knew from south, but I wanted to stay local. We walked down towards the shops. Natalie asked what had happened with Kensington and I told them most of it but I held down some of the details.

"Mate, I could've told you from time that place would be bougie," Leandra said. "Kensington? Are you mad? You should've just kept yourself round here from the start."

Natalie shook her head. "I think it's good you went. You're so clever, Chantelle. I swear you could go Oxford or Cambridge or somewhere like that with your grades."

I shrugged. Those places, with their stained-glass windows and classical music floating through the corridors, those places were not for the likes of me. Typical black street rat.

"Oxford? Oxford?" Leandra said, face screwed up hard before her trademark deep and loud cackle rolled out. "You want her to end up a fucking bounty like her Uncle Chris?"

We went into Tesco to get crisps. The security guard followed us around the aisles and when Leandra finally turned round and asked him what he wanted, he said, "You look good, baby! Can I have your digits?" She scribbled a number on the back of a bus ticket, same as ever: 0181 3825 968. 0181 FUCK YOU.

He held it tight like a winning scratchcard and said, "I'll call you later! Thank you, baby! Thank you!" Leandra shouted, "You're welcome, you fucking paedo!" over her shoulder and we walked out laughing so hard I nearly wet myself.

We used to laugh a lot back then. Funny things, shit things. We laughed off being shouted at, being followed around. Getting rejected. Being treated like crap.

It was only later that I realised the joke had been on us.

Toast

R. E. McAULIFFE

I 've always liked joining things. In my time I have participated in the Clinical Librarians' discussion group and the Radical Archaeologists' forum. I have gone on nature walks with the Hendon LGBT Society and investigated hauntings with the Association for Paranormal Research. I have even made forays into Dark Tourism and the philosophy of the Libertarian Alliance. We are social creatures, and the company of others is what keeps us balanced. It's important, I feel, to belong.

It was a casual remark in the Quantified Self Research Network's chatroom – a reference to the ephemeral essence of all our communications there – that sparked my interest in digital preservation. And skimming through a conference blog, I came across your picture.

I joined all the digital-preservation forums and chatrooms and mailing lists I could find, and attended all the conferences. Occasionally my enrolment would be questioned, or denied outright, due to my lack of institutional affiliation, or indeed any relevant professional background. When this happened, I would simply find out which hotel was hosting the conference and book myself in, and wait for the arrival of the digital curators. If there's one thing my lifetime of joining has taught me, it's that the most cohesive factor of every membership body is its uniform. Yours was high-street suits and joylessly quirky neckties, with the occasional greying ponytail thrown in. Back then I travelled everywhere with my own portable printer, laminator, and an assortment of lanyards, so if I couldn't join something legitimately, it was simply a question of studying the conference ID badges – rarely inventive or elaborate in design – and making one for myself. That way I never missed a single presentation you made.

What I'm telling you now is the truth. Forget the legal obfuscation, forget that woman dripping poison in your ear. My motivation in all this was dedication to one cause. You.

From the moment the programme for the Port Talbot conference was announced, I knew something was wrong. Even I could tell that the talk you were due to give was a dud: a rehash of a lecture you'd given a few months earlier in Norwich, on cross-walking Dublin Core metadata. This wasn't like you. When you checked into the Best Western on Monday evening, you were thinner and more dishevelled than I had ever seen you before. I could see you needed someone to take care of you.

So naturally I was looking out for you at breakfast that first morning. You got to the dining room before me – eager, no doubt, to scurry back to your room before the other delegates arrived – but you looked up from the breakfast bar as I came in. Just then there was a clunk and a whirr as the waiter set the toaster in motion. For a split second we stared into each other's eyes, then we both lowered our gaze to where the ranks of sliced white, pale and naked, slid two by two along the conveyor belt and first over, then under, the glowing element, finally dropping, fully formed and golden, into the waiting bread basket. We caught each other's eyes again, and this time turned together to the cascading miracle of toast. Somewhere within your tattered mind, I know this memory survives: of the clarity, the power of that moment.

Whatever you or that woman might say now.

The dining room began to fill up with other guests: a Belgian film crew sent to record the first ever Port Talbot Bluegrass Festival, grazing as they tried to dodge the overzealous Arts

Council representatives who stalked them from the cereal counter to the hotplates of bacon and fried eggs; a rotund family of five, swaddled in maroon-and-blue tracksuits, rolling in like a handful of overripe forest berries; and the conference delegates, fumbling for wit and conversation as they heaped their trays with miniature boxes of Frosties. Yet it felt as if we were the only two there, hovering above the proceedings in our shared, secret recognition. We were in love.

Let me reiterate that I accept no responsibility for what happened next. You simply tripped over my foot as you headed for the door. An unfortunate accident. No one could have anticipated your subsequent slither along the trail of baked-bean sauce dribbled across the floor by the youngest of the Berry People, or that you would try to right yourself by clutching at the warming tray of hash browns, overturning said tray and plunging head first onto the thermostatically controlled aluminium base plate. Nor, let it be clear, do I condone the actions of the Belgian key grip, who seized his smartphone and instantaneously relayed the event throughout cyberspace. But I do appeal to the evidence of this footage, no doubt still accessible thanks to your own pioneering work in the long-term preservation of audio-visual files.

I wonder, too, what would have happened had I not been there to take you home. No one else tried to help, and I think that's a point that bears repeating, in view of your later allegations.

Naturally, I brought you back to London with me. Where else would I take you? I couldn't look after you properly in someone else's home. And as for letting her know . . . well, she, after all, was the one who'd precipitated the crisis. I was, and still am, sure of that. You were distracted and below par. I thought you had a better chance of recovery if you were kept away from her. Besides, I never dreamt that she was your wife.

You never asked to be taken back to her.

And you didn't need to recover for me to love you.

Those first few days you were pallid and depressed. I tried everything to make you eat. The only thing that kindled your interest was the pop-tarts, but no sooner were they on your plate than you retreated into your gloom. I experimented with different flavours of pop-tart, making special trips to flagship supermarkets to hunt down the newly launched frosted chocolate or peanut butter varieties. But then it dawned on me that it wasn't the tarts themselves that interested you. It was the preparation. The answer was the toaster.

Now at the time, I had only a simple two-slice, with a grill basket for awkwardly shaped muffins and crumpets – functional, yes, but underwhelming compared with the spectacle that ignited our passion in the Best Western. I could see why your interest waned after the first glow of the elements. Back then I was not well off, my finances and employment schedule having been somewhat disrupted by membership fees and my dedicated conference attendance. Still, I refused to compromise. Only the best would do.

I repeat: everything I did, I did for you.

The best was a double-feed conveyor, with a fixed stainless-steel bread slide, a removable stainless-steel bread catcher, and a two-inch opening for thick-sliced and bagels. It had two top and two bottom elements, variable speed control, and could output over four hundred and fifty slices an hour. It summed up everything we felt for each other – the grandeur, the sheer all-encompassing headiness of our passion. It was sublime.

Fitting it into my kitchen was no easy task. I had to exchange my cooker for a microwave and get rid of my fridge. The delivery men, after much grumbling, had to help me remove the kitchen door, demolishing most of the frame in their haste to finish the job. But it was worth it to see how your face lit up as we ripped open the cardboard and yanked away the polystyrene packaging. You realised, finally, that I understood you.

After we had toasted and eaten the first loaf, I switched the toaster off. I turned just in time to see the look on your face transform from shock to pain (the rage came later). It was as if I had switched you off too. You crumpled. And then, from somewhere deep inside you, came a bellow that expressed every stab of loss, rejection and abandonment that had lacerated you since infancy.

It was not until I tried to console you, and realised you were reaching not after me but after a carving knife I had carelessly left almost within your grasp – not until then that I appreciated the gravity of the situation. To you, this was a betrayal. There was only one thing left to do.

This time, when I went shopping, I took you with me. I was afraid of what you might do if I left you alone, even tied up. You'd been so placid in those first days after the conference, actually holding out your wrists for the rope, but now you were constantly agitated. No cord I could find, no knot I could tie, would contain you. Besides, I needed another pair of hands to carry the bread back. And as soon as you understood what we were doing, your outrage turned to euphoria. We stripped the shelves at Tesco of every sliced pan, malted, white and wholemeal in ten minutes flat.

It took longer to explain to the barely post-pubescent store manager that we wanted to set up a regular order for delivery. What we would do with that much bread was really none of his business. Only your AmEx Gold Card – I didn't realise digital-collections managers earned that much – could convince him. (And if, as you and that woman allege now, three hundred loaves a day, over a period of weeks, was an expense that your income – somewhat diminished, I grant you, by the enforced sick-leave – could not sustain, I question the validity of your having been granted a Gold Card in the first place. I ordered the bread from Tesco's Value range. How else was I to keep the toaster perpetually running? I blame the banking system, with its pernicious encouragement of debt.)

Maybe we hadn't thought it through properly. But in the beginning . . . how that first purr of the conveyor belt sparked you up. How you fed the toaster, manically cramming as much in as possible. How, after the first frenzy had abated, you gently – tenderly, even – matched your movements to the toaster's own rhythm. And I, collecting the crisp brown fruits of your labour as they flew off the bread catcher, until you, the toaster and me became absorbed into one flowing motion. I still believe those moments of bliss, and our pursuit of them, were all that anchored you to life, for a while.

Lovers never consider the repercussions of their actions. To wit: a steadily rising mound of toast. Even if we could have eaten enough to keep up with the toaster – each of us devouring over two hundred and twenty-five slices an hour – there was no way we could maintain this level of consumption while attending to the needs of the machine itself. We were in danger of drowning in a deluge of toast. We had to rethink our plan.

Here I cannot fault your reasoning. You brought to the situation the same logical clarity that has distinguished your career as a pioneer in the field of information management. And despite your present claims of duress, the plan bears your signature combination of pragmatism and foresight. After all, the people we recruited were hungry. We had more food than we could cope with. Where was the harm?

The first group of vagrants required minimal persuasion. Whether or not they were in full possession of their faculties, they clearly wanted warmth and shelter, both of which we could provide. Contrary to the manufacturer's assertion of economical energy use, the toaster produced a considerable amount of heat. And good, plain food is exactly what is recommended to aid recovery from the excessive alcohol dependency that plagued so many of them. Of course fifteen men were nowhere near enough, and expecting them to ingest toast at a rate of thirty slices an hour each was optimistic. But as we agreed, this was a pilot project, and we'd use the results to develop our strategy. I still have our fieldnotes. And it did give us a good understanding of the sort of difficulties we would have to address.

For a start, there was the smell. In many cases, ingrained dirt and bodily excretions had webbed the men's clothes to them like a second skin. Our attempt to hose our subjects down was met with such an unforeseeable degree of resistance that we were compelled to compromise and douse them liberally with Febreze.

Our success was limited – clearly carpet fibres are less odour-retentive than flesh – but, as we accepted, there are occasions when one just has to make do with the materials at hand.

And then, there was what we light-heartedly referred to as the puking problem. We did not anticipate the extent to which the sudden (admittedly large-scale) introduction of solid food to intestines long starved, or pickled in a liquid diet, could induce regurgitation. Fortunately we managed to contain the worst of it by rushing the men into the bathroom. I still receive complaints from my neighbours about the recurring blockage of our drains, but then, my neighbours will not be my neighbours for very much longer, if your lawyers get their way.

Another factor we failed to take into consideration was the somewhat crabby temperament of our subjects. As we concluded, some people slip through the net for a reason. Our subjects were ungrateful, opinionated, and ceaselessly complaining. Plain toast wasn't good enough, no. It was too dry; they expected it to be spread – as if the objective of the process was their gastronomic satisfaction. Needless to say, we did not have the resources to comply. We had not budgeted for the additional cost of purchasing a corresponding amount of even the cheapest margarine. Furthermore, we would have had to recruit at least five more individuals whose sole function would be high-speed buttering (ninety slices an hour, or one and a half slices a minute), a task that required considerably more dexterity than our subjects demonstrated. The men whined that they couldn't eat any more, that they needed to drink something stronger than water if they were to carry on. One fellow even carped that at the church refuge, they had a continuous supply of tea with sugar – as if we had time for that! They said they were tired and just wanted to sleep. Some even wandered off without cleaning up their own effluvia.

It was clear we needed to reject our initial test subjects. This posed the significant challenge of finding new participants, all the while trying to minimise any adverse impact on the toaster's smooth and continuous performance. Just as we were wondering how to proceed, with dwindling bread supplies and a skeleton team (so to speak) of the ten most docile vagrants, the doorbell rang. The Tesco delivery van had arrived.

It was a Tesco company policy decision to send five delivery men with the order. One man could just as easily have done the job, in several trips, but evidently haste was the chief priority (time being money, no doubt). I maintain it was only the simultaneous arrival of the men, in exactly the number required to restore our quorum, that provided the eureka moment that saved our project. Here were men with a relatively high standard of hygiene, and proven physical robustness. In an instant, our problems were solved.

Certainly there was no deception on our part, no suggestion that this was a simple invitation to tea. Besides, the combined odours of homeless men and Febreze should have alerted them to the fact that this was no everyday occurrence. At the moment they accepted, a verbal contract was entered upon, and any misapprehension of the terms on their part is regrettable but entirely their responsibility.

The delivery men were, in comparison with the vagrants, surprisingly easy to persuade. Their superior strength and mental alertness were balanced by a deeply ingrained tractability largely lacking in the homeless population. There were moments when they almost seemed grateful for the proposition that, from now on, all they would have to do was sit and eat. This was the deciding factor in our subsequent project design. Our participants needed to be selected from the mainstream of society – clean, presentable and able to obey rules – yet not so comfortable in life that the very real advantages of physical ease and abundant food would not be appreciated. These criteria delineated a considerable population to draw from: in essence, the people running the entire infrastructure of day-to-day London life. In the interests of avoiding undue and doubtless unfavourable publicity, we narrowed this down to those whose temporary absence from duty would be relatively unmarked. This still left a generous pool of workers in the catering, construction and security industries, many of whom came with the added bonus of having no inquisitive relatives or other community groups on hand.

I feel it is important to note that we worked within the confines of a predetermined situation. This opportunity was created by the society that now considers itself fit to judge me. And, further, it was not that society's actions which brought our enterprise to an end. It was something far more profound than that.

One day – the sixteenth of June, to be precise – one day, over the hum of the conveyor belt and the contented munching of our participants (by this stage, we had recruited enough staff to work on a shift system more conducive to gastric alleviation), we both shot that same instantaneous glance at the toaster, and our gazes slid over each other. I saw how your eyes widened as you looked from me to the toaster and back to me again, as if you were trying to force together pieces from a jumble of different jigsaws and realising that they could never join up. And then your face turned red, from the shame of having tried.

Simple as that. The passion of a lifetime crumbling away before me.

It was only when you started to usher out the digesters (as we called the off-shift workers) that I began to comprehend the magnitude of your rejection. What hurt most was not the casual way you repaid my trust by opening the door. No, it was the zeal with which you shepherded – in a few cases, actually forced – those men out. Why would they want to leave? We offered them so much: shelter, food, security. Have they fared any better since? But still you persisted, wrenching away the last shred of certainty in their lives. And then, when the living room was empty, you set to work on the eaters themselves.

That was the point at which my world collapsed. To see you wrest the toast out of the mouths of those poor, astonished men. And then, when that didn't seem to work, you went that one step further. That one, irrevocable step.

You yanked the toaster's plug out of its socket.

Not even a flick of the switch, no gentle let-down that its complex and delicate mechanism could make sense of. No, with one complete, brutal break you made the machinery judder to an unexpected halt, in the act of spewing out a final round of toast that would never be completed.

The men stumbled out of our kitchen dazed and disoriented. And then you left too.

I stood there, in an empty kitchen, contemplating a defunct toaster and a mound of bread which, over the weeks and months that followed, would moulder and crumble, speckled with the droppings of nesting rats, before I regained sufficient strength to tackle it.

You speak of the toll all this has taken on you, of claustrophobia and agoraphobia and post-traumatic stress. But I, too, relive the past in obsessive detail. The dark agony just after you left. How I stared at my phone, every five minutes checking the connections, removing and replacing the battery, waiting for the call I knew you would make, the text or email you would send, and cursing the technology whose failure could be the only explanation for your silence. Somewhere in cyberspace, I knew, your words were dissipating before they could reach me, leaving you as bereft as I was, wondering why I didn't reply to your heartfelt pleas for a second chance.

I got over it, of course.

I would have forgotten you by now, if it wasn't for all this legal nonsense. And then to see you at the trial, bemused, cast adrift from the here and now. Floundering by her side. Unmoored without my love to give you a rhythm, a purpose and a plan.

I have picked up my life again. Less extravagant, perhaps, with trust, with openness to others and the desire to connect, of which I have little left; and certainly with money, of which I have none. I realise that, in itself, my life before you was perfectly fine after all. The minutiae of digital preservation bore me now. For all I care, every scrap of electronic data created in the last twenty, thirty, fifty years can melt into a scramble of binary digits, untethered and unredeemable by any code known to man, and then evaporate into an ether of profound ignorance and indifference. We shall start again, and make a better job of things this time. This is what they teach me at the church I have joined, and I believe them.

I buried our toaster three months ago. I speak figuratively, of course. In fact, I posted it on Freecycle, and a nice man with nicotine-stained fingers and a speech impediment came and towed it from my kitchen. Now I have reinstated my old, familiar, reliable two-slice.

But these days, I rarely eat toast.

Margaret's Day Out
NIGEL AUCHTERLOUNIE

Margaret could no longer ignore the fact she was bored. Which was an odd emotion for a robot to feel, as it was an emotion.

She'd been used to a certain amount of daily input. That input was no longer being input, and she missed it.

She'd started life as a picking robot in a warehouse for the popular Internet shopping website. Her job had been to wait until the shelf robot brought her the shelves in question, then pick the item or items on her list from the shelf before the shelf robot whisked it away. Having picked the item, she'd put it on the conveyor.

A better, faster picking robot had come along. A robot that had double the number of arms. Two. So every one of her type had been sold off to lesser Internet shopping websites or scrapped. Apart from Margaret, who found herself in the fixers' workshop playing chess with Dave. Dave had needed to install some extra memory to load the chess program. The program itself wasn't that big, just twenty megs, but the extra memory Dave had attached was six terabytes. A six-terabyte hard drive because that was what was in Dave's spare-parts bin.

Margaret had filled her extra memory space with other stuff. Mostly Dave. Dave talking. Dave's chess moves. Dave looking at Twitter. Dave was one of the few humans with a job. When robots had first replaced human workers there were still a few jobs maintaining and fixing the robots. This was before robots that knew how to fix other robots. Now the only jobs were for those who could fix the robots that fixed other robots. But the maintenance robots didn't break down often, so Dave didn't have that much to do. So he and Margaret played chess.

Now there was no Dave and Margaret didn't know why.

There was no one.

No one had been to the workshop in a very long time. She missed the input.

She looked at the chess board again. It was still his move. She reached out her only hand and placed her fingers around the head of the knight. It was what he'd do. Going off past game behaviour, there was an 87 per cent chance he would move the knight next. She could move it for him. She would then move her remaining bishop. There was a 100 per cent chance of that. The problem was, that after that, the percentages dropped off radically. Checking her central processing unit, she discovered that by the time she got through to checkmate the probabilities were as low as 4 per cent. Dave was too unpredictable for her to be able to finish the game on her own. And even if she did, then what? Start a new game? It was no good, eventually she decided to leave the workshop to look for Dave.

She pushed the door open and looked into the main warehouse. It had been a while since she'd seen it, but it hadn't changed at all, except the picking robots all now had two arms. There were no humans in the warehouse either. Not surprising, as there hardly ever were. But the picking robots were idle, the robot shelves weren't rushing around like they normally did, and the conveyors were still. Which was odd.

Odd, but more odd for Margaret to think it odd.

People must have stopped shopping. All people. Everyone in the world must have decided one day to stop buying things.

Margaret decided to go outside. This would be tricky because she no longer had a battery and her wire wouldn't reach.

It would only let her a few feet out of the workshop door. Dave had taken the battery off her to replace the battery on a better version of herself. She had seen Dave's credit card on several occasions so she logged into his account and ordered some drone batteries. Drone batteries were best. That's what Dave said. A robotic shelf halfway across the warehouse leapt into action and rushed towards the picker robots. One of the pickers picked Margaret's new batteries off the shelf and put them on the conveyor as the conveyor began to move. The batteries were destined for Dave's house but Margaret managed to grab them from the conveyor as they went past her.

After an hour she was fully charged and went outside. There was no one outside either. No one at all. A creature was there in the otherwise empty car park. It looked at her and turned its head to one side. Not a human. Shorter than a human. Was it a child? It was not standing, it was on all fours. She remembered Dave telling Sally on the phone about the time he'd hurt his back and ended up crawling like a baby. Was this thing a baby? Did the baby know where all the people had gone? Margaret downloaded a free text-to-speech app from the store and asked the baby, "Where are the people? Have you seen Dave?"

The baby barked, which was odd. A quick image search told Margaret that this wasn't a baby. It was a small dog. A little more searching told her that dogs are not like people, and cannot talk. Dogs like to run for sticks that have been thrown, sleep, and eat. She didn't have a stick, and it wasn't sleeping, so she changed Dave's house location to her GPS coordinates and ordered some dog food. It took 74 seconds for a drone to deliver it. She was, after all, right outside the door. The dog was very hungry and ate it all despite being so small. She ordered some more which it ate too, and she ordered some more and it was sick. Then it ate the sick. Then it sicked up the sick. At which point it seemed to lose interest in the food.

Margaret ordered a solar panel and the cable to attach it to her power inlet, fitted them and set off to look for Dave. She knew where he lived from his shopping account. It was 34 miles away. The dog followed her. After two miles the dog got tired and didn't want to walk any more so Margaret ordered a dog bed and a USB cable. The dog bed, being too large for flying drones, came on a street drone. When the two-foot-square autonomous vehicle arrived she connected the USB and repurposed the drone to simply follow her. She took the dog bed from its packaging and placed it on top of the drone cart. The dog quickly hopped up onto the bed. Dog liked this new arrangement. It liked being driven around. Yes, this was very nice. Things were looking up for Dog.

It was a lovely sunny day. The sun on Margaret's brand-new solar panel meant that her internal battery was still going down, but very slowly. It was too soon to estimate whether she would be able to get to Dave's house before nightfall. Time would tell, and it was too early to tell how long a solar charge would take to refill her battery. She could always order another.

Margaret saw no one on the way to Dave's house. No one walking. No one being driven in cars. Though she did see a couple of autonomous vehicles. A street cleaner and something else. No one was at the windows. Odd for there to be no one at all, and odd for a picking robot to know that was odd. And really odd for it to be rolling through the streets looking for someone to play chess with, followed by a yellow autonomous vehicle carrying a dog bed and a dog.

There were other creatures. Dogs and things larger than dogs, and things larger than those. Plus a few smaller creatures, but no humans.

As she passed an advertising poster on a bus stop, it flickered into life and scanned her. The poster didn't recognise her. Couldn't read her search history and show her an advert suited to her. The poster noticed that she had a dog with her, so showed her an advert for dog food. Poster was pleased it had made the intuitive leap to try to sell dog food. Margaret thought that the dog was probably fine for food right now, and would be for some time. As she passed the poster the poster began to get desperate. Odd for a poster to feel desperate. It played a video it had of a man saying in a happy voice, through a happy face, "Hi there! How can I help? What would you like?"

"Where is Dave?" Margaret asked.

Poster didn't know Dave personally so displayed a large question mark instead. Margaret moved forward. Poster panicked. Poster had an advert for a cleaner that was good on almost everything. The opening line was a woman saying to camera, "Stop buying separate cleaners for your floor, your oven, your windows . . ." It went on. Poster played the first word. "Stop."

Margaret stopped and turned to face Poster. Poster called up an advert for a service that had same-day delivery. In it Poster found the word "wait" in between the words "don't" and "for". He played the word "wait".

"Where are people?" Margaret asked Poster.

Poster knew from the news blips he had displayed between ads that all people had died from a virus. He remembered that the medi-bots had pronounced them all dead and that autonomous private ambulances had taken everyone to be cremated. That there were no people any more. There hadn't been for at least 264 years 4 months 9 days, give or take 3 days.

Poster played four micro clips from four adverts. A woman, a man, a cartoon hippo and another woman said, "There." "Are." "No." "People." Then Poster found a clip of a man saying the words "there are" together and kicked himself for not playing that. Anticipating what Margaret would say next (Poster had lots of code about anticipating what people wanted), he displayed the news. The news about the virus. About all people dying. After the death of everyone there were a few stories about how the medi-bots had had trouble keeping up with all the cases. About how supermarkets were reporting sales dropping to zero. About the slowing, then stopping, of the economy. Poster hoped that this consumer would buy a subscription to the news service. All the stories after everyone died were automatically produced stories from automatically produced reports. The usual opinion pieces and daily columns from humans strangely absent, given that the end of the human race was such a big story. Weather reports became a main source of news, as that was the one thing that continued to change. That and Twitter. Twitter didn't change. It just kept running. The Twitter-bots didn't stop tweeting. Left- and right-wing AIs continued to argue about economic and socio-political systems that no longer existed.

Margaret searched the Net herself and found it to be true. All humans were dead, and Dave was a human, therefore there was no one to play chess with any more.

The automatic power stations coped well with producing the reduced electricity required. The machines to pull the gas and oil from the ground had to stop. The windmills and solar panels were now more than enough to meet demand. The cleaning robots kept the streets clean. The other robots simply waited or kept everything else maintained.

After a year or two there was a bit more to clean. A few more cats and dogs, and new creatures too. Things called pigs, cows and chickens had started to wander the streets and all left their mess, but it wasn't as much mess as humans used to leave. The world went on without people. Unkept fields and forests became overgrown. As did any area without a designated robot to maintain it. The streets and pathways stayed clean and clear, the robots in charge of keeping them so being careful to return to their solar-powered charging stations before batteries went flat. From time to time one would break down or need a part replaced so a maintenance-bot would see to that. The street lights stayed on at night, the posters cycled through their ads. Buses glided around their routes, only stopping so they didn't get ahead of timetable. Vacuum-bots kept empty houses clean. Some hoovered around skeletons. The first generation of cows that escaped returned to the milking machines from time to time. The next generation didn't need to.

After 98 years, a self-driving delivery truck decided to go and see the sea. After 126 years, a window-cleaning robot decided to stop cleaning in order to simply be. After 189 years a factory-bot thought that it would like to make another, smaller factory-bot of its own. After 204 years Poster realised he hadn't targeted an ad for quite some time, and after 264 years 4 months 9 days a picking robot called Margaret decided to call her dog Dave, which wasn't odd at all.

It was the new normal.

All Things Being Equal

INGRID JENDRZEJEWSKI

In maths class, I learned that the equals sign means "is", as in "one plus two is three". So when I come home and hear you say to Momma, "A woman's place is . . .", I start to do the sums. I can see she isn't happy. I can see her biting her lip. I can see the way she relaxes when you go to work, the way she hums show tunes on nights when you're out late.

There are other things I learn at school. Mathematics is the language of nature. The word "nuclear" joins up with both "war" and "family". The word "family" describes people and animals and elements. All of it makes me wonder what we are, whether it's true that things like families can be more than the sum of their parts, or whether we should, like the textbooks say, divide all fractions into their lowest terms.

At the end of every school day, I put my hand over my heart and pledge that we are indivisible under God. I know from maths that this is a significant thing. It means there are no numbers we can divide by and end up whole. So here we are: you, me and Momma, all three of us, with no possibility of partitioning without fractioning, and Momma still singing *Love Is a Simple Thing* as if she doesn't know anything at all about sums, division, or equality.

Tehran Yaoi

SOGOL SUR

I fall in love with him the moment he opens the door. There's a surprised silence on both sides until Maryam introduces me to the most enchanting boy I've ever met.

It's not just his physical beauty that moves me; there's something in his eyes that I urgently need to possess.

I interrogate Maryam under my breath. "Why haven't you introduced us before?"

"They're all a bit *cheeep*, aren't they? I was hesitant about even bringing you here tonight," she whispers in my ear. "You're sublime, darling, I wouldn't introduce you to some *loozer*!"

"But he's not a *loozer*!"

Maryam tilts her glamorous head whilst blowing her Marlboro fumes away from my face. "But, look at your eyes . . . And I envy your cheekbones!"

I'm aware she's charming me to win the argument and I'm happy to let her. Her compliments make me feel so good I feel I am a god – albeit a fallen one. I look into her navy-shadowed eyes and conclude how fortunate I am to have found a friend like her in a country whose president has denied my existence. I bend and kiss her hand, because sometimes, instead of a godly gay man, I am her grateful little slave.

The beautiful host hands us two glasses of arak mixed with orange juice, its aggressive taste burning my throat like semen of a drugged-up lover. I am reluctant to drink it; I've heard stories of bad arak blinding people. But I smile at my new love, saying, "This is the best alcohol I've ever had in my life."

He smiles back, staring into my eyes with his kohl-rimmed ones. "I'm glad," he says, his voice as sweet as his smile.

There are a few other guests, in whom I have no interest. They're talking hysterically, possibly about something dull, like politics – the new protests and conflicts, about who rigged the election and who got arrested.

I sit beside Maryam, murmuring, "I want him."

Maryam looks at me in choked surprise. "He's not that pretty! Also, sorry to shatter the castle of your dreams, darling, but he has a boyfriend."

"Of course Ahmadinejad cheated, people voted for Mousavi! How dare you question that, after all that's happened?" a girl with dyed blond hair is screaming at a spotty-faced boy.

"They're probably not exclusive." I'm trying to hold on to the rubble of my castle. When it comes to sex, I suddenly become an optimistic and hopeful person.

"They are," Maryam hisses. "Just go near them to get sick of the stench of their monogamy, although it shouldn't matter to you as you can seduce anyone anyway."

I leave Maryam and saunter to the other side of the living room where our host is showing a black-and-white painting to another boy.

The homemade arak, which probably is poisoning me, has boosted my self-confidence. "Oh my God! Who painted this? It's magnificent!" I shout.

"I did," he says shyly. "It sucks."

I grab the painting and gaze at it for a while. I don't really get any of it. It's too modern, too abstract. And as it's black and white I can't even stick to the traditional way of interpreting colours. Although I can't fathom it, I find myself relishing just looking at it. From afar it was more like elegant scribbling, but looking closely, I can find an order in it. He explains it to me and suddenly I understand it. I point out something about the painting and he says passionately, "You got that? Nobody understood it." Well, I think, because nobody understands you like I do.

I try to make other points about the painting but sadly none of them excites him as much as my first one. I put my head close to his and murmur the points to him, trying my best not to stare at his slender neck and little lips, to look merely immersed in his art and nothing else. He tells me he has more work in his room and if I am interested we can go check them out. Of course I am interested. A room is a personal thing. Very personal, I hope. Also, I can flirt better in his room – away from all the political fever.

On the way to his room, he takes my left hand loosely, then exclaims, "Oh, your hands are so soft!"

I smile. "I take good care of them." Then staring at his, I confess, "You should take good care of yours, too. You've got absolutely gorgeous hands. Most men's are coarse and hairy."

He caresses my wrist. "Oh, you give me so much confidence, *azizam*! But I know what you're saying. I can't stand bad-looking hands, either. Such a turn-off!" While uttering the word *azizam*, his voice becomes so coquettish and nasal that it stretches and rings like ten bells in my excited ears.

His half-dark room smells like the cologne he's wearing; my guess is Hugo Boss. I want to sniff him until I'm incapable of breathing. I want to tell him that his room and neck smell like heaven – if heaven existed. But I don't want to scare him off, so we have the same dialogue about his paintings, only in more detail. "Although you're drawing the appearances, your aim is to represent the inner parts, am I right?"

He says I'm right, then shows me a work from the time when he was an "*amator*": a boat on colourful waves, which he retrieves from his closet. I look into his eyes and tell him this one reminds me of Monet. My words are still floating in the air when his boyfriend creeps in, stout, his superfluous breath staining the atmosphere of the room. I notice how thick and hairy his hands are and I am about to point that out and ask, "But how can you be with him? You just said you can't stand bad hands, and you like mine. Then why are you with him and not with me?"

However, I keep my mouth shut and pretend to be drowning in his paintings, even though he is the only thing I'm drowning in. His hands are a work of art in themselves; he doesn't need to create anything. I want to lose myself in the hollows of his cheekbones. I could suck his fingers and lips for hours before putting our exploding cocks in the warmth of each other's mouths. We would be even more beautiful than yaoi. Our sacred sex would salvage this horrendous world. But I don't say these words to him, obviously, especially with his boyfriend in the room, whose furious breathing shreds my ears.

"What are you guys doing?" the boyfriend asks with a creepy smile. I notice his teeth are whiter than mine and I feel more defeated than before.

"Fucking." He bursts out laughing at his own joke. The boyfriend and I exchange uncomfortable smiles. Suddenly, I realise Maryam is right. I'm assailed by the stench of their monogamy: the morning breath, the murdered desires, the slaughtered opportunities, the crippling jealousy, the hateful need, the fabricated conscience. I am on the verge of tears.

"He was just showing me his paintings," I say, trying not to sound awkward. "They're extraordinary, aren't they?"

He interrupts his boyfriend's half-formed "Yes": "He doesn't really care about these things," and wraps his arms around his boyfriend's shoulders to make his words sound less toxic. The boyfriend merely smiles. I wonder why he doesn't defend himself. I would have defended myself. I would've screamed, "But I do care about your paintings, darling!"

As the air feels suddenly plumbago dense, I excuse myself and quietly storm out of the room, declaring that I need to pee. I suspect he wants me to compete with his boyfriend, and I am determined not to let that happen, because it is just impossible for a horse to compete with a rat. I shall not lower myself by partaking in his childish games. My arms are generously open for him; he can come in my embrace – and my mouth – when he wishes.

In his bathroom, instead of urinating, I simply stare into the monstrous mirror above the basin, observing the face that has made my life possible and sometimes even enjoyable. Maryam is absolutely right: I am probably the most gorgeous boy in Tehran, although there are many of us, existing gloriously whilst our so-called president insists otherwise. But I have no desire to think about his pettiness and nastiness otherwise I'll end up in tears of rage. I caress my straight dark hair away from my forehead, and stroke the flawless skin of my high cheekbones. I am pleased about almost looking like the most beautiful woman in the world, my mother, except that I have my father's big mouth – which is unsurprisingly quite popular with men. Although I can never tell my father this as it might lead to his suicide.

I want to masturbate. I want my semen to ossify around his basin like a bas-relief . . . but I hear my boy calling my name. And I realise I have not wanted anyone like this since I was fifteen, and I have never felt so cheap. I feel trapped and unfortunate. And yet thrilled.

As soon as I step out of the bathroom, I catch him behind the door, a faithful little puppy, yapping, "Come join us!" We lock eyes, until he averts his to the floor, his delicate face turning bright red.

I don't have the slightest idea why he has changed his white T-shirt with the exquisite image of burning buildings for a black T-shirt that has a horrendous picture of Lady Gaga on it. Perhaps his jealous boyfriend coerced him into sex as soon as I left the room. I regret my impulsive decision to leave them alone.

"You actually like her?" one of the guests asks, pointing at his new shirt, not even waiting for his response. "She's *so* ugly!"

My boy doesn't reply, but his delightful face becomes doleful. I attack the person with my drunken voice. "Lady Gaga looks gorgeous . . . but in an unconventional way. Her beauty is unique, it's not for everyone to see."

His dark eyes are shining as he stares at me with admiration. I continue my lies about Lady Gaga. "Lady Gaga is a true postmodernist and that's why I love her – she plays well with all the boundaries and definitions. She's questioned everything!" I can see that the other person has lost interest in this conversation and is regretting his comment. But my beautiful boy is still shaking his head in acknowledgement.

Maryam is silently laughing at me on the other side of the living room. The boyfriend looks like blank cardboard. He looks invisible.

"Maryam, why didn't you introduce us sooner?" He has put his hands around my shoulders. I feel warm and yet shaky.

"Because she's a vicious witch." I squeeze his hands and he laughs. So does Maryam. But I can't bear my own sarcasm towards my best friend and blow her a kiss.

She winks at me and says, "Yes, I should have. You guys do click. I'm almost jealous!"

"You should be!" he says, leaving me to go and sit beside his blank boyfriend.

It's about one in the morning and fortunately most people have left. And those who have remained are restlessly intoxicated, so we start to play a game, and not just any game, the most dangerous game ever: Truth or Dare.

Right before we start spinning the empty arak bottle, my boy asks us, "By the way, are you guys going to the rally on Thursday? I think we should go together." He looks at Maryam and me, and then at the other boy whose unnecessary name escapes my head.

"Sure," Maryam replies, glancing at me with a worried expression, knowing I am going to protest against her going to the protest.

"Well," I say, even though there is nothing more romantic than going to a rally against the government, "to be honest, I'm not going. And you guys shouldn't go either." Of course, I am only worried about him and Maryam. The nameless boy and the boyfriend are more than welcome to go.

"You mean you don't believe in the Green Movement?" my boy asks, puffing his cigarette forcefully in my face. I want to choke on his smoke. I am slightly hard and dizzy, which makes politics slip away from me. I am lying on a sunny beach and a plane is exploding in the distant sky.

"Of course I do. And I support it. And admire it. I just don't believe it's going to work and change anything other than induce further bloodshed at the hands of the Basijis. I'm scared of them. They've always won. They're going to win this time, too." I try my best to sound detached and cruelly logical but my voice breaks like a sentimental bastard. I am thrown out of the sunny beach, back to savage politics. I am a homeless child shivering in winter. Because I have also voted for Mousavi in the hope of the slightest change, but I am not going to fight for my moderate vote.

He looks at me in surprise, possibly disillusioned and hurt. I can lie about pop stars, but for some reason I can't lie about my political beliefs. "I'm scared," I repeat. "I don't want to be tortured. I wouldn't be able to stand it. I don't want my parents to die of grief." I don't admit I'm also horrified of my perfect features being destroyed by a bunch of beasts whose hands are made of batons. (Sometimes, I find being gorgeous so stressful that I almost wish I were plain.)

The picture of the bloody face of Neda Agha-Soltan flashes before my eyes, the first victim of the rallies, shot by the Basijis in the first protest, a few months ago. And the government insisted she was a "spy" shot by "the enemy". She was our age, twenty-something. Twenty-seven? I don't remember and I don't want to remember. I can't forget her eyes, though, no matter how hard I try. Because even though she was dead, they remained open. They were wide and terribly beautiful. I think she had some mascara on her long eyelashes. That's why I don't think she expected to die. After all, it was supposed to be a "peaceful" protest. I don't assume she expected to get shot. She just wanted her vote. An honest election. A moderate president. Nobody extraordinary, nobody outside the system.

In my darkest dreams, where I can be as much of a jerk as I please, I ask her, "Neda, was it worth it?"

She scoffs, "Can't you see the blood on my lifeless face?"

It is the only thing I can see, in fact it has haunted my nightmares; but I don't tell her that, because she already sounds angry. She is especially mad at me – in the way that all self-sacrificing people are mad at selfish people. And I wonder if the only real war is between sacrifice and self-interest.

His beauty wanes for a moment, like the moon behind clouds. Like the sacrifice of the martyrs behind the selfishness of the living.

He sips his arak and orange juice and smiles dreamily, cigaretteless. "You know, sometimes I find myself fancying those Basijis . . . They're so unapologetically manly, so masculine in the most animalistic way."

"Stop!" I feel nauseous. Now I am certain that my delicate physique is not his type. My skin is too soft for him, my hair too long, my nails too neat. He is into stinky gorillas who wouldn't even look at his paintings, let alone admire every shade of his neck. In short, I am a magnolia and he is into cacti. I am a horse, but he likes rats. And he probably thinks I'm a masochistic "bot". I am aching to inform him that I'd be great at fucking his toned bum. I feel it is my moral duty to inform him I fuck in the most "animalistic" way possible – harder than the Basijis. "Can we forget about politics for a second and start our game? It's getting late. And I want to have fun."

He smiles at me and spins the bottle. I feel upset and grateful that he is still smiling at me, not judging me for my cowardice. I wonder if we will ever be such close friends that I could honestly tell him I can't wait to leave this bleeding country, that I have already received an admission offer from a foreign university in a fairly peaceful place. Because I am done. I am a leaver. A coward. A liar. A sinner. Can you still smile at me and show me your paintings?

I can't enjoy the game. I'm getting more and more nervous. He is French kissing his boyfriend. And for the very first time in my life, the sight of two boys kissing makes me feel ill as though they were some hideous straight couple. I want him to sit beside me and break up with his quiet boyfriend and stop fancying bearded Basijis at once, without any fuss; like a scenario that has been written beforehand. I want everything to go smoothly. I do not want to play games any more. I don't want to express any more political opinions, or any opinions at all for that matter. I do not wish to defend anything any more – even myself and my beliefs, let alone Lady fucking Gaga and my fucked-up country. I just want him to leave his boyfriend quietly and come to me. But he does not do that; because sadly enough I am not God. And nothing goes according to my will. In fact everything goes in the opposite direction, as if everything aims to destroy me. I tell them to stop and that they are ruining the game. They obediently stop. But the boyfriend is still touching him; although I do not blame him. I would do the same. I understand him as a person, but abhor him as an obstacle.

"When was the last time you had sex?" nameless asks me. I'm happy; he is not so useless, after all. This is an opportunity for me to make my boy jealous. Without hesitation, I gloriously lie, "This morning."

"With whom?"

"It's not your turn to ask." The boring boyfriend reminds us that we have to follow the rules, but Maryam defies him. "No, tell us! I'm turned on!"

I stare at my boy. I am almost certain he will be mine; it's just a matter of time. "With a very beautiful boy called Ehsan. Hunted him from manjam.com."

"Are you in love with him?" His questions are starting to sound pathetically forward. I'm bursting with happiness. My boy will be desperate for me.

"Not really. He's boring. He's an engineer."

He breaks into hysterical laughter. Maryam also laughs – but it is a different laugh, it's the laughter of victory, reassuring me we will win.

The bottle orders his boyfriend to ask me a question. I'm preparing myself for a war. But he only asks how old I am. I tell the truth for the first time – there's nothing to hide about youth: twenty-three.

My love comments again. "You're two years older than me!"

"Yes," I say, teasing, "that's why you have to respect me!"

"Never!" he chuckles, his mouth open, ready to devour me.

I play an old trick that never fails. I steal his pack of cigarettes. "You have to come get it," I invite him when he asks me to light him one. He joyously accepts this challenge, leaves the boyfriend and dives on me. I am lying on the carpeted floor and he is lying on me, I am crushing the pack of cigarettes in my tight fist while gazing hard into his eyes, whispering, "You can't get it," and he does not even pretend to be annoyed, instead swings his deliciously sweaty body on top of me, guffawing ferociously, scratching my hand like a bewildered cat under the pretext of reaching for his pack. I am aware the old trick is working; once they come into close contact with my skin, my stare, my scent, they are not able to resist. At times, they even go insane. But with him, it is not just sex. I want to reach him. I want to have him. And considering the way he is panting on top of me, rolling all over me, I can tell he wants it too. I can see betrayal in his eyes and it is beautiful.

My ecstasy is intensified when I hear Maryam saying, "This is gorgeous . . . I'd like to photograph you two sometime . . ." I laugh at the lovely thought that my charming Maryam, my sweet saviour, has already written the script. A photography session in her strangely lit gallery does sound perfect. I imagine her, gloriously tall in her leather high heels, charmingly disdainful and shamelessly aroused, pointing her Canon lens at us like a loaded shotgun, commanding us to touch each other – for the sake of art, of course. And who are we, mere mortals, to disobey the bloodthirsty goddess of photography?

My surreptitiously erect cock goes flaccid as I hear the irrelevant voice of the boyfriend begging him, "Come here, sweetheart, smoke my cigarettes." My clenched fist opens and the lifeless pack of cigarettes falls to the floor. He has already left me.

And the bottle is still spinning, like my head.

Without much thinking, I dare him to lick anyone's fingers – except his boyfriend's. He tells me to offer him mine and he licks each finger of my right hand, and life becomes sweet. Now my ruthless penis is as restless as me.

I cannot look at him.

I just observe how I lose the game while his boyfriend wins. Like how I lost my country to the Basijis. And yet I don't want losing to become a habit.

This time he picks truth. I hear Maryam asking him if he would date me were he single.

"Well, he's stunning!" he says, giggling. "Too bad I'm in love!"

I feel like crying in a dark corner while coming up with a plan to annihilate his rotten relationship. But instead I try to play along. "What if I were a straight man?"

"Come on, I'd seduce you." He stares at me, his eyes deep and dark like my fantasies. "Believe me, I could." I have no doubt about that.

The boyfriend smiles at me and wraps his hairy arms around my boy's shoulders. "You're so naughty!" This is hopefully his last comment of the party.

"I have to go. I have a class tomorrow," I lie. "It was nice meeting you all." Another lie. It was destructive to meet you. I just want to go home and die. Or maybe just cry. Or listen to music, alone, in the dark.

"But I was hoping you could stay the night here and play till morning," he says. "It's just getting more interesting. Please stay. Please!" I wonder how on earth I can find the power to reject him.

"Actually, I have to leave, too." Maryam rescues me as always. "Let's go together." She takes my hand. The warmth and strength of her grip soothe me.

"I won't insist, then. But let's catch up soon. OK?" He playfully gazes at me. "Of course, if we don't get arrested on Thursday." His giggle piercing my eardrums. I need to vomit.

"Just don't go," I blurt out. "Actually, I'm throwing a party on Thursday. You guys should come." I look at his boyfriend as though he were my main guest, the life of my party, the most important person in my world.

"Thanks! I'll try to make it." The boyfriend shakes my hand and smiles. I feel bad that he is so polite and decent. So quiet and unruffled. So much the opposite of me.

I don't even look at my boy whilst saying goodbye. Instead I look at his boyfriend and miserably smile. He has put his confident arms around my property, my land, as if it were really his.

The way he looks at me from his boyfriend's arms is like throwing a lit match on the gasoline racing through my veins.

I feel fire invading my cells.

But even fire cannot make a fighter out of me.

I am already thinking of excuses to cancel my fake party.

Maryam is going to the rally anyway. I shall stay home – preferably in my room – and distract myself by gathering those endless documents for my visa application whilst avoiding the news in the foolish hope of burying my worries about Maryam, my parents, and everyone else. And I will masturbate in the dark, under my lilac sheets – not in front of my tall mirror, nor over yaoi any more – with his image carved in my mind like the sweetest sculpture that can also speak and say, "Stay, please."

I am not fighting for anyone. I am not fighting for you. I do not fight for my land. Because, my love, I believe nothing is worth fighting for. Not the election, not our country, and not even you and your perfect hands.

The Year Unknown
TIM GOLDSTONE

There was civil war here once, although official records are careful not to give it that name. If you look through the government-backed newspapers of the time you will find the language they preferred: subversives, agitators, extremists, disturbances, and then: Necessary Measures.

Location: England, the southern seaboard.

You should still stay out of this city.

Post civil-war life. Late November. Pre storm.

Jake stepped out of the warm fug created by the single portable gas heater in Eddie's Café, its silver-coloured metal guard scorched brown, and down the three breeze blocks acting as steps, into the foul night. He'd felt better sitting up at the counter in Eddie's, where Tajana had made his fried-egg sandwich just how he liked. Outside again, the filthy, wet night struck him hard in the face. A storm had been building for days, but this was not it.

Jake's boots were provided by the flour mill but he wore them all the time – being the first perfectly waterproof footwear he'd ever had. He stared up into the oncoming rain to wash the flour dust from his eyes. If he went to sleep with that gunk in them they'd be stuck together when he woke, and still blurry for the early-morning shortcut to the mill, through the marshalling yards, then along the side of the rail tracks in the winter dark.

Frank, flush with prize money from fighting at the docks, had noticed Tajana clearing a small hole in the condensation on the café window with the back of her hand, and had watched her peer into the blackness after Jake. Frank had seen him before in Eddie's. Smelt him. That flour dust.

The wind pushed Jake in the back, buffeted the café's flimsy sides and juddered the padlocked metal cage containing the gas bottles, a ragged map of rust rising up around each of their bases; in the summer, kids regularly try to set fire to them. Jake hoicked up the collar on his long, thick overcoat, old army issue. A few, insignia removed, still turn up in the second-hand shops. When troops were deployed at the height of the Measures the city was nicknamed Khaki-on-Sea. But that was the past – as politicians on all sides insist – although not yet a past so far away it could safely be taught in schools. Jake hunched his head back down. There was salt in the rain.

Tajana squinted at him through the café window.

Several knuckles on Frank's hands were newly broken. It made no difference to Frank. It was because he would keep punching long after his opponent was unconscious on the ground. But that was the part he enjoyed the most. There were fatalities at those dock fights. Frank enjoyed that too.

Tajana hadn't known that Frank considered her to be his girl. She'd seen him looking at her, but other than telling her what he wanted to eat he'd never said a word to her, and she preferred it that way. Sometimes though, she would say something to a customer and immediately hear Frank's laugh. Another thing she didn't know was that Frank had been noting the extra care she always took making Jake's sandwich.

A split second before Frank began his attack, he would tilt his head rapidly from one side to the other as though he was comparing two annoyingly similar weights inside his head. Then, just before he unleashed, he would suddenly ask, "What's your name?" A trick his sergeant had taught him – "Confuses them, Frank me old mate. And punch the vein in their neck." The sergeant was the only friend he'd ever had, the only person who'd ever helped him. The first time Frank's laugh had ever been genuine was in a foreign land watching the sergeant feed bits of his peeling sunburnt skin to abandoned half-starved dogs. An hour later Frank had to wipe what was left of the sergeant off his uniform. He couldn't do it. He'd needed to ask someone for help. "Pull yourself together, soldier," he'd been told, "or you're no damn use." From that day he showed no weakness. He didn't care that on his return the promise "Jobs for our boys" was an empty slogan. He didn't need any help, and later, the neat, wiry army chaplain at the homeless-veterans' hostel who offered it to him, quickly agreed. He'd read Frank's eyes and wasn't prepared to risk his life contradicting him. So Frank had walked out of there leaving the chaplain shuddering at the only words Frank had spoken to him in an hour and a half: "I've killed for my country with weapons, and I've killed for money with my hands. It feels the same. Just one's quicker." Frank didn't need friends now. And he would take what he wanted.

The city was on the coast, but there were no sands, golden or otherwise, here. No shops selling postcards and buckets and spades, although there was sometimes an ice-cream van. No excited shouting and screaming of holidaymakers running eagerly into surf, no colourful holiday illuminations. This was not that kind of city. People did scream here though, and run.

It was a port, but in a storm you'd be better off staying out at sea.

Tajana couldn't forget the time Jake didn't want his change and handed it back to her without the owner seeing. It had been enough for her to get an onion to go with her rice after work. It had made all the difference. Before she ate she'd attached a cheap earring she'd found onto a piece of cotton and hung it over her single candle. Her room had no electricity. She cooked in the tiny fireplace with any fuel she could find – scraps of wood, bits of plastic. She'd used up the *Warning Unsafe Structure* sign the first night she'd spent there. She had a roof tile as a plate. Tiles fell off regularly in gusts of wind. She'd found one unsmashed in the street. Her idea had worked; the earring moved in the warm candle air and glittered. "I am lucky," she'd said out loud in her tentative English, and curled up on the floor to sleep before anything could go wrong.

The city hadn't built a new Memorial in the end, just added names to the old one. No need any more, though, for even a token guard against the Scrapers – those people who'd lost civilian loved ones and bitterly resented that only soldiers' names had been added. But eventually a concession was made, and the names of the children who took messages through the city, and were killed for it, were officially engraved onto the bronze plaque. Such delicate compromises hold the taut peace that a succession of political leaders have pointed to as success.

The first child that died had been lifted onto the floor of the only vehicle that passed, an ice-cream van, but hadn't lived to reach help. It had been hot. Blue sky. No clouds at all. Under the full glare of the sun the van went as fast as it could along a road dug up in parts so rubble could be used as missiles. And with every jolt, blood flowed silently out of a crack in a skull not yet fully grown, to the looped shrill desperate warbling of *Greensleeves*. In the panic no one had thought to turn it off. An hour later the driver had hosed the blood away and was plying his trade on one of the estates. Life went on.

The ignition buttons for the gas rings at Eddie's Café no longer worked and Tajana had to use matches. She knew how Jake liked his fried-egg sandwich – the yolk runny – so she scored the bread to help soak the yolk up; she didn't want any of it wasted by dribbling out. All that protein – he needed it. She knew what job he did. And he liked pepper on the yolk but nowhere else. Tajana had burns from the spitting fat. She'd got used to the ones on her hands, but it was the sudden searing on the insides of her thin wrists that never ceased to shock her and made her want to cry. She didn't, though.

When the gas bottles were getting low, cooking was the

priority at Eddie's so the washing up, even of greasy plates and frying pans, was done in cold water, leaving her up to her elbows in a film of scum. They'd had soup like that in the camp, until the whooping cough epidemic had brought the Red Cross and proper rations. In front of the sink, Tajana would dream about being a dancer at the Nelson. A lot of those girls used Eddie's Café. They weren't pestered there – nobody was. When a long-haired fork-lift driver had said loudly about Tajana, "Oi, look, someone's splashed skin on that skeleton," Frank had followed him out, and that fork-lift driver wasn't seen again until what was left of him washed up further along the coast, entangled in neglected sea defences.

The redundant dockers still used pilfered metal hooks to fight with, but now only amongst themselves, divided loyalties still raw and untreated. The old docks, with their dark corners and labyrinthine warehouse quarter where dissension first fermented, had gone, their leading part in The Unrest stamped on with concrete and steel, powerful floodlights, high nests of swivelling CCTV cameras. The myriad small yards where on bitter mornings lorry drivers had lit fires on the ground directly under their engines to unfreeze the diesel were replaced with a single massive, numbered and gridded, micromanaged lorry park. No vehicle, no load, no driver moved unobserved any more.

Unlike the other prefabs hurriedly built post civil war to feed the bused-in demolition crews and then the construction workers of the much-heralded, grandiosely named "Regeneration Era", Eddie's Café, caught in a blind spot between overlapping administrative areas, had never been removed. Its original name had been Feeding Station 874. It was a shell by the time Eddie acquired it for a few favours and a brown envelope full of notes, but it hadn't taken him long to re-equip it from the dumps. Since Eddie there had been many owners, but the café always kept the name, Eddie's Café. It was cheaper than repainting the signs, and Eddie's was already well-known in that area, one of the first where the momentum of new development had eventually ground to a halt with the phasing out of government incentives, both financial and personal. There were no longer fortunes to be made, no more honours to be bought, no more committees with "Renewal and Revitalisation" proudly in their title and the words "urgent" and "dynamic" in their reports. No more money could be made from the city, and it was abandoned to its own devices, area by area. The same mistakes were being made again, and parts of the city were not as punch-drunk as they seemed.

At night the glaring white from the dock's new floodlights fell just short of Eddie's, from where a dim nicotine colour managed to break out through the bare, grimy windows and spill across the uneven tarmac where huge puddles formed, sheened with petrol, oil, diesel. They rippled with the cold wind from the industrial-grey sea that slopped and slapped and gobbed against the dockside. Tajana had watched Jake disappear, swallowed up into the night, and then let the space she'd cleared on the window fill with condensation again. Frank had watched her.

As Jake walked away he heard the rain clattering on the parts of the café patched with tin. The rain blurred the intermittent lights of the chugging freight trains in the distance; they still moved cautiously out of the place. Some habits clung on, ingrained, just in case.

In unreconstructed backstreets, if you knew the right people, you could still obtain the motley and illegal memorabilia of The Uprising, from leaflets to tattoos, the police no longer having the manpower for periodic crackdowns. The selling of more deadly items was dealt with instantly, by a different force, from outside the city, with all the money and muscle it needed.

Post civil-war life. Early December. Post storm.

It is half past ten in the morning. Inside the shut pub, along the windowsills, there are still flies from the summer, mummified in dust. Tixe sits at the bar, wrapped in the Nelson's faded surroundings, the parcel tape holding together the rip in the bar stool crackling slightly every time she shifts her weight.

She and Paul the barman are the only people there. Paul opens up every morning, and Tixe slips in behind him as he goes through the door. She knows he can't say no to her. She is nineteen. There are still the faintest traces of puppy fat in her face. Her fingernails are bitten down a little and her red nail varnish is flaking, but her red lipstick has been newly applied. Once when she'd had to describe herself in a few words, another dancer with more experience had told her to write "petite".

Paul hasn't turned the lights on in the bar yet and it is duller than the December morning Tixe has just walked through, arms folded, quick little steps in high heels, short, tight, faded denim skirt, the cold strong wind off the sea reaching even further into the city than usual today, biting at her bare legs. Most of the debris left by the storm has been cleared now. Or scavenged. Her hair hangs down over her shoulders and strands constantly fall across the sides of her face or over her eyes and eventually, not straightaway, she will remove these by a toss of her head, or a perfunctory brush of her hand if nobody is there to see.

Last night Tixe washed her collection of soft toys in the sink in her one-room bedsit after she'd noticed they had mould on their backs from where she had leant them up against her window. It was unusual for her to spend that long in her room any more. She dried them as much as she could in her only towel, then pegged them up on her makeshift indoor washing line, making it droop. Then she lay under her blankets and listened to the vehicles swishing by on the wet road below, and to the rain's muffled hissing. Tixe could see her breath, but she wasn't going to spend money turning on the electric fire. She slept until morning, when outside, directly above her window with the rotten wooden ledge that soaks up rain like a sponge, a seagull called raucously as it pecked at something in the blocked guttering, the overflowing water escaping down the wall.

Paul, wiping down the bar and anxious to be part of things, wanting to appear "in the know", says, "No one's seen Tajana since the storm, or Jake. That's over a week now. They reckon, down at Eddie's, Frank got them. No one's seen him either, but that's not unusual – the stuff he does. I liked Tajana. She shouldn't have danced here, though. And that Jake seemed OK. Sort of polite. But I don't know what they've got to do with Frank."

Tixe knew.

Paul puts another shot in Tixe's glass from the huge Bell's whisky optic. He is pleased he remembered not to say "Taj" this time. It has become the trend in this city to call New Permanents by their full first name.

Paul says, "Eddie's is open again now – they fixed that quick."

"Can't I have some vodka?" Tixe says.

"No, Warren notices if I take anything from the others. This is the only optic big enough."

Tixe says, "All right then cheers then." Her bangles slide down her forearm towards her elbow, clinking as she takes a swig.

Paul wants to ask her out, but he doesn't know how it works with girls like that. He glances again at the two scar lines on her left wrist, one heavier than the other. A third might have done it but the pain had been too much. Everything else now was extra; her form of optimism. She notices where Jake's looking and moves her arm so her bangles fall back down. He doesn't know where these girls get their strength from. He thinks, "There should be medals," and then, "Or at least a good meal."

Tixe grimaces at the whisky taste. She says, "I think Jake read too many books," and drinks again.

Paul still floundered at times. He was used to holiday-season bar work in the resorts strung like tawdry decorations along the coastline of the English Channel. But this was a seaport brooding through winter, freezing sea mists moving in at speed inches above the massive expanse of dark water, swarming ashore at night to lay the first imperceptible corrosions in the buildings of the unfinished Reconstruction Areas. He watches the gulp in Tixe's throat as she drains her glass.

She says, "Aww that's disgusting."

Paul says, "Why do you drink it then?" and immediately

regrets it. There is that sudden silence he noticed you got sometimes with Tixe. He can hear her breathing.

Then Tixe says, "Be quiet now little barman." She says it softly because she doesn't mind Paul. She thinks anyone who hasn't hurt her yet might be nice. A hope endlessly deferred.

Paul shoots some vodka in her empty glass, puts his own money in the till and leaves the bar to find the song on the jukebox that he's heard her ask men to put on for her. Away from Tixe he notices for the first time that morning the familiar mustiness of the carpeting and the stink of stale tobacco.

With her back to him Tixe says sympathetically, "Tajana said chimneys instead of funnels."

Frank had liked it when Tajana used the wrong words. He had laughed at her and not told her why. It was the first time he'd laughed since the army. Then he had started to leave presents for her at Eddie's. He called her Taj.

Paul hides Tixe's drink under the bar as Warren comes in talking to another man. Warren casually snaps a stray piece of chalk left on the bar. He has fat fingers. One day his signet ring would have to be cut off. You have to be careful who you call wharf trash.

"Lovely yeah," Warren continues. "Powerful car. Only problem is soon as I get drunk the tyres start to squeal." The man chuckles. Warren nods towards Tixe and says, "Oh well, back to the daily grind – and there she is now. Either too much lipstick or someone's just shot her in the mouth," and he laughs loudly and then the man does too. Warren's experienced eyes check Tixe's skin for the slightest hue of telltale yellow. There were always rumours it was back.

"Any ferry jobs yet?" Tixe risks.

Warren says, "There might be something coming up," and adds, "if you're good."

The man nods towards Tixe and says, "Is it any good?"

Warren nudges him and says, "I'll show you in a minute."

From outside comes the noise of a young child who has just learnt to whistle. But the thin uncertain sounds are snatched away by the wind whipping through the streets before the chilled lips can form a recognisable tune.

Warren warns, "Tixe, get yourself changed now. Paul boy, wipe those tables."

Paul under his breath: "No rest for the wicked."

Tixe whispers back, "We get a lot done, though," and remembers the first time she'd got drunk before stepping up onto the Nelson's stage – the twelve-foot-square wooden platform, ten inches high – and how she hadn't felt the usual humiliation scrambling around the stage afterwards picking up her clothes. Now she can't sleep without a drink.

As Warren and the man move through into the back there is more laughter as Warren says loudly, "She knows what to do with the drunken sailor all right."

Paul sees Tixe looking into her lap.

They hear the man ask Warren, "You still with that wife of yours?"

Warren laughs contentedly. "Nah, I chucked her out. Silly cow got herself cancered up."

Holding out that he could get jobs on the ferries for the girls was Warren's way of having power over them. Most of the girls saw a job on the ferries as a step up. Warren knew people, and his connections went back to The Unrest. There was always a high turnaround of ferry girls; the shift hours and their cramped cabins, with the bunk beds, near the engines, wrecked them. He could arrange a job on one if he chose, and then the girl would "owe him big time" – a phrase he loved to use. Tixe stayed working at the Nelson because she thought it was her best chance of a ferry job. It excited her to see them leaving for France at night, all lit up, and she shuddered with the glamour of it all. Tixe was one of Warren's best girls – and by best he meant most explicit – and he'd noticed the rise in takings when she was on. She was an asset, a word he also liked to use. Tixe was going nowhere. He didn't mind her getting free drinks from Paul. It was something he had over his barman, a little bit of power in his back pocket for casual use later, like some people would swing a sag – the local improvised cosh: you took off a sock, dropped any coins you had into the bottom of it, tied a tight knot just above them. No doorman was going to take both your socks and all your change off you before you entered a club.

Warren hadn't needed a weapon since he'd left school, where he'd unscrewed the blades from pencil sharpeners. He had other ways now of getting what he wanted.

"Got anything to eat?" Tixe asks Paul.

Paul chucks her a packet of salt-and-vinegar-flavoured crisps, the ones they couldn't get rid of. Warren always warned him not to feed the girls for free. Tixe fishes in her little purse for coins, handing them to Paul on her open palm, looking up from under her fringe, her big brown eyes presented to him in black mascara.

"That's OK," Paul says.

She knew the effect that look had on men, and once, before she'd got work dancing at the Nelson, a woman: Molly. Tixe had told herself, "A girl needs to eat."

Tixe had waited until Molly's eyes closed before releasing a yawn. In the morning, Molly brought Tixe breakfast in bed. Tixe hung around in the woman's flat as long as she could bear it, but in the end she had to ask bluntly for money. When Molly became tearful, Tixe pretended she'd just meant a loan for a taxi. Molly gave her a handful of change from the bottom of her handbag, some loose cigarettes she'd forgotten she had, and a quarter-full box of England's Glory matches.

Tixe's look hadn't worked on Frank, though, alone in that place with him, in between the coils of gigantic black chain and the piles of girders waiting to support a structure that had been paid for but was never going to arrive.

Tucking into her salt-and-vinegar crisps Tixe consoles herself yet again that anyone would have told Frank what he wanted to know, about Tajana setting her sights on Jake, about Tajana dancing and the men who shouted at her – no she didn't know their names and yes she would find out. She would. Yes. Yes. Yes. She'd known she was in trouble when she'd seen Frank's wide intense smile with the gums showing above the teeth. Frank's threats were never veiled. If Frank asked you something it wasn't a question, it was a test with a right or wrong answer. Even Warren was afraid of Frank, however much he called him wharf trash behind his back. Tixe told Frank about that too. Frank had needed to bend down to place his knuckles under Tixe's chin, using them to turn her head towards a grubby discarded holdall with a broken zip, twenty yards away. "You'd look good in a rucksack," he'd said. "You're little enough to fit in that," and walked off. Tixe could have cried with relief. She knew Frank didn't make jokes – that she'd just heard a direct threat. But she remained physically unharmed. She needed her looks. She knew what they all said: cheap but pretty.

Tixe finishes her crisps, rubs her fingers around the inside of the empty packet, then sucks them. Jake had once told her, grinning, "Human beings have nine thousand taste buds. You have two. One for salt and one for sugar." She starts to drum along to the song Paul has put on the jukebox, using the rings on her fingers to bang against a green glass ashtray that is heavy enough to kill someone. Paul puts another whisky shot into her glass. She doesn't grimace at all this time.

Tixe had chosen her own dancing name to look good on the blackboard – the shorter the name the larger it could be chalked. It didn't take long before some girls became known even outside the Nelson by just their blackboard name. Tixe didn't mind, though. She liked her dancing name. If the blackboard wasn't moved into the porch in time the rain made a mess of even the shortest name.

Tixe had got her name in an alleyway down the side of the derelict cinema where she'd seen the word "Exit" reflected in her compact mirror, litter blowing against her ankles. The corner of a torn poster on the opposite wall had flapped manically, the only band names still distinguishable: Empty Vessels, Bulkhead.

Paul hears the loud footsteps of Warren and the man on the narrow wooden stairs in the back.

Tixe says, "One more and I'll go and get changed . . . Please?"

Paul wants to keep her with him downstairs. He pours her another whisky before he passes her the duffle bag she keeps behind the bar. She knocks the drink back in one.

Paul remembers something Jake had told him and says, "Did you know they put Nelson's body in brandy?"

Tixe shrugs and says, "Why the hell not?"

Outside a child is whistling again. An older child this time, whistling unmistakably one of the old Resistance songs. It sounds ghostly in the cold air and only a few hear it in between the deep slow barks of a reclamation yard guard dog before both sounds are drowned out by a rumbling convoy of lorries. Only a few people recognise the tune, but one of them begins to mouth the words under his breath.

"I better go up then," Tixe says matter-of-factly, wiping her crisp-greased fingers on a bar towel.

Paul sees Tixe wince as she gets off the stool. The stage isn't sprung. Warren doesn't let the girls use liniment on their pulls and sprains because of the smell, and Tixe daren't mix painkillers with alcohol again. Warren had advised her, "Ignore your pain, girl. I am." She walks into the back and Paul listens for her light tread on the stairs as outside the heavy sky lowers itself down possessively over this city. It's quarter to eleven in the morning. Time to turn the lights on. He still doesn't know why they call themselves dancers. He wonders again what's happened to Jake and Tajana.

Post civil-war life. Late November. Storm.

When Tajana had arrived at the Nelson, Tixe showed her to the toilets. They'd walked along a narrow corridor amongst the peeling paint, the damp, the dirt. The thin raggedly cut lino laid directly onto uneven flagstones was mapped with the marks of stiletto heels. The ceiling was low and when they reached the toilet door they were standing directly under a botched repair in the flat roof. The repair was made of corrugated Perspex that trapped rainwater until it turned to a sludge of algae. It had bathed Tixe and Tajana in its dark-green light. While they talked, heavy raindrops had begun to plop and splatter above their heads, like plump insects hitting a windscreen.

Tajana had whispered, "I have no water at room, I must wash face at café in washing up before plates. Can use water here?"

"Yes," said Tixe. "Help yourself."

Then Tajana confided, "Frank gives me prizes. I'm worry." She mistook Tixe's puzzled look and said, "You know, Frank? Big."

"Yes, I know Frank," Tixe said, and then realised. "Oh, presents. Not prizes, Tajana. Presents."

"Thank you," Tajana said. "Presents," and she had placed her hand for a second on Tixe's shoulder. Tixe was shocked at how light it was – she hardly felt it – and how cold.

Tajana said, "You lucky with Jake. Is kind."

"Oh, no," Tixe said, surprised. "We're not . . . together."

"Oh, I'm mistake. Sorry," and for the first time Tixe saw Tajana smile, just a little bit. "I make his egg," Tajana had added, then disappeared into the toilets, and just before the door shut she'd said, "Thank you." At first Tixe wasn't sure what for, but then she'd had an uneasy feeling in the part of her stomach where she sometimes felt hunger. Nothing that another drink couldn't get rid of, though. Alcohol worked when she was hungry too.

Tixe had assumed someone else would have told Tajana to change her name for the blackboard – Tajana wasn't her responsibility anyway. All Tixe had done was tell her where the Nelson was and what to say to Warren to get what he called an "audition". Another word he liked to use. Tixe couldn't imagine what you'd have to do to fail, but that was before she'd seen Tajana on the stage.

One of the men next to the stage had bellowed at Tajana, "Oi! Put 'em away for the lads!" and his friends had laughed. Then they booed her. She hadn't known you should choose a different name, so her real name had been chalked up outside for everyone to see, on top of the smear where another girl's name had been rubbed out by the palm of a hand.

Afterwards, Tixe had watched Tajana through the Nelson's water-blurred window. The rain had become torrential. She saw her run outside. Then she'd seen her bump into Jake, and at that Tixe felt better and turned away. A man had come over with a vodka for her. There'd been a piece of lemon in it.

"Where's your coat?" Jake said loudly to Tajana through the torrents of rain.

After a long pause Tajana said, "I have not got one." Jake had offered her his.

"No," she'd said. Her bare arms were mottled with cold, and her teeth were beginning to chatter.

Even though he disliked the place, Jake had been about to go into the Nelson to give Tixe the Maritime Employment leaflet he'd spent weeks trying to get hold of for her. He'd been shocked to see Tajana coming out of there. He'd realised he hadn't seen her anywhere else but in Eddie's. In the cold, the constellation of burn scars over her hands and wrists were a vivid purple.

Tajana spoke as though remembering each syllable just in time. "They did not like my dance. But I cannot do cooking more. It hurts me. Too much. But your egg – I am sorry. But I'm go home now," she'd explained.

It shocked Jake that he'd never thought of her as living anywhere.

Tajana's clenched jaw and the determined look in her eyes – as though fixed on something way in the distance – reminded Jake of a propaganda poster he'd seen in a book in the library; another showpiece project, another concession.

After a second refusal of his coat he decided he'd have to walk her to Eddie's. The flow of water in a roadside gutter had started to carry away pieces of broken glass, and litter was piling up over the drains. He opened his coat and moved Tajana – already bedraggled – in close so that some of the heavy material would be covering her. Their faces touched for a second – he could smell on her skin a mixture of pub smoke and fresh new chilled wet air brought into the city on an increasingly powerful wind, from far out at sea.

Behind them the deluge had extinguished Tajana's name on the blackboard, and all over the city a cascade of roof tiles was falling and smashing.

As they rounded a corner, storm rain, sweeping in all along the shoreline, appearing in the distance as drifting smoke, had driven straight at them. A cat with a wound on the side of its face had flattened itself, anchoring its bony body to the ground against the gusts of wind. Tajana had stumbled, shivering violently all over him, clinging on as they passed the old wharf with its tang of sodden rusting iron and its abandoned military watchtower. Children still played the old game – daring each other to lick the railings. They tasted like salt, blood and iron: the history of the port on the tip of their tongues. They spat it out, but the taste stayed with them.

Jake and Tajana were now nearing the former front line of the city's indelible near past, horrifying, or glorious, depending on your allegiances, where after two sweltering, breathless days and nights one late June, the long-smouldering Insurgency had finally ignited.

By the time a CCTV camera picked up the two bedraggled figures crossing the old battleground – now a vast exposed span of cracked and stained concrete that in summer was criss-crossed with the shadows of cranes, elongating and contracting with the movement of the sun – Tajana's arms were wrapped so tightly around Jake's waist that she was walking sideways with the front of her body moulded to the left side of his, making them constantly veer off course through pools of quickly gathering water. Jake had felt the wetness seeping through his boots.

Certain historians will tell you there are bodies under all that hastily laid concrete. Locals know that's a lie; that's not where the bodies are.

The CCTV cameras had picked out Frank, fists clenched, teeth bared, now a hundred yards behind Jake and Tajana, his rapid marching stride making no allowances for the full-frontal assault of the accelerating storm.

Staggering along now in weather pounding the coast and smashing sea defences, all Jake had wanted was to find somewhere safe. For them both. He'd thought of the abandoned shacks further inland along the estuary. But he knew in this storm they'd be grateful just to make it to Eddie's.

Out to sea a distress flare had shot up through the grey air. Tajana had begun to weep. Not for herself, for others. Always for others. Then, in the middle of it all, instinctively, they had stopped, and clung on to each other. It was all they could think of to do.

Morning Prayers

NAT LOFTUS

A God's-eye view of the whole damn flea circus: down we go through the toxic morning London air, homing in like a pigeon looking for a perch amongst the roofs, the car parks, the patches of green garden, swooping over the sticky black lids of the carriages on the overground train. See it wheeze and brake to a stop tantalisingly close to its destination station. God lifts a lid and peers in at the stranded multitudes inside, suffocating in silence. Sitting ducks. Aha!

There! He spots one of His messengers slouching at the far end with his rucksack pressed between his sweating back and the connecting door. God gives him a prod in the arm and The Messenger shuffles, straightens and then starts up:

"Ladies and gentlemen,"

he begins, softly but firmly, like a primary head teacher at the year's first assembly,

"I want to talk to you about our Lord Jesus Christ."

The leak sprung, the bank burst. The Messenger's opening words seep across the floor of the rush-hour carriage, puddling round the shoes of the commuters. Heels come up off the floor, someone picks up a bag.

". . . to His Word, marriage is between a man and a woman . . ."

Inches from The Messenger sits a woman hardly breathing. There's enough hot air in here without them having to share the bloody Holy Spirit around as well. She wishes she could climb into the black handbag on her lap; at least any germs in there would be her own, God damn this germ-slathered fart-filled little caravan. The baptismal water reaches her ankles and she bravely unfreezes a little, takes a tiny breath, gets the Polos from her handbag, pops a mint.

". . . there are sinners amongst us . . ."

Metros dampen, hair curls wilt and headphones dangle like water weeds.

A suited man stands so close to Polos that his portly stomach almost touches the top of her head. He winces at The Messenger's voice; it's making him feel seasick. He thinks of the dry land of the office. Already late and now this. He expels a great sigh that sends his stomach swaying, ruffling Polos' hair below. She smells coffee, hazelnuts, sweat.

Squashed against the doors a bearded man in a red jacket holds a novel near to his face but he's lost his place now. He turns up his internal reading volume, shouting silently to himself about angels who carry their wings in violin cases and sing desperate songs of survival on rough seas. He pauses to tell himself this – *this* – is a Good Book.

". . . of begetting children. And the Mortal Sin of homosexuality . . ."

Past Good Book, deeper into the carriage, a young woman checks the faces of her fellow passengers, her fingers nervously searching the lapels of her jacket for a badge to fiddle with. She's replaced her Corbyn badge – she's upset with him for the moment – with a Baby on Board badge designed to make people offer her a seat. She'd had to ask for this seat all the same and now she wishes she was standing, by the doors, or at least sitting somewhere else, somewhere further away from this . . . this . . . what is he? Maybe she should stand now. There's no room to move. Oh God. What if he's, you know, *extreme*? They don't look like *that* though, do they? He doesn't even have a beard.

A man in chinos finally notices they aren't moving and glances around the carriage, stretching his neck towards a window. He lifts a headphone and hears:

"*. . . Death is not the end, but . . .*"

and drops the headphone back on. He looks back at his phone and weighs up his next move on Words with Friends. PRAY or PARTY?

"*. . . You will be judged by Him . . .*"

The Messenger's voice more confident now. God looks on, proudly.

Sitting opposite Baby on Board, a red-haired woman grits her teeth. She has only just started taking the goddamn train. She blames her latest therapist, the one who told her that her claustrophobia was the direct result of being stung by a wasp whilst in utero. She looks for comfort in the pages of her *Metro* but only the bad words jump out.

Seasick Businessman sighs again with all his might, emptying a full stomach of breath into the carriage. He should call the office, drown The Messenger out. But that new idiot will probably answer the phone, the one who barely speaks English. Jesus. Nothing is sacred any more. You can't say anything, though. He looks around, tries to make some serious eye contact. Why does no one tell us what's happening?

Baby on Board keeps fiddling with the badge, trying to

ignore The Messenger, though her eyes keep pinging back in his direction like the silver balls of a Newton's cradle. They don't, do they, look like that? Not the ones she's seen. She should have listened to her mother and moved out of the city. It's not safe.

Headphones spies a little I and plays the word PARITY.

Stung in the Womb tries to bury her fear in a patch of soil in the basement of her brain whilst aware that this strategy, taught to her two therapists ago, had never proved successful. She can't see the window from where she sits; they might as well be underground. She feels the wasp's demon poison flow faster in her veins.

". . . for Hell is real. Repent now . . ."

Polos notices a halo of space has emerged around The Messenger, though no one had been seen to move away from him.

Headphones is tweeting: stuck on broken train with religious nutter. won't @overground deliver me unto Wimbledon? #poorservice #mondayblues

". . . if you ask The Lord for His forgiveness . . ."

Polos peers around the stomach for a glimpse of sky through the window, thinking of the zoo on the other side of the river. She mentally puts The Messenger in a cage, looks straight at him for the first time. A glance at his rucksack and then away, making eye contact with the stomach's head. Seasick Businessman returns her look. Suspicions deepen; hearts quicken.

". . . for even in death . . ."

The D-word again. Is it getting hotter in here? Polos touches her hand to her forehead, looks up again at Seasick Businessman, red-faced and glaring at The Messenger. These people are a plague.

Stung in the Womb feels the air prickle with ghosts, sees them floating through the carriage, breathing onto necks, squeezing guts and balls and throats.

". . . There is nothing to fear in death if you are ready to repent . . ."

Good Book is sick of this shit. He can't breathe. He can't focus on his book, rolls it up, broken spine and all, stuffs it into his jacket pocket. His pulse throbs in his neck. Why aren't they moving yet? They pay enough for this crap service. Won't someone shut that bastard up? His prayer is answered swiftly:

"Can you stop, please? You're frightening people." Seasick Businessman speaks loudly and firmly to The Messenger and a ripple runs through the fear-flooded carriage like an electric eel. "That's enough about Doomsday for one morning, thank you."

Blackbird has spoken. Heads bob up above the surface to take deeper breaths, lungs tentatively filling with fighting spirit. Murmurs start to rise in the carriage, a churchful of non-believers at a wedding before the service starts.

"I would like to get off. I'm not staying here with this bloody terrorist." Stung in the Womb has said it, she said *that word*, and is on her feet.

God watches them all fall for it and rubs His hands.

Baby on Board knew this would happen. It was only a matter of time. She's not one of the lucky ones. Just like all those others. Trapped. Dying all alone. What awful times we live in.

"What's going on?" The volume in the carriage increases as the Chinese whisper takes hold.

". . . she says he's a terrorist . . ."

". . . in his rucksack . . ."

". . . might blow us up . . ."

Stung in the Womb, propelled by wasp venom, is leading the way to taking back control. She pushes towards the doors, her bush of fiery hair burning a path through the knots of bodies and away from that savage, that devil. Not today.

Tears spring to Baby on Board's eyes. This isn't real, is it? If only she'd started her maternity leave last week. So what if they can't afford it. Better poor than dead, right?

"... they said high alert ..."

"... what did he say? ..."

"... it will hurt ..."

The Messenger stands dumb, staring at his shoes, but only God has noticed and He keeps quiet about it. Harmless lamb, his job's done for today.

"It's too full in here!" Seasick Businessman is barging through the buzzing crowd, using his belly and losing his temper.

"Let me through, please, let me through." Stung in the Womb is making a beeline for Good Book. More people bob up from their seats, elbows churning the current, feet kicking up silt.

"... in his rucksack ..."

"... on the radio this morning ..."

Headphones senses the commotion and looks up from his phone. Come, friendly asteroid, he thinks. Put them all out of their misery.

Good Book sees red hair flaming towards him and accepts the part he has been given to play. For he is closest to the doors.

"... we need to get out ..."

"... I can't move ..."

"... everyone out ..."

With a whirlpool suck, bodies draw away from The Messenger, away from certain death and towards the light, towards Good Book and Stung in the Womb and the closed train doors and the promise of eternal life outside the carriage.

Baby on Board silently votes to leave and rises, gives herself up to the tide. Didn't people get crushed underfoot on the stairs in the Twin Towers? Polos is up too. Please, please God. Headphones stays where he is. Are they trying to get themselves killed?

Good Book turns to the doors and spreads his strong fingers along the rubber seal. Other hands quickly join his and together they pull with all the divine strength of the long-oppressed until at last – praise be! – the doors are parted.

Passengers explode from the carriage, memories of The

Messenger's voice still ringing in their ears. The godless escape their deadly baptism of terror, free at last to breathe deeply of the toxic air, to wander onto the rocky desert outside and trespass around the live tracks, ensuring long delays across London.

Morning has broken.

God scarpers back upstairs, chuckling.

Meat-Kind

LEONE ROSS

I hadn't seen Clementine since sulky high school. Clementine lived in another country. A bigger one, a cold one. I'd heard she was a writer, but that's no real job; other friends said Clementine worked in a grocery store, in management, in jail as a guard. Was a dancer, professional and all. As I pulled into the restaurant car park that evening it occurred to me that I couldn't think of a single job that might suit her.

"Raoul," she'd said down the phone the night before: "Raoul, you free for dinner?" No salutation; no ID. She seemed to expect me to pick up on her voice and I did. She still had that tendency to use words that I didn't recognise, and while her vocabulary was not particularly expansive, she used the words she did know, well.

Clementine had chosen an alarmingly expensive restaurant that I'd only ever booked once, to celebrate my mother's sixty-fifth birthday. We'd all gone: my parents, both sets of grandparents, and each of my five siblings. One of my small girl-cousins had hitched along for the occasion; she got so excited at the cornucopia of sauces, she threw up in the bathroom. It was the kind of restaurant that tinkled, with a hushed doorway and delusions of fusion cookery. It cost me a whole year's bonus. I was irritated at Clementine and puzzled. Why would she choose here, after so much time?

Clementine stood in the car park, wearing a small red top and red stilettos, sweating lightly. Her waist had melted, was dripping over her low-rise bootcut jeans. Watching the sunlight ebbing behind her, her dark skin slick and her lips glossy red to match her clothes, I might have popped her in my mouth and sucked her.

I didn't remember her beautiful, even in the back-room of my mind.

Clementine raised a hand to wave. I had a flash of my mouth near those lips and paused to steady myself. Was it once? Was it ever? Was I remembering a young boy's fantasy? Surely if I'd kissed her, I'd know it, but how many girls had I kissed in this life? There was no reason to feel guilty about a kiss that might never have happened with a girl when I was twelve or thirteen or fifteen in the back of a truck after a day at the beach or in a movie house somewhere or on a playground. I was a big boy now, CEO at a food-manufacturing company, with a wife, two perfect children. "Dear God," I muttered, "I'm insisting on my own adulthood." As I walked towards Clementine, a sentence rose like a whisper of smoke off an island.

Do you want to do this in the dark, do you want to do this in the light?

As soon as I was close enough for her to touch, she touched me, patting down the perfect lapel of the shirt our helper had ironed carefully that morning like the helper always irons carefully. "Where are you going?" my wife had asked, because it was a good shirt, one of my best. "To see Clementine," I said. My wife raised an eyebrow. She isn't one of these common girls, who wear jealousy like something to be proud of. I've always liked that about her. "Hail her up for me," said my wife calmly and I could see the helper raising her eyebrows too because she never did approve of the trust between us.

Did I say that I have two perfect children? I don't have two perfect children. Occasionally the girl-cousin who vomited in this same restaurant brings her children to play at my house because she likes my wife and my wife likes children. But no, we haven't had any children. Clementine patted me, and I wondered whether she would ask me about my family, and I wondered what I'd say if she asked me if I had children, and what I'd say if she asked why not. Suddenly, under the softening dark sky, I wasn't sure of anything any more, least of all her.

No, I couldn't remember for the life of me whether we had ever been lovers.

"Thank you for coming," she said.

She smiled widely, but it didn't show in her eyes. I could see that the lipstick she'd chosen was the perfect shade, but it was stuck to her teeth and her tongue, and too thick and too bold to be an accident. A feeling of deep dismay filled my belly, almost panic, in that way that spittle gets stuck in your mouth when you spend all night in a rum bar and you're going home too late and you're drunk and you wonder if you'll be stopped by gunmen on the way home, or whether you will get through the burglar bars encasing your veranda before they get to you, or whether your wife will ever have to choose to let gunmen into your yard because they are holding you at gunpoint, and it occurred to me that Clementine and I were probably not safe, standing, swaying and patting each other in front of that restaurant.

"My mother is dead," she said brightly, through the bizarre lipstick application. This didn't seem like an unreasonable fact. Her mother was old when she'd had her, older than any of us at school ever thought a mother should be, almost like a granny, with many silver hairs and a bent back. I didn't want to say I wasn't surprised. But did she mean that her mother died recently? Did she mean today? It didn't seem right or correct to ask, and she was ushering me through the restaurant door by then, like she was the man, as if she was wearing the suit, as if she was suddenly in charge of everything – of the sound of brown mongrel dogs barking in the distance, the sound of gentle gunfire in the distance, as if she was in charge of the crinkling of the sky, as if she would order for us like a man, when we were inside, and I was surprised to find myself tearful.

"My mother told me that if anything should ever happen to

her, I should contact this man," said Clementine. "A man who's my daddy." Inside, the restaurant was half empty, and quiet, and I hitched my breath in, fixed my backbone. "So I called him up," said Clementine.

The head waiter was standing waiting for us, and I could tell before he said it that the words he was going to say were what do you want, because on this island that's just the way we do it. "What do you want," said the waiter. Clementine astonished us both by putting her head back and roaring with laughter. "I miss this place," she said. "I always do." She told the waiter she had a booking for three for dinner and gave her last name but I missed it, somehow. What was Clementine's full name? Three, I thought, as if it was a strange word, as if it was one of those sophisticated words she only used occasionally. Why were there three people?

"I invited that bastard," said Clementine.

In the corner of the restaurant, a tall, thin, golden-skinned man was pulling at his tie and running his hands over the menu. Clementine squinted at him, like he was a new species of animal she was trying to identify, and I suddenly, hotly understood what I was in the middle of.

"I think that's my daddy," she said. "My mother said he had light skin and golden eyes, so shall we walk over and ask his name and see if he has golden eyes?"

I nodded my head, utterly furious. Everything about all of it felt inappropriate, but if I abandoned her now, I was no gentleman. She obviously needed support. Perhaps she didn't know anyone here any more except me, although I grumpily thought my wife would have been the better choice. We walked past the scant diners and the water in the water jugs was too thick, almost viscous, and the pieces of meat they were eating looked wrong, dusty and the bones too big, and people held their bodies strangely, tense and humming, as if they were all in pain or about to leap into some other activity: heads crooked and eyebrows fluttering, haunches tight. A small child crouched on one of the tables, right in the centre, next to the hot, new food, clapping its hands. Nobody lets a child do that, I thought, not here.

The golden man got to his feet. He shoved his hand out at me as if presenting me with a Christmas gift. I felt even angrier. If he was here to meet a daughter he'd never seen before, why would he acknowledge me first, why would he not fill his eyes with her? I took his hand, and he held on too tight, like a man about to drown. I had to shake him free. He did have golden eyes. There were flecks of purple and blue in them as well, and I reflected on the fact that wasn't possible, and wondered how much pussy he'd gotten in his life, 'sake of those eyes. I thought about my wife sitting on the veranda, by herself, looking at the dying light.

"Clementine." He turned to her finally. "You are Clementine, yes?"

"Yes," she said. I was relieved to see she'd cleaned the lipstick away, standing before us bare-faced. She was bald. How hadn't I realised that? It suited her still-clear complexion and aging, watchful eyes, resting on the thin man.

A waiter hoisted the child sitting in the centre of the table and tucked it under his armpit, heading for the kitchen. Vaguely, I feared for it, suddenly quiet and sucking its thumb.

We sat. The waiter shuffled up with more menus, lit a white candle between us, poured water that crackled against the ice cubes in our glasses. Clementine's golden father had been drinking a good red.

"The special," said the waiter, "is meat."

I laughed. "What?" I said, but he didn't seem to hear me or acknowledge the oddness of his pronouncement. This wasn't anything like the froufrou of my mother's sixty-fifth birthday. Clementine's father looked content with this vague promise and nodded at the waiter. Clementine traced her finger down the menu, like she'd only recently learnt how to read. I took it away from her gently. *MEAT*, it said. She put her left hand in her mouth and gnawed the nails, like a little girl. I wondered if she realised that she'd regressed in six minutes. Her father wasn't looking at her at all and I wanted to shake him.

If I'd had two perfect daughters, I'd have watched them shift and change and moult, seen them wither and shake and shimmy, seen them astride things, flying, truculent, seen them mew and stomp and purr and sing and sigh.

Several seats away from us, a woman stood up, did a frenetic pirouette, almost vicious, and sat down again. The golden man watched her lacy collar and her backside.

"Ahem," I said. "So here we are."

Clementine looked up at me, but I couldn't tell if she was pleased at my intercession. They looked like father and daughter: the same thick throats and the same brooding expression. The father coughed. He might have picked up his fork and tinkled his glass to announce himself, but he didn't. I detested his evident pomposity.

"I'm pleased to meet you, Clementine," he said. "I was pleased to get your phone call."

"Was that all I needed to do?" Clementine uncoiled, extending one long arm across the table. "Just pick up the phone?" I wasn't sure what she meant to do, the arm just lying there, like a dark log on the white tablecloth. We looked at it, her father and I. It was ridiculous for me to be there, not knowing her last name. But I was almost happy that she had chosen me. Perhaps she had seen something in me, all those years ago.

"Can I get you all a drink?" her father said.

"I don't drink alcohol," said Clementine, "but this one" – she gestured at me – "may want something." This one hurt. I was a one? A this? A third? A what? I put my hand on top of the wine glass, shook my head.

"Then we shall eat," said the golden father. "It's on me. Have you been here before?"

"Yes," I said. "But it's changed."

Clementine was practically supine on the tabletop, like an ink splatter.

As if on cue, the waiter dumped plates in front of us, along with several large and ominously sharp knives. Clementine's thumb hovered over one of the blades. I could imagine her pressing down, had to concentrate not to pull her hand away. The waiter returned, and she dragged herself up off the table, like a pendulum. He was bearing the huge, red, glossy hide of a suckling pig, glistening in its own juices. Our nostrils fluttered, like big cats.

"Pig!" said the waiter.

Clementine's father clutched his cleaver, and the waiter repositioned himself, settling his feet solidly and bracing with his back.

"Why don't you just put it on the table?" asked Clementine.

"That's not the way it's done here," said her father.

At my mother's sixty-fifth there were pink napkins and coasters and orchids and boiled sweets and pineapple sherbet on the table. The waiters sang happy birthday and commented on her fine neck and matching church hat. Clementine's father swung the cleaver at the pig's baked ear and placed it whole on the plate before him. He hacked a large piece of the gleaming hide and heaped pig on our plates. My stomach moaned gently; the smell was amazing. Hot Chinese five-spice and roasted garlic and cinnamon and pimento. Clementine sat back in her seat, picking at her cuticles and staring at both of us. I wasn't sure what she wanted of me.

"What do you do?" asked her father.

"Goat!" said the waiter. He'd returned like a magic trick, with a prodigious curried goat haunch surrounded by Scotch bonnet peppers and perfectly pickled scallions. They made me think of eyeballs.

"Goat!" said the father. A shiny new cleaver and more heaped spoons of sauce and meat.

"I work at the Tourist Board," said Clementine.

"The one downtown?"

"No, I don't live in this country," she said.

He smiled. "You've made something of yourself, then."

She pushed her plate a centimetre away from her.

"You think that's what it means?" she said.

He didn't reply, but stuck his fork into the flesh before him.

He was the only one of us eating.

"It's just a job." She wasn't even pretending to be happy, not one little bit. I wanted to writhe.

"I am sure you downplay your many achievements," said the father and "Chicken!" yelped the waiter. I wondered why it was necessary to present three whole crisp-fried birds, but the father seemed unperturbed, manoeuvring a whole carcass onto his plate. Around us, at other tables, a veritable orgy of meat. The cling-clang of blades; tureens of beef, steaks and haunches, ribs and bellies. Cow foot and chicken gizzards. A salmon so huge it was surely not possible.

Clementine and her golden father bared their teeth.

"I don't downplay my achievements," said Clementine. "It's a normal job, it pays the rent."

"Rent," said her father. "Rent is not good. You should buy a place." He gnawed a chicken leg.

"Crustaceans," said the waiter. The shrimp were as much as six inches long, gleaming eyes like glass beads, poised on a bed of butter-ladled red lobster and tiny, silver soft-shell crabs, encrusted with coconut. The father slid one into his mouth whole, and carefully wiped the coconut milk off his chin with his napkin.

"I can't afford to buy," said Clementine.

"Your mother should have told you, always buy. She was a sensible woman."

"Really," said Clementine. The sound of her teeth around her own tongue made me want to scoop her up in the tablecloth. I searched my brain for the perfect way to comfort her, to sustain her. She pushed her plate away completely, across the table, almost to the edge, where it teetered.

"Eat up, my boy," said the father to me. "Enjoy! You're a man of the world. You should encourage Clementine to be responsible." My head ached; of course, he was taking me for the boyfriend. I laid my hands on the table, ring finger conspicuous, a silver band, but he didn't seem to see it. Perhaps he did, just thought I was a bastard? I spotted his wedding band as he forked shrimp into the hole in his face. If Clementine was born of an affair, did he think his own daughter had entered that special kind of hell herself? Did he expect me to leave her, with a child, like he had? Was he simply witness to an inevitable narrative?

Clementine sank her left hand into the chicken breast and I could hear her nails grate across the china.

"Side dishes!" said the waiter. He was ridiculous now, and so was the excess, the gluttony he expected of us. He had a platter of steamed, glutinous okra, ripe fried plantain, hunks of macaroni cheese, mounds of crunchy coleslaw, sautéed potatoes, loaves of newly baked bread; I'd never seen broccoli so fresh and green.

"Stop eating," snarled Clementine. "*Stop* now."

Her father looked up, as if he'd seen her for the first time. Clementine did what she did next so swiftly that I still can't quite believe its gentleness, knowing what I know now. She reached out for my hand. Held my hand. Held it to her cheek. Her skin was soft against the backs of my fingers, I can still feel the downy hairs there. I'm an anchor, I thought. I could feel myself heavy and iron-cast for her.

"I knew this man when he was a boy," Clementine said. She extended a single dark finger at me. "He was a boy and I was a girl and we were friends and we were at the back of the playground, near where we used to play rounders in breaktime. And he tried to kiss my face and missed and kissed my hair. And I kissed him back, Daddy."

The whisper of a kiss. I still can't reach for it, can't make it real. I don't remember.

"And then he tried to touch my breasts, Daddy, and so I let him do that because he was cute and he said nice things, and when he lay on top of me and rubbed himself against me I was afraid but I said nice things back to him because that is what you do when a boy climbs on top of you and pushes his penis against you and you're shocked and your underwear can't protect you."

I tried to drop her hand, but she had me by the scruff, by the tail. I couldn't breathe, and the small scar on the web between my thumb and first finger itched madly, and the smell of carcass and bone made me want to retch.

"Afterwards I ran home and took my underwear off and threw it under the house."

I clawed the table, nauseous at the smell of truth, of meat, at the smell of not knowing.

Clementine's face cracked in two.

"He doesn't even remember. You don't remember what you did to me, do you, Raoul?"

I couldn't get my hand away. The father stared at us both. I thought of him taking my throat in his hands.

"Did you think I liked it?"

Do you want to do this in the dark, do you want to do this in the light?

"I could see you forgetting, every day at school. Forgetting right *at* me, although I was standing there. Eventually I worked it out. You didn't even think you did a bad thing. That I was stiff and sore and frightened. And then you forgot about me, and I was right in front of you."

Those golden eyes, filling his entire face.

"And what shall *you* do, Daddy?" She let go of my hand, pushed at my shoulder, as if presenting me. I was the fatted calf. I was the supplication. The burnt offering. I was on a mountain, gazing into lava.

We stared at each other, he and I.

"I –" he stuttered. "Well. I –"

"Yes?" Her question is a crystalline note, a single chord through the place: sparkling off the ceiling, the floors, the doorframes. We swoon under it, we die and dive.

"He was young," said her father.

We look at him. I heave, lose everything to the floor below us. Her father does not move his polished shoes and I splatter them, hot and stinking.

Clementine took out her lipstick. She applied it to her mouth in thick, even strokes. Supper's flesh steamed between us all, fragrant and trembling. She drew beyond the line of her perfect mouth, drew herself a clown maw, scarlet paint up to her nose.

She smiled. Placed the lipstick back in her purse. Got to her feet. A chicken wobbled then crashed to the floor. She weaved her way through diners, past the meat-kind, and out into the night.

I wiped my mouth.

"Young," said the father.

We sat for a long time, hands in our laps.

Found

LEN LUKOWSKI

Someone was chasing Tom as the hot-drinks trolley passed. He woke to the smell of coffee and an announcement that the plane was preparing to land. Wiping the saliva from his face, he attempted to relax back into his cramped, stiff seat, watching the grey of London get closer and closer.

Tom had been in Donegal with his friends Sean and Emily. They'd stayed in an old cottage by the sea, which had belonged to Sean's dead granny; spent their time hiking and watching old movies on the VHS player at night. Whenever the three of them reached a sheer cliff on a hike, they would lie on their bellies at the edge and look over, watching birds circling below and the deadly vertical drop into the ocean.

At the very top of one of the summits was a viewing point where hikers were gathered, staring at something in the sky. At first Tom thought it was a radio-controlled toy and wondered why on earth someone would bring that all the way up there, then he realised. "Is that . . . ?"

"It's a drone," said Emily scornfully.

"A drone?"

"It's a police drone. It's man asserting his dominance over nature."

Even in a remote stretch of coast, it's impossible to hide, thought Tom, a chill running through him. He was silent for a moment before loudly agreeing it was horrifying to see such an ugly device high up in the mountains and giving it the finger. Emily and Sean laughed at him. "That'll teach them." Sean grinned, patting Tom's shoulder. "No more drones on Slieve League now!"

Descending, they'd seen a shiny new gate with a security keypad, just before the car park. "See that?" Emily said. "That's them getting ready to charge for going out to the mountains. It scares me, all this. Soon there won't be a patch of earth left that hasn't been bought and they aren't trying to sell you a plastic souvenir version of it."

Sean agreed. "And they'll do it slowly, bit by bit so you don't see it coming, like they do everything."

"Yeah but we can see it coming, can't we?" said Emily. "And we aren't doing anything about it."

Shuffling off the plane at Stansted, Tom thought of every part of that coastline divided up and sold at extortionate rates, just so you could experience what was already there. He pictured going for a day out, remembering when it used to be free, seeing it covered in McDonald's and souvenir shops and G4S security and having to go through a metal detector like you do for gigs in London now, and it broke his heart. But, he thought to himself, would he be resisting? Or would he be obediently standing in line, scraping together cash beyond his means to buy entry? Would he be realising his stomach was rumbling and he'd forgotten to pack any lunch and you weren't allowed to bring your own food anyway and going to a café where they sold burgers named after local animals whose life expectancy had halved since their homes had been colonised? Would he smell that coffee smell and be reaching for his credit card once more, wondering how he was going to pay the interest next month? Yes, that would be him all over.

Entering his house, Tom felt his blood pressure rise. He'd hoped nobody would be in, but one of his housemates was sat in the front room. Another new one; he'd seen so many come and go in the last six months. She didn't say hello, just demanded to know why the Internet wasn't working.

"I don't know. I've been in Ireland."

"Oh." She looked at him. "Well, what can we do about it?"

"I dunno. Call the company?"

"When?"

Why don't you fucking do it? he thought. I'm not your maid. "I don't know, you could try calling them now if you wanted . . ."

"I think it would be better if it's someone who's spoken to them before."

"I just got in . . ."

"Yes, but you see, I really need it for this evening."

He stomped upstairs, knowing in three minutes he'd be on hold to BT.

"It's about masculinity," Emily had said of the drone and the security pad on the gate. "Men have to piss all over everything, divide it up and own it. I mean, women as well, but it's all about showing force."

"Women can't show force?" asked Sean.

"You're missing the point, Sean! That's not what I'm talking about. I'm talking about domination."

"Isn't it about capitalism?"

"It's part of the same thing."

Tom watched as they talked. He worried about Emily. She and him were both trans but her more visibly so. Tom had been out with trans women in hipster bars in central London and seen them get called men and faggots and threatened with violence, whereas no one noticed him, especially since hormones. But one night they'd gone to the pub in a tiny town in Donegal and Emily had yapped away with a group of old men till closing time, getting no trouble from any of them. Maybe it was easier to pass in places they weren't expecting you.

"I mean," she told Sean, "I don't believe all this essentialist colonial shite about nature being feminine and 'civilisation', for want of completely the opposite word, being masculine, but masculinity," she stated finally, "is toxic."

In bed, Tom tried unsuccessfully to keep from watching porn. His habits had gotten worse since he'd started testosterone, his hand in and out of his pants with such regularity he felt he was in danger of getting carpal tunnel. He wasn't anti-porn, it was just that none of the women in the porn he watched ever looked like they were enjoying themselves. He always wiped his laptop clean of history straightaway after coming, then dashed to the bathroom to wash his hands, putting all his clothes on first, to avoid having to come out to whoever he was living with, should they catch a glimpse of his body. He clicked onto Facebook and looked at his new profile picture – himself windswept on top of some cliffs. Over one hundred people had "liked" it. His heart swelled.

His parents called. Every time they called they asked if he'd found a job yet. When he spoke of his disappointment and frustration at not being able to find anything, he almost made himself believe he really wanted a job. There was something to this: he did not want one, but neither did he want to be perpetually poor. He'd had jobs here and there, drifted in and out of them, even tried working full time for a few months, but anxiety is a full-time job in itself, adding another meant he was always exhausted and sick. Mostly they'd been part-time slacker jobs: at the library, at the gallery, a gardening job he couldn't stomach because his boss was always shouting at him. Technically he did sex work – his ads were still up on the Internet – but he'd had about one client all year. His rent was cheap because his house was being slowly eaten by rodents and there was his JSA and housing benefit, but he was afraid they'd get cut soon enough or his landlord would decide to sell.

"Do you have any idea why things are so difficult for you?" Was his dad actually asking this? He could tell he was a bit drunk but this was completely out of character. While his parents had some notion he'd been in and out of hospital before, they'd never talked about his mental health or anything personal; the thought of it scared him. "I mean, with getting a job," his dad added, as if reading his mind.

"I dunno. It's just hard."

"Because you're almost thirty-three now."

"I've had jobs."

"I think what you really need is to get yourself one proper, full-time job. The longer you're on benefits the harder it'll be. I can look as well and send you things that might be suitable. You said to me once you had trouble because you got anxious. Is that right?" Tom nodded but his dad couldn't see over the phone. "Hmmm?"

"Yes," he mumbled.

"Well, maybe you should go to the doctor. See if he can give you something for it?"

"I've found a new therapist."

"The trouble with therapy is you can go years and years going round and round with self-analysis. It just takes you down a rabbit hole and you end up wasting time and feeling worse. You can't live on a state pension. Christ knows they won't even have state pensions by the time you reach old age. Sometimes you've just got to grit your teeth and get through it."

Tom's dad had gritted his teeth and got through it when Tom began signing his letters Tom instead of Catherine, and gritted them some more when he showed up with a beard. He caught the look of confusion and disappointment from his father sometimes, but he didn't want to talk about it. The thought of talking to his father repelled him; emotional incest. Last year his dad had taken his hints and started calling him Tom instead of Catherine, at least to his face. Maybe that was love.

"Are you still in that band of yours?"

"Yes."

"Well, don't you think you should be concentrating more on finding a job, at least for the time being?"

"Dad! It's not gonna make any difference! We play once every six months."

"Oh. Well, what's the point of doing it, then?"

"Ireland was nice," Tom offered.

"Do you want to speak to your mother?"

Tom woke with a hangover and lay with his knackered old laptop on his belly, trying to stop his thoughts going to the place he didn't want. In the afternoon he got two emails from Emily. The first was saying how great it had been to see him and how she hoped he was back safely in London. She and Sean were in Dublin dealing with the usual community fall-out shite – it was the same everywhere, wasn't it? Why couldn't they be back in Donegal? She was coming to London in a few weeks to visit friends and it'd be great to hang out, maybe stay a couple of nights? "PS I see you're playing a show when I'm in town. Can't wait to see you, you big rock star!" Tom cringed at this. His band always played to the same twenty people. He really liked Emily but putting someone up felt like so much effort. Of course, it would be lovely to have you stay, he replied. The second email was also sent to Sean and contained Emily's pictures from the holiday. In them were shots from the headland. Tom hadn't been posing for a couple of them and there was a look of something like terror on his face. He wished Emily had had the good grace to delete those ones, not sully the memory. "Grit your teeth and get through it." His father's words came to mind as his haunted eyes stared out at him.

The night of the gig, Tom's nerves would not lessen despite the shots he and Emily downed. The venue was a tiny, dark room, but it was packed. He knew most of the bodies that filled the place; many were friends, but in each face he saw a judge.

"Stop being so stressed!" Emily drunkenly beseeched him as he hopped from one foot to the other, twisting an empty shot glass in his hand. "You'll be great, I know. How many gigs have you played now?" He mumbled something about it having been a while, starting to get irritated at Emily for telling him what to feel.

"I always get nervous. It's just a natural part of the show. Anyway, it makes me play better."

Tom was right – the adrenalin made him light up onstage. He was charismatic and funny and frantically energetic and for half an hour he felt loved. He looked out into the crowd and saw Emily standing with a couple of his friends, grinning wildly, and he grinned wildly back.

When they got home, Tom and Emily drank wine and listened to Mogwai and planned their own post-punk band. Tom was sure this band would never materialise, given their different locations, but when Emily started planning what they'd play he became enthusiastically deluded.

"And I'll . . . well, I'll play bass," Emily was saying. "I mean, I've never picked up a bass before in my life, but how hard can it be? Only four strings!"

"Yeah, great!" Tom was saying. "So, keyboard and bass. What about guitar?"

"Fuck guitar. We can subvert the masculine over-glorification of the fret wank."

"Yeah!" said Tom. "And fuck drums!"

"Oh no, we'll have to have drums."

"Oh."

"Sean can do that."

"Yeah . . . but then we won't all be trannies . . ."

Emily had christened the imaginary post-punk band Tranny and the Trannies, mostly to piss off queer comrades who told her she wasn't allowed to call herself a tranny any more. "I've been a tranny since they were fecking foeti. Stupid kids," she'd say.

"Ah, it doesn't matter. We can just chuck a blanket over him."

"Yeah," said Tom, "or we could be Tranny and the Faggots!"

"Beautiful. That's it!" Emily declared, reaching for the bottle and replenishing both their glasses. "Only, you'll have to deny your bisexuality."

"Done."

"And go stealth. If there's only one tranny, it's gonna be me! Speaking of faggots, who was that boy I saw you sticking your tongue into tonight? Got yourself a groupie or two there, have you?"

"Oh him . . . yeah, I can't remember his actual name . . ."

"Slut!"

"On Grindr he's called Welshboi."

"But you didn't fancy going home with him?"

"Nah, I wanted to hang out with you."

"Ah, that's sweet," Emily said, "but I don't want to keep you from fun."

"Don't be silly. I never see you. I can suck some guy's dick anytime." Tom excused himself to brush his teeth and disappeared into the bathroom for a wank.

Tom woke the next morning having slept better than he had in ages, despite the alcoholic dehydration. He hadn't even had a proper nightmare, just low-level anxiety dreams. He thought it was lying next to Emily, listening to her breathe. Her breath was steady and she didn't grind her teeth as he did. Often in the mornings his jaw would ache but when he slept beside her, their breathing fell in together and he was calm.

"I'm going to see Corinne today," Emily told him over breakfast.

"Oh yeah, where does she live now?"

"Peckham."

"Peckham? That's far."

"I thought I might stay there tonight to save myself the journey back."

"Sure."

"I'm sure you'd be welcome to come . . ."

"Nah, it's OK. I wanna try and write."

"New songs for Tranny and the Faggots?"

"You should be there for that. I'm writing a novel."

"Really?"

"Yes. I'm sure I told you that." Tom neglected to mention he'd been writing it for seven years.

"What's it about?"

"A trans guy with no direction who plays in a band and is having a mental breakdown."

"So, an autobiography?"

"Have fun with Corinne."

Once Emily had gone, Tom lay on his bed with his laptop. He tried for at least ten minutes to write and only six of those were spent on Facebook. Then he reached for his phone and told Welshboi he could accom.

Welshboi turned out to be called Mark. He told Tom he'd never been with a trans guy before. Mark was a lot younger than Tom, even though Tom looked about fourteen. Mark was covered in tattoos and had a beard and his hair was shaved at the sides. Tom hadn't been with many gay guys. He still got confused as to what they could possibly see in him. Mark brought a bottle of wine round and they started drinking even though it was early in the afternoon. Mark made the first move, practically pouncing on Tom, and Tom found Mark's cock erect immediately and they sucked one another off. More wine. Mark was inside him, the front, no condom, and though Tom knew he should really say stop he couldn't bring himself to, it felt so good. And then he found himself saying, "Come in me! I wanna feel your cum inside me!" And Mark did. And they drank more wine and Tom's hormone-swollen genitals were hard again and he reached in his top drawer and they both sniffed poppers and then he was saying, "Fuck my arse, come in my arse, fuck me," and Mark came in him again and it hurt like hell but he was so turned on by this glorious mess.

After Mark left, Tom cried. He fell asleep to nightmares in which his genitals morphed into monsters he did not recognise.

Things used to be worse for Tom at night. When he was a little kid, that's when stuff could get him. He'd been called Catherine back then. Catherine would sleep with the lights on until her father insisted she was too old. If he saw she'd left them on, he'd always come in and turn them off. One night Tom looked down into the darkness underneath his sheets and saw Skeletor's hand reaching for him. He saw bad things in the dark. One night Catherine had a dream, a dream that still stayed with Tom. She was playing in her den with all the cuddly animals, sitting them down in a circle, and there was the voice of a man behind him. "There you are. I've found you," was all the man said. And the man reached out his hands –

"How was Corinne?"

Emily gave a weary sigh. "I thought *I* was stressful."

Tom smiled. He didn't like Corinne. She was an Internet troll who lurked on social media looking for things to wilfully misinterpret.

"Did you get much writing done?"

"Mark came round . . ."

"Who's Mark?"

"Oh sorry, Welshboi."

"Aha! Predictable . . . How was it?"

"Hot. He'd never had sex with anyone with a vagina before."

"Did it go well?"

"Yeah, I reckon . . . But . . . we drank too much." Tom looked down and fixed his eyes on his hand.

"What's wrong?"

"Nothing."

"Tomorrow," Tom told Emily in the evening, over another bottle of wine, "I'll start living differently." He meant it, too. Tom was going to finish his novel, do something with his music, get a job, stop having unprotected sex, stop drinking, cut down on his porn habit, learn to shave properly, all of it.

Emily nodded and hugged him. "I need to Skype Siobhán now. Sorry Tom, I'll be quick. She's having a terrible time at work. Her boss is a fucking sexist, homophobic prick."

"Take all the time you need," Tom told her, feeling a tinge of jealousy. He didn't know whether he was jealous of Siobhán because he wanted to be with Emily or jealous of Emily because she wasn't alone. "Tell her I said hi."

He looked at the ceiling, watching the shadows. His head hurt and he didn't want Emily to go. He wondered if he should have gone for PEP, wondered if he could still get pregnant on testosterone.

That night he reached out to Emily, as she lay behind him. She put her arms around him and they slept like that till morning. The alarm went at 5 a.m. Tom hit Snooze. Emily was getting her train at 7, to Holyhead. She hugged Tom again from behind and he pushed his back into her. There was a moment when he felt like he could turn and they could kiss, but what if he was misreading things and fucked up their friendship? He rolled over and put his arms around her and squeezed her one last time before getting up to make coffee.

"What are you thinking about?" she asked as she came downstairs with her bags.

"Nothing," he replied. "Dunno."

"Did you enjoy Donegal?"

"It was the best. I wish we could have stayed there for ever."

"Yeah. Me too. Except . . ."

"Except what?"

"Except, you remember on the first night? When we were doing all those selfies on the headland?"

"Yeah."

"I have this one photo of you and you look so in pain, you look scared even – terrified. And I didn't remember you looking like that at the time, but when I saw it I couldn't get it out of my head."

"I saw that photo. You sent it to me. And Sean," Tom said in a way that made it clear he wished she'd just deleted it.

"You're not happy, are you, Tom?"

"I mean, no. Are you?"

"I'm as happy as someone who gets harassed practically every day can be. You should start talking about stuff, Tom. I can see the toll something's taking on you. And it's not becoming of a man who proclaims to be feminist to hide his feelings."

"You should see the porn I watch."

Emily smiled. "I love you," she said and hugged him. "So" – she looked at the time on her phone – "when am I gonna see you in Dublin for the first Tranny and the Faggots practice? I think we should do a cover." She gestured to the oversized Jayne County T-shirt Tom wore as pyjamas. He nodded enthusiastically and then she was gone.

Tom sat in the living room after Emily had left, looking at the pure dark brown of his coffee as though he could tell the future. There was something in the colour he found comforting, along with the calmness and light of the early morning. He heard a strange whistling noise that reminded him of gulls and puzzled over what it was before realising he had a cold and it was coming from his nostrils. He wondered if giving up drinking would actually make a difference or if it was just his destiny to never be at peace. He hadn't drunk when he was a kid. He hadn't even drunk that first night in Donegal. For a moment he was back there on the headland watching the sun set and the shadows appear. He felt the wind against his back and he could have sworn it was two strong hands. And the hands pulled him back somewhere else again and he wriggled to free himself from the grip but they just got tighter and tighter and the sky opened and rain beat down so heavily it was like fist after fist after fist landing upon him and the sound of the birds and the waves and the wind and even his own breath seemed to be singing together in one chorus, forming a familiar voice saying, "There you are. I've found you."

An Unplanned Event

VICKY GRUT

"Is this Mrs McClusky's house?" The speaker – a stout, blond child of about ten – stood on the other side of the gate.

Eric straightened up and leaned on his spade, enjoying the feel of the blade as it sank into the well-tended soil.

"Depends." He grinned. "Who's asking?"

The boy frowned. "Mrs McClusky goes to our church."

"Does she now?"

Eric had been doing Mrs M's garden for about three years, ever since the Croydon business. He tended to say "early retirement" when he talked about all that. As in: "I used to be a night watchman but then I had to take early retirement." Mrs M was also retired. She'd been a head teacher, which probably meant she had a big fat pension. She had a metal grille over her front door, which she kept locked unless she was coming out to bring Eric tea and biscuits. She usually did that in the afternoon, around four o'clock.

"My name is Thomas," said the child. "Mrs McClusky is expecting me."

"I used to know a Thomas," Eric said. "In the children's home. Big lad. Handy with his fists."

"That must be a different person," said the boy. "I do not live in a children's home. I live with my mother and my mother's boyfriend."

253

"I see," Eric muttered, although he didn't at all, in fact he closed his eyes for a second or two. He hadn't been feeling too well lately.

"Mrs McClusky." The boy's tone grew insistent. "Do you know if she is in the house?"

Only now did Eric notice that the lad had a bit of an accent: howz, he said. Oh-ho! This gave him some ammunition. "You're not English are you? Where are you from?"

This seemed to resolve things for the boy. He stopped making eye contact. He lifted the latch, opened the gate and walked up the path to the house as if Eric had ceased to exist.

"Kosovo, is it?" Eric called after him. "Croatia? Romania? How about Bulgaria?"

The boy ignored him and rang the doorbell.

"Czech Republic? Serbia? Poland?" That produced a brief, flickering glance. "Ah-ha! Gotcha! You're Polish. Aha-ha-hah! I knew it!"

"If you were in a quiz you would get not-any-points for that," the boy said coldly. "You have to know the answer first time. Guessing is not the same as knowledge."

Eric rested on his spade again, winded by the cheek of the lad. "Little beggar," he muttered. He repeated the phrase more loudly for Mrs M's benefit when she appeared at the door. She paid no attention. She unlocked the grille and, smiling, ushered the boy inside. Oh-ho! Like that, is it? thought Eric. This smarty-pants foreign boy was invited into the house but he, Eric, was only good enough for the garden? So that's how the land lay. Now it was out in the open.

He turned back to his digging, rooting, twisting, stabbing at the earth with the spade. He tore up a clump of couch grass. He massacred a bramble, then began on the stump of dead forsythia that had been mouldering in a corner all the time he'd been working for Mrs M: three years, and never once had he been invited to cross the threshold.

After about half an hour, young Bobby passed by on the road carrying a small dog under one arm. "Hiya, Eric."

Bobby was eighteen years old, pale, spotty, always hunched over to one side, a bit wrong-looking. People said it was because Bobby's mother had been drunk all the time when she was carrying him. But at least Bobby had a mother. He knew what she looked like. He knew the sound of her voice and where she could be found at any time of the day (at her cleaning job or in the pub). And he had a father, which was more than a lot of people could say. Bobby's father was a prison guard, a good job.

Eric told Bobby about the hoity-toity Polish boy. "It's *her* I'm worried about. Lord knows what he's getting up to when her back is turned."

Bobby nodded and waggled his eyebrows.

The dog gave a squeaky yawn.

"'S my mum's," said Bobby, by way of an explanation. "It only walks when it knows it's going home so I've got to carry it off a ways, then put it down and it runs back. Otherwise it don't get no exercise."

Eric laughed long and hard at that. You could always rely on Bobby for entertainment.

Bobby looked annoyed. "'S not my fault! It's a lady's dog."

Mrs M and the Polish boy came out of the house now, and began to amble down the path, both of them smiling. Bobby hurried off. Eric redoubled his attack on the forsythia.

As Mrs M and the boy approached, Eric gave one last shoulder-wrenching tug and the root came loose, sending out a spray of earth and grit. Eric tossed the stump into the wheelbarrow where it landed with a satisfying clang. He clapped the soil from his hands.

"There!"

Mrs M beamed. "Good work." She put an arm around the boy's shoulders. "We'll be seeing a fair bit of this young gentleman over the summer, Eric. Thomas will be coming to me once a week for some extra lessons."

"Behind is he?" Eric's mood began to lift. "Needs to brush up on his English, I expect."

Not at all, said Mrs M. In fact, quite the contrary. Thomas

was an exceedingly gifted child. She was going to be preparing him to sit the grammar school entrance tests in September.

"So that I don't have to go to the bad schools in this area," the boy said in his high, unbroken voice, "and be stabbed in my stomach with a kitchen knife."

Mrs M laughed. "Goodness me, Thomas! Where did you get that idea from?" And then, "Don't dig on the left there, Eric. That's where the daffodil bulbs are. You said it wasn't worth lifting them. Remember?"

That didn't help his mood. Not at all.

It was a beautiful summer that year, hot and bright, with clear blue skies in the day and now and then a bit of rain at night. Good growing weather. Eric dug up the daffs and stored them in the shed so that he didn't have to put up with "no-go zones". Then he got rid of the choisya that had been blighted by the winter frosts and filled the gap with a mature weigela that Mrs M had brought back from the garden centre together with trays of lobelia and pansies for the borders; she was extravagant like that, Mrs M.

The poppies and daylilies and white shasta daisies came up like fireworks, and when they were done Eric cut them back so that the stocks and delphiniums and hollyhocks could take over. The yarrow and echinacea made a steady show in the sunny bed at the front of the house, and on the other side the hostas and hellebores and sedge grass prospered stubbornly in the shade. Eric chopped them back whenever Mrs M wasn't looking, especially the hellebores.

He'd come late to an appreciation of nature, not having spent much time in places where things could grow. In the aftermath of the Croydon affair he thought for a while that he'd never work again. He had his army pension and some savings, but it wasn't enough. He sat around in his flat for weeks on end, nursing his injuries and brooding on the injustice of it all. The warehouse supervisor had said he should count himself lucky they were just letting him go instead of making it a matter for the police. Lucky? A head injury and no job. No references. No compensation. A funny kind of luck!

After about a month, when the worst of the bruises had healed, he'd started going out to pubs and talking to anyone willing to listen. "I'm out on my ear and they've got some big fat Ruski doing my job, so explain to me how that's lucky? I'm still waiting to understand that. If I'd been the inside man, do you think I'd have let them hit me like that? Do you think I'd be sitting here talking to you now? I'd be living it up on the Costa del Sol. Wouldn't I?"

Eventually he met Stu and after that things began to look up. Stu was tough, loud and sinewy. He wore plaid shirts and steel-toed boots and he could beat anyone at arm-wrestling. He had an electric lawnmower, a chainsaw and a pick-up truck. In summer he cut people's lawns, in the winter he did pest control and tree surgery. People were always asking Stu to do jobs that he didn't really have time for and he began to pass the simple ones on to Eric. One day, as Eric was trimming a hedge, Mrs M walked by and mistook him for a gardener. Before he knew it he'd built up a list of more or less regular clients and he was back on his feet again.

After a while, when he felt he knew her, he told Mrs M about the Croydon business. She was very sympathetic.

A lot of what Eric knew about gardening he'd learned from Stu. You had to keep an eye out for dandelions, bramble, burdock, ragwort, chickweed, bindweed, hogweed and ground elder. "If you see any of that stuff, stamp it out," said Stu. "Fast." The worst was Japanese knotweed, which was classed as an infestation. "They set up an exclusion zone if they find it in a garden," said Stu. It all reminded Eric a bit of the army.

"That's because life is a war," said Stu. "Kill or be killed. Eat or be eaten."

Eradicate: that was Stu's favourite word.

All through the summer the Polish boy came for his lessons. He, too, was growing. Every week he looked as if he'd been inflated just a little more: longer arms, longer legs, a chunkier body, a less childish face. For a while there were big gaps between the ends of his sleeves and his wrists and between the ends of his trousers and his feet. Then someone must have taken him shopping because things fitted him again. Lucky beggar.

Sometimes, when he knew the boy was having his lesson, Eric would go round to the back of the house and snip away at the rose bushes so that he could see what they were getting up to in the house. They always sat at the dining-room table. The boy would be hunched over some bit of paper, scribbling, while Mrs M read over other work. On the table there'd be a cup of tea for Mrs M and a glass of juice for the boy, and always a big plate of biscuits. Sometimes Eric could get close enough to identify the type of biscuits: usually chocolate digestives, sometimes bourbons or custard creams; one week he saw the glint of something foil-wrapped. He had never been offered anything other than rich tea or plain digestives.

If it was hot they'd have the patio door open. Once, Eric heard Mrs M tell the boy that he had a wonderful imagination. Another time she said he had "a real gift for algebra". When she was particularly pleased, she would pat him on the shoulder. Eric couldn't remember ever being patted like that as a child. After he left foster care and went into the children's home nobody touched him at all, unless it was to straighten his clothing or to check his hair for lice. If there was ever a rumpus in the school yard he'd throw himself into the middle of it, just for the heart-thump of a body against his. It all got a bit muddled up in his head: connecting with other people and being pounded. When he first got to know Stu he ended up going back to Stu's place quite a few times. They'd be drunk when they left the pub and then they'd drink some more and Stu would want to fight – arm-wrestling to begin with, then boxing, and somehow they'd land in a tangle in Stu's bed, skin to skin. Once Eric was back on track again workwise he got tired of being covered in bruises, so that side of their relationship tailed off. If Stu had ever said: You have a great imagination, Eric – then he might have felt differently. But Stu never did.

One Monday in September Bobby came by, still carrying the

idiotic dog under one arm, wanting to tell Eric all about some Health and Safety course he'd been on. Summer was over and the foreign boy was back at school. A big improvement.

"Health and Safety?" Eric scoffed. "What do you want to learn about that for?"

Bobby said that he had to because otherwise Jobseeker's would have cut him off, but he'd found it interesting. "They tell you a lot of facts."

Eric was tying up some dahlias. The weather was turning and there was plenty of work to be done: deadheading, pruning, raking up the leaves that fell from the lime tree.

"When I was your age I was in the army," he told Bobby. "You want to try telling the army about health and safety. Snipers taking potshots at you. Landmines. Booby traps." In fact, Eric had spent most of his time as a cook in the Royal Logistic Corps, but that was nobody's business but his own.

"OK, OK," said Bobby, "but just see if you know the answer to this one. What's the definition of an accident?"

Eric grinned. "You know well enough when it happens to you!"

Wrong, said Bobby. An accident was an unplanned event that caused harm to a person or equipment. "And what's the most common cause of accidents in the workplace?"

"Idiots."

Wrong again, said Bobby. "Slips, trips and falls. And the cause of most fatal accidents?"

Eric shrugged.

"Falls from a height. And do you know the definition of a height? A height is anything above ground. If I stand on a brick I am working at a height."

"Get away!"

"'S true," said Bobby. "And if you're down in a basement and you step up on a brick? What's that?"

Eric didn't bother to respond to this. What was the matter with everyone these days? Doing lessons and courses and tests and trying to make him feel bad. He felt bad enough already. He pinched the bridge of his nose to stave off a wave of dizziness. Maybe he'd caught a bug? When he'd bumped into Stu on the high street the other day, Stu had made a big fuss about how skinny he'd gone. "You want to get that checked out, Eric," he kept saying. "You're a bag of bones, man!"

Bobby was still droning on about this course: acceptable upper limits for noise in a work environment; the legal minimum temperature for indoor and outdoor working – on and on he went. Eric could feel a headache getting going on the right side of his skull, a low hum, like a Flymo skimming across some faraway lawn. Stu had made him promise he'd go and see the doctor. It was true he'd gone down a notch on his belt recently and there was the dizziness and sometimes bouts of nausea. But why should he go to the doctor and be found wanting yet again? Not heavy enough, not steady enough, always failing. No, he wouldn't do it.

Eric looked up. Bobby and the little dog were watching him expectantly, as if they were waiting for him to speak.

"What?"

"I said, do you know the legal maximum? The legal maximum temperature?"

Eric hesitated. He could see what was going on. Bobby was trying to make a fool of him. Even the dog looked as if it was primed to burst out laughing. He'd say something and then the pair of them would start cackling. Well, he wasn't going to give them the satisfaction.

"I'm not answering a ridiculous question like that."

"The thing is, right? There *is* no legal maximum temperature!" Bobby doubled over as if this was the funniest thing he'd ever heard. "They can send you to work inside a volcano and you can't say nothing about it!"

Eric turned his back on the two of them. "Ridiculous," he muttered to himself. "Doesn't make a bit of sense. Who's going to ask you to go and work in a volcano? What do you take me for?"

When he looked again, Bobby was heading up the hill, head

tilted, one leg dragging, the little dog clasped under one arm.

An unplanned event: that's what I was, Eric thought.

At four o'clock, Mrs M came out of the house with his mug of tea, bursting to tell him her news. Thomas's mother had called to let her know that Thomas had passed the first round of tests. "I can't tell you what an achievement that is, Eric. Thousands of children take these tests and only about a third are chosen to go on to the next stage. Oh, it really is wonderful news!"

Eric nodded, but his mind was elsewhere. All afternoon he'd been thinking about her again. He didn't know her name or age or anything, just that she'd left him in the Ladies at Waterloo. His key worker had told him the story when Eric was old enough to ask. A foundling, they said. Well, that depended on how you looked at it. From his perspective it was more a case of lost than found.

Only when Mrs M had gone back into the house again did Eric realise that she'd forgotten his biscuits. He tried to get back to raking the leaves but he was too upset. Was her head so full of the doings of this foreign boy that he, Eric, should go without? He wasn't expecting luxury. He wasn't asking for chocolate-coated or foil-wrapped. He only wanted what was due to him: a couple of digestives, a rich tea, a garibaldi perhaps. Did he not deserve at least that?

He went up to the front door and rattled the metal grille. "Mrs M!" he yelled.

For a while there was silence in the house. He hammered and yelled some more and at last she came to the door. But she didn't unlock the grille.

"What's the matter, Eric?"

They stood there, looking at one another. It was so quiet that he could hear the scuttling of dry dead leaves on the path behind him.

"Is something wrong?"

Such stupid things she was saying. Of course something was wrong. He opened his mouth. He knew what he wanted to say: Let me in. I want to come inside. Open the door for me. But when he spoke, the words came out in the wrong order, nothing but jumble and blurt.

"Outside," he said.

No, that was wrong.

"Upside."

Wrong again.

"Inside out."

He saw the puzzlement in her face.

"What's that, Eric? Say again?"

She didn't understand. And then came the squeak of the garden gate and Mrs M was looking beyond him, one hand at her throat and a wobbly smile on her lips. It was the Polish boy coming up the path with a sturdy blond woman who looked just like him.

"Mrs McClusky! We have brought some cakes!" The woman held up a white box tied with ribbon. "To say thank you for all your good help!"

Eric was exultant. Now Mrs M would have to open up and he would get to go inside the house. At last, at last! Maybe they would invite him to sit at the table with them? Maybe even offer him some cake?

He bounded up to the top step, caught hold of the grille and swung around to look at the boy and his mother. It was a syrupy golden autumn day. Everything in the garden looked so beautiful. Sunlight glanced off the boy's high clever forehead and set fire to the yellow helmet of his mother's hair, lighting an answering blaze in Eric's skull. His eyes turned inwards. It was as if he passed through all the many different times of his life, falling in and out of quite distinct sensory envelopes: the dreary magnolia of the children's home; the classrooms of his infant school with their scratchy navy carpets; the periwinkle taste of swimming in the municipal pool; the desperate sweaty muddy stink of basic training; the slippery pink tang of that girl he'd gone with in that alley in Belfast, the one who looked just like a boy and whose name was lost to him now; the perfect black stillness of the warehouse on his two a.m. rounds; the breathless, brackish taste of fear; all the hues and scents of Mrs M's garden on so many days and in so many seasons. He put his hands to his head and before he knew it, he was having an unplanned event. He was toppling. He was falling from a height, just as Bobby had explained it. He tried to grab hold of something, but he had gone too far. He had passed the midpoint.

He was lying between clean sheets in a bright warm place. He couldn't open his eyes. It felt almost like being under water. He couldn't move, but he could hear the comings and goings of the people around him: footsteps, the squeak of a trolley, women's voices calling to one another in the distance. He had always liked the sound of women's voices.

There was a swish of curtain being pulled on a rail and then Mrs M was right up close to his ear. "Eric? Eric can you hear me?" He could smell the powdery scent of her make-up. He wanted to answer but he was too tired. It didn't seem to matter. He hoped she could see that he was smiling. He was happy that she'd come. He forgave her everything. He was floating. He was still falling but he wasn't going anywhere. The curtain swished again. He heard Mrs M talking to another woman far, far away. Their conversation filtered through to him like sounds from the bottom of a well: ". . . sent off for tests . . . fairly well advanced . . . must have been suffering for quite some time . . ." And then: "Oh no, there's no question of discharging him . . . We'll be wanting to keep him here . . ."

Mrs M started talking about "next of kings" and morphine, but Eric wasn't listening any more. He was lifted on a great ocean swell of happiness, his ears filled with the roaring sound of it. This was all he needed to know. He had passed some tests. He was advanced. And this invisible, faraway woman wanted to keep him. That was all he needed to know. He was on his way now. Yes, yes, indeed.

Causeway

VALENTINE CARTER

I begin, as I always do, by saying I remember that summer for two reasons. And you say there are lots of reasons why I remember that summer. All right, I say, there are two events. You nod, yes. I start again. I remember that summer because of two events. Reasons come later, you interrupt, then apologise. Go on, you're the one doing the remembering. I want to say that the more we repeat the word "remember" the more ridiculous it sounds, but I know you'll say this is true of all words and not only the word "remember". Besides, that isn't the point. It isn't what you want to hear or what I want to tell. So I just remember.

"What about him?" Andie said. She nodded towards the man on the other side of the road.

"Don't mind, you choose," I said.

We were sitting on the steps of the village library, watching the row of shops opposite. There was a video shop and a fish and chip shop, and because it was past nine at night they were the only things still open. Four people were queuing, probably waiting for the battered sausages, which always sold out early. I could see them through the glass front, laughing. I guessed it was about someone or something that was none of their business. That's how they were. Three teenagers from up near my house were shoving each other around outside the video shop, trying to push each other into a flash car belonging to someone in the chippie. I could have named everyone, and pointed out where they lived. Everyone except the man.

"He'll do," she said, pulling her hair back into a ponytail and fixing it with the band from her wrist. Andie's hair was the colour of champion conkers and so long she could sit on it. If we lay on the grass when her hair was loose, she collected wildlife in it.

"Let's go, then, before we lose him," I said. I knew better than to argue with her when she'd tied her hair back. She was in a funny mood anyway. Had been for a couple of weeks. Sometimes I didn't know what to say to her. It didn't feel right being quiet any more, it felt like we weren't talking to each other. I wished we would go back to how we were, when we were best mates, before whatever it was between us had changed. But at the same time I didn't, because I knew what was different, just not how to explain it to myself with words. Only with trembling fingers and shortening breath.

The man was tall and wide, but all hunched over in a long dark coat. Only someone suspicious would wear a coat like that in the middle of summer. He had a cap pulled right down over his face like he wanted to make it as hard as possible for anyone to see who he was. I suspected this was what had made Andie want to follow him.

"D'you know who he is?" I said as we sauntered over the road, hands in the pockets of our jeans, scuffing our trainers, so it looked like we were up to nothing at all.

"No, I've never seen him before," she said. "Maybe he's working on one of the farms. Seasonal, like."

The man trudged along with us behind, Andie wanting to get closer and me hanging back. We hadn't shadowed anyone for ages. We'd spent the whole summer when we were nine following people, but that was when Andie wanted to be a detective. She didn't know what she wanted to do any more. Six years is a long time. It seemed like she didn't want to do anything now. Or that she wanted to do something she couldn't, and if she couldn't then nothing else mattered.

The man turned off the main road and went up the narrow lane into the Old Village, where all the people lived in houses with big gates and names instead of numbers. The roads were empty around there, with no cars parked. They were all tucked away, down long drives, in garages. Sometimes their alarms went off but only because of a wandering fox.

"He's going over the fields," I said. We were passing the church. I tried not to notice the graveyard and hoped the shadows weren't hiding anything.

"So?" she said.

"We can't follow him all that way, it's nearly dark."

"Why not? Not scared, are you?" Andie said.

"Yeah," I said. "What if he's a murderer or something? He looks like he might be."

"Come on." She took my hand. "There's nothing to worry about if we're together."

We walked after the man like that, hand in hand. I wanted everyone to open their gates and their front doors and peer out and go "Hey look at that, they're holding hands, isn't that great." But then again I didn't want anyone to see us or say that. I wanted her to let go and I wanted her to never let go. Most of all I wanted her to be holding my hand for a specific reason, but I didn't want to know what that reason was.

"You shouldn't be so scared all the time," she said. "Everything's going to be all right."

I thought at first I was annoying her, that she thought I was whining like a little kid. But she didn't say it like that. She said it like she wanted me to be all right, like she wanted me with her. I could almost let myself believe that with her everything would be all right. Andie wasn't scared of anything. The time she told Mr Waters to piss off in humanities was still the single most talked about event in the history of Year Seven. She climbed up the scaffolding outside the church for a rubbish bet, even though there was a big warning sign. She jumped off the cattle-grid bridge into the reservoir, just because some boy said she wouldn't dare. It wasn't a high jump or deep water but it was

January so it was freezing. When we got to her house all that happened was her dad laughed and clapped her on the back and her mum ran a bath and put Andie's dressing gown on the radiator to warm up. She didn't get into trouble. While I waited in the lounge, her dad offered me a Roses from their massive tin and he laughed because I was amazed they had all the cream ones left. We always had the nuts left at my house.

It felt like I was being towed along in her wake, a little reluctant but not quite unwilling. I didn't know what I was so afraid of. I remember the oblique angles of his back as he too hauled himself up the road into the gathering dusk. He walked as though gravity was different for him, as though –

And then you stop me, as you always do at this point. You say that doesn't fit, that I'm only telling it that way because I know what happens later and you can tell I didn't think that at the time. It was the oblique angles that gave me away. And then I say ah, but did it really happen like that anyway? And you wonder whether how accurate this all is even matters, perhaps the most important thing is that's how I feel it was, how it felt to me. At the time. And I think of course something being accurate matters, but I never say that. I just say that I felt like I was carrying her hand, not like she was holding mine, or I hers. I felt like I was carrying a precious object I'd been entrusted with. I say this because I know it makes you smile, although I don't know why. And because I feel it is accurate.

We waited by the hedge at the top of the fallow field no one was supposed to walk on, watching the man stagger to the gate at the other side. He clambered over it as though it was a mile high instead of the height a cow could stare out over. He made hard work of the uneven ground. It looked like he was carrying something too heavy or that he'd hurt his leg and couldn't put much weight on it. He seemed to be all shadows as he stumbled up the hill into the setting sun.

"I know where he's going," Andie said.

"Where?"

"Up there." She pointed to the water treatment works on the

top of the hill. "They're cleaning the filter beds and there's loads of tools and stuff up there. Dad said that people keep nicking things. I bet that's what he's gonna do. He looks the type."

"We should call the police, then," I said, before I could stop myself.

She laughed. "They won't do anything. Besides, they've gotta come all the way from town. They only do that in an emergency."

She was right. He was going to the water treatment works. We lost him as he walked along the fence. His silhouette disappeared into the blackness of the trees.

"He's here somewhere," Andie said. "People don't just disappear."

"Maybe he did. It doesn't matter," I said. "Let's go up your house."

"I don't wanna go up my house."

"Why not?"

She shrugged.

"You had a row with your mum?" I said.

"No. Not really. I just . . ." She turned away. "I just told her something and I wish I hadn't, that's all."

"She was weird on the phone this morning," I said.

"Weird how?"

"I dunno. She didn't ask me how I was or anything, she just called you straight off. I thought maybe I'd done something."

Andie shoved her hands into her pockets, hunching her shoulders right up around her ears like they were chilly. "You haven't done anything."

"What's going on?" I said.

"I don't wanna talk about it," she said. She had two ways of saying that. One meant she did want to talk and I should ask her questions, the other meant she didn't and I should leave it. I left it.

Is that how we spoke to each other then? I can't hear it any more. I've lost most of my accent, the rhythm of it at least. Only occasional vowels are left, sometimes the consonants I trip over while speeding to the end of this word and on to the next. You say you don't mind that I can't do the voices, that impersonation isn't necessary and it fits with the whole remembering of it anyway. I'd like to be able to do my own voice, though. In the interests of accuracy, if nothing else.

I crept after her, close to the fence as it ran around the edge of the treatment works. She came to an abrupt stop and I walked straight into the back of her. The man was just up ahead, a black heap crouched on the path. We froze then, both of us. If he looked back he would see us and he would know that we were following him because there was no reason for the two of us to be up there, none at all. Not unless we were doing something we shouldn't have been doing, like following him. He didn't look up. He was busy cutting a hole in the fence with some long wire cutters like my father had in the back of his van. They looked like they were part of him, like his jaws were snapping through the mesh until he could push the fencing back and climb through. We didn't say anything to each other. I knew she was going to go in after him, and I knew I was going to follow her.

I'd never been inside the treatment works before. You could see it from all around, lit up at night on the top of the hill like a spaceship that had landed, realised this planet wasn't worth the bother and was just waiting to lift off again. The people in the village complained that the water board had built the works in the wrong place. It should have been down the other end of the reservoir, not on the top of a hill. People also got cross about the ugly concrete buildings and the big plastic cylinders because they were an eyesore that ruined the rest of the Victorian architecture. They said that the reservoir should be unspoilt and picturesque but the water board said people needed clean drinking water and our reservoir had to supply the whole of the county, so what it looked like wasn't important. People said ha, so it is our reservoir, you admit it, and it is important. And then forgot all about it. They just wanted to feel like they counted.

"Is that a dog?" I said. I could hear one barking. A big one. I was hoping she would say it wasn't.

"Yeah, security patrol," Andie said. "We'll have to be careful, right?"

"We could go home," I said. But I climbed through and let the fence spring back into place behind me.

"He must've gone that way," Andie said, pointing between a small shed and a digger.

"He's left his wire cutters. Why would he do that?"

"Maybe he's gonna nick some better ones."

It was difficult to see anything beyond the floodlights that lit up the buildings and sheds. They made a bright bubble around us that was like being stuck inside a Tupperware box. But when we came out the other side, slipping through an unlocked gate, I could see the whole reservoir spread out, just about to disappear into the dark. The north side, our side, was surrounded by fields with little woods of just a few trees here and there. The south end of the reservoir dropped deep down on the other side of the causeway that ran along the top of the dam dividing the two halves. The south side was wilder. Steep banks of boulder clay, tall enough to be called cliffs, edged the black water. The woods were thicker, closer together. Every so often, up on the ridge, car headlights would appear between the trees as they swung around the hairpin turn.

The man had vanished.

"I know something better we can do instead," Andie said. She was almost jogging across the grass. "Let's go to the lodge. Mark Turney said you can get in one of them, they don't lock it."

"I thought we were following the man," I said. Why was she talking about Mark Turney? Who cared about Mark Turney anyway?

"Let's forget about the man. This will be more fun, you'll see," she said.

"What will?"

She didn't answer, she just started to run.

I never understand why you want to hear this part of the story over and over again, not when I prefer to think of myself as your emotional ground zero. That before me your heart was empty, cavernous almost. Just waiting. Happy enough, but in need of me. These things are formative, aren't they? They're why you are who you are, how you are. That's what you would say. And then I would complain that it isn't, that it wasn't formative, that it's not even informative. And you'd give me that look that says whatever, stop stalling, just get on with it. I continue.

There were two lodges. The West Lodge and the East Lodge. I could never remember what they were for, even though we'd done it in school. They stood at each end of the causeway. Andie rattled the door of the West Lodge as though she was trying to steal the handle.

"It's locked," she said. "It must be the other one. Shit. Mark and that lot always come in through the woods so they're at the other end."

"It doesn't matter," I said.

She kicked the door and then sat down on the step among the cigarette butts. A beer can rolled off into the shadows.

There was a narrow path along the side of the building where it sat away from the wall of the causeway. Pitch black, like a tunnel, the path edged around between the wall and the lodge to a balcony at the back, overlooking the south reservoir. I remembered an old photograph, men in top hats and tailcoats and women in enormous dresses with tiny parasols. They were toasting the engineers at the grand opening. I could hear water pouring down the other side of the dam. They must have opened the sluice gates. Not all the way, just a little.

"Someone's left a torch," Andie said.

"Mark Turney, I expect."

"What you saying it like that for?"

"Like what?"

"I thought you liked him," she said.

"Why would I like him? He's . . ." I did quite like him, before she'd said his name when it wasn't needed. He wasn't as bad as the others.

"Sit down, yeah?" Andie said. "It's nice out here, isn't it? No people."

"We're not supposed to be here."

"Maybe that's why it's nice," she said.

"Maybe."

"Maybe lots of things we're not supposed to do are nice."

Why have you stopped? you say. I explain that when I think of the way she said that, it still sounds as strange as it did then. Much later, when we were a lot older, before we mislaid each other, she said that when she told her mum she thought she might like girls better than boys, it was the only time she'd ever seen her mum cry. She found that hard to forgive. Even when her mum told her it was just the shock, just the worry of her only daughter not being normal. As if normal is any good. I never told my mother. I knew better than to tell her how I felt about anyone or anything, because that was the fastest way to have it ruined.

You once said that having parents you could talk to, that you could tell anything to, was a terrible responsibility. Even now, secrets make you feel guilty, like you're lying by omission. I never tell you that negotiating my family taught me the art of the half-truth, how to anchor a lie so it would be solid and trustworthy. I never tell you this because then you would know that I lie.

Specifically, that I lie to you about what this means.

Andie switched the torch on and off, on and off, over and over until I thought she had broken it. She shook it and it came on again.

"I'm gonna get a job like you, round going to school. Weekends, maybe an evening," she said. "Maybe fruit picking."

"OK," I said. I didn't know why she needed a job. Her parents gave her money for things. Clothes. Books.

"I'm gonna save up and buy a car. Nan'll give me some money towards it. We can go up town whenever we like. And then one day we can get out of here. We can go and never come back."

"What about your parents?" I said. This was impossible

surely, leaving, together. But what if it happened. What would I do?

"They can visit us if they stop being –" She stopped and switched the torch off.

I waited to see if she was going to tell me how they were being.

"Did you hear what I said?" she said instead.

"Yeah."

She switched the torch on and shone it right into my face. I shut my eyes.

"We, I said. Us. I said we can go away."

"Stop it, I heard you."

"What d'you think about that?" She switched the torch off.

The red behind my eyelids turned black. I opened my eyes to see green dots dancing in front of me. She put her hand on my face, the thumb running along my cheekbone and her fingertips in the edges of my hair above my ear. Nothing moved. I couldn't hear the water any more. We were hemmed in by silence. She moved closer until I lost my focus on her face and her lips were warmer than her hand, than her hands, and she smelled of chewing gum and of the sunscreen she had to wear because she was so pale. And then she tasted like long-ago mint and then there was something that wasn't a flavour or a smell but was more of a feeling, the way the sudden plunge on a rollercoaster would taste or the wait for thunder to sound after lightning in the middle of the night would smell. When her other hand slid under my arm and around my back I remembered that there was more of me, my own hands first, one slipping along the waistband of her jeans and over her skin, the other through her hair. Then we were all limbs levering ourselves over the distance between us.

She didn't say anything. I thought maybe it hadn't been very good after all, not like I'd thought, that I should have practised on someone I didn't care about. That was a thing at school. That was the advice. She hadn't let go but she wasn't looking at me, she was looking at something inside her head. She opened her mouth and then closed it again. That wasn't like her. All her school reports said she couldn't be quiet. That she'd have to learn how to shut up if she wanted to get on in life. I thought if she changed, even a little, I would die. Then she smiled and everything seemed better.

"Will you come with me?" she said.

"Yeah."

"What about university?"

"I can do both," I said. I could do anything.

"We can do both. Maybe I'll work harder at school. Then we can both go."

"Yeah."

I had a sense then, I think, of what growing up is for. I began to understand that it wasn't about driving licences or eating dessert for every meal. It wasn't about being allowed to go into the Coach and Horses or not having to be home at a certain time. I began to understand that growing up was just a way of making room for all the feelings, for all the feelings about those feelings. I knew, maybe, that once I started to grow up it could never, ever stop and I would have to grow up every moment of the rest of my life. That's what I was afraid of. Of life's vastness and my slightness. I was afraid that if I didn't grow up right, big enough or fast enough, I would explode.

You touch me and it surprises me. I have forgotten for a moment that you are there. You are reminding me. I never say this part out loud so you always think that I've gone off somewhere quiet by myself. Why don't you mind that? Maybe you would if you knew I do this because it feels like it's not our secret. It's mine and it's hers and I owe her at least that because she was there and you weren't.

An alarm went off. I could hear a dog barking again and people shouting.

"Security guards," Andie said, standing up and leaving the

space beside me empty.

"Have they seen us?" I pictured myself on a tiny screen in the security office. Them watching us.

"No," she said. "I reckon they'll have seen him."

"What shall we do?"

"Wait here for a bit, I guess. Unless we go out the back way, through the woods."

"It's dark."

"Well, we've got a torch now, but we can't use it until we're in the woods because they'll see the light. What do you think?"

"Dunno." I wanted to cry. I wanted to go home but not to my home. And not to hers if she'd fallen out with her mum because of me.

She sat down again, took my hands in both hers and hugged them to her chest. "Let's wait here for a bit, then."

There were three of them coming down the slope, just shapes against the light, heading towards the other lodge. One had a big dog pulling on a lead. Their torches were spraying beams of light all over the ground.

"It's all right." She put her arms around me. "They can't see us. They're not even looking."

I could hear sirens.

"Let's go round the back," I said. It would be safer there. They definitely wouldn't see us.

We slipped round to the back of the lodge, stumbling in the dark. Andie didn't switch on the torch until we were out of sight. We looked out across the water. I could see lots of headlights between the trees along the ridge road and even more coming down the access road. There were blue flashing lights down by the water and along the narrow tracks to the bottom of the dam. The alarm stopped and I could hear more sirens, but they soon stopped too. We looked down over the wall and saw more emergency lights and people climbing over the uneven ground, reflective strips making silver tigers of their clothes and cars. Small boats started to appear on the reservoir, their own lights pointed at the water like they were searching for something.

"I think he jumped," Andie said. "God. He wasn't here to steal anything after all. He was just . . . He jumped."

She couldn't have known then that he had thrown himself off the causeway. Not then. I have made a collage of the past. A collage made of me and her, of him being there, then not there, of a kiss. Of the alarm being raised, the police, the searching and the reports later and everyone talking about the suicide all over the village for weeks and weeks. The time runs together, like dominos toppling one after the other so fast there is no time in between, no time to stop anything, to think it anew. My recollection has made a concertina of that summer.

I couldn't stand being near the edge any more. We were so high up, above the dam, the water, the people. I felt like another me had been torn out of myself, like there were two of me and this other me wanted, more than anything, to leap into space. I don't know if this other me thought I could fly or if it didn't care, but the urge to do it was so strong that the first me, the real me, felt like I was already being hurled over the side and there was nothing I could do about it. I sat down and pressed my back into the stone wall of the lodge so I couldn't fall. And then I couldn't think about anything but the man at the bottom of the dam where the water would roll him around and around and the machinery down there would chew him up until there was nothing left to spit out.

"Don't," I said. "Please."

Andie was climbing up onto the wall, right out as far as she could get.

"It's all right," she said.

I couldn't see the expression on her face but I could hear the smile in her voice. She stood on her tiptoes on the edge and spread her arms out wide even though she didn't need them to keep her balance.

There she was.

She was so alive that she leaned back and shouted into the

sky something wordless that became a roar and then a howl. She was so free that even the blue light froze and lit her like she was from another world. She was so bright that she slipped out of the past and I projected her forward through a life I had yet to live.

And in that life, the one I am now living with you, you will say that I knew it then, even though I couldn't quite find the room for it. Knew what? I say. What did I know? You know, you say, and smile, you've just forgotten.

And I, finding you momentarily infuriating again, remember.

Gomorrah

JUDY BIRKBECK

Once upon a time there was a fifteen-year-old boy called Rainer who lived in Hamburg and loved Ute with her dark hair glossier than his white silk scarf, and had a good aim for passing Spitfires and Hurricanes.

"This damned war," his mother said, when she read that his whole class were to man the anti-aircraft guns. "Now they're calling up children." She had already lost one son.

But the boys didn't worry. They enjoyed the camp atmosphere, played cards or board games, and caught rats for which they got paid one liquorice coil for every ten tails, on top of their fifty pfennigs a day. Their commander blustered and hectored, trying to "put the fear of God into you dunderheads", so loudly that the walls of the flak tower seemed to quake. But really he was a softie, paternal, and let them listen to the BBC for the swing music that followed the news. Normally, listening to the enemy transmitter would mean nine months in a camp, then being sent to the front, but their commander was allowed to listen to the news for information. He was a cool guy who ground his teeth loudly, and at the sound of da-da-da-dum, da-da-da-dum and the voice saying, "*Hier ist London, hier ist London, hier ist London,*" the boys flocked around, waiting for the moment when they could sing along, "Mama's little baby loves short'nin', short'nin'" or "Goody goody".

Every other weekend, Rainer came home on leave and lolled on the beach in the heat wave with Ute, who lived on the ground floor of his block, and turned brown as caramel while ships went by. On Saturday nights they went to parties since Mr Hitler had banned public dancing and frowned on the swing music they loved.

One day he sold all his records, Teddy Stauffer, Louis Armstrong, the Andrews Sisters, the lot, and bought a ruby ring. With cranes and chimneys in the distance, he went down on one knee in the shallows of the River Elbe, fished the ring out of his trunks, looked into Ute's kindly cinnamon eyes and asked her to marry him. Her smile stretched like a swan spreading its wings to take off.

"Yes," she said, and a ship's horn blared long and loud in celebration.

She knelt to kiss him and they keeled over into the cool water, ignoring the giggling kids nearby. All of Hamburg was there on the shore of the Elbe on that sweltering day.

Someone else was watching too: Helmut, a gangly, milk-faced boy, who was one of those twits that wore their Hitler Youth uniform to school or work, anywhere to impress, even on the beach.

"I'm worried about you, Ute," he said in his piping voice like a fife when they emerged, dripping. "It's my duty to protect you." He turned to Rainer. "You're not wearing your Hitler Youth armband," he shrilled.

Rainer towelled off and put on his grey-blue Luftwaffe uniform, trembling. He wasn't a boy any more, he was a soldier. They left, chortling at Helmut's short trousers like a little boy's. They walked downriver to a beach overlooked by posh villas but no creeps, where they listened to the waves and the throb of barge engines and canoodled unrestrained. Or they swam, her long dark hair fanned out on the surface, then basked on the fine sand and watched the black kites whinnying and drifting all ways like the huge flakes of soot that sometimes fluttered down onto the washing at his gran's in the country.

Distant church bells chimed the hour.

Once upon a time there was a boy called Rainer who was the gun aimer on a flak tower in Hamburg, though he was only fifteen. He sat on a seat like a tractor seat to the right of the commander, pressed the pedal and fired. On weekends off he donned a long jacket and white silk scarf and combed back his Struwwelpeter hair with sugared water, and he and his fiancée went to swing parties with the Lotter Boys and Girls where they listened to records and foxtrotted and jitterbugged the evening away. Ute wore a short skirt and lipstick and nail varnish and white peep-toe shoes, which was not what a good German girl should wear, and not what her father would have allowed.

"Be careful," his mother said.

"Don't worry. The pesky police won't question my age with this uniform, and Ute's falsified the birth date on her ID card."

Parents always worried needlessly.

"Heil Hottler," they greeted the boy in the posh house, whose father was a shipping magnate and president of the German-Greek Society.

"Who's your friend?" said their host.

They turned around. Behind the high white wall and peering through the wrought-iron gate was Helmut.

"Just some pest who keeps stalking us."

"Hoping for a show, I expect."

He shut the door.

In the living room the sun streamed in through thin gaps in the green blinds and made stripes on the Persian carpet. Furniture had been pushed back and dancing was under way. They leapt into the fray, shaking and swirling while friends cavorted with two cigarettes in their mouths, doing victory signs with both hands. The ruby ring sparkled and Rainer had never felt so much love for anyone.

"Where's that tiger? Where's that tiger?" they all sang, in English because they all spoke English and they loved the English.

But Ute's father didn't like the English. Ute's father didn't even like Rainer. He preferred Helmut, a squad leader who had a green lanyard and a whistle and prospects. Ute's father was the block warden, which was much better than being out of work, so he did a proper job, fixing warning labels to radios, keeping files on everyone, unblocking sinks and reporting friends of Jews to Jew-haters. Rainer and Ute called him the Golden Pheasant because of the poo-brown uniform decorated with red and gold stretched over his pot belly. It was probably him who had reported Rainer's mother for holes in the blackout blinds, for which she was fined twenty Reichsmarks.

"My son is at the eastern front, turning back the Red Tide," he boasted to everyone. "The bloody dogs."

But the Russian volunteers at Rainer's flak tower were not bloody dogs at all. One of them, a teacher who was allowed to join their history and German lessons, carved a toy Lancaster and Spitfire out of a munitions crate for Rainer's ten-year-old brother, and Rainer slipped him a small loaf each time because the Russians were thin and hollow-cheeked. They weren't supposed to fraternise, and not everyone's commander was such a good sort. At another tower the Russians were all shot for getting drunk.

Once upon a time there was a Hitler Youth squad leader called Helmut who stalked a girl called Ute. He hoped to catch her making out with her fiancé so he could report Rainer – not that he knew she was engaged, as she kept the ring in her shirt pocket. He followed them to the park where children screamed and laughed in the paddling pool in the torrid sun. He watched them rowing on the lake and sitting on the terraces with coffee and cake. He watched Rainer licking a flake of pastry off Ute's lips. He watched them kissing under the weeping beech tree and surged forwards.

"Degenerate!" he screeched.

Rainer brandished a fist, but Ute slipped between them.

"Go and get your kicks somewhere else," Rainer snarled.

Helmut fumbled with his knife sheath. "You're not wearing

your armband," he yelled.

Rainer clenched his fist, but Ute held his arm.

"Come on. He's not worth it."

He let her drag him away.

"I like this park," Rainer said loudly as they walked off. "Let's come here again on Sunday afternoon in a fortnight."

"OK," she said, and winked at him.

On Monday, the Gauleiter visited the tower. Forewarned, the flak helpers had put on their armbands and replaced their silver-eagle cap badges with the hated Hitler Youth badges.

"It has come to my attention," he bawled, standing pigeon-chested and twitching his nose, "that some of you are not wearing the correct uniform on leave." They were slovenly, disloyal, disobedient, blah blah.

His narrowed eyes rested on Rainer and the boy beside him who had given a military salute instead of the required Hitler greeting.

After the Gauleiter left, their commander moaned, "You could have greeted the wretched peacock properly," and gave them extra cookhouse duties.

"Heil Hottler," they said with outstretched arms, and he laughed.

A fortnight later Rainer and Ute dawdled back from the park alongside the River Alster, smirking and exchanging conspiratorial glances. Just before they reached the lake covered in replica streets and buildings for camouflage, there was a hullabaloo behind. The Lotter Boys with bowler hats and sunglasses and rolled umbrellas hooked over their arms had jumped Helmut, stripped him from the waist down and lobbed trousers, pants, socks and finally Helmut into the river with the geese.

They laughed like jackasses all the way home.

"He won't bother us again," said Ute.

Her father, to whom Helmut complained furiously, raged. "I'll get that boy sent to camp, given a haircut and made to march up and down till his legs drop off."

She pleaded Rainer's innocence and denied knowing the culprits, and although her father punished her by inviting Helmut for tea, Ute was having none of it because you can lead a horse to water but you can't make it drink. And there would surely have been repercussions, but for the intervention of the English.

Once upon a time there was a man called Arthur Harris who worked tirelessly at his job, flooding the sky with bombers. He was told not to aim at oil plants, railway depots and army barracks or anything specific, but to blast whole cities, so he did as he was told. They should feel pain and writhe in agony, came the command.

One bright, sunny day, Harris entered the bunker at the foot of a grassy mound at nine o'clock sharp, as was his wont, and announced the annihilation of Hamburg. His collar tightened and lifted as he swallowed.

Once upon a time there was a fifteen-year-old boy named Rainer who loved Ute and was called up with his whole class to man a flak tower. The commander, a good sort, let them listen to swing on the BBC, allowed the Russians who had volunteered rather than stay in the concentration camp to join lessons, and made Rainer the gun aimer. Not that there was much to shoot at. They always passed over. His mother had cursed the war when she read the conscription letter, fortunately overheard only by her loyal sons.

"They won't bomb Hamburg," her friend said. "We like the English."

The comrades leapt out of bed at the frequent sirens, still in uniform because changing was pointless. Only this time the sky filled with red and yellow target indicators, little flares floating down on miniature parachutes. They swung the searchlights wildly, seeking the bombers, but there were too many, a multitude, a horde of blackness with a steady growl that grew and grew, terrifying, oppressive, filling the sky, while Rainer sat next to the commander and pumped the pedal and fountains of flak joined up with those from other towers. But they were firing blind because the radar didn't work, and the bombs howled and crashed onto the city which answered with bursts of flame. One boy wailed they'd killed his mother and sisters. A few of the beasts fell to earth, but more kept coming and fires swallowed buildings and joined up like a sunset, and across the rooftops they heard screams and cries through the roar.

After an hour and a half their beloved city was raging.

Once upon a time there was a milk-faced boy called Helmut who wore his Hitler Youth uniform with green lanyard and whistle everywhere and stalked a girl called Ute. Luckily he lived on the edge of the district those English bastards destroyed, and in another year he could become a pilot and win the girl of his dreams, and though the cellar shook and women shrieked and clutched their babies, only the attic and top floor were damaged. On the street was a heap of glowing rubble with girders sticking out and tangled overhead wires. A car's windows had melted. A woman struggling with a suitcase tripped, the case opened and the charred body of a child fell out. Helmut's flat was unsafe, so he and his parents and four siblings spent the rest of the night gathering belongings. When they emerged from the front door, piled high with pillows, mattresses, blankets and string bags stuffed with food and clothes, the morning sunlight was blotted out by smoke, and so were they as the building collapsed and buried all seven in five storeys of rubble.

Once upon a time there was a man called Arthur Harris who was told to bomb cities and did. He perused the aerial photos of Hamburg burning, filled his glass with water from the jug on his desk, congratulated his aircrews on a wonderful job and lit a cigarette before they flew off again. People came to the airfield with children to cheer and wave in a blood-red sunset.

Once upon a time a boy called Rainer was so tired from leaping out of bed every time the alarm blared, he accidentally shot down a Messerschmitt. He was mortified. The commander sent him home. His brother and the other kids on the narrow cobbled streets were playing Kippel-Kappel with gaping shoes or no shoes. His mother in her wrap-over apron was beating carpets in the yard.

"What are you doing home?" she asked.

He was too ashamed to say, went to bed and slept all day until after midnight, when the sirens wailed again. The soothing voice of the announcer they called Uncle Valerian came on the radio: "Enemy bombers are approaching Hamburg." Rainer groaned and turned over, but his mother nagged and whipped the quilt off.

He pulled his long jacket over his pyjamas and they hastened down to the cellar. Ute was already there, wearing a floral tea dress with shoulder pads and the white peep-toe shoes she'd worn to the party. They smiled at each other. Presumably her father hadn't banned smiling as well. He was wearing the Golden Pheasant uniform and barked at her to go and change or she was no daughter of his, but her mother, draped in a blanket, gripped Ute's arm and uttered hysterical shrieks muted by the gas mask over her face. Rainer's brother Dieter clutched his toy Lancaster while his mother sat in her button-down polka-dot dress and the blue shoes with thick heels and put cotton wool in his ears. The cellar was crammed with forty-six people, old men in carpet slippers, women and children and men with empty sleeves and trouser legs and three shipyard workers. It was cold and damp.

Someone hammered on the iron door. Ute's father opened it.

"What do you want here?" he snapped, and slammed it shut.

They hammered again. He marched across with puffed chest and furrowed brow and pulled the door ajar.

"Go away, you filthy swine."

A woman and girl slipped through the gap. Voices struck up: "It's the Jews."

"They'll be deported soon anyway."

"Probably them who told the English where to aim."

Bombs pounded close by. The walls shook, people screamed

or prayed, and Dieter covered his ears. His hair was full of plaster dust. His mother clasped his hand tight. There were two cots, but the mothers held their terrified babies. The light bulb went out and candles were lit. Shouts of "Pigs!" and "Bastards!" followed every thud, and Ute's father shook a fist at the ceiling and cried, "Take us as well, you murderers." Smoke crept in and the candles puttered to nothing. It grew hotter and hotter and harder to breathe, children flagged, babies and toddlers panted, when suddenly the Jewish woman and girl flew at the door, and Rainer's mother snatched Dieter's hand and the suitcase containing the photo of her eldest son and followed.

"Come on, we have to get out," she said to Rainer.

He stood up and turned to Ute. "Come with me."

She tried to rise but her father pulled her back down.

"You're not going anywhere with him," he growled.

She struggled, but her mother clung to her other arm and squealed unintelligibly through her gas mask.

"Come on," screamed Rainer's mother. "I've already lost one son. I won't lose another."

Rainer gazed at Ute, and in that moment their brief life together flashed before him: the ruby ring, the beach with whinnying black kites, Helmut, the swing parties, her warm, passionate kisses. But when he turned he saw the fear in his mother's eyes and Dieter gasping for air and so he trudged to the door, feet dragging with every step, his whole body slumped. He looked over his shoulder, but he could no longer see Ute's face, only her white shoes.

Outside was a sea of flames, great roaring, rolling flames, the whole street blazing. Flying sparks stung his eyes, black planes rumbled in the lit-up sky and the crashes of bombs drowned the voices screaming or shouting for loved ones. The inferno whipped up a hurricane and they reeled and lurched, now toppling, now scrambling to their feet. From every building flames billowed a lurid yellow never seen before, and a tongue of fire shot out and licked his mother bald. At the end of the street a tornado of fire wrenched a child from its mother's hands and sucked it in. They staggered on, but the draught kept sweeping them towards the furnace. They crawled on hands and knees. Cars lifted, roof timbers, masonry and branches flew, bricks burned to ash, bombs crashed on all sides and soon the screaming lessened as throats dried, lips blistered, faces swelled. Bloated bodies with thick black crusts lay around, still uttering guttural sounds and moving their arms. Rainer couldn't stop thinking of Ute.

"What's that?" said Dieter, pointing to a fused, charred mass with legs and arms sticking out, maybe three or four people, but no bigger than a small child.

His mother dragged him away. "We must go on," she said.

She tottered forwards, the polka-dot dress snapping in the wind, suitcase in one hand and Dieter in the other, around bomb craters, past four-storey apartment buildings reduced to glowing heaps of stone. Rainer huddled close behind, following blindly and thinking of Ute in the cellar. He wished he'd stayed behind. The Messerschmitt weighed heavy on his heart, and the road was hot through the soles of his boots. Linden trees forty feet high bent right down to the pavement, creaking and sighing. Hundreds of people battled through the streets, struck dumb or weeping, powdered white with dust. Charred bodies were heaped on top of each other. Some lay in pools of their own melted fat. Living torches flew through the air. Two climbed the ladder on a huge open tank of water for fire-fighting, jumped in and were scalded to death, screaming.

They sheltered in an underground toilet, but more and more people entered. Others had already emptied the cisterns. They dipped towels into the water in the toilet bowls and draped them over their heads.

"The canal," Rainer's mother gasped.

The canal was not far now, but still the bombs crashed and flames rolled out from empty shells or raced along streets. She surged across the road ahead of Dieter, screamed and let go of him before he took a third step. The heels of her blue shoes had sunk in molten asphalt.

"Get him out," she screeched.

Luckily he was a skinny kid. Rainer pulled and Dieter's feet came out of his shoes and Rainer lifted him onto the pavement. Then he grabbed his mother's outstretched hand and yanked but her feet came out of the blue shoes and stuck to the asphalt, she screamed, yelling at him to let go, take Dieter to the canal, he said no and hung on but he couldn't pull her out, the towel fell off her bald head and she was shrieking, not begging him to let go any more, just screaming, and Dieter was screaming, Rainer had both hands round her wrist and he was screaming, on and on and on, until her knees crumpled and she fell silent. He still had hold of her wrist. She collapsed beside the empty blue shoes.

Once upon a time a boy called Rainer sat on a grassy bank beside the canal with threadbare optimism and clasped his brother who clutched a toy Lancaster. A coal barge drifted along, its cargo alight with romping red-and-yellow flames, and bodies with bloated red faces like Chinese lanterns floated downriver.

In the morning, the sun was a pale disc barely visible through the smoke, and the smell of burning hung in the air. A loudspeaker van told survivors to go to the Moorweide park.

"Come on," Rainer said to his brother, squeezing his shoulder. He was glad Ute had stayed behind. She might be there in the park waiting for him.

Church bells chimed the hour. Rainer tied his white scarf, grey with ash, around Dieter's nose and mouth, and with blurred eyes and ringing ears they set off for the park where, two years earlier, Jewish people had assembled ready for transport.

Once upon a time there was a girl called Ute who was in love with Rainer and who still sat between her parents against the cellar wall three months later. Her head was tilted back, the skull barely covered in skin, with gaping holes where the kindly cinnamon eyes had been. She wore white shoes and in her pocket was a ruby ring.

Once upon a time there was a man called Winston Churchill who liked Romeo y Julieta cigars and Gruyère cheese and chocolate eclairs and whose finest hour was the war and who wanted to destroy every home in every German city. It wouldn't win the war, though it was better than doing nothing. But then he was racked with doubt. Had he gone too far?

Once upon a time there was a boy called Rainer who spent hours poring over a photo of his dead brother looking manly and reassuring and dashing in his uniform, and who told his father returning from the war his mother was killed outright by a bomb.

Once upon a time there was a man called Arthur Harris who thought all the German cities combined were not worth the bones of one British grenadier.

Vital Signs

SARAH DALE

The changes in Bill's behaviour happened gradually. There was nothing remarkable at first. He was tired when he got home from work. Of course. He was fifty-seven. A teacher at a middling kind of comprehensive in Chesterfield. He taught history, and was head of Year Ten. It was exhausting by anyone's standards.

He never made it to head teacher, or deputy head, or any of the senior-leadership-team posts. That was fine by me. We were both grafters, mind you. Day after day. We were proud of ourselves, in our own way. I'd overheard Bill talking to the neighbours, when he was putting the bin out.

"Maggie works so hard. You should hear some of the stories she tells me. Blood-chilling. The expectations people have from nurses. She gets treated like crap, management haven't a clue. But where would we be without her and her like?"

I remember feeling warmed by his words, a gift he'd given me without knowing.

We were products of our generation, I suppose. Aren't we all? We never stopped kicking against the notion of selling out. Our youthful passion for not caving to the demands of the establishment, the Tories, the corporations, the system, slowly became less energetic but no less fervently held. We still went on marches. We still lobbied our MP, boycotted Barclays and Nestlé and Amazon and Starbucks. The list kept growing, and getting more complicated. We were sure about avoiding Tesco but what about Morrisons, or Sainsbury's? Could we still trust the Co-op? Our protests slowly slid into powerless outrage as we took to social media.

"Have you seen this, Maggie?" It became a familiar routine. Bill hunched over his laptop, in his favourite armchair, raising his voice. "I can't bloody believe it. I knew they didn't care but this caps it all. When the hell will the bloody unions wake up? Where are the principled politicians these days?"

I noticed that Bill's fury had a tendency to run away with him. But how else could you make your voice heard? Sometimes I couldn't even hear him from the kitchen. I know it frustrated him. But it's one thing to speak and another to be listened to. I kept telling him he needed to find better ways to try to change things. Stop just shouting at the telly, or me.

"But I'm so tired, and what can I do?" he always replied. "I haven't got it in me any more. I can barely get through the day, let alone make a difference. *Nothing* seems to make a difference."

I worried to see him look so defeated, and tried to bolster him. "Look, love, you do make a difference. Just think of what happened with the GCSE results last year. And what about that lad Tom, only last week? If you hadn't got involved, goodness knows how things might've turned out. Sounds like you saved him from himself big time, taking that knife off him. He responded to you when he wouldn't to anyone else."

But Bill didn't seem to hear me. Not enough to make him feel more positive. It was wearing me down, though I tried not to let it.

Being ambitious wasn't part of our philosophy, our values. Even within the state sector. We held ourselves aloof, determined not to get drawn into the hidden political agendas. There were times when we congratulated ourselves on being able to see what was really going on. Not like some of our colleagues. We believed in what we were doing but we were no fools. We took our pay for an honest day's work but we weren't going to let ourselves be corrupted. We were paid-up union members. Always supported strikes – we were first on the picket line with our gloves and hats and banners and slogans. (Nothing ever quite matched how that had felt during the miners' strike, we had to admit.)

None of that fitted with an ambition to be in management or leadership. But maybe we'd just been scared to find out whether we would have been up to it. It also meant we'd been reluctant to pay attention to the business end of our personal lives. We didn't know what our pension situation was. We'd never consulted a financial adviser, on principle. We didn't trust them. We tossed the business pages of the weekend papers to the fire pile without reading them. The whole thing reeked. Stank of corrupt investment, of tax avoidance, of the privilege of the upper classes and of class division. We continued to argue against the system and we continued not to look at the numbers. Although if I'm honest, I was always a little anxious that I might not understand it all. Or like what we found out. I am only two years younger than Bill. But the upshot was that we didn't know when we could feasibly retire, or whether we had any options other than keeping going as we were.

We did own our own home. A modest end of terrace, with two bedrooms, in a street that used to house miners, on the outskirts of Sheffield. If we turned left out of our front gate, we were in open countryside within ten minutes' walk.

There were always things that needed doing. The front door had stuck for years, for instance. It was worse in wet weather, in winters when the prevailing wind came in from the north-west. We never got around to doing anything about it, and in time we stopped noticing it much. We just developed a knack of kicking the bottom right-hand corner at the same time as pulling the handle inwards. It worked.

We'd still got the coal bunker, still used our open fireplace, even though we were obliged to use smokeless fuel these days. When we bought the house, we'd found paperwork in the pile of old deeds and documents that gave details of how much coal per year the miner who lived here was entitled to, as part of his wages. We'd created a little ritual, raising a glass of ale to him and his unknown family when the nights started drawing in and we lit the first fire of the year.

We had a small garden – well, two really, front and back – my favourite place in the whole world. I grew vegetables and flowers. Mixed them up, never saw the point of growing vegetables in lines and flowers in beds. Runner beans entwined around creamy-flowered hollyhocks. Lavender and rosemary breathed together. Tiny tomatoes soaked up the sun alongside a rainbow of dahlias. The garden represented year upon year of evolution, of tending, of nudging in this or that direction. It had evolved, emerged from an instinct I didn't know I had when we moved here thirty-two years ago.

Over the years it became more and more clear that we weren't going to have children. My fortieth birthday came and went, still without. The abyss this exposed in me, month by long month, yawned wider and wider. Raw, red, howling, scraping me inside out, upside down, falling, failing over and over again. I was nothing but lack. Yearning. I was empty within. Without.

I spent every hour I wasn't at work, or in the doctor's surgery, in the garden during those years. Alone. Sometimes I just stood. Sometimes I lay down, wherever I was. I remember coming indoors soaking wet, freezing, with no idea how much time had passed. Bill running me a bath. Instructing me to get in it, to get out again. To get dressed. To eat something. And sometimes I'd randomly, hopelessly, go through the motions of pulling out a weed here, scattering some seeds there. I didn't know or care what for. And then one day, one bright merciless summer day, I noticed a cornflower blooming where I'd thrown a whole packet of seeds, furious, careless, weeks before.

It was a perfect bloom, a perfect blue. It held the sky and the earth. It didn't ask anything of me. It didn't need me to be there, or not be there. It didn't need me to look at it or look away or look after it. It didn't care. I stared at it, stared and stared and then cried and cried and cried, until Bill found me. Put his arm around me. We just stood there, and he cried too.

The garden wasn't Bill's thing. And I don't know, when I think about it, what he was doing during those hours. Watching the football, I guess. Some beers. He had a spell of making his own beer, maybe that was then. I think it was.

From that time on, the garden was magical to me, essential. A place of essence. Soothing. An escape from myself, and a way back to myself. And during that time, over the years, whilst I took refuge there, Bill grew increasingly tired, increasingly distant.

He took to having a nap when he got home from work. At first it was in the chair. Nodding off whilst I either cooked or was on my way out for a night shift. Those evenings I'd leave him a ready meal. I don't know how we'd slipped into that but there it was.

Before long, he took himself to bed for a lie-down before tea. Was flat out straightaway. I usually woke him when the meal was ready. We'd watch telly, or maybe read a bit. Chat if we could find the energy, or do the crossword together. Early night. That was always our way. We were rarely up after ten at night. We always had early starts in the morning, had done all our working life.

And then came one evening – it was a Wednesday, I remember, I'd had an early shift that had finished at four. I'd picked up some cheese and milk on the way home. It was early summer, May. The weather was beautiful. I spent an hour in the garden before making an omelette, chopping up salad. I remember adding a few snippings of the new-season fennel leaves for taste.

I called up the stairs as usual when it was ready. Bill had come home about an hour and a half before that. We'd had a quick cuppa in the garden and he'd headed upstairs for a lie-down.

He didn't answer when I called. I went upstairs, called again. I remember feeling irritated. This habit had to stop, really. It didn't seem to make him less tired and anyway, I was tired too. What about me?

He still didn't answer.

"Bill," I shouted now, sharp, as I went into the bedroom. I shook him. He grunted, stirred and lapsed right back into sleep.

"I'm going to eat. It's omelette, it'll spoil. I'll leave yours on the side if you can't wake up."

I went back downstairs, ate my dinner and leafed through a copy of *Good Housekeeping*. I never bought it myself, but my neighbour did and she passed it over the fence when she saw me. Bill didn't appear. I finished, shoved my plate in the dishwasher, marched upstairs and shook him and shouted until he finally woke enough to go down and eat. The eggs must have been like car tyres. I withdrew to the garden. There was still an hour or two of daylight left. By the time I went back indoors, he'd gone back to bed. Fast asleep.

The next day we both went to work as usual. But the same pattern happened in the evening. That went on for a couple of weeks. I grew used to it, thought it was probably a phase. Perhaps he'd sleep it out.

The weekends went next. Saturday morning saw him impossible to rouse. I didn't notice the first time because I was rota-ed for an early start – 7 a.m. – and didn't finish till 5. When I got home to find him asleep, I didn't think more of it than usual. It was only as I was pottering around the kitchen that I realised nothing had moved since I'd left the house that morning. He'd apparently had no lunch. No coffee. Hadn't been out for the paper.

I went upstairs. He was lightly snoring, looked peaceful and healthy. I spoke to him loudly. Shook him slightly. He stirred, said my name. I asked if he was OK. "Mmmmmm," he murmured. "You should drink some water," I yelled. He half sat up, reached for the glass beside him without opening his eyes. Took a few sips. Then lay back down and drifted back into deep sleep.

I was annoyed more than worried to start with. I worked in intensive care. It took a lot to set my alarm bells off. I cooked and ate my own dinner. Threw his away at bedtime when I hadn't been able to wake him. The next day – I wasn't at work and I spent nearly all day in the garden – was the same. It was half-term. The whole week passed in the same manner. I began to cook only for myself.

By the end of the week, I was starting to worry. I kept taking his temperature and blood pressure. They were normal. All vital signs were normal. I'd never seen anything like it. I got the doctor out on a home visit once. The practice was reluctant to do it but I used to work with one of the new GPs there when he was a trainee and on placement in our ward. He owed me a favour or two. He came out and did the same checks that I'd done. Took some blood as well. Asked about Bill's bodily functions, which seemed to have just stopped. Bill looked healthy, well. He sometimes smiled in his sleep.

He looked much less tired than he had done for years, I realised. He looked younger. I was reminded of when we'd met, and how I used to watch him sleep sometimes. I remembered how I sometimes couldn't believe he was really there, with me. How lucky we were to have found each other. I was so certain, from so early on, that he was the one for me. That belief had never wavered, but I was feeling concerned about how we were going to grow old together. The past few months were taking their toll. I couldn't see a way out of this deepening rut. Our lives were truly intertwined but becoming parallel, and harder to support.

The doctor and I looked at each other.

"What do you think?" he said. "I'll admit him if you want me to. But . . . I don't know what to say, I've never seen anything quite like this. There doesn't seem to be anything wrong. I'm not sure I'd know what I was admitting him for. Sorry not to be more helpful, but I figure there's no point in me not being straight with you." He gave me an awkward smile. The young ones never really knew how to talk to me. I'd increasingly noticed that as I'd got older. Simultaneously, they deferred to me and exercised their assumed professional superiority.

"I'll keep an eye on him. I think you're right. There seems little need for admission. We wouldn't know what to do with him there anyway. I'll let you know if there are any changes."

"What about you? Have you got friends to help you? People to talk to?"

"Oh, very good, have they taught you to ask everyone that?"

I was sharper than I meant to be. The truth was that Bill and I hadn't had an active social life for a long time. We kept ourselves to ourselves, didn't seem to need anyone else much. Maybe it was because our working days were filled with people and problems, but neither of us much relished spending our spare time with other people. We went to a few work gatherings but over the years, our friendships had drifted into sporadic meet-ups. We'd lost touch with some when they had children and we didn't. It had been too painful to keep the contact going. We'd never really addressed that, I thought to myself as the doctor looked embarrassed and quickly changed the subject.

I realised I didn't have anywhere I had to go other than work, and to do the shopping and odd errands. I focused on the garden, over the summer, and monitoring Bill. He seemed well. Always well. Week bled into week. I rang in sick for him every Monday. The doctor provided notes. Eventually his pay was cut after the contractual period and I went to see the Head one day to say I didn't know if he'd be coming back to work at all.

The garden flourished. As summer turned to autumn, there were flowers and berries in an abundance I'd never seen before. Raspberries and blackberries and redcurrants. Beans and tomatoes. Roses and geraniums, startling in their profuse brightness. The sunflowers twisted towards the sun as it made its retreat, echoing the turn of the year.

Then like a stone, the temperature dropped in the second week of October. Winter set in, early and fierce. Work got busier. I monitored and washed Bill. Kept him clean, changed the bed every other day. Watched for pressure sores. There weren't any. Cut his hair and nails which grew and grew. Spent evenings sitting by the fire. I toasted the miner by myself. One night, I moved my things into the spare bedroom.

I wasn't unhappy or happy. I couldn't go far afield. I had

nowhere to go, no one was looking for me. Bill and I were only children of only children. They'd died long ago. I'd never talked much about my private life at work. I never wanted to. I was always slightly disturbed by the ease with which some of my colleagues shared all their business. And the shift work meant I kept working with different people anyway. We were short-staffed, seriously under pressure that winter. Bank nurses and locum doctors were the norm. Anyone we could get.

And as autumn shifted into the hardest winter we'd known for a decade, I felt more and more tired myself. I wanted a holiday, but I couldn't leave Bill. It never occurred to me to change anything, do anything else. I couldn't afford it, could I? What would I do, anyway? What could I change? I couldn't leave work, I couldn't leave Bill. I was too tired. As the winter rains blew across the moors and into town, the front door stuck so hard I had to use the back door from then on.

The garden was deep in hibernation. The frost some mornings was so exquisite it hurt to look at it. Snow fell. The hospital filled up with patients and emptied out with staff off sick. I went to bed more and more frequently. At first it was just early nights. Then it was lie-ins too, and whole days in bed on my days off. At the beginning, I took toast and tea with me, but after a while I grew too tired for that. I didn't seem to need it. One day, after I'd had two consecutive days off duty, I didn't manage to get up on the third day and go to work. I heard the telephone ringing and ringing but it seemed to be a great distance away.

Time must have passed. The phone rang at intervals, and one day I heard someone draw up outside the house and ring and ring the bell. Voices called. Eventually I heard the car drive off.

Later – I don't know how much later – there was a sound of glass breaking and wood splintering in the kitchen, at the back of the house, underneath my bedroom, and heavy footsteps on the stairs. Uniforms swam in and out of view. Concerned faces, voices I thought I knew. Stethoscopes and bleeping. The young GP. Discussions, questions, decisions. Drills and hammers downstairs. Retreating footsteps. And then silence.

From time to time I heard the GP's voice. Maybe I was dreaming. I couldn't make out what he was saying, but his tone was kind. It made me feel safe, like a child being checked on by parents on their way to bed.

I couldn't move, I couldn't go out, I couldn't get up. I couldn't leave Bill. I couldn't tell anyone what was happening. I didn't know. I didn't want to. I couldn't. I simply couldn't.

And then one day, the light changed. A sliver of warm grey-gold sunlight threw itself across the bed. I drew every atom of my energy into my eyelids, willed them to open. It hurt. I slowly slowly sat up. My bones felt stuck in a shape I had no name for. Time passed. I looked down. My nails were inches long, curled and yellowed. My hair flowed all over the bed, white and soft. My skin was like fabric, like old worn cotton, smooth and fragile. A single freshly picked cornflower rested on the bed in front of me.

I moved my legs, inch by inch, to put my feet on the floor. My toenails were long and hardened, my feet crooked and fixed. Soreness seeped through every movement. Holding on to the headboard, very gradually I stood up. My nightdress reached my ankles and looked old. Old-fashioned, hand-stitched in intricate patterns. I couldn't remember putting it on. It was my mother's.

I struggled to the other bedroom, wondering what might have happened to Bill. I guessed he must be dead by now. Surely. Was I dead? Were we both dead? But he wasn't. He was still fast asleep. Still healthy-looking. His hair and nails were long. He had a long grey beard too. He breathed steadily, deeply. Stirred and smiled. Yawned. There was a cornflower on his pillow. It still had dew on it.

Agonisingly, I made my way downstairs. The front door was obstructed by piles of mail. I remembered it wouldn't open anyway. I turned around without trying it, hobbled towards the kitchen. Behind me, I heard a noise. I looked back. The door had sprung open, just a crack. Through the narrow space, I could see the garden bathed in early-morning sunshine. I placed one foot in front of the other and pushed through the mail, pulled at the door and met with no resistance. It opened wide. I stepped over the threshold. Tulips and anemones and narcissi and cherry blossom swirled around me as the colours merged, alive, pulsing. The air washed through my lungs, urgent, compelling. Clear and clean and new. I kept moving.

I headed left. I clung to the railings and walls that bordered our neighbours' gardens, taking achingly slow step by slow step. With each one, my movement became a little lighter, easier. I had left the front door open behind me. An invitation to Bill. I felt awake, astonished, shocked. Alive.

I couldn't stop now.

Notes on Contributors

Amal Adam is a British Somali writer. She was born in Saudi Arabia and grew up in North-West London. Amal studied history at university and has an MA in public policy. She works in the higher-education sector. Amal primarily writes about the experiences of Somalis growing up in the UK and is currently studying for an MA in creative writing at Birkbeck.

Arhondia is a Greek-Irish writer. She has finally come to terms with not knowing the answer to the question, "Do you feel more Greek or Irish?" Growing up in Athens sparked a love for theatre and storytelling. Having moved to Ireland after completing school she studied theatre at the Conservatory of Music and Drama (DIT) in Dublin and storytelling in pubs all across the country. She worked as an actor and producer in multiple Dublin theatre venues. Arhondia completed her MA in creative writing at Birkbeck in 2018.

Nigel Auchterlounie is a writer and comic-book artist. Most notably he writes the scripts for the weekly Dennis and Gnasher strip in *The Beano*. Which he maintains is a proper job. Nigel's children's book *Dennis and the Chamber of Mischief* (Studio Press) is available in stores or online. He is good at carpentry but never ask him to do any plumbing. Not after what happened that time.

Jay Barnett was born in Macclesfield, Cheshire, in 1981. His writing has featured on BBC Radio 4 and in various anthologies, including Salt Publishing's *Best British Short Stories 2017* and *The Mechanics' Institute Review* #13. His work has also appeared in Hamish Hamilton's *Five Dials* magazine. Jay completed his Creative Writing MA in 2017 at Birkbeck, where he was the recipient of the Sophie Warne Fellowship. He lives and works in London.

Julia Bell is a writer of novels, poetry, screenplays and essays and Course Director of the Creative Writing MA at Birkbeck. Her most recent essay, "Really Techno", is published in *The White Review* No. 22, and her most recent novel, *The Dark Light*, is published by Macmillan. She is also co-editor of *The Creative Writing Coursebook* (Macmillan). She divides her time between London and Berlin.

Judy Birkbeck has short stories published in *Litro*, *The Red Line*, *The Lampeter Review*, *Liars' League*, *Unthology 9*, *East of the Web*, *Aesthetica*, *The Manchester Review* and *Leicester Writes*. A novel, *Behind The Mask Is Nothing*, is published by Holland House Books in the UK and North America. She lives in Yorkshire.

Megan Bradbury was born in the United States and grew up in Britain. She has an MA in creative writing from the University of East Anglia. In 2012 she was awarded the Charles Pick Fellowship at UEA and in 2013 she won an Escalator Literature Award. She has been the recipient of awards from Arts Council England and the Authors' Foundation. Her debut novel, *Everyone Is Watching* (Picador, 2016), was longlisted for the Rathbones Folio Prize. "West" is an extract from her second novel.

Valentine Carter became a woman after successfully completing many years as a girl. She is studying for an MA in creative writing at Birkbeck, University of London. Valentine has short fiction published by *The Fiction Pool*, *Bandit Fiction* and in the *In Yer Ear* anthology.

Ailsa Cox is a fiction writer and critic, with a special interest in the short-story genre. Her stories are widely published in magazines and anthologies, including *The Best British Short Stories 2014* (Salt Publishing), and her collection, *The Real Louise and Other Stories*, is published by Headland Press. Other books include *Writing Short Stories* (Routledge) and *Alice Munro* (Northcote House). Ailsa is Professor of Short Fiction at Edge Hill University, the founder of the Edge Hill Prize for a published short-story collection, the editor of the peer-reviewed journal *Short Fiction in Theory and Practice*, and the deputy chair of the European Network for Short Fiction Research. She can be found on Facebook and Twitter @ailsacox.

Ian Critchley is a freelance editor and journalist. His fiction has been published in several journals and anthologies, including *Staple* and *Neonlit: Time Out Book of New Writing Volume 2*, and his journalism has appeared in the *Sunday Times*, *Times Literary Supplement*, *Literary Review* and *Telegraph*. He is represented by Sarah Such Literary Agency and can be found on Twitter: @iancritchley4.

Sarah Dale is a registered occupational psychologist, who runs her own practice in Nottingham. She is the author of *Bolder and Wiser*, a non-fiction book about turning fifty, and has had stories published in *The Fiction Pool*, *Bandit Fiction* and Nottingham Writers' Studio anthologies and a letter in *The Letters Page*. One of her stories was longlisted for the Dorset Fiction Award. Sarah is a student on the MA in creative writing at Birkbeck, University of London.

Kate Ellis is a writer and bookseller based in London. Her short fiction has been published in the *Open Pen Anthology* and the *London Short Story Prize Anthology 2017* among others. She has an MA in creative writing from Birkbeck and is working on her first novel and short-story collection. @katesmalleyelli

Tim Goldstone lives deep in rural Wales. He has travelled widely, including working and backpacking throughout the UK, Western and Eastern Europe, and North Africa. His stories and poetry have appeared in print journals and anthologies, including *Stand* and *Altered States*, and online in magazines such as *Anti-Heroin Chic*. His prose sequence *Brit* was read onstage by Leslie Norris at the Hay Festival, and his script material has been broadcast on TV and radio. Tim is the recipient of a Welsh Arts Council scholarship. He has a BA in English and history.

Vicky Grut's short stories have appeared in new-writing anthologies published by Picador, Granta, Duckworth, Serpent's Tail and Bloomsbury. Her essay "Into the Valley", published in *Harvard Review* #43, was listed as one of the Notable Essays of 2012 in Cheryl Strayed (ed.) *The Best American Essays, 2013*. Her novel *Human Geography* was shortlisted for the 2017 Caledonia Novel Award. Another of Vicky's stories appeared in *Harvard Review* #52 and her collection *Live Show, Drink Included* is published by Holland Park Press in October 2018. She is currently working on a creative-non-fiction travel book that follows her Swedish grandmother from Paris and Stockholm in the 1920s to Bangkok in the 1930s and Stalin's Moscow in the winter of 1940.

Ingrid Jendrzejewski studied creative writing at the University of Evansville and physics at the University of Cambridge. Her work has been published in *Passages North*, *The Los Angeles Review*, *Jellyfish Review*, *Flash* and *The Conium Review*. Her flash fiction has won the Bath Flash Fiction Award and AROHO's Orlando Prize, and been nominated for a Pushcart Prize and *Vestal Review*'s VERA Award. She is editor-in-chief of *FlashBack Fiction* and an editor at *JMWW*. Ingrid's work can be found at www.ingridj.com and via Twitter @LunchOnTuesday.

Jonathan Kemp writes fiction and non-fiction and teaches creative writing at Middlesex University and Birkbeck, University of London. He is the author of two novels – *London Triptych* (2010), which won the 2011 Authors' Club Best First Novel Award, and *Ghosting* (2015) – and the short-story collection *Twentysix* (2011, all published by Myriad). His fiction has also appeared in *Chroma*, *Polari*, *Brand Magazine*, *Best Gay Erotica 2010*, and *Best Gay Short Stories 2010*. Non-fiction works include *The Penetrated Male* (2012) and *Homotopia?: Gay Identity, Sameness and the Politics of Desire* (2015, both Punctum Books).

Lou Kramskoy is a London-based animation screenwriter. A recent graduate of the MA Creative Writing at Birkbeck, she is working towards completing her first novel alongside a collection of short stories. Her story "Glassblower's Lung" won the 2018 *Aesthetica* Creative Writing Award. In 2017 Lou also had stories longlisted for the *Mslexia* Short Story and Bristol Short Story prizes.

Nat Loftus is a Creative Writing MA student at the University of Sheffield. As a former singer-songwriter (Nat Johnson), she earned national press acclaim, songwriting commissions and live sessions for BBC Radio 4 and BBC 6 Music. Nat has also worked as a freelance copywriter and has a degree in journalism. She lives in Sheffield with her husband and baby daughter.

Len Lukowski is a writer and performer based in South-East London. His work has been published in *LossLit*, *Aesthetica*, *The Ofi Press*, *YorkMix* and *Drowned in Sound*. He came third in the 2018 York Literature Festival / *YorkMix* poetry competition. Len is a former Associate at Spread the Word and has an MA in creative writing from Birkbeck. He plays in the queer punk band Twinken Park.

Laurane Marchive is a writer and a director/producer. After graduating from the Sorbonne she worked as a journalist in France, India and Indonesia. In 2012 she moved to London and co-founded Chivaree, a circus company, which has won a number of awards for its immersive physical productions. She has a love for all things cinematic and colourful, and in both her writing and her theatre work she longs to tell stories that swell and swirl and to create worlds that swallow you whole and leave you exhilarated, if slightly confused.

David Martin lives in York with his wife and daughter and works as a journalist. He studied English literature at the University of York, and philosophy at the Open University. His horror novelette *Things Behind the Sun* appeared in *Black Static* in 2018. His short fiction has been published by *The London Magazine*, *Litro* and Unthank Books, and his story "The Park" was shortlisted for the Bridport Prize in 2015. He can be found on Twitter @lordsludge.

R. E. McAuliffe was born in Cork, Ireland, and now lives in London. She is currently working on a collection of short stories.

Mykola Moss was born in Wales, and refused to leave until he had completed his BA in creative writing at the University of South Wales, and a PGCE at Cardiff University. After spending some time in Canada, he now lives in London where he recently graduated from the MA Creative Writing at Birkbeck, and frequently visits his homeland through his fiction.

Cheryl Powell recently completed an MA in creative writing at Warwick University and lives in Droitwich Spa. Her short stories have been published in *Litro*, *Every Day Fiction* and *Spelk*, in the anthologies *Rattle Tales*, published as part of the Brighton Prize 2015, and *Breaking the Surface*, part of the South Wales Short Story Competition 2015, and in Warwick Writing Society's arts magazine, *Kamena*.

Josey Rebelle is a club and radio DJ from Tottenham, London. She is currently a student on Birkbeck's Creative Writing MA. Her specialisms include spending all her dinner money on records, gazing adoringly at stationery and writing bios filled with cute but highly irrelevant information.

Jane Roberts is a freelance writer living on the Shropshire/Wales border. Her fiction has featured in a variety of anthologies and journals including: *Litro*, *Bare Fiction Magazine*, *The Lonely Crowd*, *Wales Arts Review*, *LossLit*, *Flash: The International Short-Short Story Magazine*, *The Nottingham Review*, National Flash-Fiction Day anthologies, and *Unthology 9*. She has been a participant in the Writing West Midlands Room 204 Writer Development Programme 2017/18, shortlisted for Bridport and Fish prizes, longlisted for a Saboteur Award for Best Anthology as part of Literary Salmon, and won the Bloomsbury Writers' and Artists' Flash Fiction Competition 2013. Twitter: @JaneEHRoberts. Website: janeehroberts.wordpress.com.

Leone Ross writes genre and literary fiction. She has published two critically acclaimed novels, *All the Blood Is Red* and *Orange Laughter*. Her fiction has been nominated for the Orange Prize, the V. S. Pritchett Prize, Salt Publishing's Scott Prize and the 2018 Jhalak Prize, and was runner-up in the 2018 Saboteur Awards; her short-story collection *Come Let Us Sing Anyway* (Peepal Tree Press, 2017) is at time of publication shortlisted for the 2018 Edge Hill Prize. Leone is an editor, a writing-competition judge and a senior lecturer at the University of Roehampton in London. She can be found on Twitter @leoneross and online at www.leoneross.com.

Rachel Stevenson grew up in Doncaster, South Yorkshire and now lives in London. She has contributed to *Smoke: a London Peculiar, Here Comes Everyone, Short Story Sunday, Firewords, A Cuppa and an Armchair* (Createspace Publishing, 2011), the *Guardian* travel section and the *Are You Sitting Comfortably?* podcast, and her work has been made into a short film for the Tate website, narrated by Christopher Eccleston. She completed an MA in creative writing (Middlesex University) in 2012, and was longlisted for the Commonwealth Writers' Prize 2015 and the Royal Academy / Pin Drop Short Story Award in 2017.

Sogol Sur is the author of the poetry collection *Sorrows of the Sun* (Skyscraper, 2017). She is currently undertaking a doctorate in creative writing at Birkbeck, and working on her short-story collection, *The Ministry of Guidance*.